ON THE RUN

BOOK 1 IN THE RYAN KAINE SERIES

KERRY J DONOVAN

To Meg, my angel.

CHAPTER ONE

The North Sea, UK

Herring Gull's ancient sonar showed the depth beneath the keel as eighteen metres. Deep enough for safety.

Ryan Kaine, designated "Alpha Two" for the operation, cut the engine and allowed the fifteen-metre fishing boat to drift. At only six miles out, with a slow current, he had plenty of time to complete the mission before the ebb tide took him into the shipping lanes.

Kaine frowned at *Herring Gull's* rubbish-strewn wheelhouse. Some people didn't deserve to own a boat. Next time, he'd hire one from a more responsible owner, but for this operation, filthy as she was, she would suffice.

The time on his diver's watch read 20:13. Twenty-six minutes until nautical twilight and twenty-one from the target's ETA.

Excellent.

He sucked in a deep, settling breath, released it slowly, and repeated the process.

Time to earn his corn.

He pulled on his diver's hood, grabbed the ruggedised plastic case, and stepped out onto the rolling deck. A stiffening breeze whipped a mist of salt water into his eyes. He blinked it away.

Kaine dropped to one knee, released the clasps on the case, and flipped open the lid. There she lay—safe in her black, dimpled-foam cocoon—a wide-bodied tube of awesome power and functional beauty.

He removed the matte green cylinder and balanced it on his thigh.

The prototype Portable Air-Attack System Mark IV, the PAAS-4, weighed far less than he expected—a bantamweight killing machine. Its payload, a modified Buzzer III SAM, nestled safe inside its home. He popped open the instrument cover, keyed in the code, and waited for the system to scroll through the initialisation protocol. Thirty seconds later she was ready—armed and crushingly dangerous.

According to the manufacturer's technical specs, the "ultra-light-weight" SAM "set the technological bar higher than anything else currently on the market".

Kaine snorted.

We'll see.

He stood, swung the tube onto his shoulder, and tested its balance while fully loaded. Not bad. Wouldn't want to carry it far over heavy terrain, but the ergonomic setup worked well enough. Surprisingly enough and, as promised, the pistol grip handle, targeting screen, and operating software were a distinct improvement on the competition.

In his head, Kaine noted the observations for his post-test report.

The swell deepened, and *Herring Gull*'s increasing roll forced him to brace his left thigh against the gunwale. By hinging at the waist, he matched his sway with that of the pitching deck.

Everything was ready for the green light. Even the weather, cool and mainly clear, with a growing onshore breeze, cooperated.

He checked the field of operation.

The only other vessel in sight, an oil tanker, chugged three miles off his starboard bow, heading northeast, towards Norway. Her navigation lights showed clear and bright, and her bridge threw a fractured blanket of brilliant white into the gathering darkness. As for *Herring Gull*, she ran dark and rode low in the water, hidden inside deep troughs more than half the time. If the tanker crew spotted his little tub on their radar, they'd think nothing of it.

The pale grey sky, criss-crossed with white jet trails but otherwise empty, gazed down on him, its face benign. Cloud free, the visibility couldn't be better.

The deck continued to roll and buck beneath his feet, but it didn't matter. If the weapon lived up to the hype, it would find its test target.

Which was the whole point.

According to the blurb, once the Buzzer's internal infrared homing system gained a lock, nothing could intercept it. Hence Kaine's current location, six miles offshore, twenty-five from Hull, and eighteen from Grimsby—give or take. An isolated spot.

Perfect.

The deadly weapon on his shoulder weighed heavy and begged for release. He lowered it to the rail.

All set, Kaine checked his watch once again. He waited.

———

The sea roiled beneath the hull, gulls screamed and bickered along the rail, and the keen salt air filled his lungs. Kaine smiled. He couldn't think of a better place to spend an early autumn evening.

Static crackled in his earpiece, the words unrecognisable.

Kaine released the PAAS-4's handgrip and hit the press-to-talk button strapped to his left index finger with his thumb.

"Alpha One, repeat message, over."

"Alpha Two, this is Alpha One. Are you receiving me? Over."

"Receiving you strength five. Over."

"Standby to accept the transponder code in thirty seconds. Over."

3

"Standing by. Alpha Two, out."

Kaine took a knee once more, balanced the PAAS-4 on his thigh, and pressed a button above the trigger mechanism—the failsafe lock. A rectangular flap sprang open. In his head, he counted down the seconds.

"Alpha Two, transponder code is as follows: bravo-echo-one-five-five-five-bravo-sierra-tango. Repeat to confirm, over."

Kaine repeated the alpha-numeric sequence aloud as he dialled it into the tracking system. Alpha One responded to each entry with, *"Check."*

"Sequence confirmed? Over."

"Affirmative, Alpha Two. Sequence confirmed. Over."

Kaine pressed "lock". Three green lights confirmed the code. A slow click emanating from the device showed the system as active and searching for the transponder signal.

"Launch when you have a confirmed visual. I repeat. Launch when you have a confirmed visual. Over."

"Understood. Alpha Two, out."

Kaine threw the off switch for communications blackout. After this point, nothing but a system failure could halt the test. All Kaine needed was a belt-and-braces visual confirmation of the target and the audible alarm on the weapon to confirm the lock. Then he'd squeeze the trigger, stand back to watch the fireworks, and head for home. With luck and a fair wind, he'd be back in time for breakfast.

The Principal would make the second half of the payment within thirty minutes of Kaine launching the Buzzer. It would take that long for telemetry to confirm the launch and the target's destruction.

So far, the Principal had met every milestone in each of their contracts. If the Principal ever failed to make a payment on time and in full, he knew that not only would Kaine and Alpha One never work for the man again, they'd spread the news around their world. Then where would the Principal go?

In Ryan Kaine's world, trust was everything. Trust and a ruddy great big stick.

Still on one knee, Kaine raised the PAAS-4 against his shoulder and rested the barrel on the gunwale once again. Despite the rapidly fading light, the night vision scope made the image as bright as midday in June. He wrapped his hand around the contours of the pistol grip and placed his trigger finger along the guard.

Herring Gull weaved and bobbed as the sea grew more turbulent. The fresh-to-strong breeze dried the sweat on his face—the only exposed skin apart from his hands.

The gulls, annoying little buggers, still argued over sea-borne morsels.

Nine minutes. Any longer and he'd abort. The window of opportunity was precise, immutable.

Time slowed.

His world condensed into a grey sea, chill wind, a pitching deck, and the northern horizon.

Come on.

CHAPTER TWO

Wednesday 9th September – Evening

The North Sea, UK

Herring Gull swung three points to port, putting him in the lee of the wheelhouse. The heat built inside his wetsuit. Sweat formed a slick barrier between skin and insulated neoprene. Although strictly unnecessary for this specific mission, the wetsuit formed part of Kaine's personal rules of engagement. During a live assignment at sea, he wore the neoprene, no compromises. The rules had saved his life in the past and would no doubt do so in the future.

He pressed his ear against the launcher's breach-stock. The internal electronics fired out radio pulses in search of their prey.

Click-fizz-tick.

Click-fizz-tick.

He glanced to the northwest. The dark, undulating pencil line of the coast appeared thinner than before. They'd drifted further out to sea. Seven more minutes before the abort.

There!

Low to the northern horizon, a small movement caught his eye. It climbed slowly into the sky, pushing east, towards Continental Europe. Kaine rotated a knurled button on the weapon's optical display. The image sharpened.

Green starboard wingtip light flashing once per second, white light a fraction forward of that. The target! Visual confirmation made.

The clicking from the Buzzer's internal tracking system increased in speed and volume. It pinged twice.

Lock established.

Kaine smiled again. Show time.

He slid his trigger finger into the guard and squeezed.

An infinitesimal delay brought fractional doubt before the PAAS-4 roared and thumped hard into his shoulder. The Buzzer leaped from the wide muzzle, tail aflame. The tube's flash-guard screen protected Kaine's eyes and face, but the heat singed the hairs on the back of his hands. The acrid tang of burnt hair rankled.

As the missile cleared the barrel, its tail fins flipped open and the nose lifted. A moment later, the afterburners ignited. The Buzzer shot forwards, doubling in speed as it arced through the air and disappeared into the darkening sky. A perfect launch. It barely left a vapour trail.

Seventeen seconds later—he counted them—a large orange flower bloomed in the northern sky.

Kaine clenched his fist.

Success.

Time to leave.

He lowered the lighter PAAS-4 and stood.

Herring Gull lurched. Her stern fell away and then righted itself as the sea crashed against the hull. The boat dipped and corkscrewed, throwing Kaine forwards. The PAAS-4's barrel hit the guardrail and the cover protecting the targeting display flipped open. The screen glowed when it should have been inactive.

What the hell?

Amber numbers flashed.

11... 10 ... 9 ...

A countdown.

Christ!

Kaine heaved the weapon over the rail and it dropped into the thrashing waters.

6 ... 5 ... 4 ...

He dived to the side, scrambling for cover. Time stretched and contracted.

2 ... 1 ...

Two near-simultaneous explosions vied for his attention—both muffled, both from beneath the boat. The deck lurched up and slammed into his face and belly, and threw him against the wheelhouse wall. A pressure wave popped his ears and punched the air from his lungs.

Herring Gull screamed and listed to port, the angle growing ever steeper.

Kaine struggled to maintain his position on a sloping deck made slippery by green slime. He slid and crashed into the scuppers. The jarring crunch of skull and shoulder hitting metalwork stunned him, but the cries of the dying boat cut through his daze.

No thought, no plan. He acted on pure animal instinct.

He grasped the rail, heaved himself over the gunwale, and rolled into the sea. A three-metre fall into the raging water, no more.

The splash.

Ice cold water froze his face and hands. Shock killed all reason.

He kicked hard and pulled through the fluid murk.

Heart thumping, pulse pounding in his ears, he broke through to the surface.

Air!

Kaine spat filth from his mouth—sea water mixed with oil, flakes of rust, and bilge scum—gulped a mouthful of air, sucked in sea spray, coughed.

Move man. Move!

Ryan Kaine did what years of training had drilled into him—he swam. Heading away. Away from the boat. Clear of the undertow and any wreckage wanting to drag him beneath the water.

After thirty full-bore racing strokes—fifty metres—he stopped, spun through one-eighty degrees, and trod water while the stricken vessel slipped below the surface. Not with a roar or a whimper, but a barely audible groan.

Bubbles and foam exploded in her wake.

As *Herring Gull's* radio mast disappeared below the waves, a lump formed in Kaine's salt-raw throat. Any sailor who could watch the death of a boat without feeling its pain wasn't human.

Flotsam rippled on the surface and dispersed in the turbulent foam. An old tyre, one of the fenders, had broken free from its line and bobbed in the oily scum.

What the hell happened?

How could a near-empty tube have packed enough explosives to sink a fishing boat?

Not possible.

A bomb below decks. Sabotage?

Some bastard wanted him dead. Why?

He tamped down the anger. Answers could wait. First things first. Personal safety. Take care of the now, deal with the rest later—assuming he survived the now.

He coughed. Pain shot through his left side. What?

Rib damage from crashing into the scuppers.

Problem piled on top of problem.

Alone in an empty sea with a howling, mocking wind. Even the gulls had deserted him. He fought a harrowing sense of isolation.

A dangerous situation, but he'd been in worse. At least this time he wasn't taking fire from insurgents armed with AK47s.

Small mercies.

Despite the crack to the rib and the lack of feeling in his fingers, his arms and legs worked well enough. Full range of movement. The blow to his head was nothing but a minor discomfort. As far as he could tell with stiffened, numbed fingers, no broken skin, no bleeding. Probably had his hood to thank for that. The wetsuit now played its part in his survival. Good thermal insulation. Once again his personal code had saved him, so far.

But his hands. So damned cold.

He reached for the dive bag attached to his belt, but found the rough end of a broken strap. The bag had gone and with it his gloves, facemask, and fins.

Jesus. No fins!

Could the day get any worse?

How long since he'd cut the engine? Twenty-five minutes, maybe thirty. In that time, how far would *Herring Gull* have drifted on an ebb tide but with a counteracting onshore breeze? One mile? Two?

Without flippers or facemask, the eight or nine mile swim would be tough, especially in the heavy swell. He'd also be fighting the receding tide for at least three hours. After that, the moon would give him a gravitational push if he still needed it.

The first tremor of a shiver tightened his gut, a stark reminder of the danger he faced. He had to move.

Fingers without feeling. Lips tingling. Thoughts muddled. Reactions slowing. The cold had already begun its deadly work. Despite the insulated wetsuit, in thirty or forty minutes, hypothermia would take him if he didn't start swimming. Generate warmth through exercise. The only option.

Swim, man. Go!

Which way? Which way to shore?

West. Follow the fading light of the setting sun.

No, southwest to keep away from the Humber Estuary's shipping lanes. The diver's watch was finally going to justify its heavy price tag. He breathed warmth onto his fingers and ran them along the watch's bevelled edge. Numb fingertips eventually found the button and activated the light. Three perishing, trembling minutes later, he'd locked in the direction—225 degrees from true north.

Southwest.

He took a breath, flipped up his legs, and struck out for shore.

Pain flared along his ribs with each stroke, but the tight wetsuit helped hold him together. Head down, reach, catch, rotate the shoulders, pull, double kick. Check the compass every thirty-fifth breath to correct for tidal drift and swim inefficiency.

Muscle contraction generated heat. Exercise pumped warmed blood through his body, warming his extremities, easing the rib pain. But something else stoked his furnace—anger.

Pure bloody anger. The thirst for revenge.

Someone had turned against him, and that someone would pay. Dark vengeance fuelled the rage boiling deep within Ryan Kaine. The fire kept him warm, kept him alive.

He ploughed through the water, hour after endless hour.

Dusk turned to coal-dark night, broken only by the luminous dials on his watch and the light of a billion stars. On he swam. On and on.

Midnight passed and brought with it a barely perceptible change in the sea's dynamics. The tide now drove him forwards, towards the safety of shore.

Long, slow, and economical, the endurance stroke's easy rhythm soothed. Its metronomic simplicity gave his brain time to recover and work properly for the first time since *Herring Gull*'s shattered death.

Through the long night, Kaine replayed the operation in his head from contract placement to explosive finish.

The pale northern sky at sunset ... the lighted arc heading for the Continent ... too slow for a private or military jet and too small for an intercontinental airliner. Nor was it the unmanned drone he'd been contracted to destroy—the explosion had been too big.

What in God's name had he shot from the sky?

CHAPTER THREE

Thursday 10th September – Predawn

The Lincolnshire Coast, UK

Kaine fought the waves and the swell in the pitch black. The seas and oceans of the world had done their best to take him, and one day, no doubt, they'd succeed, but not this day.

No. Not this bloody day.

Salt water stung his neck where the wetsuit's Velcro strap had rubbed it raw. A chafing at his inner thighs was of a lesser concern, but the discomfort would only increase over time. The wetsuit that had protected him from hypothermia and saved his life, demanded layers of skin in return. Its pound of flesh.

A price worth paying.

Shoulders and neck ached, calves cramped, but still he swam on.

Slowly, the background crash of surf drove into his consciousness.

Dim at first, the sound grew above the pounding in his ears and his rasping breaths.

Surf meant the shore was close. The excitement lifted his spirits, gave him strength. His right hand touched something hard.

Rocks?

Panic flashed across a fatigued mind.

Christ, how close had he come to death?

He stopped swimming, dropped his feet, and hit mud. No, sand.

Sand!

Kaine stood.

A wave slammed into his back and pitched him forwards. Face hit foam ... swallowed water, retched. Head up for air. Sucked in a lungful, held it. Another punch in the back.

Tumbling ... rolling ... crashing.

He dug stiffened fingers into hard-packed sand and pulled himself forwards, crawling. The undertow sucked at his feet. Crawled again. Stopped, exhausted.

A beach. A glorious beach.

Safety.

Kaine fell on his front. Hugged the land. Joyous tears formed, but the screaming wind whipped sand into his mouth and eyes, taking away the brief flash of joy. He coughed. His ribs spat fire and he only managed a gentle hack that didn't do the job. He hugged his chest and tried again, this time with more success.

Why go to sea when she hates me?

He shivered.

Still not out of danger, he had to move. Find shelter, find the lee.

He pushed up with his hands and knelt back on his heels, half-closing his eyes against the stinging wind-blown grit. Ahead, a lighter band of dry sand reflected the merest hint of light thrown out by the stars and the phosphorescent sea. Darker shapes beyond—mounds —gave him a target. A direction away from the vicious spiteful sea. She'd lost her latest victim and her anger showed in the boiling lather.

Too tired and unsteady to walk, he scrambled, stumbled, crawled towards the dark humps. Spiky dune grass scratched his face. By touch, he found a hollow. Blessed shelter from the sandblasting wind.

With his back to the weather, he curled into a ball, scooped dry sand over his feet and legs, and allowed himself the luxury of a shivering rest. Involuntary muscle contraction generated heat. Heat kept him alive, but the shivering also drained his energy.

He needed to find better shelter, but to stumble around in the dark would invite danger.

The luminous hands on his diver's watch showed 01:17. Dawn wouldn't arrive for another four hours. Until then, he'd sit. Recuperate as best he could. Wait for the daylight.

What a God-awful mess.

He had no idea where he'd landed. Conceivably, he could be as far south as Chapel St Leonard's, or as far north as Mablethorpe, anywhere along a twelve-and-a-half-mile stretch of Lincolnshire coastline.

Kaine pictured the map he'd memorised after the firm had received the contract. He'd reached dunes. Somewhere out there, a couple of miles inland, ran the north-south coastal road. It cut thought a quiet area dotted with tiny villages, holiday homes, and little else. Rich pickings for a desperate man. If he could reach his car in Cleethorpes, he might be able to reach safety. But how?

Kaine tried to rub heat into his hands, but stopped when the clinging sand abraded his seawater-softened skin. His hands would be useless for precision work—like picking a lock—but he could form fists if necessary. He breathed on them and stuck them under his armpits. Fingers tingled as the blood returned and brought with it signs of life. Small improvements, but improvements just the same.

Arms folded, hands clamped into armpits, he shivered beneath his sandy blanket.

The wind whistled through the grass-topped dunes, the surf crashed into the shore, and the dark thoughts returned. Once more, anger boiled up from deep within his aching bones.

Who wanted him dead. Why?

PAAS-4s didn't have the facility to self-destruct. It didn't make sense. Kaine had poured over the design specifications, left nothing to chance. Once the Buzzer deployed, the launcher was little more than a plastic drainpipe with a fancy electronic trigger. The sexy stuff —fuel, guidance systems, payload—was housed deep inside the guts of the missile.

Yet the empty tube had detonated with enough force to register as one of two blasts. It had been loaded with something powerful. PETN maybe? Lightweight, and with enough brisance to wreak intense damage on soft tissue, but not enough to scupper *Herring Gull*. No, the second blast had done the real damage. The booby trap on the PAAS-4 was designed to vaporise Kaine in case someone tried to salvage the little fishing boat.

Jesus!

What had he done to deserve death?

The first explosion, the target he'd shot down, had to be ultra-sensitive. An event the Principal could not allow to be traced back to him. Kaine was the trigger man, a witness. Expendable.

Disgust doused the fire of anger and turned it into cold, hard hate.

The Principal was going to pay. By God, would he pay. But who was he? Alpha One would know. Yes, he'd know.

Could Kaine risk sleep? No. The second it became light enough to travel, he'd have to go, and he needed to think, plan, take stock. Everything he'd done since the explosion had been reactive, autonomic responses driven by survival instinct. But with his immediate safety assured, he needed more. He needed a plan.

Think Kaine. What now?

First step, identify his location, source some clothing, drink and food, and reach his car. Second step, contact Alpha One, warn him. He could be in danger. Another target.

The bones of a plan. Add flesh to the bones.

What did he have in his arsenal?

The wetsuit would continue to stave off the worst of the weather. Already the shivering has subsided. The diver's knife in his calf scabbard might come in handy at some point. His emergency supply belt contained eight crisp ten-pound notes in a watertight bag, his car keys, and half a dozen matchstick heads encased in a block of candle wax.

The matches were useless. No way he could risk building a fire until he'd fixed his location. For all he knew, a holiday camp sat over the next bank of dunes. Hell, if the current had pushed him further north than his estimate, he could be sitting in the back garden of Grimsby's coastguard station.

That was it for physical assets, but he had one final weapon in his arsenal. As far as the Principal was concerned, as far as the world was concerned, Kaine was dead. He could use that.

He *would* use that.

CHAPTER FOUR

Thursday 10th September – Predawn

The Lincolnshire Coast, UK

Second followed second. Minute followed minute. The night stretched on forever.

Kaine reran the mission from contract placement, to final detonation, searching for something he'd missed. Something that should have triggered his internal defences, a deviation from the norm. He found nothing.

He kept working his fingers. Wrinkled, dry skin, but mobile joints showed improvement. Protection from the wind and the covering of sand had worked its magic. Kaine no longer wasted his energy in shivering.

———

At 03:56 the rain started as a light drizzle and developed into a driving, hammering deluge. Where most people in the open would grumble at the discomfort, to Kaine it was a Godsend. Rain kept people indoors. Dog owners delayed their walks. Children stayed inside warm houses. Car windows misted up. Visibility fell. Perfect for the man who didn't want to be found.

He had two hours—maybe a little longer given the heavy cloud cover—until predawn. The horizon would be indistinct, but he'd be able to move about on land without bumping into anything big.

His joints and limbs had stiffened in the hours spent under the sand, and he began easing the cramp out of his bones and muscles. Ankles, knees, hips, and the other major joints in the upper body. All needed loosening, yet each demanded he leave them in peace. When had he become such a miserable, frail old man?

His stomach rumbled in complaint.

Okay buddy, you're high on the list. Can't promise the full English for a while, though.

No, he couldn't promise a cooked breakfast, but an imagined bowl of cereal, humble as it was, made his dry mouth water in anticipation.

He rubbed more life into his hands, eased over to his left side and sucked air through his teeth as the damaged ribs barked another complaint.

Suck it up Kaine, you've had worse injuries on the dojo mat.

05:17.

An imperceptible lightening in the east, no more than a half-imagined glow, gave him the impetus to move. He struggled to his feet and swayed until finding his land legs.

The rain increased in intensity, tapping a loud percussion on his hood.

After a single backwards glance at the calming sea, he headed inland, over the dunes. Soft sand slowed his progress, but he was grateful to have something to do. Lying still didn't suit his psyche, and simply being on the move was enough to improve his mood.

He jogged over sand and grass, at home. He'd cut his Commando teeth on such terrain. For the first time since *Herring Gull*'s death, he felt in control. He felt alive.

In the fifteen minutes since leaving his hidey hole, the rain had eased and the wind had died to a rasping whisper. Droplets ran down his hood and into his eyes. He wiped them away with the back of his hand.

Breathing hard, he crested a house-sized dune, crouched low, and peered into the gloom. A thin line, lighter than the rest of the land, ran north-south for a few hundred metres. To his right, it twisted uphill and headed west, further inland.

A path?

He hurried down the far side of the dune and into the protection of a deep valley. The hard-packed mud, sand, and stones digging into the soft soles of his neoprene sock-boots confirmed his hopes—a path through the dunes.

Which way? North or south?

To the south lay the middle-sized town of Mabelthorpe. Not for him—not in a wetsuit. To the north, the tiny villages of Theddlethorpe, Saltfleet, and others offered more promise. Better still, it took him closer to Cleethorpes, and his Citroën.

He turned right, heading north, and increased pace on the firmer ground. The eastern sky had brightened. Twilight time was running short.

A ten-minute jog took him to a fork in the path guarded by the most glorious notice board he'd ever seen. He paused for breath, hands on knees, and he smiled. The title carved into its upper horizontal rail read: *Theddlethorpe Saltmarsh and Foreshore*. Behind the scratched plastic screen, a helpful map confirmed that his dead reckoning had been bang on.

His spirits lifted. Twenty miles to the Citroën. Not that far.

Kaine made himself a promise. If he ever worked his way out of the mess, he'd send a large donation to Nature England for being so damned helpful to a man on the run. He continued west and ran some more. A man in a wetsuit out for a predawn jog in the marshes, what could be more normal?

Yeah, right.

Sometime during his enforced yomp, the rain had stopped altogether.

Running in the wetsuit generated heat. Ironically, too much heat. Panting hard, he cut his pace to a fast walk, ripped off the hood and relished the airy freedom and the improved hearing. He reached around his back for the cord attached to the zip's pull tab, and tugged it down a couple of inches. Cool, refreshing air hit his bare back. He tore open the Velcro neck strap and completed his release from restrictive incarceration.

All the while, he kept his eyes and ears attuned for sights and sounds of danger.

Fifteen hundred exhausting paces later, the uphill path morphed into a staircase with extra-deep treads complete with a rusted iron railing. It scaled a mountainous, gorse-covered dune. Like a jaded old man struggling to climb the stairs to bed, Kaine pulled on the handrail as he climbed.

At the top, his spirits rose again. An empty car park. Further glorious signs of civilisation to match the wondrous notice board.

Kaine found the park's exit and trod a muddy, potholed trail until he reached a track leading to the sand-and-pebbled surface of Brick-yard Lane—as indicated by a helpful road sign.

A grinning, massively relieved Kaine took shelter behind a head-high buckthorn bush. Directly in front of him stood the most beautiful building he'd ever seen. The modest, white-walled bungalow with its red-tiled roof and single detached garage on the left-hand side ranked up there with Versailles, the Taj Mahal, and Buckingham Palace. But, without the slightest doubt, the best sight of all was the rust-bitten, dirt-covered Ford Fiesta parked in its drive. Even better, the grass growing tall around its tyres confirmed it hadn't moved for weeks. Another wondrous sight for the weary fugitive.

A detached building, surrounded by nothing but saltmarsh and isolation, it looked uninhabited. A holiday home, most likely. No red burglar alarm box attached to the outside wall. In the sticks, few people bothered with alarms. No one around to react or take notice.

Kaine darted forwards at a half-crouch, crossed Brickyard Lane, took a one-kneed stance behind a small bush on the grass verge outside the house, and listened. Silence save for the heavy breath of the wind huffing over the saltmarsh.

Too early for a dawn chorus; he'd beaten the sparrows to their morning farts.

His smile grew. So great to be alive after such a night.

Next decision. Frontal attack or covert entry?

He scanned the area to his left and right as far as the horizon. No other buildings within earshot. He stood, marched to the front door, and rapped loudly.

"Hello? Anybody there? I need help."

More silence. No bedroom lights snapped on. He repeated the knock and the call. Still nothing.

Excellent.

He jogged around to the back of the house, feet crunching over weed-clogged gravel, knocked at the door, and earned the same response. Kaine tried the handle. Locked. No surprises there.

Small windows either side of the rear door, curtains drawn, allowed no view of the inside. He crept across to the garage and peered through another dirty window. The crack between the garage's double doors and dirt-smeared glass let in enough light to show it filled with cardboard boxes, gardening equipment, and outdoor furniture—all packed away for the upcoming winter.

He hated the idea of damaging the place, but needs must, and his emergency pack didn't contain lock-picks—something he'd address when things returned to normal. If they ever did.

Back at the rear door, he picked up one of the two large white-painted stones planted either side of the threshold, intending to lob it through one of the curtained windows. It was light, far lighter than expected. Fibreglass. He flipped it over and found a set of house keys concealed in a magnetised recess.

Who used key safes anymore? At least it saved the owners the expense of hiring a glazier. One less thing to weigh on his conscience. A Roman Catholic upbringing could create a heavy burden.

Rusted hinges creaked in protest as the back door opened into the kitchen. A waft of stale air confirmed his theory and came as a massive relief. The house hadn't been used in weeks, maybe months, yet the kitchen fixtures looked fairly modern, less than a decade old. Definitely a holiday home.

The fridge was empty and clean, its door propped open with an empty bin. As if in exasperation, Kaine's stomach let out another angry grumble. He opened each kitchen cupboard, but found nothing edible. An old-fashioned larder contained a motley assortment of cleaning products, but nothing to eat or drink. On the positive side, the cold tap let out a stream of crystal clear water. An unexpected delight. He let the tap run before filling a glass and draining it in four long, delicious, life-affirming swallows.

When had a simple glass of water last tasted so good? Iraq, probably—after a three-week, deep-desert patrol.

He poured another glass, repeated the performance, and then a third, which he took with him on his search, sipping delicately.

And once again, life was good.

In the first room off the kitchen, a bedroom, Kaine struck gold. Amongst piles of children's and women's clothes, he found a pair of men's jeans, a clean white T-shirt, and a heavy fisherman's sweater, worn thin at one elbow. The jeans were three sizes too large at the waist and two inches short in the leg, but beggars didn't make good choosers. The T-shirt and sweater fitted well enough. A ball of string from a kitchen drawer served as a decent makeshift belt.

The freedom he felt after removing the wetsuit matched the relief of tearing off the hood. He'd have emptied one of his Cayman Islands accounts for a shower, but the old-fashioned immersion heater he discovered in the airing cupboard next to the bathroom would take hours to warm the water and he couldn't stand the idea of stepping under a cold shower. He might be a former SBS officer, a self-affirmed hard nut, but a seven-hour swim in the bitter North Sea was more than enough for one day. Maybe for a lifetime.

His reflection in a cracked full-length mirror told him he'd pass muster, provided nobody looked too close. From a distance, the diver's sock-boots could pass for designer trainers—to a blind man with no fashion sense.

Watered and clothed, he'd already outstayed his welcome. The car keys he found in a kitchen drawer provided him with a potential escape vehicle, assuming the Fiesta's battery held enough charge to turn the engine over. Still, he'd ridden his luck so far, he'd ride it some more.

At the front of the house, he checked the surroundings once again. Still clear.

He unlocked the Fiesta, threw the wetsuit onto the back seat, and stuck the key in the ignition. He said a prayer to the Gods of the sea and turned the key.

The starter motor clicked and squealed, but after a couple of laboured turns, the engine caught. It caught!

Ragged as hell, the exhaust burbled and coughed blue fumes, but it ran well enough for a car that had been left standing out in the salt air for God knows how long. The fuel gauge needle edged up to a quarter tank. More than enough to get him to Cleethorpes. Fantastic.

He left the car idling, ran back to the kitchen, and wrote a note on the pad stuck to the side of the fridge, using the pencil dangling from a second piece of string. He used his non-dominant hand. As intended, the penmanship was appalling, barely legible.

Dear home owner,

Please forgive me for taking the clothes and the Fiesta. My needs over-rode my innate honesty. I'll leave the car at Thanet Park.

Please accept the £50 in the kitchen drawer to cover petrol and the inconvenience.

Regards,

A Burglar.

23

. . .

Once written, he took a dishcloth and wiped down every surface he could remember touching—including the notepad. He helped himself to the baseball cap hanging on a hook in the hall, left the money as promised, and exited the way he entered, returning the house keys to the false rock.

Ryan Kaine, the oh-so-tidy thief.

The Fiesta's rear brakes bound tight when he released the handle, but the car clunked forwards after he slipped the clutch.

Clothes, water, transport—a treasure trove of good fortune. Kaine relaxed a little, but kept up his guard. His luck had held so far, and he didn't want to jinx it.

Kaine fed fuel into the carburettor, eased the little car into Brick-yard Lane, and pulled away. He maintained a sedate twenty-five miles per hour until reaching the junction with Sea Lane. This time he did allow himself a whoop and a holler.

He'd made it! How about that? Survived a sinking boat, a seven-hour swim, a night on the beach, a B&E, and still had time to make it to his car before breakfast.

Life held promise.

A right turn onto the A1031 gave him the chance to ramp the speed up to fifty-five—slow enough to avoid annoying any safety cameras, but fast enough to remain inconspicuous. He kept a continual check on his rear-view mirror, although he'd never outrun a police car in the clapped out Ford.

Two miles into his journey, the sun broke through the low cloud and welcomed the new day. He cranked the handle to wind down the window and let air into the stuffy car.

The only things needed to lift the mood further were breakfast and information. His emergency rations in his car would meet the first need, and the Fiesta's radio would meet the second. He powered up the system and pressed each button in turn until he found BBC Radio 4.

The first item on the news, the only item on the news, collapsed Kaine's world around his ears.

"No! Oh God. Please, no!"

Kaine stamped on the brake pedal, the rear wheels locked, and the Fiesta skidded to a screeching, juddering halt. He pushed open the driver's door, leaned out, and vomited onto the tarmac. For the first time since his mother died, Ryan Kaine buried his face in his hands, and he wept.

Life as he knew it, had just ended.

CHAPTER FIVE

Thursday 10th September – Morning

The Lincolnshire Coast, UK

"Good morning. This is Andrew Macready. During this bulletin we will have the latest from the North Sea in this rapidly unfolding story, but for our new listeners, here is a summary of events so far."

The news anchor cleared his throat and allowed a brief dramatic pause before continuing, his tone deep and sombre.

"Shortly before six o'clock yesterday evening, Air Traffic Control at Humberside International Airport lost contact with BrightEuro Airlines Flight BE1555. The aircraft, a propeller-powered Lombard Sprint 8, departed Humberside, destined for Schiphol Airport in Amsterdam.

"Flight BE1555 carried a crew of five and had a maximum seating capacity of seventy-eight passengers. Officials from BrightEuro Airlines are currently collating the passenger manifest, but unofficial reports state that the flight was full.

"All eighty-three passengers and crew are feared lost."

Macready's cultured Scottish voice cracked, and he took a breath before continuing.

"The crew of an oil tanker, the MV Sirius Three, *contacted the Maritime and Coastguard Agency to report sighting an explosion. The Coastguards, in turn, notified the Humberside maritime rescue co-ordination centre. Lifeboats were sent to the scene and have been searching the area through the night ..."*

Kaine listened in a fog of disbelief and horror as the report repeated the scant details. After a few minutes, Macready passed the baton to an outside broadcast reporter sitting on a boat in the middle of the North Sea, who described a scene of wreckage-strewn devastation. Back in the studio once again, the news anchor interviewed an aviation expert who speculated on the causes: mechanical breakdown, pilot error, terrorist attack. The usual suspects.

Kaine snapped off the radio and fought back the tears. The fire of anger tied his guts into knots.

With a simple squeeze of the PAAS-4's trigger, he'd ended the lives of eighty-three innocent men, women, and children. How many other lives would be affected by their deaths? Wives, husbands, mothers and fathers, sons and daughters. Hundreds. Maybe thousands. All those grieving people, and for what?

Why?

On the road outside, cars swept past, their slipstream buffeting the little Fiesta. Some blared horns at his skewed parking, but Kaine could only stare into oblivion, lost in a fog of despair and fury. He replayed the images in his head. The track of the Buzzer, the flickering countdown, his headlong dive into the water, the double explosions in the moments before *Herring Gull* died.

Kaine grasped the steering wheel with both hands, needing the anchor. Sunlight flashed in the roadside puddles. What had he done?

God! What have I done?

Not his fault. Although Kaine would take the guilt to his grave, it was not his fault.

The Principal funded the operation. The Principal provided the transponder code. As much as Kaine, no, more than Kaine, he was the one with the blood on his hands.

The Principal, whoever he was, would pay.

Goddammit, he *would* pay.

What did the man have to gain from the deaths of all those people? There had to be a specific target.

And what about Alpha One? Was he part of the conspiracy? Surely not. Kaine had known him for years. An honourable man, no way he'd be complicit in the mass slaughter. But he would know the Principal's identity. They had to talk. Compare notes.

Alpha One, Gravel, lived in London, but Kaine couldn't risk driving all that way in a stolen car. Despite taking it from a holiday home, he couldn't know when the owners, or the neighbours, would notice its disappearance.

No, driving to Cleethorpes was dangerous enough. Schlepping the one hundred and fifty miles to London in a stolen car was out of the question. The sooner he dumped the Fiesta the better. Besides, the Citroën held his grab-bag, which contained spare clothes, folding money, alternative identification. The car also held his Glock 19, hidden in a gun safe welded to the floor of the boot. He needed that too.

Even without a clear plan, the odds were always better with a full belly and a weapon in his fist.

He wiped his face with calloused hands and tried to clear a way through his muddled thoughts. Should he give himself up? No, the police would never believe him, not without proof. He had nothing. Gravel had the work order and all the documentation. He knew the Principal's name.

Anger built again. Powerful. Overwhelming.

He dropped the Fiesta into first, checked over his shoulder, and allowed the next vehicle, a BMW, to pass before pulling onto the road.

———

The two-lane A1031 wound through the pan-flat Lincolnshire countryside, hedge-lined fields on either side. In different circumstances, it would have been a pleasant drive, but the dark thoughts of horror and revenge running through his mind allowed Kaine no pleasure in the view.

He glanced through the rear-view mirror. How long had that dark green VW been following him? An ounce more pressure on the accelerator pedal saw the speedometer needle creep towards and then beyond sixty. The old Fiesta rattled and howled in complaint.

Fields spread out on either side of the road. So bloody flat. Being caught in the open here would be a nightmare.

The tiny hamlets of North Chapel, Marsh Cotes, and Tetney flashed past, and still the green VW followed. Kaine's senses sharpened. He spent as much time studying his mirror as he did watching the road ahead.

A single occupant, but impossible to tell whether the driver was a man or woman.

Twenty miles into his drive, he stamped on the brake and cut a sharp right onto Midfield Road without using his indicator. The green VW carried straight on along the A1031, giving nothing more than an irate parp of its horn.

Not a tail. Paranoia maybe, but it had kept him alive so far.

He took the second left into the narrow Fieldmouse Road and followed the signs to Thanet Park Holiday Camp. The route avoided the main thoroughfares and most of the sporadic early morning traffic.

At 06:23, he pulled into the grass-lined car park, drove slowly past his eight-year-old Citroën C4, and found a quiet spot in the overspill section beyond the main parking area. He reversed into a corner bay, deep in the shadows formed by the surrounding hedge and a small stand of conifers. The gallant little Ford had done him proud. He patted the dashboard in thanks.

Kaine rubbed his face hard and eased out of the Fiesta. He stood and arched his back, working through the stabbing pain in his side, and looking every inch the tired driver, stiff after a long haul. He took the opportunity to scan the fifty-space car park from a standing perspective. So far, nothing suspicious—no one peering through binoculars, no one taking a crafty break for a nicotine fix.

From his shadowy position Kaine couldn't see the hotel or the reception block. More importantly, no one in the hotel could see him. He pulled the stolen cap down over his eyes, stooped his shoulders to lose a couple of inches in height, and strolled around the car park's perimeter. In a slow amble, he took an indirect route to his Citroën, playing the part of a man in no hurry to start his working day. His eyes and ears continually searched, his senses alert for danger.

He reached a spot level with the Citroën. A row of vehicles stood between him and his car, hiding him. Kaine carried on past to check for watchers. At the end, where the path met the main service road to the hotel, he stopped, snapped his fingers as though he'd forgotten something. He reversed direction and felt rather than saw something dark step out from behind a white Nissan van.

Kaine dived forwards and to the left before the gun in the man's hand coughed.

The bullet flew past Kaine's right shoulder. He turned the dive into a forward roll, kicked out, and knocked the man's legs out from beneath him. The shooter grunted. His gun spat and again the bullet missed.

They fell in a scrambling heap of flailing arms and kicking legs. Kaine caught hold of the man's gun hand in both of his, pushing it up and away. It left Shooter with one powerful arm free to land clubbing blows on Kaine's unprotected face and ribs. His damaged ribs.

Pain, excruciating, total, drew down the red mist of anger.

Kaine turned defence into attack the only way he could. He raised a knee into the soft parts of Shooter's groin. The man grunted, but the punches continued to rain down.

Kaine dug his toes into the footpath and worked his way upwards, edging towards Shooter's neck. He pushed his face close. Shooter tucked in his chin, but too late. Kaine found the soft tissue at the big man's throat. He bit down hard on salty skin and locked his jaws.

Shooter gagged and squirmed. He flailed, kicked, and tried to buck Kaine off, but Kaine, the limpet, refused to let go. The blows stopped as Shooter's free hand found Kaine's forehead and tried to push him off. Kaine clamped down harder, tearing, rending, crushing.

It was Kaine or Shooter. No quarter, no surrender.

Fingernails dug into Kaine's flesh, gouging, frantic.

Hot blood spilled into Kaine's mouth and he gagged. He tasted salt and iron. Gristle crunched.

Shooter's gun arm weakened as he focussed all his attention on dragging Kaine's teeth from his throat. His fingers searched for Kaine's eyes. Kaine relaxed his jaws and pulled his head away.

Air gurgled through Shooter's crushed windpipe.

No mercy.

Still gripping Shooter's gun hand, Kaine swung his legs, used the gun as a lever, and twisted. Wrist bones cracked. Shooter gargled. The pistol came free. Kaine adjusted his grip, pushed the muzzle hard against Shooter's temple, and pulled the trigger. The gun coughed for a third time.

Bone, blood, and brain-matter pebble-dashed the concrete red and grey.

Thursday 10th September – Morning

CHAPTER SIX

Thursday 10th September – Morning

The Lincolnshire Coast, UK

Kaine rolled away fast, lungs on fire, coughing, spitting, vision greying. He panted, sucked in air, cleared his eyes. Spat again, trying to remove the coppery taste of death.

He scrambled to the Nissan, took a one-kneed firing stance behind the passenger's wing, and swept the car park with the blood-spattered automatic—a Maxim 9 with a built-in silencer. An assassin's weapon.

He waited. No one came. A lone gunman? Unlikely. So, why hadn't anyone come to Shooter's aid?

The Nissan and the campervan beside it gave him the answer. The vehicles had hidden the life-and-death struggle from the rest of the car park.

Kaine retched and spat onto the tarmac without looking down.

His ribs ached. His arms and hands trembled, but he was alive. Perhaps he didn't deserve it, but he *was* alive. The cornered animal inside him raged, and the fire refused to fade. He still had things to do before Death took him.

There had to be at least one more watcher. Shooter's partner. But where? He scanned the car park once more, searching for a watcher's nest. A truck, eight family cars—including his Citroën—the Nissan, the campervan, and a dark blue Range Rover Discovery.

Wait!

The Discovery drew his attention. Part-hidden behind the truck, condensation on the inside of the glass gave away the presence of at least one occupant.

Who'd sit in a car long enough to steam up the windows with a comfortable hotel less than two hundred metres away? A pair of penniless young lovers? Hardly. The expensive Range Rover proved money wasn't a problem. Unless they'd stolen the damn thing.

Shooter's partner?

Had to be.

The SUV's position, in full view of the hotel and his Citroën, stood as further proof.

Whoever rigged the rocket launcher to explode might have assumed it would kill Kaine, but he'd left a "wet team" as backup. Shooter hadn't stopped to ask questions before opening fire, a clear indication of a death order.

The wet team's presence gave him a second suspect, and the awful realisation hit with the force of a physical blow.

Nobody had followed him to Grimsby, they couldn't have—with his internal mission radar on full alert, Kaine would have spotted a tail. Another fact lent support to his certainty. Apart from the Citroën's blend-in-anywhere appearance, the main reason he used the veteran car was the absence of a hardwired infotainment system. Unlike with modern cars, no one could track the Citroën remotely— a distinct advantage to a man running a covert operation.

Clearly, the wet team had been tipped off, but only one man knew where he intended to leave the Citroën overnight.

Alpha One. Major Graham "Gravel" Valence.

Why, you bastard? Why?

Answers could come later. First, Kaine had to deal with whoever sat in the Range Rover, which shouldn't be too hard. This particular wet team wasn't the best or Kaine would already be dead. No way would he have been able to overpower a top operative, not unarmed and taken by surprise. Whoever sat in the steamed-up Range Rover wasn't Premier League either or he'd never have allowed himself to be spotted so easily. Steamy windows in a supposedly empty car were a dead giveaway. A rookie's blunder.

Time to move.

Keeping the Nissan between him and the Range Rover, Kaine returned to Shooter. Late twenties or early thirties, heavily muscled, military buzz-cut, deep tan. In life, the guy looked tough. In death, not so much.

With no identification in his pockets or labels on his clothing, Shooter was dressed as a man on a covert mission. The only thing missing was an earwig comms system, which was a good thing. It confirmed this team was underprepared and out of direct contact with each other and, possibly, their controllers. Kaine could make use of that.

A winged dagger tattoo on Shooter's right forearm, and the "Who Dares Wins" motto above it, suggested SAS, but no way could that be right. Shooter couldn't have been SAS or Kaine wouldn't have survived unarmed combat. At forty-two he was fitter and stronger than most men his age, but no match for a well-trained youngster, especially after the night he'd endured.

No, Shooter was either an SAS wanna-be or a washout from their training programme. Either the Principal or Gravel had contracted cut-price operatives, assuming Kaine was at the bottom of the North Sea, or well past his prime. Under different circumstances, Kaine might have been offended by the disrespect, but at this point in the proceedings, he'd take any advantage on offer.

His search of Shooter's pockets turned up three additional seventeen-round Glock magazines for the Maxim. Discounting the three already fired, it gave him sixty-five shots. With Kaine's accuracy and the advantage of being a "dead man", he already had enough ammo to start and end a two-platoon skirmish if he needed to. So be it.

Next task. Take out the person in the Range Rover. Shooter's absence wouldn't go unnoticed for long. Kaine had to move, and move fast.

Under battlefield conditions, he'd simply open fire and wipe out the second man from a safe distance. Clean, simple, and with little risk, but this wasn't a battlefield. What if he was wrong and the occupant had nothing to do with Shooter? He couldn't take the risk of adding more deaths to his tally. No way. He needed the "up-close-and-personal" approach. That way, he might even learn something useful.

He rolled Shooter out of sight under the hedge. The corpse would make a nasty surprise for the next underpaid gardener who made the rounds with a grass strimmer. Although, judging by the raggedy height of the undergrowth, Shooter might well lie undisturbed for a while.

The route between Kaine and the Range Rover remained largely hidden between the campervan and the truck. Another rookie mistake. The wet team should have made sure all their sight lines were clear. One more error Kaine would use to his advantage. Clinging to the shadows and crouching low, he crossed to the hotel side of the car park and reached the rear of the truck without incident.

He edged closer to the Discovery, held his breath, and listened.

A man spoke, paused, and spoke again in the unmistakeable cadence of a man on the phone. Kaine waited for silence and counted to five.

He raised the Maxim 9, edged around the back of the truck, wrenched open the Discovery's front passenger door, and slid inside.

The driver turned, smiling. "Hey, Stu. About time you—"

His expression hardened. Lightning fast, he swept an arm up. Metal glinted.

Kaine twisted away from the lunge. Pain flared along his left side, and he squeezed the Maxim's trigger. The bullet shattered the man's wrist and perforated the windscreen. Blood painted the glass arterial red. The driver screamed, dropped the knife, and grabbed the wound, desperate to staunch the flow.

Kaine rammed his gun into the driver's throat. The man jerked his head back, crunching it against the side window. He blinked. Stunned. Mouth agape, he gulped air, chest working like a bellows. Cigarette-fouled breath and body odour assaulted Kaine's nose.

Keeping his eyes on the driver, Kaine picked up the knife, doing his best to ignore the sharp pain in his side. He felt the weapon's weight. Heavy, well-balanced, one side honed to a razor's edge, the other serrated. A hunting knife. Deadly at close-quarters.

The gasping driver hugged his arm tight to his chest. Frantic, his eyes scanned the car, searching for an escape route.

"Go on," Kaine whispered, "try me."

The man—about the same age as Shooter, with flaming red hair and bulging blue eyes—clamped his mouth shut, flared his nostrils. Sweat bathed his face. The foul stench of unwashed bodies filled the car and mixed with the newer smell of gun-smoke and blood.

"Stinks in here," Kaine said. "You really should have cracked open a window or two. It might have saved your wrist."

Red frowned in question, but Kaine wasn't in the mood to explain. The man's eyes searched through the windows, no doubt looking for his partner.

"Give me your gun. Use your left hand, finger and thumb only. Move fast and you die."

"If I let go of this wrist, I'll bleed out."

"Tough. Do as you're told."

Face creased in pain, Red complied, and Kaine added a second bloodied Maxim 9 to his collection.

"Magazines, too. Same conditions apply."

As with Shooter, Red had arrived at the party with the Maxim 9 and three full mags. Kaine sneered. "Were they having a two-for-one sale at Assassins-R-Us?"

Red frowned. "Huh?"

Kaine placed the second gun and the magazines on the seat between his legs. His private firefight could grow from two-platoon skirmish to mini battle and he'd still be odds-on-favourite, all other things taken into consideration.

A trickle of warmth spread down his left side. Each time he breathed, an extra spear of pain stabbed at his injured side, sharper than the bruising. Kaine snatched a downward glance. A patch of red blossomed through a neat slice in his sweater. More than he expected.

A wave of nausea swelled and his vision dimmed. Red's knife thrust had found its mark. A long gash tore open Kaine's ribcage. He could feel the skin part each time he breathed in. Warm blood ran down the inside of his T-shirt and with it flowed his life. He clamped his left arm hard against the wound, trying to hold off Death. Apocalypse must wait another day.

Red followed Kaine's gaze. His lips twitched into a smile.

CHAPTER SEVEN

Thursday 10th September – Morning

The Lincolnshire Coast, UK

"Don't get your hopes up, son. You'll be dead before I am."

Red tilted his head towards his own injury. "This is bleeding bad. There's a first aid kit in the boot. Can I go get it?"

Kaine smiled. "Don't be silly."

Red licked his lips. "Okay, I'll be cool. Where'd you come from?"

He had a Welsh accent—south, not north—and spoke calmly. Kaine guessed he was playing for time, hoping Shooter would swoop to his aid.

"I'll ask the questions, and don't expect help from your friend, Stu. He won't be riding to the rescue any time soon."

Red shot a look towards the white Nissan. His expression changed from hope to disappointment, and then to fear.

"What was he doing over there?" Kaine asked, keeping his tone conversational. Two old friends passing the time of day.

"Having a piss."

"Taken short? Too bad."

"What have you done with him?"

"Don't worry about him. Worry about you."

Kaine raised the gun and drilled the muzzle into Red's forehead. The Welshman whimpered and closed his eyes.

"Time for a little chat. What were your orders?"

Hesitation.

Kaine pressed the muzzle harder.

"I won't ask twice."

"We were told to watch your Citroën and report back if anyone showed up."

Kaine shook his head. "That's the only lie I'll allow you. Your mate, the SAS wanna-be, shot first, didn't ask questions. The next lie from your lips will cost you a testicle." He pressed the tip of the knife against the trousers at Red's groin.

Red winced, tried to edge away, but had nowhere to go. Blood seeped through the fingers holding his shattered wrist. His rancid breath filled the car.

"Your orders were to kill me, right?"

Red nodded. "And now you're gonna kill me, yeah?"

"Not necessarily," Kaine answered, his voice quiet and steady. "You might be able to bargain your way into tomorrow. Who signed the contract?"

"I don't know."

Kaine leaned on the knife. It cut through the denim and reached skin. Red grimaced, sucking air between his teeth.

"No, no. I swear it. I don't know. We received an anonymous email from a blind IP address yesterday afternoon. It had a description of your Citroën, the location, and your photo."

"What's the going rate for murder these days?"

"Two ... two grand each. Half before and half when the job's done.

Paid into a deposit account by secure transfer. If you didn't turn up, we'd keep the deposit."

"Two grand each? Four thousand quid? Not much for a man's life, is it?"

Sweat flowed from Red's hairline, ran in rivulets down his 70s sideburns, and dripped from the point of his chin. His Adam's apple jerked twice.

"Sorry, man," he whined. "After the army kicked me out, it's the only way I can earn a living."

The line from *The Outlaw Josey Wales* popped into Kaine's head, "Dying ain't much of a living," but he couldn't bring himself to say it aloud.

"Where's the email?"

"On my phone."

"Show me."

Red hesitated. Kaine twitched his knife hand and the blade sank a fraction deeper.

The would-be murderer squirmed. "Please, don't."

"Just reminding you of the rules. Do as you're told. Open the email and show me the photo."

Trembling, blood-soaked fingers swiped the mobile a couple of times, and he turned the screen towards Kaine. The picture—one of him relaxed and smiling on a sunny day—confirmed his initial suspicions. The photo had been taken at a barbecue in Gravel's back garden the previous summer. Only Kaine's close friends had access to the photo, it would never have made his military personnel file, nor would anyone have posted it on social media.

"What were you supposed to do after dealing with me?"

Red swallowed hard again before speaking. "We were to take a photo as proof of death and get rid of your body."

Kaine nodded.

He removed the knife, wiped the blade clean on Red's jeans, and eased the pressure on the Maxim. As expected, Red grabbed the barrel of the gun with his good hand and rammed it into the car's roof. The shining light of triumph filled his eyes.

Kaine slid the blade under Red's ribcage and angled it upwards. The stainless steel sliced through muscle and connective tissue, and pierced the heart. He twisted the handle and held it steady until Red's heels stopped scraping on the carpet and the life faded from his pale blue eyes.

He could have shot the hired killer in the head easily enough, but that would have gone against Kaine's personal code. He gave Red the chance to die fighting.

Kaine wasted no pity on either Red or Shooter. If they'd had their way, he'd be in the boot of their car, on his way to a dump site. If you wage war, you need to accept the consequences.

The dashboard clock read 06:41. Time to go.

Kaine was surprised the car park had yet to start filling up. Such were the benefits of being in hiding at the end of the holiday season. Although the rolling dice came up with double six on that front, his luck had run out with Red's knife thrust. His side throbbed, and another waft of dizziness washed over him.

He squeezed the edges of his wound together with his left hand. The blood flow slowed to a trickle. God, he was thirsty and tired. So tired.

Perhaps a few minutes' rest would help?

No. Stay awake.

If he passed out in the Range Rover, his story would end. No chance to investigate, no hope of exposing the conspiracy, and no chance for revenge. All he'd have to look forwards to was a tiny cell for the rest of his days—if he lived that long.

He'd be finished.

Kaine left the knife in Red's chest. No point trying to remove his fingerprints from this crime scene with all the DNA he'd spilled into the carpets.

Keeping pressure on his wound with his elbow, Kaine wrapped the weapons and magazines in a cloth he found on the back seat and stumbled to the welcome familiarity of his Citroën.

He dropped the weapons package into the boot, grabbed a roll of all-purpose duct tape from his tool box, and dropped behind the steering wheel. He wiped sweat from his face with his sleeve. Vision darkened. Stomach threatened to erupt.

Breathe, Ryan. Breathe. You're not done yet.

Kaine peeled back the sodden sweater and T-shirt. A six-inch diagonal gash exposed the purple of muscle and the white of two ribs. Bad, really bad. Fifteen stitches at least. He packed the wound with a rolled-up T-shirt from the grab bag in the passenger footwell and bound it tight with the tape. It took six loops to stem the bleeding. How many uses had he found for duct tape over the years?

Removing the tape would be agony, but as a field pressure dressing and a stop-gap, it worked. Although, if he didn't do something soon, the wound would prove fatal.

Given more time, he'd have swapped cars. The opposition knew his Citroën and the licence plate, but he had to put distance between himself and the bodies. Flight first, medical treatment second, change of car third. No alternatives. He keyed the ignition, and the carefully maintained Citroën purred.

Kaine exited the battlefield without a backwards glance.

CHAPTER EIGHT

Thursday 10th September – MG Sampson

Sampson Tower, London, UK

Malcolm Gareth Sampson—Sir Malcolm to his business associates, MG to the few he called friends—uncrossed his legs and smoothed out the creases in his trousers. He muted the sound on Business News AM and picked up the ringing telephone. After hitting the scrambler button, he waited five seconds for the software to engage before speaking.

"What do you have?" he asked, his voice relaxed, his accent a carefully crafted blend of Oxbridge superiority and Home Counties aloof. He'd paid the elocutionist a shedload of readies for the snotty accent. It opened doors money alone wouldn't. Fuck, even Her Majesty had fallen for it during his investiture. A heady day at the Palace.

"Mission accomplished," came the equally plummy voice, this one bred and not learned.

Excellent.

MG relaxed, closed his eyes, and breathed deep. He took air in through the nose and released it through the mouth. A technique learned from an aggressively attractive yoga instructor.

"Fatality confirmed?"

A pause.

MG opened his eyes and sat up. Rudy Bernadotti, MG's Senior Vice President of Internal Security, rarely hesitated.

"Fatalities confirmed," Bernadotti corrected.

"Fatalities?"

"Affirmative. Multiple collaterals. Final number to be determined."

"Fuck's sake, Rudy, what have you done?"

Naughty, naughty, Malcolm. No need to resort to swearing.

His voice coach, Mincing Michael, would have been dreadfully upset. Well, the old poof could go fuck himself.

"I did what was necessary to complete the task we discussed."

MG willed himself to keep calm. In through the nose, out through the mouth.

"What have you done?" MG repeated.

"For expediency, I made an … executive decision."

"Details, Rudy. Give me the details."

MG listened to the terse report, trying to keep calm. "Flight BE1555, that was down to you?"

"Us, MG. It was down to us."

"You stupid prick!" he yelled, all pretence of polish gone. "What the fuck were you thinking of authorising a SAM strike on a passenger aircraft?"

"I made it look like a terrorist attack."

"And your operative?"

"Alpha Two? What about him?"

"Is he trustworthy?"

Another slight hesitation threatened to pop one of MG's blood vessels. Sod the breathing exercise. Increased tension behind his right eye promised an approaching migraine. He'd need some stress relief later. "Answer me, Rudy."

A sigh, barely audible above the hum of the voice scrambler did nothing to ease MG's growing anger.

"He's a contractor, sir. Of course he isn't trustworthy."

"Can he trace anything back to either of us or to the company?"

"Relax, sir. Things are cool. It doesn't matter. No one will ever see or hear from Alpha Two again."

If Rudy could relax, perhaps MG could, too. The pressure behind his eye eased. "Explain yourself."

"We gave him a modified GRAAS tricked out to look like one of—"

"What!" MG jumped out of his seat. "Are you fucking mad? You shot it down with one of our weapons? The authorities are gonna trace the fragments right back to us."

Despite the early hour, MG rushed to the drinks cabinet in the corner of his walnut-panelled office and poured himself a large Louis XIII Remy, spilling some of the expensive cognac on the inlaid leather surface. He drained the cut glass balloon in one fiery swallow and poured another.

"MG, I said he used one of our *modified* GRAAS launchers. I had it tricked out to look like a PAAS-4 and adapted to fire Stingers. Alpha Two, the dumb schmuck, thought he was launching a Buzzer. If the investigation team finds anything at the bottom of the North Sea, it'll link back to ESAPP, not to us. Everyone knows the French are worse than the Yanks for letting their ordnance fall into the wrong hands." He laughed. "You've been following the news reports? The media's already linking the crash to ISIS."

MG lowered the glass and rubbed his forehead. Perhaps things weren't as bad as he feared. "ISIS," he breathed, "everyone's modern day Bogie Man."

"Yeah, and the arseholes have already claimed responsibility. A win-win. Couldn't have worked out better for us."

MG dropped into the red leather wingback chair, stretched out his legs, and reclaimed the glass. Maybe Bernadotti wasn't just a psychopathic fruitcake after all. "But those deaths? Was it absolutely necessary?"

Down the other end of the line, Rudy snorted. MG imagined the cocky smile on the faggot's square-jawed face. "Let me put it this way. When the Professor booked the flight to Amsterdam and the departure time coincided with the field test on our GRAAS, I considered it an opportunity too good to miss."

"But eighty-three people."

"Eighty-four, if you include Alpha Two. Admittedly, the collateral damage is unfortunate," Rudy said, without sounding at all put out by the death toll, "but it does mask the Professor's demise rather nicely. If he'd died any other way, suspicion would have inevitably fallen on anyone who benefitted from his loss. Any fool of a cop would look at us and maybe ESAPP. This way, we're covered."

MG took a moment to absorb the information. Try as hard as he might, he failed to find fault with the logic. "Okay. Understood. As long as there's no blowback on me or the company, I'm happy."

"There won't be, Sir Malcolm."

"So, tell me why you made this Alpha Two bugger use a GRAAS?"

"You haven't read the latest modification specs?" Bernadotti chuckled at the end of the question.

MG bit back an instant rebuke. The man was definitely finding too much enjoyment from his work and starting to outgrow his fucking boots. It could soon be time to find another second-in-command.

"No, Rudy. I don't have time to read the engineering specifications of all our prototypes. What did I miss?"

"For a start, the GRAAS is a component-by-component copy of the PAAS-4—ESAPP's baby—right down to the composite materials and firing electronics. Without our badge on the barrel, few could tell the launchers apart. And then there's the nifty auto-destruct feature," Rudy announced. This time, the laugh was real and extended into the subsequent sentence. "Twenty seconds after Alpha Two pulled the trigger, the launcher blew up in his face." He took a second, presumably to let MG absorb the message fully. "Christ, MG, wish I'd seen the expression on the dull fuckwit's face. Maybe we should incorporate a camera in the next upgrade."

MG stared through his office window and marvelled once more at the magnificent London skyline. His city.

No doubt about it, Rudy had become a liability. The man had to go, but not before he'd completed the project. Killing the Professor had been a good start, but it had only wounded Blaby Small Arms Limited—the Professor's upstart employers. MG wanted BSAL crushed and defeated. Ripe for a hostile takeover. Killing their chief research scientist was a great way to do just that.

"At least we've learned one thing," the liability said.

"What's that?"

"The GRAAS passed its first real-world trial with flying colours."

"We don't have independent verification, so it's worthless from a certification perspective."

"True enough." Another laugh. "We certainly wouldn't want that particular field test to appear on any audit trail. On the other hand, there are a couple of added bonus points."

MG took a more relaxed nip of the brandy. This time it slid down smooth and easy, warming, not burning. "Go on. Make my day with some good news."

"First of all, we've saved fifty thousand pounds. Alpha Two is hardly in a position to complain about non-payment of his fees."

Still annoyed by the freak's lack of restraint, but seeing the long-term value, MG kept his voice under control. "The death toll's mounting, Rudy. We make armaments, we don't fucking use them. When's this going to stop?"

"It already has."

"You sure about that?"

"Certain."

"And the second benefit?"

"Sorry, sir?"

"You said there were a couple of benefits to the loss of Flight BE1555. What's the other one?"

"Oh, right. I've been saving the best for last. You heard the PM called a COBRA meeting for later this morning? Well, one of my contacts in the Cabinet Office told me the old biddy went ballistic. Did a Maggie Thatcher and threw her handbag at the wall."

"How does this help us?"

"She's finally agreed to fund research into a defensive umbrella to protect civilian aircraft flying in UK airspace. You know what that means, don't you?"

MG smiled, at last feeling the love. Maybe Bernadotti had earned himself a longer reprieve. "Yes, I do indeed. It means we can pull HighShield out of mothballs. We lost billions on that white elephant. If we can suck more money out of the defence budget, we could actually make the piece of shit work."

"Possibly, and we're top of the list for funding. As I said, my government contacts have been priming the pump all night. I doubt there'll even be an open tender. The PM's going to force the project through using her executive powers. Kneejerk is such a wonderful reaction in times of stress."

"That is good news."

MG sighed happily. Things really were actually starting to look up. He set the brandy aside and reached for the coffee. Any more cognac and he wouldn't last the morning.

"I had a feeling you'd like that. As per our usual contract terms, the first payment milestone will be delivery of the scoping report. Our R&D department can dust off the one we did back in 2001, after 9/11. We'll only have to change the dates and run a few new show trials to demonstrate Proof of Concept. We'll be getting all that money for absolutely nothing."

"How much money?"

"Fifty, sixty million, but with a promise of billions over the next five years. Plus maintenance contracts and future upgrades. Our Aerospace Division will be in clover."

Yes, definitely a reprieve. Rudy might have even earned himself a juicy end-of-year bonus. The queer clearly had his uses. "When will we hear?"

"The PM will make the announcement by the end of next week."

"Excellent. I applaud your initiative."

"It's nothing, MG. My absolute pleasure."

"Nah, credit where it's due. Now all we need is to hammer the final nail into BSAL's coffin."

"Leave it with me. I have a plan to exert some pressure on their manufacturing base. Do you want the details upfront?"

"No. Surprise me. But no more casualties, understood?"

"Understood. Will that be all for now?"

"There is one thing."

"Yes, MG?"

"I've just had a thought. Given the public outcry over last night's horrifying incident, it might be a good idea for someone to start a foundation to support the families of the deceased. Maybe we should put a few quid into the collecting box."

"How few, MG?"

"A quarter million ought to cover it."

"Really? That seems rather generous."

"No it isn't. Think of all those poor grieving families. The goodwill would be worth ten times that amount, and it'll be a tax write-off. You can handle the donation, but keep it anonymous. We wouldn't want our generosity to appear self-serving."

"Anonymous, sir? What's the point in that?"

It was MG's turn to laugh. "Even though we'll make it anonymous, I'm sure one of the nation's intrepid investigative journalists will be able to ferret out our little secret, eh?"

"Ah, I see, sir. Excellent idea."

"Oh, and if the journalist discovered the name behind our generous donation in time for Christmas, it would be even better, wouldn't it?"

"Brilliant. I'll set it in motion."

"You do that."

MG hit the disconnect button before Rudy could respond and dialled a memorised number. The ring tone kept going. No answer.

"Fuck."

Swearing felt good. If he hadn't given it up to please Cora's family all those years ago maybe his blood pressure wouldn't be so fucking stratospheric.

Against his own standing instructions, he dialled the number again and sent a text.

"Call tonight. The Chair needs a workout."

———

Despite the Shard—that God-awful monstrosity staring him in the face and obscuring his view—no other sight in the world could match London at night. MG stood at the window, smiling in anticipation of the delights to come.

His day had dragged through meeting after turgid meeting, but at last the time had arrived.

The phone rattled in its cradle. MG lowered the balloon of cognac to the table, hit the scrambler button, and waited for the click before speaking. "About time. The Chair's been empty far too long."

"When?" the woman answered, her tone relaxed, professional.

"Soon as possible. I've been waiting all day."

"Understood." Down the phone line, a keyboard tapped as the woman opened her order menu. "Preferences tonight?"

"A big man, plenty of muscles. And a girl to dish out the punishment."

"Any particular type of girl tonight?"

"Young, round. Dominant."

Among other things, MG's heartrate shot up.

"How young?"

"At least eighteen," he snapped. "I'm not a fucking paedo."

"Just double-checking. I have some new ... stock in from the Baltic. Very nice. Pliable. Fresh."

"Absolutely not!" He wasn't a sick fuck, they needed to be old enough to sign the consent forms.

"Will I need to make medical arrangements?"

MG relaxed, he needed to conserve his strength for later. "Yes.

Full private healthcare. Post-contract surgery might be required. How soon can they get here?"

"Within the next hour. I have the inventory available and will escort them personally. Service entrance, as usual?"

"Of course."

"I can't wait to see you again, Chairman."

The cool professionalism in the thirty-year-old voice made him harder. Terror and pain, both in the receiving and the giving, were the world's greatest aphrodisiac. No need for the diamond-shaped blue pills, not when whips and leather were available.

CHAPTER NINE

Thursday 10th September – Morning

Lincolnshire, UK

The road sign—*Lay-by 1 mile*—revived Kaine enough to help him lift his chin from his chest and pull his eyes into focus.

With no real idea how he survived the journey from Grimsby, the memory stretched into a fragmented nightmare of cascading images —traffic lights, shop fronts, pedestrian crossings, car horns, and road spray. At one point, blue lights in his rear-view caused a flicker of concern until an ambulance flew past, throwing up a grey blanket of filthy spray.

Kaine pulled into the quiet lay-by, parked as far from the road as possible, and leaned back against the head restraint. Sweat washed his body, rolled down his forehead, stung his eyes. His fingers trembled, and fatigue pressed down on his eyelids.

Immediate needs—water, food, a change of clothes, and medical attention.

The first two he could handle alone. He kept emergency supplies in the glove compartment in the shape of a water bottle and two energy bars. They went down easy and stayed down, always a good sign. No fever or nausea yet, no early signs of infection.

Item three on the agenda proved more difficult and painful. Clothes didn't present a problem—he kept a change in his grab bag—but the contortions needed to remove the sweater and pull the polo-shirt over his head reopened the wound and ratcheted up the agony.

Two minutes and a barroom brawl's worth of swearing had him burning hot and dripping more sweat, but dressed like a human, not an extra in *Zombie Dawn*. Okay as far as it went, but without medical attention, he couldn't function, couldn't survive. The wound had to be cleaned, stitched, and dressed. He also needed antibiotics, but hospitals were out of the question. In London, it wouldn't be a problem. In London, he could call on medics with battlefield expertise who'd ask no questions. In Lincolnshire, he knew no one, and he'd never make it to the south without emergency treatment.

Despite the risk of a phone trace, Kaine powered up Red's mobile phone, ran an internet search, and came up with a destination. He powered off the mobile and dropped it out the window. No need to wipe it clean of prints, he'd left enough of himself in the Range Rover for any half-decent forensics team to identify him in minutes. They only had to search the military database to find his biometrics, finger-prints, DNA, IQ, dental records, inside leg measurement. Big Brother was a lightweight compared to his modern equivalent.

With the energy from the power bars offsetting some of his exhaustion, Kaine keyed the postcode into his plug-in satnav—Laceby to Swadlow, ETA thirteen minutes—and hit the road. He had no idea what he'd find on arrival, but had few other options.

The bulk of the morning traffic headed towards Grimsby, which left the A46 westbound lanes relatively free and clear. He gained time on the satnav by powering over the speed limit on the dual carriageway. A calculated risk, but he could feel himself fading, the energy leaching away. Without medical attention soon, his escape from the Thanet Park wet team would be for nothing.

He ignored the fixed speed cameras, but watched out for white cars with orange and green side flashes. None appeared. On a long straight stretch of empty road, he edged the speed over ninety, but his fading vision and slowed reactions made it too risky and he eased his foot off the accelerator. A crash would help no one but his pursuers, whoever the bastards were.

A roundabout after a sharp right-hand corner took him by surprise. He clipped the inside kerb, lost the rear end, and terrified a granny in her yellow Fiat 500. He stamped on the brakes, regained control, and ignored her blaring horn. The road changed from dual-carriageway to two-lane road flanked by tall hedges.

Two minutes later, Kaine lost focus for a second and nearly rear-ended a petrol tanker.

Jesus.

Eyes streaming, head pounding, he made the left turn into Lumber Road, which turned into the single-tracked, unmetalled, Cuckold Lane. Another half-mile on the bone-jarring, badly surfaced track took him to a farm entrance defended by a three-bar gate. A sign on the gate announced: *Lodge Farm and Veterinary Clinic, Dr LB Orchard, RCVS (Prop).*

The GPS's, "You have arrived at your destination," had never sounded so damned good and had never arrived in better time.

Next, he faced the tricky part, finding the strength to open the farm gates and drive the Citroën off the lane and out of sight. He took as deep a breath as possible given the binding, gritted his teeth, and reached for the door handle.

The farm gate wasn't that bad, well-oiled hinges and a sprung latch made the job easy, but getting in and out of the Citroën had been a fumbling ordeal of dizziness and torture. Twice he nearly fell and had to lean against something solid—the car, a fence post—until his balance returned.

He parked in the deep shadow formed by oak trees and a low

stable block and staggered across a muddy courtyard. The lack of tread on his diver's boots made progress treacherous, but he picked out a half-decent route to the three-storey, brick-and-tiled farmhouse.

Unsurprisingly, the solid front door—iron-studded and panelled oak—was locked. Kaine hammered on the cast iron knocker with the last of his strength. The metallic clanging echoed through what sounded like a large hallway.

"Steady on there," a woman shouted from the stable block behind him. "No need to break the door down."

As Kaine let go of the knocker, the stone doorstep floated up to crack him on the forehead.

CHAPTER TEN

Thursday 10th September – Morning

Cuckold Lane, Lincolnshire, UK

Kaine woke with half-remembered images and sounds swimming through his head. Hands reached under armpits ... supported by someone small but strong ... dark hair ... nice smell ... fresh hay and coffee, clean ... softly spoken words of reassurance ...

"You've been in the wars ..."

"Lean on me ..."

"Let's get you inside ..."

The images and sounds continued. He was half-dragged, half-led from sunshine into shade ... A padded surface, back raised to a reclined position ... A cool, damp cloth wiped his face. Liquid dribbled into his mouth. He swallowed, gagged, and swallowed some more.

More darkness arrived but brought no fear along for the ride.

"I'm sorry to have to do this to you," a woman said, her voice clear and commanding, "but the tape has to come off before I can assess the damage."

Kaine opened his eyes to a room tricked out as a small operating theatre. All shiny surfaces and bright lights. The dark-haired woman he'd seen near the stable before passing out stood close. An angel welcoming him back to life.

Trim figure beneath a white lab coat. Intelligent, hazel eyes appraised his wound. Clear skin, fine laughter lines showed the first bloom of youth giving way to confident maturity. Her full lips pursed and her forehead creased into a serious frown.

"You ready?"

"Huh?" he managed, voice dry and cracked.

"I have to remove this tape to examine the wound."

"Who are you?"

Her brows creased in question. "You ought to know. You were the one who tried to break down my front door. I should be asking you that question."

"Who are you?" Kaine repeated, louder this time, more insistent.

"Dr Lara Orchard, at your service. Now, are you going to continue with the interrogation, or should I make a start?"

Lara. Nice name.

The memories returned. The wet team's attack and a desperate search for medical help. "A vet. You're a vet, right?"

"And you're the first human I've ever treated. Ready? Hold the dressing. What is it, by the way?"

"A rolled up T-shirt. How long have I been here?"

"Two minutes, maybe three. Come on, hold it in place while I tear off this parcel tape."

"Duct tape," he said, ever the pedant. "Better glue than parcel tape. More waterproof."

"I stand corrected. Now, ready?"

As he had done in the Range Rover after the fight, Kaine clamped his upper arm in place over the wound and reinforced the pressure with his free hand, while she cut the tape either side of the dressing with a pair of round-nosed surgical scissors.

"Did you call for an ambulance?" he asked to take his mind off the anticipated pain.

"Not yet. Ready?"

"Yes."

"Fast or slow?"

"Fast, please," he answered, gritting his teeth.

She helped him sit up and grasped one end of the tape in her gloved hand. Up close, she smelled of earthy leather and something floral coming from the dimple of her collarbone. A damn sight better than the last people he'd been in close contact with.

"This is going to hurt a little."

"Carry on, I'll be brave. Won't cry."

She left the piece over the wound in place, and removed the rest is one long, agonising rend. It hurt like stink, but he took it without a murmur. Wouldn't want show pain in front of a woman. So what if he was a big macho chump? Ingrained. Couldn't help himself.

The tape took a three-inch-wide strip of hair with it, leaving behind a horizontal red stripe of bare, tender skin.

Dr Orchard, Lara, eased him back against the bench.

"Well done," she said, her eyes and voice showing concern, empathy. "That couldn't have been pleasant."

He stretched his grimace into a thin smile. "No problem."

The pain had snapped him awake, sharpened his senses, reminded him to be on the alert. From his position on the examination couch, Kaine searched the room but found nothing to cause alarm. A stainless steel worktop over wipe-clean cupboards lined the wall beneath a large window. Equipment he didn't recognise dotted the surface, one looked like a large microwave oven. An autoclave, he guessed, used to sterilise her instruments. Wall cabinets, some with locks on the doors, carried labels with medical words he didn't understand.

"A strange man stumbles into your animal hospital covered in blood and you don't call the police or ambulance. Why not?"

"No time. From all the blood on your trousers, I was worried you might have bled out before I finished the call. I didn't realise you'd bandaged yourself with the ... duct tape. It probably saved your life."

He looked down. The fresh polo shirt lay in a heap on the floor. It hadn't lasted long, and his jeans looked as though they'd soaked up half his blood supply. He didn't tell her that some of the claret belonged to the unfortunate Red and his mate with the SAS tat.

"It's an old trick. One I've used before."

She waved a hand at scars decorating his torso, the reminders of a life spent fighting to survive, and nodded. "I can see that."

Was that a smile?

Still below par, vulnerable, Kaine shook his head, tried to clear the wool clogging his mind. "Do you have any plasma? To ward off shock."

"None rated for humans, but the paramedics can sort you out when they arrive. From what I can tell, the wound is clean. Not as bad as I originally feared. It's even stopped bleeding. I'm going to leave the dressing in place. Don't want to risk opening it again. Treatment is best left to the doctors. I'll go fetch my phone."

She turned to leave. Kaine snaked out a hand and caught her wrist. "Really sorry, Doc. Can't let you do that, I'm afraid. You need to patch me up."

"Let go!" she shouted, trying to tear her arm free. But, strong as she was, she didn't stand a chance.

"I'm sorry," he said, and he meant it.

The flash of panic in her eyes turned his stomach. She'd only wanted to help and here he was, terrorising the poor woman in her own clinic. How low could he stoop?

Kaine dropped his feet to the floor and dragged her to the door. He turned the key in the lock and slid it into his pocket. His vision greyed. The room swam. He leaned against the wall.

"Let me go!"

She slapped his face with her free hand. He didn't have the

strength to block the blow, but barely felt it land. A love tap, no more. The ballsy vet looked more angry than scared. Surprised too, maybe by her own reaction.

"Please," he said, weakening fast. "Stitch me up and I'm gone, I promise. If I leave like this, I'm a dead man."

The steel anger in her eyes softened. She stopped trying to break the grip, but braced her shoulders in defiance. "No way. I'm not about to lose my license for the likes of you. You can bleed to death for all I care."

God, she was brave.

They faced each other, a frozen painting.

On one side, a veterinarian, panting as though she'd just completed a ten-kilometre yomp in full battle gear, her face the picture of stony resistance. On the other, a veteran with a scarred torso, a weeping gash in his side, wearing nothing but blood soaked denims and diver's shoes. What a sight.

The moment stretched into seconds, the seconds into a minute. Her breathing calmed, but she refused to look away, refused to buckle.

Damn her.

She'd beaten him. He released her wrist and slumped harder against the wall, staying upright by force of will alone. She stepped back, rubbing a red mark on her arm that would probably bruise.

"God, I'm so sorry. Did I hurt you?" He spoke softly, head lowered.

"No," she said, eyes fixed on his cheek, not her wrist. "You didn't hit me back."

Fighting another wave of nausea, he replaced the key in the lock and opened the door. "You win. I'm going."

"Wait."

"No, I've put you in enough danger just by being here." Without relaxing the pressure on the remains of his improvised dressing, he pushed away from the wall and turned. "Forgive me, please."

Her lab coat swished and she arrived at his side. "You can't drive in that condition. I won't be responsible for a road accident. Come back and I'll see what I can do."

She took his arm, and Kaine allowed her to help him climb onto the couch.

The cut had opened during the struggle. A thick line of blood trickled down his ribs and puddled on the paper towel covering the padded upholstery. That it seeped rather than pumped was a good thing, no arteries severed. His knowledge of human anatomy didn't run to an in-depth map of the human circulatory system. Did hers?

"How did you get this?"

"Would you believe a fishing accident?"

"No."

Sharp woman.

Sufficiently relaxed to turn her back on him, she rifled through a cupboard and some drawers and filled a trolley with equipment Kaine recognised from a dozen visits to field hospitals around the world—plastic bottle full of a dark brown liquid, another bottle of clear fluid, suture kit, gauze and other dressings, and a yellow sharps bin for clinical waste. She snapped on a pair of surgical gloves and tied a paper facemask.

"Again, this might hurt, but you've clearly been through this procedure before. I'm not sure of the correct intravenous dosage for humans, so you'll have to make do with a topical local anaesthetic."

"No problem, Doc. Do your worst."

"Didn't think I'd have to shave your pelt, but you're a hairy individual. Will you trust me with a razor?"

He nodded. "The duct tape made a start for you."

The Doc smiled. It was a nice smile. It shone in her eyes and he returned it. Then she stiffened as though remembering who she was talking to. She took the bottle from the trolley. It had a bent straw-like thing sticking out of the stopper.

"This," she said, showing him the label that might as well have been Greek but was probably Latin, "is a combined local analgesic and antiseptic. It will deaden the pain in a few minutes."

To soften the semi-congealed blood, she dribbled a small line of the liquid over the top edge of the rolled-up T-shirt, and kept the fluid trickling as she peeled away the cloth. Kaine clenched his teeth and fists against the pain as she revealed more of the wound with each gentle tug.

Ugly and red, the cut oozed blood and plasma but, apart from the metallic tang of iron it didn't smell bad.

"Shall I continue, or wait for the pain to ease?"

"Keep going, Doc. The sooner you're done, the sooner you can have your clinic back."

"This is going to hurt. Keep still now."

By the time she'd shaved the area around the wound, bathed it with more of the liquid, and loaded the needle, the painkiller had taken effect, and he watched her work with almost academic interest. Nine deep stitches pulled muscle and connective tissue together, closing an injury that would leave yet another scar. She doused the surface wound with clear antiseptic fluid, dabbed it dry, and started closing the skin. The top sutures were neat and small. Professionally done, almost painless, and at least as good as the field surgeons who'd worked on him before.

"Nice work, Doc. How much would you charge to darn my socks?"

Her cheeks bunched as a smile formed beneath her mask. "Be quiet, you idiot. Let me concentrate."

"Yes, Doc. Sorry."

After another three stitches, she reloaded the needle. "I expect you're wondering why I'm using sutures instead of staples?"

"Nope, but do tell." It didn't matter to him, but she seemed to want to talk.

"Staples aren't any good for small animals, cats and toy dogs, and rarely hold for horses. Sutures are best."

"Good to know next time I have an injured puppy."

"You're a dog lover?"

"Nope. My grandma's best friend once had a tabby, though. Does that count?"

"Nope," she said, mimicking his voice.

God, she was cool under pressure. He could grow accustomed to her sense of humour and the way the light caught in her hair.

Damn it, what was he thinking? Blood loss did strange things to the head.

He waited in silence a few more minutes but questions had been nagging at him from the moment he woke on the examination table, and he couldn't put them off any longer.

"This is a big house. Are you on your own here?"

Her head snapped up, pupils narrowed, wary. "Why?"

Kaine raised his hands in surrender. "Don't worry. I'm not going to hurt you, again. I promise. Just making conversation."

She started another stitch, the eleventh. The needle pinched like the sting of a wasp.

"It's just the two of us at the moment. Me and Lady Sundowner."

"Who?"

"A client's mare. I've been treating her for colic and post-partum complications."

"Serious?"

Lara wrinkled her nose. "Sounds worse than it is. Her owner's an old family friend. Thinks more of her horse than her husband. Mind you, if you'd seen the way Charles treats her ... I promised to stay up with her through the night ... Lady Sundowner, not my friend." She shook her head. "Sorry, I talk too much when I'm nervous."

"No need to be nervous. You have nothing to fear from me."

She paused mid-stitch and shot him a quick glance. "I know."

"The minute you're done, I'll be out of your hair."

He waited until she'd completed two more stitches before speaking again, keeping the tone conversational. "You've been in the stable all night?"

Maybe she hadn't heard the news reports.

"Since about six o'clock yesterday evening."

The memory of sitting in the dunes through a howling gale returned. Kaine shivered.

Lara stopped sewing and looked up. "Did that hurt?"

"No, no. It's just that ... it was pretty cold last night, blowing a gale. You must have been freezing in a stable."

She tilted her head. The ghost of a frown creased her brow.

"Listen here, whoever you are. I'm a veterinarian and my work stables are centrally heated. Better equipped than many NHS hospitals. I have piped music to keep the horses calm—"

"Piped music?"

"Yes. Lady Sundowner is partial to Mozart. She'll put up with Pop and Rock, but hates Heavy Metal and Rap."

He shook his head in wonder. "An animal with impeccable taste. What does she think of TV? Does she watch soaps or maybe ... horse operas?"

She closed her eyes and groaned. "Oh dear, this is no time for bad jokes."

"Sorry, I'm saddled with a terrible sense of humour. I'll stop horsing around until you've finished."

"That's awful. If you must know, Lady Sundowner was mistreated as a foal. Male voices terrify her, which is why I play CDs, not the radio."

No radio, no TV, and most importantly, no news. He'd probably stumbled into the care of the only adult in the UK who hadn't heard of Flight BE1555. Kaine's lucky streak had returned, and not before time.

He settled back and carried on watching her.

A strong woman. A woman of character. He admired her spirit, her steady hands, the way she filled out the lab coat. Ten minutes later, she'd finished. A shame. Despite the multiple wasp stings, he could have watched her work for hours.

"There you go," she said after covering the wound with a sterile dressing. "Nineteen sutures. Most of my patients aren't large enough to survive that big a laceration. Apart from the horses, I mainly treat companion animals."

"You mean pets, right?"

She made a sucking sound between her teeth. "We don't call them pets anymore. Very non-PC. Shame on you."

"You're trying to teach political correctness to a military man? Doubt you'll get very far with that curriculum."

The minute Kaine opened his big fat mouth he knew he'd said

too much. That sort of error could get people killed and the last thing he wanted was to put the vet in any more danger than he already had. He tried to hide the worry. "You talk to all your patients like that when you operate?"

Her cheeks bunched again. "Unless I have to anaesthetise them completely. Did it annoy you?"

He shook his head. "It did the trick. I stayed calm, didn't bite or kick out when you started attacking me with the needle and the cat gut. Did I earn a lump of sugar or an apple?"

She tore off the gloves and mask, and dropped them into the same bin into which she'd thrown soiled dressings.

"What really happened?" she asked, pointing to the wound.

"For your own good, the less you know the better. When you call the police, tell them I held a gun on you and forced you to operate. Okay? And make sure you keep the used bandages to give their forensics team."

"There's an incinerator out back for medical waste. Can't I destroy them?"

Kaine shook his head emphatically. "No, don't do that. It'll look suspicious, and I don't want to drag you any further into this."

She stepped back and leaned against the counter, both hands gripping the surface behind her, studying him. He waited for the inevitable barrage of questions, most of which he wasn't prepared, or able, to answer. Instead, she nodded thoughtfully as though having made up her mind about something. "You're about the same size as Ollie. I'll get you some of his clothes."

"Won't he be annoyed?"

"No," she said and hurried from the room.

Kaine tensed. For all he knew, she could be heading for the nearest phone, not that he could do anything about it. He couldn't even stand, let alone chase after her. But something in her manner— a sadness, a kinship—told him to trust her as she'd trusted him.

She returned a few minutes later, hugging a pile of clothes. She placed them on the work surface, keeping her distance. "What size shoes do you wear?"

"Tens."

"Ollie took size eleven. Do you wear trainers? You can't go round in those things. What are they?"

Kaine shrugged, unwilling to give her any more information than necessary. If she knew what he'd done, her attitude would change in an instant, and he didn't want to have to restrain her again. If she stayed calm it would be better for them both.

"Thanks for these. Couldn't trouble you for some water as well, could I?"

"Of course. I didn't think."

She filled a glass from the tap over the sink and walked it to him. Their fingers brushed as he took it from her. She didn't recoil from his touch.

"Sorry," he said. "My hands are filthy. I'm surprised you could stand being so close to someone who smells this bad."

She tilted her head forwards. "You think a bad smell would upset a vet?"

Kaine snorted. "Point taken." He took a deep pull. The water slipped down cool and sweet. He drained the glass and handed it back.

"Thanks. I needed that."

She stepped back as he eased his legs over the side of the couch and, still holding the wound, used the impetus to help him sit upright. The room swam in his vision and he held onto the edge of the bench until his balance returned. He thought about trying to stand, but gave it up as a lost cause, at least for a while.

"Mind if I ask a question?" he said to fill the silence while he recovered.

"Feel free."

"Why did you help? I might be a dangerous fugitive."

It was her turn to shrug. "When I see an injured animal, I have to do what I can." Her eyes opened wide and she threw a hand to her mouth. "Not that I think you're an animal."

"It's okay. I know what you mean."

"Besides, I saw more worry in you than aggression. Looked as though you were more scared of hurting me than anything else."

If she only knew.

"Thanks for everything, but I need to go."

She stepped forward but stayed out of arm's reach. "You can't leave now. After losing all that blood, you need time to recover. A doctor, hospital."

"I told you," he mumbled, unable to muster the energy to raise his voice, "no hospitals, no doctors."

"There's a chance of infection. You'll need antibiotics. And look at you. I mean you're practically asleep sitting up."

The alarm bells in Kaine's head screamed at him to stay awake, stay upright, leave, but every other system was shutting down. He couldn't fight it anymore. "Perhaps after half an hour's rest and some food?"

She nodded eagerly. "Yes, food. That'll help. How does a bacon buttie and a cuppa sound?"

Kaine's mouth watered at the thought. "Perfect."

"And a bowl of muesli for the slow-release carbohydrates?"

"Please."

She helped swing his legs around and back up onto the bench, her arm supporting his shoulders. He eased back, but the skin around the stitches tugged and he raised his knees to ease the tension. Sleep, he needed the dark recovery of sleep, but his mind nagged away. The clothes. Where did they come from?

Despite telling him she lived alone, Dr Orchard had access to men's clothes. She didn't seem the type to lie.

What was she hiding?

He looked into her eyes but found no evasion, only concern for his wound.

"Ollie's your ... husband?"

"He ... was," she said, avoiding eye contact.

"He passed away?"

"Eighteen months ago. Helmand Province, Afghanistan. An IED tore him apart. I ... I wasn't there for him, but I am here for you."

"You pegged me for military?"

"That tattoo on your forearm is a bit of a giveaway," she said without emotion and hurried from the room.

The door closed softly behind her, leaving him alone and thoroughly ashamed. His innate mistrust had led him to interrogate and probably upset the one person he'd met that week who'd hadn't tried to kill him.

Damn it.

Kaine dropped his head onto the bench and stared at the white-painted ceiling. If he had the strength, he'd have slapped himself and rushed to apologise. He grimaced.

"She's right. You are an idiot."

CHAPTER ELEVEN

Thursday 10th September – Lara Orchard

Cuckold Lane, Lincolnshire, UK

Once out in the hallway, Lara slumped against the closed door to her clinic. Confusion blurred her thoughts.

What was she doing? Standing there with a stranger in her clinic. A stranger who'd smashed his way into her life.

She looked up. Her eyes found the telephone hanging on the wall by the front door. She should call the police and run for help. But the injured man with the desperation in his voice hadn't attacked her or forced her to treat his wound. She'd volunteered.

He'd been prepared to leave. Despite the pain he must have felt, the weakness. He would have gone away and probably bled to death rather than hurt her. She'd seen it in his eyes. Desperation, and hurt, but no anger, no hostility.

When she'd first caught sight of him hammering on the front

door, for an impossible joyous microsecond, Ollie had come back to her.

Not that the stranger lying in her clinic looked anything like her dead husband. Too hard-faced, almost ugly. No, he looked nothing like Ollie. Perhaps the shape of his head, the hair colour, the cant of his shoulders. Maybe that had thrown her mind into a spin. Or maybe the need to have Ollie back in her life had been too strong and she saw what simply wasn't there. The human mind, while powerful, is not always reliable.

As well as his harsh features, the man was strong, lean, powerful. Or he would be after he'd recovered.

Something about him conveyed honesty and resilience, but sadness, too. The same sadness she saw each time she passed a mirror. Lara knew all about loss. It had been her constant partner for eighteen months. She'd deflected her pain by immersing herself in work, taking on more and more patients. The sick and injured animals needed her and didn't ask awkward questions or offer useless platitudes.

Even when the man grabbed her, she'd sensed no real danger. The horror on his face when he let go and saw the red mark on her wrist told a tale. He was someone to help, not to fear.

And the blood. Lord, he'd lost so much.

The knife wound, deep to the bone, was fresh, the blood hadn't had time to coagulate fully. He'd received it recently. That morning. He'd been in a knife fight. But at half past eight? Where? How?

Like her Ollie, the man in her treatment room was tough, battle-hardened. Half a dozen long-healed scars showed that.

How he'd managed to keep still for the sutures, she'd never know. The analgesic couldn't have worked that quickly or that completely, yet he didn't complain, hardly even twitched. He just stared at her through those deep brown eyes. Sad eyes.

Ollie's eyes.

Oh Lord. He really did look like Ollie. A tougher, grimmer version, he could have been Ollie's older brother.

Lara pushed herself away from the clinic door, turned her back to the phone, and hurried towards the kitchen. She'd promised the man a cooked breakfast. The domestic routine would calm her spirits and cure the hunger pangs nibbling at her stomach. Perhaps after being fed and watered, he'd tell her about himself. Maybe she could help him win whatever war he was fighting. At least he'd be stronger from the food. It would help speed his recovery.

Yawning wide and deep, she filled the kettle and set it on the hotplate to boil. The long night in the stable with Lady Sundowner had sapped her energy, but sleep would have to wait.

Breakfast, questions, decisions, and then rest.

Ollie, the careful one in their marriage, told her never to do anything serious without a plan of campaign. Now she had one.

Lara grabbed the vacuum-sealed packet of smoked bacon from the fridge and returned to the cooker. Out of habit, she reached for the radio on the windowsill.

CHAPTER TWELVE

Thursday 10th September – Sabrina Faroukh

SAMS HQ, London, UK

Sabrina Faroukh watched the mayhem from her quiet corner of the office, side-lined by a boss jealous of her superior IT skills. For nine hours, the bank of monitors on the far wall displayed her colleagues' efforts as they scrambled to answer the question, what happened to Flight BE1555?

She normally had the office to herself overnight, free to continue her clandestine investigations while her so-called superiors slept—but not tonight. Tonight, she had to sit and watch, and bite her tongue at their slow progress while pretending to carry out the menial task allocated by her boss, Department Director Joshua "Knowitall" Knowles.

The *putain*.

Knowitall, the design template for a chinless wonder, had been the prime target of her anger since her second week at Sampson Armaments and Munitions Services Plc when she pointed out a small but important flaw in one of the company's search algorithms. She'd presented him with an elegant patch to cure the problem. Knowitall told her he'd "look into it". The next day, she'd seen the same block of code spliced into the design matrix. Worse still, Knowitall had manipulated the root directory's timestamps to show the upgrades had been installed before her arrival at the company.

Not only a *putain*, but a plagiarist and a thief.

Ever since then, Knowitall had made her work permanent nights, probably hoping she'd resign, but Sabrina had her own agenda. It would take more than Knowitall's petty jealousies to deflect her from her goal. She would have the final say, and he would pay for his acts.

For the current emergency research, Knowitall had split the others into sub-teams. One monitored UK telephone traffic, a second listened to Middle Eastern chatter, a third searched email traffic for specific words and phrases. A fourth sub-team interrogated the petabytes of digital information pouring in from around the world. They were looking for patterns, hoping to assign blame or find a cause. The fifth team—Knowitall's Chosen Few—searched the satellite data.

As for Sabrina, she used the hidden sub-routine built into her system patch, and unwittingly delivered by Knowitall, to monitor the investigation's progress while appearing to do nothing but her routine task.

At 03:17, Gary Oakbridge, a member of the Chosen Few and the only one in the office to treat Sabrina as anything like an equal, jumped out of his seat, fist pumping the air. "A boat. The SAM was fired from a small boat off the Humber Estuary."

Sabrina smiled at him and nodded her congratulations while the other teams burst into spontaneous applause. She had reached the same conclusion thirty minutes earlier and had turned her attention to the data recorded by the Atlantic satellite *before* Flight BE1555 exploded. After reverse-plotting a small dot from the missile's launch site, she discovered its original berth in a coastal town called Cleethorpes.

Sabrina's heart had lurched at the revelation. One of the subcontracted observation teams, whose communications she'd been tasked with monitoring, was based in Cleethorpes.

Merde, what were the odds of such a thing?

Curiosity piqued, she pulled up the tasking sheets for the Cleethorpes observation team, designated OT7. She didn't have internal security clearance to access the file, but that had never stopped her before. In any event, why would SAMS hire people with Sabrina's skills if they didn't expect her to use them?

Through the night, she watched her bank of screens with keen interest, paying particular attention to the hourly reports from OT7 in Cleethorpes.

———

For hours, routine messages from around the country melted into a blurry mess. Even the arrival of a grey dawn failed to provide its usual boost. Sabrina's dry eyes stung, her back ached, and her shoulders took on the texture of concrete slabs.

Her immediate fantasy, a hot bath and sleep. *Dieu*, how she needed her sleep.

At 07:47, a blinking red "Communications Interrupted" warning message flashed up on one of her screens, and her morning sparked into agitated life.

Real action. At last.

Excitement mounted as her fingers worked the keyboard. It took five minutes to splice into the servers controlling Thanet Park Holiday Camp's surveillance system. One of their feeds threw up a surveillance image taken from a camera attached to the same cell tower used by OT7. It showed a high-level shot looking down on a car park surrounded by landscaped gardens. A sandy coastline ran diagonally from the top left corner of the screen to the middle right edge.

She zoomed in on the cars, searching for the distinctive shape of OT7's Range Rover, but the image blurred.

A few keystrokes sharpened the picture and enhanced the colour contrast.

At the top of the shot, a dozen people stood at the car park's entrance. A man in a bright yellow jacket spread out his arms to keep them well away from a specific car ... a dark-blue Range Rover!

Je t'ai! I have you!

Blue lights flashed at the bottom of the picture. The first responders had arrived.

She zoomed in on the Range Rover as much as she could and increased the resolution. A red patch smudged the windscreen and white jagged lines spread out from the edge of the glass.

Blood, it was blood.

Enough of her private work. The information was too serious to keep to herself. Reluctantly, she dialled Knowitall's office number.

"Yes," he said, brusque and aloof.

"It's Sabrina—"

"I know that. Make your report."

Putain de merde.

She took a breath. "Sir, the system flagged a break in communications with one of our observation teams. The one near Grimsby. Designation, OT7."

"Go on." He drew out the words, suspicion heavy in his tone.

"The team leader should have reported in twenty minutes ago, but he failed to make contact."

"Have they been late checking in before tonight?"

"Never more than five minutes."

"You've tried to reach them?"

Of course I have, you moron.

"They are not answering, sir. According to the overnight log, they have been in the same location since six o'clock last evening. As a test, I pinged the nearest cell tower. The service is still active, but I have no signal from the team leader's mobile. I found a surveillance camera close to where OT7 parked their vehicle. Sir, it has been compromised."

"In what way?"

She told him and waited for a response. None came.

"What are your instructions, sir?"

"Shut down your interface, close the file. Get on with what you've been tasked to do and leave the rest to me."

In her head, Sabrina threw out a string of invectives. Aloud, she said, "Are you sure, sir? I'd like to help."

The phone line clicked. The arrogant bastard had cut her off, mid-sentence. A minute later, Knowitall burst from his office and hurried to his Chosen Few, issuing shouted instructions as he approached. The exhausted men gathered around the wall of monitors, and Sabrina's ears filled with their animated conversation. Someone tuned into the Humberside local news channel, but the Cleethorpes story had yet to break. Only one item occupied the programming—the loss of Flight BE1555.

A number of local residents had captured the explosion on mobile phones. The news feeds replayed the footage time and again, and the tickertape banner running along the bottom of the picture repeated the few known details in a continuous loop.

Sabrina returned her attention to her own screens and continued watching the live events in Cleethorpes. She also hacked the Humberside Police's radio traffic. What she learned had her senses tingling from the roots of her hair to the tips of her fingers. Two men —the OT7 operatives, she assumed—had been murdered in a place less than twenty miles from the launch site of the missile that destroyed Flight BE1555. The events had to be linked. It could not be a coincidence.

Her opportunity to impress the executive team had arrived and she would not let the *putain* stand in her way.

The radio messages flying between the crime scene and the Humberside Police HQ in Hull mentioned eyewitness reports of a man fleeing the car park in a dark blue Citroën.

A Citroën?

The information rang a claxon in her head. She pulled up the tasking reports again and there it was, a single mention of OT7's target—the very same vehicle. The Citroën.

"Sabrina?"

She gasped and threw her hand to her chest. *"Dieu."*

Gary Oakbridge smiled down at her. Fortunately, he couldn't see her active screen from his position at the side of her desk. She hit a function key and the image changed to the SAMS logo screensaver. Lost in her own world, she had failed to hear Gary's approach. A schoolgirl error of such magnitude could end her project. She breathed deeply, trying to calm her tripping heart.

"You startled me," she said, hoping the warmth in her cheeks passed for girlish fluster rather than guilt.

"Sorry," he said. "Maybe I'll cough next time."

She exhaled slowly. "That would be a good idea. Can I help you?"

"Are you seeing this?" He pointed to the far wall. "One of our observation teams is in trouble."

"In Cleethorpes, I know. It was I who brought the situation to Mr Knowles' attention." She kept her voice low.

"Any idea what happened?"

"None. The team leader's last report said everything was, and I quote, 'quiet as the grave'."

How prescient.

Despite the cool air pulsing through the office, sweat pricked her scalp.

"If you're not too busy, fancy giving us a hand?"

"I would absolutely love to, but Mr Knowles told me to carry on with my other work. I would not want to upset him."

At the mention of Knowitall, Gary sneered and made a crucifix with his fingers. "Okay, understood." He checked his watch. "You'll be off the clock soon anyway. Fancy catching up later?"

Now? He chooses now to ask me out?

The Brits and their penchant for bad timing. She fluttered her lashes, but stopped when she realised how ridiculous it would appear. In her situation, romantic entanglements were completely off the table. She wouldn't be in England long enough and didn't consider Gary Oakbridge at all suitable. For her preference, he needed to add ten years to his age and around thirty kilos of power to his weedy frame.

"That would be lovely, Gary. Maybe when things are a little quieter?"

He beamed and touched her shoulder. "Excellent. I'd ... better get back to work before *Knowitall* sees me slacking." He whispered "Knowitall" and added a conspiratorial wink.

"Where is Mr Knowles?"

"No idea. He buggered off after delivering his orders and isn't in his office. With this flap on, he's probably upstairs brown-nosing."

"Sorry, 'brown-nosing'?"

"Toadying. Being a smarmy git. Trying to curry favour. You know, with Shafiq Patel? I saw the Great One in the loo earlier. Never seen him in this early. Someone upstairs must be in a panic. No idea why. It's not as though BrightEuro Airlines is one of SAMS' companies. Anyway, laters." He gave her a toothy grin, waggled his fingers at her, and hurried back to his desk.

Sabrina watched him go, her thoughts a mixture of relief tinged with suspicion. She couldn't help wondering whether Knowitall had instigated Gary's approach, and if so, why. She dismissed the thought as paranoia and returned to her private task.

She rolled the Thanet Park surveillance pictures back to before the last contact with the OT7 team leader, 06:31, and pulled out the shot. After watching for a few seconds, movement in the periphery caught her eye.

Between two vehicles on the far side of the car park diagonally across from the Range Rover, two men lay on the ground, one on top of the other. Sabrina zoomed back in on the quadrant and ran the picture forwards at normal speed. A man in a grey sweater appeared to be kissing the neck of the one underneath. Gay lovers making out in the early morning? A little chilly.

After a few moments of writhing, the man in the sweater rolled away and wrenched his partner's arm. A small flare lit the screen. Dark spray flew from the second man's head. He stopped moving.

Murder. *Mère de Dieu.*

She'd witnessed a murder. One of the OT7. A real murder, not a video game. Shock brought home the enormity of her task. She watched the action continue, unable to tear her eyes away from the screen.

The *tueur*, the killer, rolled the body under a hedge and then crouched behind the van, facing the Range Rover. The film took on the appearance of a fly-on-the-wall police show, but without the editing for safe public consumption. She could not stop her eyes wandering to the dark patch on the ground behind the killer—the patch of blood and porridge from the head of the dead man. It turned Sabrina's stomach. She breathed deep and returned her attention to the killer.

Focus, Sabrina.

Although horrific, gut-wrenching, she could cope with the shock as long as she kept her mind on the greater prize, her goal. But, *Dieu*, was it worth the risk?

After dragging the body and hiding it under a hedge, the assassin moved. He followed a stealthy route around the perimeter of the car park, hugging the shadows and using the parked vehicles for cover. He paused for a second behind a *campingcar*, and then slid into the front of the Range Rover. Seconds later, the red splodge and cracks appeared on the driver's side of the windshield, signalling the death of the second member of OT7. Two dead, both killed by the same man.

Qui es-tu? Who are you?

Three minutes passed before the killer exited the car and shuffled across the car park towards the Citroën. With his back to the CCTV camera, Sabrina couldn't work out why he carried himself hunched over on his left side until he reached the Citroën and turned to slide behind the wheel. The dark patch on the grey top had not been there when he finished his vampire act behind the white van.

More blood.

The killer, he was injured!

The second member of OT7 must have fought back. Good man.

A plume of white exhaust fumes trailed the Citroën as it exited the crime scene. Sabrina noted the time on the recording, 06:42:13, and the direction the car took after leaving the holiday park—west. Inland.

She rolled back the film to the part where the terrorist staggered towards his car, paused, zoomed in, and hit the "enhance" key.

Et voila. Got you!

Here he was, the person whom everyone in the country was looking for—the terrorist who had taken so many lives.

The aerial image caught the top of the man's head but didn't show enough detail for a digital reconstruction or facial recognition. That would have been too much to expect, but at least it was a start. From that still photo, and the length of the surrounding shadows, she made a reasonable extrapolation of the killer's height and weight—one metre eighty and around eighty kilos.

Barely able to contain her excitement, she pulled up a map of the region and searched the SAMS database for surveillance and traffic cameras in the locale. Using the combined system, she followed the Citroën along the A46 until it stopped in a lay-by under trees and out of sight of the camera. After approximately four minutes, the Citroën pulled away and continued west, still on the A46. She lost track of the car when the surveillance coverage fizzled out and the urban landscape changed to countryside.

A question shouted at her. Why the rest stop? Why would an injured man on the run stop in a lay-by for nearly four minutes when he'd surely prefer to get as far from the crime scene as possible. The words "injured man" rattled around in her head.

That was it! He needed medical treatment. Where would he go?

She pulled up an internet browser, keyed in a search string that included the terms "medical centres", "doctors", and "hospitals", and hit enter. Twenty-four hits—too many—but some were east of where she had lost the Citroën. She retained the ones to the west of the lay-by and extended the search to the next major town on the route, Caistor. After that, the killer's destination would be impossible to guess. She refined the search further by removing the hospitals and medical centres; the killer would surely avoid them and target clinics in smaller towns or villages. But there were no towns between the lay-by and Caistor, only villages and farms.

Farms, of course. Foolish girl.

She added one word to her search string. It returned three hits, one of them situated close to the Caistor Road, no more than fifteen miles west of where she'd last seen the Citroën—a Veterinary Clinic.

Heart pounding, she reached for her desk phone and dialled, but Knowitall didn't answer. She stood and looked at Gary and the Chosen Few. One man was busy trying to enhance the images of the Citroën in the lay-by, the rest were searching the traffic cameras in Caistor. If she told them what she'd found, they'd take the credit and control. Alternatively, she could take a risk and move her plan to the next level earlier than expected.

Bypassing Knowitall had the potential to drop her into deep *kaka*, but what did that matter? She'd been skirting the *merde* ever since joining the company.

In any event, Knowitall's days as *le petit roi*, The Little King, were coming to an end, and she already had plenty of ammunition to hasten his removal from the throne.

She dialled again, choosing a different number.

CHAPTER THIRTEEN

Thursday 10th September – Sabrina Faroukh

SAMS HQ, London, UK

Sabrina clutched the folder to her chest, her shield against the anticipated battle. On the chrome nameplate—which read Chief Information Security Officer, Shafiq Patel—she checked her teeth for
smeared lipstick and rapped on the door.

Patel summoned and she entered.

The rich smoky aroma of fresh coffee welcomed her into a bright,
warm office strangely devoid of personality. Patel sat behind a huge
chrome and glass table which dominated the centre of the room. The
walls to the right and behind him—floor-to-ceiling glass—revealed a
magnificent panoramic view of London, the Shard, and a cloud-filled
sky. A massive flat screen TV hung on the wall to Sabrina's left. Two
visitors' chairs completed the decor. Patel exposed nothing of himself
in the room. No family photos, no certificates of achievement, no

artwork, no display cabinets containing trophies. The office of a hard-working enigma. At least that was probably his intention.

"Come in, Ms Faroukh. Come in," Patel said, in an accent sharp enough to shatter glass—Eton followed by Cambridge, followed by a short spell in the army.

Before starting at SAMS, Sabrina had read the résumés of everyone in the company who might prove useful. Had he known, *grand-père* Mo-Mo would have been so proud of her preparedness, as much as he'd be worried for her safety.

Patel stood and approached her. "My PA tells me you have some information I need to hear immediately."

His smile revealed a set of gleaming white teeth, the canines so pointed, she imagined them tearing at a virgin's neck in a vampire movie. On autopilot, her hand reached up to play with the silver cross at her throat, but changed direction to tuck the folder tighter under her arm.

"Come, come," Patel said, "don't be shy. I won't bite."

Had he read her mind?

Patel offered his hand. Sabrina transferred the folder from one arm to the other and they shook. He had a firm grip, but soft hands. His manicured fingernails were protected by a layer of clear polish. Barely a crease spoiled his white cotton shirt, and he'd rammed his perfectly knotted, red silk tie tight against his collar. If not for the hook nose and the razor teeth, she might have considered him handsome.

"Can I pour you a coffee? It's Bolivian. Rather good."

She swallowed hard, trying to ignore the caterpillars gnawing at her insides. "Yes please, Mr Patel. Cream, no sugar."

She took the chair he'd waved her into and placed the file on the edge of his desk. Patel returned with a small cup and saucer. The coffee was delicious and the caffeine kick stimulating.

"Now," Patel said after reclaiming his seat, "what is it you have to tell me?"

Again, he smiled, and again the image of a predator slinked into Sabrina's mind.

Courage ma fille.

Bypassing Knowitall countermanded the rules of engagement, but it was the one certain way of drawing attention to herself. If she played her hand well, it would work. Mess up and she'd lose her chance, maybe irrevocably.

"Sir," she said, "I think I know where the target is."

Patel sat up straight, eyebrows raised. "Target? You mean the man who shot down Flight BE1555?"

"Yes, sir."

The blunt approach seemed to work well enough. She scooted her chair forwards and flipped open the folder. She passed him the hard copy of the image she'd captured of the killer. While he studied it, she took her chance. "Sir, I've put together a short presentation. It's on the primary server. Do you mind if I open it?" She pointed to the monitor on his desk.

Patel lifted his eyes from the photo and studied her for a moment, the creases on his forehead deepened. "One moment." He pressed a button on his desk phone. "You can come in now, Joshua."

The office door opened. Sabrina turned to see a scowling Know-itall framed in the doorway.

Merde.

He entered the room as though striding into battle and stood over her, fists resting on his skinny hips. A vein bulged on his temple.

"This is outrageous. How dare you bother Mr Patel without talking to me first!"

Sabrina kept her seat and her calm. "I tried calling you, sir, but you didn't answer your telephone and this information"—she pointed to the file—"is time sensitive."

"Time sensitive? Time bloody sensit—"

"Joshua, please sit." Patel's quietly refined voice cut him off at the knees. "I'd like to hear what Ms Faroukh has to say. It's not as though your much-vaunted Chosen Few can claim to have found the ... target."

"She's done what?" Knowitall looked down his nose at her, but his eyes came to rest on an area somewhat lower than her throat.

"I know where the terrorist is, or at least where he was sixty minutes ago."

Knowitall snorted. "We all know that. He was in Cleethorpes, killing two men!"

Sabrina kept her voice low and her tone neutral. "No. He left the car park at six forty-two and headed west. It is now"—she glanced at her watch—"eight thirteen. Ninety-one minutes later. Sixty minutes ago, he would have reached a tiny hamlet called Swadlow."

Patel spoke next. "Where is Swadlow, and why would this man go there?"

Sabrina took her chance before Knowitall could interrupt again. "I created a presentation and uploaded it onto the system. If you bring up the file, I shall walk you through the data."

Patel and Knowitall exchanged glances before Patel turned his attention to his keyboard and started hitting the keys. Although not exactly a two-fingered typist, he wasn't particularly fluid either. He took some time to select and run the file. Despite Patel's job title, his personnel file suggested he had little more than a working knowledge of systems architecture. His faltering typing speed confirmed it.

"If I might borrow your mouse, sir. I can show you on the big screen."

Patel nodded his consent.

Sabrina moved her chair to his side of the desk and picked up a hit of over-spicy aftershave. She eased away a few centimetres, loaded the file, and ran her quickly prepared presentation. The TV screen on the wall split into three windows, each showing the subject's Citroën from different angles and in different locations.

"I tracked the vehicle using roadside cameras until he stopped at this lay-by on the A46 for three minutes and forty-eight seconds. After that, I lost him when he reached open country. I tried everything, but he vanished."

Knowitall snorted, dragged his eyes from her cleavage, and turned them on Patel. "We know all this, Shafiq. My team used similar tracking methods and lost him at this very same spot. This is a waste of—"

"So," Sabrina continued as though Knowitall hadn't spoken. "I began wondering why the terrorist would stop in a lay-by when he should have been fleeing the area."

"And what did you decide?" Patel asked.

"What if that injury was even more serious than we imagined? What if he was running an internet search for the nearest medical centre or doctor's surgery?"

Patel lifted an eyebrow and smiled appreciatively. "What did you find?"

"There are dozens within thirty miles of that lay-by," she said pointing at the screen. "But, there are only three veterinary clinics."

"Vets! You can't be serious." Knowitall threw his arms wide and let them flop into his lap. "This is preposterous."

"So," she repeated, dragging out the word, "I hacked the Lincolnshire Police communications hub and found a traffic report. A man in a dark-coloured car lost control and nearly caused an accident at a roundabout on the A46, near a village called Laceby. After that point, the road narrows and there are few turnings until it reaches Caistor. There are dozens of surveillance and traffic cameras in and around Caistor, but the Citroën appears on none of them. However"—she hit the play button and one of the images became a map—"there's a veterinary surgery outside Swadlow, run by a Dr LB Orchard. This is likely to be the only place the target could find treatment before Caistor, unless he switched cars." She paused briefly before adding, "There have been no reports of vehicular theft in the area within the timeline."

Patel looked hard at her, his eyes slicing through her. "What are your recommendations?"

Oui! He was asking her opinion. She'd passed the initial test and was on her way.

"If I were you, Mr Patel, I would notify the Lincolnshire Police, send them to Swadlow, and warn them to take extreme caution." She pointed at the photo she'd given Patel. "The way that man defeated the members of OT7 shows how dangerous he can be."

Patel picked up the photo and studied it, thin lips pursed. After a few seconds, he nodded. "This is very good work indeed, Ms Faroukh, and shows a great deal of personal initiative, despite pressure to the contrary."

Although he tried to hide it, Sabrina caught the silencing head-shake he threw at Knowitall.

Patel dropped the photo and turned to face her, his expression deadly serious.

"As you know," he said, "SAMS has a close working relationship with the Home Office and the MoD. This intelligence will show how essential our support can be. It will, no doubt, help us win a number of imminent outsourcing contracts. Now, if you leave this with me, I shall set things in motion. Thank you very much for your excellent assistance. It will not be forgotten."

He tilted his head to the door and dismissed her with a thin smile.

"Joshua, remain here a moment, we need to coordinate our response."

Sabrina took care to keep the look of triumph from her face. She turned her back on the spluttering Knowitall and hurried to leave.

"Oh, Ms Faroukh." Patel's voice stopped her in her tracks.

She spun. "Yes, sir?"

"Need I tell you to keep this information to yourself? As I'm sure you understand, this operation is highly sensitive."

"Yes, sir. Of course."

She closed the office door behind her and leaned heavily against it. The PA's desk stood empty and Sabrina lingered, eyes closed, catching her breath, but the blood thumping in her ears didn't prevent her hearing Patel shouting.

"What the fuck are you doing, Knowles?"

"I don't know what you mean, Shafiq."

"Working on her own, that girl found Ryan Kaine when your so-called Chosen Few came up with fuck all."

Sabrina's smile fell and her ears pricked up.

Ryan Kaine?

The assassin?

"Really, sir," Knowitall said, rushing his words. "The vet thing's nothing more than speculation. Ridiculous."

"Makes perfect sense to me, you moron. We need to sort out this mess before the police find him."

Confused and concerned, Sabrina hurried away before Patel's PA returned and caught her eavesdropping. Her shoes *click-clacked* on the tiled flooring as she replayed the overheard conversation in her head.

How did Patel know the killer's name? The fact that Knowitall hadn't asked to whom Patel referred suggested a shared knowledge. This information, together with OT7's location—lying in wait for the man, Ryan Kaine—reeked of conspiracy. Patel and Knowitall were definitely involved, but were there others?

Did SAMS have something to do with the destruction of Flight BE1555? Surely not. What would be the motive? What on God's good earth was going on?

Desperate to hear the rest of Patel and Knowitall's conversation, she picked up the pace, almost breaking into a run before reaching the lifts at the end of the corridor. The doors to one stood open. She dived inside, hit the button for the twelfth floor, and waited. Nothing happened. As usual, jabbing the button three more times didn't help.

Venez vite. Come on, hurry.

Finally, the doors slid together. The lift descended too slowly, and Sabrina paced the carriage, begging it to move faster. Patel's revelation had made her task, her long game, a great deal more delicate and even more dangerous. She had to find out what they knew, and if that meant more unpaid overtime, so be it.

At her floor, Sabrina squeezed through the opening before the doors had fully retracted.

Most of what she needed was already in place—the Knowitall-installed bug. She knew it worked and had bypassed SAMS' much vaunted in-house security with ease during her first week on the job. Having internal access codes made the task simple. She only had to expand the program to include Shafiq Patel's node, and she'd have full access to his office, in both sound and pictures.

The modification took seconds. Now all she needed was to make sure Patel wasn't looking at his PC screen when uploading the worm to his system. She paused to collect her thoughts before picking up her desk phone and dialling Patel's number. His PA answered and put her straight through.

"Ms Faroukh, is everything okay?" he said, pleasantness itself.

Sabrina shivered as something nasty seemed to walk up and down her spine.

"Mr Patel," Sabrina said, "I'm so sorry to interrupt, but did I leave my folder on your desk? I can't seem to find it."

She took the calculated chance that he'd look straight ahead at where she'd been sitting and hit "enter" on her keypad. It was a small risk, but the message on Patel's screen would have appeared on the task bar and lasted a few seconds. It would have taken an expert to notice and, as he had already demonstrated, Patel was nothing of the sort.

"Can't see a folder," Patel said, amid a rustling of papers.

Sabrina shuffled papers of her own. "No, sir? ... Oh dear, I found it in this pile. I'm terribly sorry—"

"Not to worry, Ms Faroukh. Good day to you."

Sabrina ended the call and wiped sweaty hands on her trouser legs. She made sure no one, Gary included, was watching before donning her headset and loading her surveillance program. The ambient mic and built-in camera on Patel's thin client monitor picked up the sound and pictures from his office in glorious stereo and high definition. Her patch made sure the camera's green light remained off.

Her view was restricted to Patel's right shoulder, the window behind it, and the still-cloudy sky beyond.

Patel was speaking. "How the fuck did Kaine survive last night?"

"No idea, Shafiq," Knowitall answered, out of picture. "We have absolute confirmation of *Herring Gull's* destruction, but he clearly wasn't aboard at the time."

"This is a monumental fuck-up. We underestimated the man's

capabilities. Damn it. He has to disappear, along with anyone he's talked to since the crash. Understood?"

"The vet and any staff at the location?"

"Of course. We have to contain this. Get on with it. We can't have Kaine survive long enough to talk to the police. What's happening with the assault team?"

Assault team?

Sabrina's blood chilled. Did Patel really order Kaine's death and the deaths of an unknown number of innocent people?

"It's in hand, Shafiq," Knowitall answered, every bit the sycophant Sabrina knew him to be. "I've tasked a helicopter and two back-up wet teams from Hull. As far as they know, they're targeting a terrorist nest. They're conducting an MI5-sanctioned slash-and-burn operation."

Patel's shoulder hitched. "And they believed you?"

"Those people will believe anything if the money's right."

Sabrina ground her teeth.

The callous salauds! *The bastards!*

Knowitall continued. "The chopper will arrive at the farm in around twenty-five minutes, but the cars will take a few minutes longer. I have the co-pilot on comms now. He wants to speak with you."

"Put him on."

A third voice joined the conversation. His words were metallic and the flattened drubbing in the background suggested a helicopter. She recognised the effect of noise-cancelling electronics.

"This is Shotgun in Air One. Can you send us everything you have on the targets? I'd like to know what we're facing. Over."

Patel's shoulder moved and his face appeared full centre on the screen. Gone was the smile on the darkly handsome face. In this guise, his eyes were dead, and his lips formed a thin gash. He pecked at his keyboard.

"Information's on its way, together with all we have on the location. A vet's clinic based at a farm. Isolated. Should be a clean take-down. There might be some collateral, but you'll be paid well for each hit. Be careful though, the primary target, Ryan Kaine, is ex-special forces gone rogue. He killed two of our men in Cleethorpes and shot down that plane last night. He won't make it easy for you."

"*Sweet,*" Shotgun said, his accompanying laugh cruel. "*I love it when they fight back. Makes my job all the more fun.*" A bleep sounded from somewhere inside the helicopter. "*Information received. ETA at Lodge Farm. Twenty minutes. Let's go smoke some towel heads. Shotgun, out.*"

For a second, Patel smiled at his screen and then looked up.

"Now then, Joshua. What are we going to do about the delicious Ms Faroukh?"

Sabrina's mouth turned sand dry. She awaited Knowitall's response, heart pounding, unable to breathe. *Dieu,* what had she started?

"I'm open to suggestions, Shafiq."

"Keep your eyes on her. She could prove useful if we can learn to trust her. Might even bring her on board. She's better at your job than you are."

"If you say so, Shafiq," Knowitall replied, anger in his tone. "I'll keep my eye on the interfering bitch all right. As for letting her into the inner circle, that's up to Rudy and the boss."

"For once, Joshua," Patel said, leaning back again, leaving only the view of his shoulder, "you are absolutely right."

Sabrina recognised the name Rudy—Rudolpho Bernadotti. The "boss" could only refer to Sir Malcolm Sampson. So, Patel and Knowitall were not simply a rogue cadre inside the company, the rot spread down from the top, not out from the core. In time, she would use that information, but first, she needed to undo the damage she had caused.

The vet, his staff, and Ryan Kaine were about to die. Sabrina's work had led these people to the vet's door. She cared nothing for Kaine. He'd chosen his path and could face the consequences, but the vet and his staff? What had they done wrong? With trembling fingers, Sabrina terminated the connection.

She had but a few minutes remaining.

She cleared her spy program from the system and deleted her digital footprint as only she knew how—clean and untraceable. The clock on her screen counted off the time. Sixteen minutes to save a vet and Ryan Kaine. Not enough.

She closed her system, grabbed her handbag, and rushed from the room. Both lifts were in use. Running down twenty-four flights of stairs would be slower than waiting. She paced the hall for what seemed like hours before the doors finally opened. The ride down took forever, and she spent it staring at the timer on her mobile.

The seconds ticked away the lives of Ryan Kaine and who knew how many in the veterinary clinic. Oh Lord, she shouldn't have wasted the minutes cleaning the system. People were going to die because she wanted to protect her mission.

By the time she reached the ground floor, her heart was pounding, and sweat stuck the blouse to her back. The doors rolled open. She fixed a smile to a face that wanted to scream and strolled through the reception area while every cell in her body begged her to run. As usual, she threw a nonchalant wave to the pair of security officers guarding the entrance. She stepped though the revolving doors, feeling the guards' eyes bore into her neck the whole way.

Outside, she turned left and picked up the pace. Once out of sight of the entrance, she grabbed her unregistered mobile and dialled the number burned into her memory— the number for the vet's clinic.

She hit enter and prayed.

CHAPTER FOURTEEN

Thursday 10th September – Morning

Cuckold Lane, Lincolnshire, UK

Kaine eased back into the firm couch. How nice would it be to have a few hours' quiet R&R in a nice warm room with the nice warm vet? He closed his eyes for a moment, but the stink of stale sweat and dried blood wafting up from beneath the thin cotton sheet made his nose wrinkle in disgust. If it smelled that bad to him, what would his medic think?

After struggling to his feet, he stood on shaky legs until his balance returned and used the counter as a crutch to help him reach the washbasin.

He untied the string-for-a-belt and dropped the filthy jeans to the floor along with his salt-and-sweat-stained trunks. Ten minutes later, after judicial use of flannel, liquid soap, two towels, and delicate avoidance of the new dressing, Kaine felt and smelled almost human.

He made it back to the bench and carefully worked into the clothes Lara had left. As she'd promised, the rest of the pile, briefs, white t-shirt, plaid lumberjack shirt, and black Chinos were a pretty good fit. The trainers presented a challenge—tying the laces while trying not to bend at the waist took time and effort. He spared a moment to luxuriate. Only someone who'd lived rough for any length of time could truly appreciate the restorative effect of clean clothes. All he needed to complete the delight was a full stomach, but he'd have to make do with the promised bacon buttie on the move. The sooner he left the farm, the better it would be for the vet.

The enticing aroma of frying bacon drew him from the clinic and pulled him down the hall. From the open doorway, he studied the kitchen layout.

A rustic affair with a gas-fired range, oak units, pots hanging from beams, and a large oak dining table with six chairs welcomed him with their homeliness. Classical music—a light piano piece he didn't recognise, tinkled over the sizzle of bacon, the crackling pop of frying eggs, and the boiling kettle. A CD, or Radio 3? Either way, no news. Kaine breathed easier. With luck, he'd make it out of the farm without her learning what he'd done. He'd do anything to avoid seeing hatred in Lara Orchard's hazel eyes.

She had removed the lab coat, and he managed a good look at his saviour for the first time. Wavy brown hair cascaded over slim shoulders. A green polo shirt tucked into her tight blue jeans showed a narrow waist and wide hips. She filled the jeans with long, slim legs and a firm backside he could stare at for weeks without losing interest.

He coughed to announce his presence. Lara, pouring boiled water into a teapot, turned. She gasped and dropped the kettle onto the hotplate. It landed with a metallic crash and a watery sizzle.

Kaine raised his hands. "Sorry. Sorry. I didn't mean to scare you."

"No, no." She turned away and reached for a dishcloth. "It's just that, for a moment, I thought you were Ollie. The clothes."

Damn it. The last thing he wanted was to upset her.

"The water. Are you okay?"

"I'm fine. It didn't get me."

She mopped the spill while Kaine failed to think of something to say that might ease her shock and disappointment. He stayed in the doorway, keeping his distance until she pointed him to the table.

"Take a seat, breakfast is ready. The tea won't be long. How do you take it?"

"Sorry, I need to go. It's too dangerous for you if I stay."

Kaine swayed and threw his hand against the wall for balance. She rushed forwards but he raised his free hand. "It's okay. I'm good."

"Look at you. You're in no condition to leave. Eat something. It'll do you good and it's ready."

Reluctantly, Kaine gave in and allowed her to help him into a chair. He bit back the pain of movement.

"So, tea?"

He managed a weak smile. "White, please. No sugar."

After the night he'd suffered and the news he'd received, watching Lara pour him tea in a country kitchen with breakfast on offer and orchestral music playing in the background was delightfully bizarre. He'd give it ten minutes, no longer. Already, he'd ridden his luck, and hers, too far. Way too far.

With the most delicious breakfast he'd ever tasted demolished within the allotted time and his stomach pleasantly full but not enough to strain the stitches, Kaine drained the last of his second mug of tea. His stomach gurgled with content, and he patted it.

Told you I'd see you right, buddy.

Lara had made do with two slices of toast spread with generous licks of butter and dollops of honey, and a bucket-sized mug of coffee. She ate quickly and sat at the opposite end of the table. Her eyes never left him.

Scared or curious? He couldn't tell. Probably a little of both.

The questions must have been running around in her head ever since he'd arrived on her doorstep, yet she maintained excellent restraint. In her place, Kaine would have made a passable impression of Torquemada and the Spanish Inquisition.

"Mind if I ask a question?" he said after lowering his mug to the table.

She shook her head.

"Where are all your pets, sorry, companion animals? I'd have expected a vet's house to be overrun with hairy wee beasties." He grinned to lessen any perceived insult to her chosen career.

A ghost smile lifted the edges of her full lips. Dimples formed. Smiling, she looked about twenty-five and absolutely beautiful.

"I'm between dogs at the moment. Baroness, my golden retriever, passed recently and I need time to recover before ... I've never been one to fill the house with 'hairy wee beasties'. And I'm not a fan of cats. Supercilious creatures. Don't tell any of my clients, though."

He matched her smile, said, "It'll be our secret," and lowered the mug. Time to leave. Every extra second he stayed put her in greater danger. He cleared his throat and the wound jabbed fire into his side. The topical painkiller hadn't lasted long. "I need to go and—"

"You should stay until you're stronger. Someone needs to monitor your wound for signs of infection. And as I said, you might need a course of antibiotics."

"It's okay. I have friends down ... elsewhere I can call on. I'll be right. As you noticed from all the scars, this isn't the first time I've been stitched up."

In more ways than one.

"When I listen to the news, what will it tell me?"

Kaine straightened. He had to hold his side as the skin stretched around the wound and stung like hell.

"Whatever you hear ... Whatever you're told, it's not true. When the police come, remember to tell them I forced you to treat me. Tell them you were frightened for your life. Promise?"

She sidestepped the question with one of her own. "What have you done? It's serious, right?"

"And complicated, but at the heart of it, I'm innocent. You probably won't think so by the time the police finish talking to you, but ... Hell, sorry. I've said too much. I need to get far away from here as fast as I can." Kaine wanted to tell her, to unburden himself, but that would have been too damned selfish.

The clock on the wall over the cooker read 9:07.

That late?

"I have to go. Thank you for everything. I've left some money in the clinic to cover the cost of treatment and that wonderful breakfast." He used his hands to push off the table and stand. "There is one more thing. My car ..."

"It will be recognised?" she asked, also standing.

Kaine nodded. Of course the bloody thing would be recognised. The wet team at the caravan park proved that. The Cleethorpes car park would have been covered by surveillance cameras, too. He should have checked before, but the overnight operation in its original form had been legal and, according to Gravel, sanctioned by both the MoD and the Civil Aviation Authority.

Bastard.

That morning, fatigue and blood loss had made him sloppy.

Stupid, stupid, stupid.

Gravel was going to pay. He'd pay soon and pay hard.

Lara took a set of keys from a drawer in a big old Welsh dresser. "There's a Land Rover in the barn. It's old but reliable and well-serviced. Nobody will know you have it. Leave your Citroën here for the police. I'll tell them I don't know how you left. Go now and be safe."

"Where's the nearest police station?"

"Caistor or Grimsby. Both about half an hour away."

"Okay, good. Call 9-9-9 the second I leave."

"Shouldn't I give you more time?"

Why was she helping? Simple loyalty to her dead husband, or was she trying to keep him there while the cops raced towards the farm? Kaine couldn't waste time on the internal debate. He had to go with it and hope for the best.

"Make sure to tell them I'm armed. They'll throw up some road blocks and wait for the armed response teams for backup. It'll give me more time."

"Okay. I will."

He took her hand. "I'll never be able to thank you for this, Lara. When I'm safe, I'll have a friend return the car to you, fully serviced. It'll be running like a Ferrari and have a full tank. I know one of the best mechanics in the UK."

"Thanks, but it's not important, I have another car. I never expect to see you or the car again. Do I make myself clear?"

Fighting the impulse to kiss her cheek, Kaine followed her through the hall to the front door. The sun had made a watery appearance and the courtyard glowed under its yellow light. Lara pointed to a huge wooden barn about fifty paces from the end of the stable block.

"The doors are on the far side. Are you fit enough to drive?"

He tried another smile. "Breakfast made me a new man. I'm as strong as an ox."

"Liar," she said and held out her hand. "Keys, now."

"No. I don't want you leaving a trace of evidence in the Citroën. Lead the way. I'll follow."

She frowned, but seemed to understand his logic. "Okay. Follow me to the barn. I'll open the doors," she said and trotted away.

Kaine watched her cross the yard, impressed, and not only with the way she moved. A great woman. Quick on the uptake. Someone to rely on in a crisis. If things were different ...

Halfway to the Citroën, he pointed the key-fob at his car and hit the button. The car's locks click-fizzed open and the hazards blinked twice. He took a jacket from the passenger's side and threw it over the driver's seat before sliding behind the wheel. Before he could fire up the engine, the rattling drone of a helicopter approaching from the northeast sent his internal alarm bells clanging.

Jesus!

The pain in his side receded as adrenaline powered through his system.

He fired up the car, found first gear, and took off. The Citroën slipped sideways as the drive wheels fought the muddy surface for traction. The driver's door slammed shut under the forward momentum, and he followed the route Lara had taken around the side of the barn.

The sun flashed in his eyes as he turned the corner to the far side of the building. A shadow skipped over the ground in front of him.

Lara had the double barn doors open. Kaine careened the Citroën into the darkness without checking whether there was enough room to accommodate it. He jerked up the handbrake and threw open the driver's door.

The chopper eased into a hover, thirty metres off the ground and the fuselage rotated sideways on. The loading bay door stood open, the inside dark. The muzzle of an assault rifle poked out through the opening.

"*Ryan Kaine,*" a sardonic voice boomed from a loudspeaker slung beneath the cockpit, "*we know it's you. That Citroën's a dead giveaway. C'mon, arsehole. Show yourself! Don't keep us waiting!*"

Lara turned to face the helicopter, looking up. Framed in the doorway, lit by the sun, she made an easy target. An easy kill.

"Get down," Kaine screamed. "Now!"

She turned, a questioning frown creased her brow.

Loud cracks sounded over the thrum of helicopter rotors. Puffs of dirt raked towards her. One missed her heel by inches.

Kaine dived from the Citroën, rugby tackled her to the ground, and scrambled the two of them out of sight behind a wall of hay bales.

"What are you doing?" she screamed, pushing his chest with her palms. "Get off me."

"Lara, stop. They're shooting at us!"

CHAPTER FIFTEEN

Thursday 10th September – Morning

Cuckold Lane, Lincolnshire, UK

"What?" Lara screamed. "You're insane!"

Five more rounds drilled through the wall and thumped into the bales by her head. Her face crumpled and she scrambled away as Kaine rolled to his knees.

"Stay low. Keep behind the bales and for God's sake, don't let them see your face."

Kaine crawled to the back of the Citroën, keeping to the shadows as more bullets punctured the barn's wooden walls and thudded into the ground around him. The holes let in narrow shafts of sunlight. Behind him, metallic clangs and shattering glass blended with the growing cacophony of helicopter rotors chopping air.

A bullet whined past Kaine's ear. He felt its heat. Tailgate open, he grabbed the package of weapons he'd taken from the wet team and scooted, head down, to the far side of the Citroën. With a Maxim 9 in each hand, he took a moment to catch his breath.

Focus. Calm.

Panic and fear had no place in battle. No value.

Somewhere, in the deep recesses of his consciousness, he knew some of the stitches had popped, but that injury could wait.

The chopper maintained a static position for aerial assault, hanging above the meadow, clear of the tall hedge behind. Sideways on, the pilot kept the cockpit tilted down to maintain a good sightline and the tail lifted to maintain the hover. The pilot—black helmet, mirrored lenses—turned his head towards the barn, monitoring the scene.

The open side door revealed a huge man in military fatigues. Muscular arms, thick neck, flat top buzz cut. Teeth bared in a savage smile. The L85 assault rifle in his hands bucked again, but the helicopter shifted on an updraft and the bullets missed their mark and punched three more holes into the wall. The L85 had a sniper's scope, but Buzzcut ignored it and opted for the spray-and-hope approach. Fortunately for Kaine and Lara, he'd chosen the wrong weapon for that application and the wrong platform for accuracy.

Another bastard firing indiscriminately in a civilian zone. Anyone could have been inside the barn. Women, children. Anyone.

Kaine's hands squeezed the Maxims' textured grips. For all the good a couple of 9mm handguns would do against a military helicopter, with its bullet-resistant glass cockpit and armoured fuselage, he might as well throw rocks. He searched the freshly ventilated barn. Looking for what? An anti-aircraft weapon? A cannon? A bigger rock?

Get real, Ryan.

Wait. What was that?

A closer look at the aircraft gave him hope. The white-on-blue livery and the Humberside Police decals confirmed it.

Not military. No armour. Good.

The machinegun spat again and his Citroën rocked under the

impact of 5.56mm calibre bullets. Kaine worked his way further into the darkness of the barn.

They'd killed his car and were only minutes away from killing him and Lara.

Damn it.

"Lara, can you hear me?" he yelled above the din of aero engine and gunfire.

"Yes," she screamed, voice high-pitched, terrified.

"The hedge behind the chopper. What's on the other side?"

"Farmland."

"Any buildings? People?"

"No. Just a field and beyond that, woods."

More lead flew past his head—part of the softening up process before the pilot landed and disgorged Buzzcut to finish the job. A horse whinnied. Hooves hammered on stable doors. A ridiculous part of Kaine's mind wondered whether they were properly bolted.

"Lara, lie flat. Cover your head."

Kaine chambered a round into each Maxim, inhaled and held it. He waited for the next pause in the barrage—the pause to reload.

Buzzcut looked down, pulled the spent magazine, and popped in a fresh one. Kaine jumped up, raised the weapons, aimed at the cockpit glass screen, and fired in one continuous movement.

Eight shots. Eight hits. All dead centre.

The glass cracked and the pilot's expression changed from cynical smile to open-mouthed scream. He yanked up on the collective, a reflex action Kaine had seen a dozen times in novices under fire. The aircraft's nose lifted and it backed away at speed. Buzzcut yelled as he fell back inside the cabin.

"Lara, stay down!" Kaine shouted.

As the pilot wrestled with the controls, trying to gain altitude, the nose leapt up. The boom dropped, the tail rotor touched the ground, and the whole assembly sheared off.

The airframe flipped. The main rotors dug into the earth and shattered, sending a shower of carbon fibre shards flying. A howl of overtaxed engine drowned out the men's screams. Flames rose and the concussive force of an explosion punched the air from Kaine's lungs. He dived backwards, scrambled for the protection of the Citroën, and covered his ears.

A blast of superheated air buffeted his shoulders, back, and legs. Like battlefield shrapnel, pieces of dead helicopter rattled into the barn. They tore through the thin wooden walls and dropped in smouldering pellets into the dry hay.

"Lara?"

As he struggled to his feet, the pain in his side returned. No time to do anything about it now. Smoke and dust thickened the air. He sneeze coughed and popped another stitch.

"Lara! Come on. We've got to go!"

Kaine found her cowering behind the bales. Two feet above her head, the tip of a rotor blade stuck out from the top bale. Heat from its torn edge scorched the hay. If it caught fire, the whole barn would go up in minutes.

He reached for her hand.

"We can't stay here. Get up."

She recoiled from his touch and tried to burrow into the foot of the hay wall but he grabbed her wrist and pulled hard. She fought him, eyes wild, screaming. He pulled her into a bear hug and held on until she calmed enough to hear his words.

"I'm so sorry I got you into this. Don't know how they found me, but we have to go. That was the advanced party. There'll be more on the way. Probably coming by road."

"You shot it down. You murdered those policemen!"

"They weren't police. They were hired killers. Come on, Doc. It's not safe here."

She screamed. Hysterical sobs wracked her body. He slapped her cheek, and her mouth snapped shut. She stared out through the barn doors at the orange and yellow flames and the black smoke in her paddock. Tears fell, but her shoulders stilled.

"Why?" she asked, her voice barely making it over the roaring flames.

"Now isn't the time." He held out his hand. "Keys to the Land Rover. Now."

She opened her fingers and a bunch of keys fell to the floor. He scooped them up and dragged her to the vehicle—a grey beast that looked as though it could climb a vertical cliff face and punch through a brick wall without buckling. Protected by his Citroën, the Defender had survived the explosion unscathed.

He bundled her into the passenger seat, dived behind the wheel, and turned over the engine. It coughed, died, and then fired up with the rattling, throaty roar of an elderly but well-maintained diesel. He reversed it alongside the remains of his Citroën and left it on idle.

Struggling against the wound to his side, Kaine spent a couple of precious minutes transferring the grab bag, his overstuffed military backpack—his Bergen—and the remaining magazines into the Defender. With time flying, he left his weapons case undisturbed and dived into the driver's seat. He drove out of the barn, handbrake turned, and raced into the courtyard.

"Stop," Lara shouted. "Please stop, I need my medical bag."

"What? We don't have time."

"Look, you're bleeding again. Please. I won't be long."

Kaine looked her in the eye, searching for deception but finding only shocked concern. He nodded.

"Be quick. No telling how far away the back-up team is."

She raced into the house, leaving the front door open, and was gone no more than a few seconds before she reappeared at the run, red-face, breathing hard. A large medical bag hung from a strap over her shoulder, and she clutched a handbag in her fist.

Kaine almost smiled at the absurdity. Women and their handbags.

As she slammed the front door, a telephone rang, the repeater bell in the porch loud enough to be heard over the roar of the flames and the whinnying horse. Lara stopped, reached for the handle.

"No, leave it!" he yelled. "We've got to go."

Lara shook her head as though snapping out of a daze. "Yes, right. Sorry."

She raced down the path and stole a glance at the stables before throwing her bags in the back and jumping into the passenger seat.

"Lady Sundowner. Do I have time to call Jackie, my assistant?"

"Later," he said and rammed the Land Rover into first. "Is there a back way out of here? We need to avoid the main roads."

She pointed at the barn and Kaine threw the Defender into a U-turn. Stuttering movement in the rattling wing mirror caught Kaine's eye. A big car, dark blue, crashed through the wooden gates at speed.

"Shit!"

The backup team.

CHAPTER SIXTEEN

Thursday 10th September – Morning

Cuckold Lane, Lincolnshire, UK

Kaine stamped on the throttle and the Defender shot forwards. The middle rear window exploded in a shower of fractured glass. Lara screamed.

"Get down," he shouted, grabbing her by the upper arm and pushing her into the footwell. "Stay there."

As they passed the end of the barn, Kaine spun the wheel left. A volley of bullets tore into the ground, throwing up pellets of concrete. As with Buzzcut, the men in the backup team fired indiscriminately, giving up accuracy for weight of firepower.

Kaine ground his teeth and ran through his options. There weren't many.

The pursuers in a Renault SUV—complete with bull bars and flashing blue lights—were less than thirty metres behind and gaining quickly, the ancient Land Rover no match in terms of speed.

Through the wing mirror, Kaine could make out a man in a dark military uniform and sunglasses leaning through the front passenger window. The automatic carbine in his hands spat bursts of flame. A second man in green fatigues fired a pistol from the rear on the driver's side. Together, the men threw down a withering hail of death.

Kaine aimed the Defender at the burning helicopter, praying the smoke would hide them. He eased off the throttle and allowed the gap between the vehicles to close quickly.

Twenty metres.

Fifteen metres.

Point blank.

He spun the wheel to the right, exposing his side of the Defender to the firing line, and then stamped on the brakes.

The Renault driver reacted too late. The front wing of the Renault drove into the Defender's rear bumper in a grinding, howling crash of metal on metal. Lara screamed again. The Defender's rear end lifted and snapped around, throwing them into a clockwise spin.

"Lara, keep your head down!"

Kaine punched open his door while the two heavy vehicles performed an ugly, slow-motion pirouette.

Gunfire coughed and barked.

Maxims drawn, Kaine dived from the Defender, twisting as he hit empty air.

Hot metal plucked at his shoulder. A wasp stung his thigh.

Still flying, Kaine fired three rounds. The first bullet punched a hole through the Renault's rear door. The next two blew the rear passenger's head apart.

The driver, eyes wide, mouth open, fought the steering wheel, but couldn't halt the two vehicles' dance.

Kaine hit the ground, rolled, found his feet, and fired in the same motion. The driver's lower jaw disintegrated. His head slumped against the steering wheel. The screaming stopped.

The man in the shades, crushed between the side of the Renault and the Defender's exposed spare wheel, offered no more threat. The cars stopped, the concertina opened. Shades slipped from sight between the panels of crumpled metal.

"Lara, stay where you are. This isn't over yet."

Kaine clamped his left hand over his rib wound—bleeding again—and dashed to the far side of the Renault. The driver and the man behind him were dead, but Shades still moved. Blood bubbled from his mouth. He stretched out an arm to reach for the H&K carbine he'd lost in the crash, but his fingers fell ten centimetres short.

One look at the would-be killer—pelvis and thighs pulped, shattered right forearm, splinters of white bone piercing the skin, blood flowing from the wound—confirmed he didn't have long.

Kaine knelt, grabbed the man's hair, and pulled his head up. Blood gurgled in his throat.

"Your mates. How far behind?"

Shades grimaced. "Help me—"

Kaine nodded. "Yes, I promise. Now, tell me. Your mates. How many and how far behind?"

The man's eyes closed.

"Answer me, damn you."

Kaine jabbed the butt of his Maxim into the man's destroyed forearm. Shades screeched and his eyes opened.

"Three ... three men. Couple of minutes behind us. Maybe ... maybe less."

"Okay. That's all I need."

Kaine stood and left the man to bleed. Nothing quick or painless. No better than the bastard deserved. He'd shown Lara no mercy and deserved none in return.

"Hey! Are you alive?," Lara yelled, still hidden in the footwell of the Defender. "The guns stopped. What's happening?"

"Stay where you are. Be right back. Some housework to do."

Kaine scooped up the carbine and sprinted to the barn, checking the weapon's readiness on the way—thirty-round magazine, still more than half full. He skidded to a stop, bouncing against the building's gable end, ignored the pain in his side, and poked his head around the corner.

A second Renault, a duplicate of the first, ploughed through the wreckage of the gate. It skidded to a sideways stop inside the courtyard, blocking the entrance. Three men—all wearing dark military fatigues, all carrying H&K G36k carbines—jumped out and took cover behind the SUV.

One of the men raised a hand to his mouth and talked into his wrist mic. "Brooke, this is Charlton. You got him? Over."

The other two men, weapons shipped and ready to fire, crouched either side of Charlton, taking in the smoky devastation. The carbine muzzles moved in sync with their eyes, checking the area for danger. Prepared. Cautious. More sensible than their mates.

The burning straw bales superheated the air inside the barn and soaked into its wooden walls. Heat toasted Kaine's right side as he leaned against the barn's gable wall. Behind him, thick, black smoke billowed from the downed helicopter and flames licked up from the fuselage. The smoke-filled warzone gave him cover.

"Brooke? Where the fuck are you? Over."

Quietly, slowly, Kaine worked the charging handle on his carbine, forcing a round into the chamber. He clicked the fire-selector to "E", semi-automatic—single-shot mode.

Charlton repeated his question once more and received the same silent response. He turned to his men, keeping his words slow and deliberate. "This, I don't like. Kaine's a dangerous fucker. Keep your eyes open. Let's go see what's burning on the far side of the barn. Remember, swift kills, no prisoners. Understood?" He paused a beat while both men acknowledged their orders. "Okay, Bob, right flank. Ali, take the left. Move at the double on my three count."

Despite keeping his voice low, the wind carried Charlton's words clearly over the crackle of the burning helicopter and groans of the smouldering barn.

Staying crouched, Charlton edged to the front of the Renault. Bob and Ali fell into position behind him.

As a right-hander, Kaine's preferred firing arc flowed right-to-left and took in Bob, Charlton, and Ali, in that order. He raised the carbine, targeted Bob centre-mass, took a breath, held it, and slowed his heartrate. Three against one. Bad odds, but he had surprise and good sightlines once the men left the cover of the Renault. He could have taken one or two out where they stood, but he needed the Renault undamaged.

Charlton, eyes scanning the route ahead, raised his left hand. His gloved fingers made the count.

One …

Slowly, Kaine released his breath.

Two …

His heartrate slowed further.

Three.

The men darted forwards at the half-crouch, fanned wide.

Kaine fired. Three shots. Three hits. Three men fell. Two moved. Bob didn't.

Ali, the last man down, squeezed off a shot before hitting the ground, but his bullet smacked harmlessly into the wall three metres above Kaine's head.

Kaine fired again. The bullet tore through the gap between Ali's ballistic vest and armpit. It ploughed through his upper chest and exploded out through his neck. Like his mate Bob, Ali stopped moving.

Charlton lay face down, arms splayed wide. Boots scraping concrete as he struggled to find safety, struggled to breathe, his carbine apparently too heavy to lift.

Kaine hurried across the courtyard. He turned the man onto his back with the toe of his shoe. The bullet had torn a chunk out of the team leader's neck. Spurting arterial blood pooled on the concrete, forming the curl of a question mark. Angry, dark eyes turned on Kaine. Charlton's right arm moved, he tried to lift the carbine, but the weapon stayed on the ground as though bolted to the concrete.

Kaine clamped a hand over the neck wound. "Who sent you?"

Charlton's lips moved, words formed, but no sounds came.

Kaine released his grip. Blood pumped again, this time with less force. Charlton's eyes lost focus. He stopped breathing.

Kaine wiped his hand on the dead man's jacket, but the sticky blood refused to budge. Confirming three dead was easy, but he still had no time to waste. A neighbour was bound to have dialled 9-9-9 already. Even here, out in the sticks, it wouldn't take the emergency services long to arrive.

As he found the keys to the Renault in Charlton's trouser pocket, something inside the barn succumbed to the heat. A explosion ripped through scorched timbers. Thick black smoke spewed skyward It stank of rubber and creosote. Kaine coughed and another stitch gave up the struggle.

He sidestepped the corpses, climbed into the Renault, and drove it towards the carnage of the first car. Seconds later he had to coax a pale and trembling Lara from the Defender.

"Are you hurt?"

She shook her head. "I-I don't think so."

"You sure?" Visually, he checked her for wounds and found none. The Defender, although badly crumpled and riddled with bullet holes, had lived up to its name.

"What happened? I-I heard shooting again."

"Nothing much. Come on. We need to change cars. This one's a gonner."

Her eyes flitted across his body and she gasped. "You're ... bleeding."

He raised a hand to dismiss her concern. "Keep popping those stitches. Sorry for messing up your good work, but it can wait. We have to go. Now."

She shook her head and pointed a shaky finger at him. "No, not just your side. Your shoulder and leg, too."

He followed the direction of her gaze. More bloodstains. "Scratches, no more. We'll stop when we're safe. Are you okay to help me move the gear to the Renault?"

"Y-yes. Of course."

She reached for the Defender's rear door and tugged on the handle. It wouldn't budge.

"Step back."

Kaine smashed the window with the butt of the carbine, reached inside for her medical bag, and placed it on the ground at her feet. The handbag still hung from her shoulder. He gave her an encouraging smile.

"I'll get you out of this mess."

"Will you?" Her glazed eyes showed little recognition.

"I promise. But we need to go. Load your kit into the Renault.."

He emptied the Defender and threw his gear into the back of the Renault. By the time he'd finished, Lara had made her way into the passenger's seat and fastened her seatbelt, apparently on auto-pilot. In the distance, sirens wailed.

Lara shook her head as though trying to wake from a nightmare. She turned scared eyes on him. "Lady Sundowner ..."

"The stables are nowhere near the fire. The horse is safe. Where to?"

"Sorry?"

"We need a back way out of here." He spoke quietly, keen not to spook her any more than a team of gun-toting mercenaries destroying her home already had. The sirens grew louder.

She pointed straight ahead, her fingers trembling. "There's a ... track through the woods. Leads to a road."

Kaine threw the Renault into gear and stamped on the accelerator.

CHAPTER SEVENTEEN

Thursday 10th September – Midday

Cuckold Lane, Lincolnshire, UK

Lara's directions took them past the remains of the still-burning helicopter.

Buzzcut had been thrown clear of the wreckage and lay in a broken heap. A twisted metal rod stuck out of his crushed chest. Blood flowed from the wounds. Dead eyes stared at the sky. The big bastard had been happy enough to kill Lara and anyone else on the farm and deserved nothing but a painful, lingering death. Pity he'd died so quickly, although Kaine doubted Lara would see it that way. As they drove past, she turned away from the gore and closed her eyes.

"Don't cry for him, Lara. He'd have killed us both."

She lifted her chin and said, "I know, but ..."

They reached a crossing where three tracks merged and split in two. "Where to now?"

She pointed left. He engaged four wheel drive and picked up speed.

Lara's instructions—delivered in a considered, but emotionless monotone—took them to a rutted, potholed lane running along the hawthorn and oak hedge, heading deep into the woods.

"Turn right at the next fork," she said, rubbing her forehead, "and keep heading south until we reach Fulton Lane, then take a left. After that, it's up to you. I ... Oh Lord, is this really happening?"

He shifted into low gear as they entered the woods. The lane became a dirt track, barely wide enough for the Renault to pass without scraping branches and brambles. The mottled light played havoc with his vision, one second gloom, the next dazzling sunshine.

Lara raised her hands to her mouth and gasped. Tears filled her eyes. He'd seen the same post-battle reaction a hundred times in men trained for conflict, but Lara was a civilian. Kaine needed to give her something to do or he'd lose her to the pain. She needed a practical task. Something normal. Something within her control.

"Lady Sundowner," he said.

"What?"

"You wanted to text your assistant."

Lara blinked and looked around the car, as though realising where they were for the first time. "Yes, yes. Of course. Thank you."

She searched her handbag and dug out a mobile. With flying thumbs, she tapped a message and hit send.

"Let me see the phone."

She held up something Kaine's younger friends might have called a "brick". No bells, no whistles, no internet, just a phone. He relaxed a little. It seemed that Kaine the technophobe and Lara the vet had something in common after all.

"Remove the battery and SIM card and lob them out the window."

"Why?"

"So nobody can find the mobile easily and track you through

your contacts. No GPS on a phone that old. You'll need to go into hiding until I can fix this mess."

Like that's going to happen any time soon.

She broke open the mobile and did as he asked.

Seconds later, they burst through the trees and bounced along too fast for comfort. A hedgerow guarded their left and a field of ripening wheat spread out on the right. Or was it barley? He never could tell. Another hedge met them at right angles and a three-bar gate blocked their way.

Kaine jammed on the brakes, but before he could reach for his door handle, Lara jumped out, opened the gate, and waved him through. He looked on in amazement. It hadn't taken her long to recover from her first gun battle. In fact, she'd recovered faster than some highly trained rookies he'd seen.

He drove through, waited for her to close the gate and return to her seat, and stared at her. The determination on her striking face did something to his insides, but he locked those rogue feelings away. He'd entered her life unannounced and torn it apart. Now, someone wanted her dead to cover their tracks. Although he was nothing but a pawn in the Principal's sick game, it was one hundred percent his fault that the vet's fate was tied to his. She was his responsibility.

"Do you have anywhere safe to go? A non-family member? Somewhere miles away from here. Preferably abroad."

"I'm going nowhere until I've patched you up again."

She lifted his shirt to inspect the bandages. Fresh blood leached through the gauze and a thick trail had soaked into his borrowed Chinos.

"You've torn at least three stitches. I'll need to repair the damage as soon as you think it's safe."

"That won't be until we reach London," he said, showing her a grim smile. "But we can stop somewhere for a few minutes if you insist. We need to dump this car anyway. Whoever's chasing me will have a locator on it." He deliberately avoided saying "chasing us" and began driving again. "Do you know anywhere around here we could pick up a vehicle? Preferably an old one—one without a built-in satnav?"

She closed her eyes for a moment. "My friend, Roberta, has an old Beetle, but ..."

Kaine stopped at another fork in the track. "Which way?"

She didn't answer.

He grasped her hand and squeezed. "It's okay, I won't involve her directly. We can dump the Renault a distance away and walk. But we do need to hurry. Which way and how far?"

"Take a left here and then the next right. It's not far."

Ten minutes later, and under her instruction, Kaine pulled the car off the track and into a thicket of oak, chestnut, and beech. He parked under the heaviest canopy, popped the bonnet, and emptied a magazine into the electrics. He also disconnected the battery. Chances were it wouldn't disable the tracking, but it was worth a try.

Heavily laden, they tramped through dense undergrowth. Brambles tugged at trouser legs and low branches clawed at exposed faces. Clearly used to the terrain, Lara kept up a stiff pace. After a few hundred metres, she led them to a footpath, and their speed improved.

Kaine might have enjoyed the half-hour stroll through the woods with an attractive companion, but the bags, the seeping wound, and the reason for their trek weighed heavily on his mind and his body.

By the time she stopped at the treeline, Kaine was a gasping puddle of sweat. Blood loss and fatigue had taken its toll. Light-headed, vision blurring, he took a knee and dropped his bags to the leaf-strewn path.

Lara stood in front of him, studying him closely. She rested the back of a cool hand on his forehead for a moment before pressing two fingers to the side of his neck.

"Pale and sweaty, pulse racing. You need rest."

He shook his head and struggled to his feet. "Not until you're safe. How far to your friend's place?"

"We're here. Look."

She pointed through a gap in the trees. A meadow—tall grass and wild flowers waving in a light breeze—sloped gently down into a shallow, sunlit valley. At the bottom of the slope, a black tiled roof showed above the feathered grass.

"That's Roberta's house." Lara checked her watch. "She won't be there for at least four hours."

"You sure?"

"She teaches at the local primary school. Walks to work and doesn't come home for lunch. I know where she keeps her spare keys. Ready?"

Kaine stood, breathed deep to fight the headrush, and nodded. "Lay on, Macduff."

Lara arched an eyebrow. "And damn'd be him that first cries, 'Hold, enough!'"

"A fan of the Bard?"

She shrugged. "By default. Ollie kept dragging me to plays at Stratford. Macbeth was one of his favourites. Most people misquote that Macduff line. Ready?"

"Born ready."

———

As promised, Roberta's isolated cottage stood empty. Lara took the spare keys from under a planter by the back door—highly unoriginal, highly insecure—and let them into a kitchen similar to Lara's in design, but half the size.

"Sit," she said, pointing him to a dining chair. "Clothes off. I need to clean all the wounds."

Kaine stripped down to his briefs—no embarrassment needed with a medic—and leaned back in the chair. He closed his eyes and allowed her to work. Again, she gave a running commentary.

"The thigh wound is little more than a scratch. It's already stopped bleeding. Just need to clean and dress it. The one in the shoulder is a little deeper, but we'll get away without stitches. You were lucky. Both missed anything vital."

Still with his eyes closed, and almost resting, Kaine sighed. "Call me Fluke. With my luck, I should book a trip to Vegas."

He opened his eyes to the wonderful sight of her gentle smile. How could she be so relaxed around a man who'd brought such destruction to her life?

She must have picked up on his confusion. The smile fell and she stopped stitching his rib wound. "Back in the barn, before you fired at the helicopter, you asked what was on the other side of the hedge. Why?"

Kaine shrugged. "No particular reason." The last thing he wanted was for her to form a bond. She needed to keep her emotional distance.

"What would you have done if I'd told you there was a school over there? Or an old people's home?"

Busted.

He shook his head. "No idea."

He'd have probably thrown up his hands and surrendered, praying they'd leave Lara alone. No way he'd have endangered a school full of kids or an old folks' residence. His life, even Lara's life, wasn't worth that.

"And in the yard, when that Renault attacked us, you exposed your side of the Defender, not mine. And you kept shouting at me to keep my head down. You were risking your life to protect me."

He needed to stop her dissection of his motives. "I brought the trouble to your door. I wanted to—"

"Whoever those men were, whoever they worked for, they didn't care about who they killed. Whatever you've done to attract that kind of trouble, you cared about ... what's it called? Collateral damage. You saved me and I'm trusting you with my life. Doesn't mean I have to believe everything you say, though." She spoke with an authority and a finality that allowed no dissent.

"Fair enough. Now, I don't mean to rush you, but we need to get as far away from here as fast as we can."

She lowered her head and returned to her darning. The minutes ticked by. Kaine's lids grew heavier by the second. He needed rest, but this was neither the time nor the place.

"There," Lara said, snipping the final piece of tape from the roll and attaching it to the dressing, "that ought to hold until the next time you decide to practise your gymnastics."

She removed the surgical gloves, rolled them into a tight ball, and tucked them into a plastic bag with the used dressings and suture kit. She rested her hand on his knee and looked hard at him.

"Sorry for how I reacted back at the farm. I ... panicked. You had no choice and saved our lives, but ... God, they tried to kill us. Why?"

Kaine placed his hand over hers and squeezed. It was a strong hand, used to manual work, but tiny in his big calloused mitt. He considered telling her everything, but she'd hate him, and he didn't want to see revulsion in those big hazel eyes. He hated himself for the cowardice.

"It's a long story," he said at last, "but I can't tell you or you'll be in even more danger. Just remember what I told you before. Don't believe everything you hear about me in the media. Most of it won't be true."

Although some of it will.

She didn't respond, but stared intently at him, her expression unreadable. At least she didn't spit in his face. The longer the silence dragged on, the more uncomfortable it made him. He blinked first. "Okay, where's this Beetle?"

"In the garage. Do we need to go so soon? Roberta won't be home for hours and you'll be stronger if you rest here for a while."

"Thanks, but no. We're too close to the Renault. They're probably already running a full background check on you, looking for friends and relatives in the area. If I thought it was safe, I'd leave you here, but ... I'm sorry."

She fixed him with a fierce glare and shook her head. Firm and adamant. "There's no way I'd let you go alone. Considering that nightmare we just escaped from, I'm safer with you, and you're in no fit state to drive."

Kaine had been expecting an argument, but once again, the gutsy woman surprised him. All he could think to do was smile and thank her for understanding.

"Can I leave a note for Bobbie?"

"Okay, but be quick and no details. I'll need five minutes to wash and change clothes. After that, we're gone. Where's the bathroom?"

She pointed to a door. "Through there. First on the right."

"Thanks. Won't be long."

He pulled a pair of jeans and a polo shirt from the Bergen and left Lara to her note.

————

The canary-yellow Beetle, of the same vintage as the recently deceased Defender, grumbled and growled as they forced it along otherwise quiet country roads. This time, Lara drove and Kaine rode shotgun. The stiff seats didn't recline, which helped him stay awake and alert.

"How much cash do you have on you?" he asked after fifteen minutes' driving and with no sign of a tail.

"Seventy-odd pounds and some loose change."

"I have a few hundred. It'll be enough for our immediate needs. You can't access your bank accounts for a while. The transactions can be traced. When we reach London, I'll have a friend transfer all your funds into a sanitised account to keep your location hidden. He'll also give you access to my emergency funds."

"My God. Sanitised accounts, emergency funds—who are you? And who the heck is chasing us?"

Kaine ignored her questions, but appreciated the way she used the collective pronoun and didn't just lay everything on his shoulders. But she was wrong. Everything was down to him. The faster and further he could distance himself from her, the safer she would be. It would be safer for him, too. He'd be able to act without worrying about what this remarkable woman thought of him.

"That's just the point," he said. "I have no idea, but I know a man who does."

"Why don't we go ask him?"

He grinned. Straight to the point. Another thing to admire about the veterinarian.

"I intend to, but it won't be as easy as that."

"Why not?"

"For one thing, he lives south of London and would never answer my call. For another, he's a mean SOB who makes me look like a wimp."

"That," she said, taking her eyes from the road for a moment to look into his, "I don't believe."

She tucked a strand of her dark hair behind her ear and fell silent until they reached a T-junction. "Are we heading for London?"

"Yes, but we need to ditch the Beetle as well. Where's the nearest train station?"

Lara checked the rear-view mirror and took the right turn, heading west. "Lincoln Central's about an hour away but it runs a slow train to King's Cross. Newark North Gate is thirty miles further, but the express service is faster."

Kaine took a moment to make the decision, fatigue slowed his thought processes. "Lincoln sounds good. The sooner we can ditch the Beetle the better. There's a chance our friends will think we'll stick to the roads."

She fed in more petrol and the little car leapt forwards. The speedometer needle crawled all the way up to a lightning fast sixty-five mph.

In London, he'd be on familiar ground. He'd have access to people who'd protect an innocent stranger in need of a bolt hole— even if that same innocent stranger didn't want to use it.

Meanwhile, a couple on a train would attract far less attention than a scruffy, single bloke in dire need of a shave. A self-serving action at best, but he'd keep her safe until London. After that, God alone knew what he'd do.

CHAPTER EIGHTEEN

Thursday 10th September – Early Afternoon

Lincoln Station, Lincolnshire, UK

A heavy, dark mantle of cloud rolled in from the east, blocking the sun. Before long, the beautiful late summer's day had morphed into drab autumn.

It started raining half an hour into their journey. Light at first, but persistent, it grew into a heavy downpour. The rubber seal on the passenger's door, perished with age, allowed a constant dribble of water to soak the bottom of Kaine's left trouser leg. Wonderful. He'd only just dried out from his overnight dip. Were it not for his delightful companion, the journey would have been hellish.

Along the way, Lara threw an inquisition of questions at him, most of which Kaine couldn't or wouldn't answer.

They passed through the tiny hamlet of Thorseway, its tranquillity shattered by the ancient Beetle's rattling engine and holed exhaust. Three miles later they took a left onto the attractively named Peppermill Lane. Tree lined hedges covered them from the air and potential satellite identification.

After a further four miles, they slowed to negotiate a sleepy Market Rasen and kept to the minor roads. If someone had asked him to explain the difference between major and minor roads in Lincolnshire, he wouldn't have been hard put to answer. The potholes and unrepaired tarmac appeared much the same. The Beetle hit every bump and rut on dead springs. Kaine had ridden in more comfortable Armoured Personnel Carriers on his way into battle. Whatever happened to the simple life of the soldier battling insurgents? He knew where he was back then ...

Something squeezed his knee. He jumped. "Wha—"

"We're here."

Kaine blinked, rubbed his eyes with the heels of his hands, and tried to ease the crick from his neck. Everything hurt—legs, back, shoulders, neck, side. Everything. To cap it all, an evil troll was attacking the inside of his head with a lump hammer, every blow timed to match the steady beat of his heart. His eyes scratched when he blinked and stung when he didn't.

"Where?"

"Lincoln. The station's around the next corner. You've been asleep for half an hour."

Asleep? Fine bloody shotgun he made.

"You should have woken me."

She'd stopped at a red light, the indicator flashed for a left turn. The rain had stopped and a pale sun lanced through broken cloud.

"You needed the rest. How do you feel?"

He scrunched up his face and rolled his shoulders. "Never better."

"Liar. You look awful."

After less than a day, she already had him pegged.

"Thanks. You, however, look wonderful."

He meant it, too.

The lights changed and she made the turn.

"I meant medically. Pale skin, red eyes, sweating. You look hung over." She placed the back of her hand against his brow. "No fever, though. Give me your wrist."

"That's okay. My pulse is running at around fifty bpm. A little fast for me, but not in the worrisome zone."

"You know your resting heartrate?"

"It's a good way to monitor fitness and health."

And mental state.

"Fifty is low for an adult male."

He shrugged. "Fully rested, mine bottoms out in the low forties." At the risk of telling her too much, he added, "I'm endurance trained. A long distance swimmer."

She ignored his attempt at wit, indicated right, and waited for a gap in the oncoming traffic. An elderly man in a shiny BMW gave way and waved them through. Lara nodded her thanks and turned into the station entrance. Filter arrows painted on red brick pavers directed them past the station's main entrance and into the Pay & Display car park.

Miraculously, they found an empty spot at the front, under a row of chestnut trees. She reversed into the space and cut the engine. After nearly ninety minutes inside an ancient tin can of a car, the silence brought rest and delight. Only the ringing tinnitus and aching back left an unwelcome reminder.

Kaine rubbed life into his face and flexed his fingers. He turned to Lara, studying her expression.

"What's wrong?" she asked, looking worried.

"Before we go into the station, I need to give you some instructions. Please don't ask questions. I know what I'm doing. Ready?"

She nodded and frowned in concentration as he reached into his grab-bag and handed her one of his baseball caps.

"Pull your hair up and put it under the cap."

He waited for her to follow his orders.

"Try to relax. Especially your head and neck. Tension there is a dead giveaway. The station is Victorian, and probably impressive, so don't be afraid to look around a little. If there are any CCTV cameras, try not to stare directly at them but don't make it obvious that you're avoiding them. With me so far?"

"Yes," she said. "I've watched spy movies."

He clenched a fist. "This is real life, Lara. We don't have a director to shout 'Cut' if we screw up."

Her chin jutted. "Dial it back, *mister*. You might be used to all this, but I'm not. I'm doing my best, darn it. I just want this to be over."

You and me both.

He wanted to apologise, but anger was good. She could use it to help her through the next part.

"Buy two cheap returns to King's Cross, not singles. Most people buy returns, and singles will stand out in the clerk's memory. You're going to be one of the few who pays cash, so you'll already be out of the ordinary. I'll be at your side when we arrive, so the clerk will expect you to order two tickets, but I'll slope off to buy some food and water, and guard our backs. I'll join you at the barrier or on the platform. Okay?"

"Okay."

She swallowed and took a faltering breath.

"And one last thing, be friendly, but on no account smile if the ticket clerk's a man."

"Why not?"

"You have a stunning smile, Dr Orchard, and the last thing we need is for you to knock some poor guy off his seat."

She sighed heavily and shook her head. "Idiot."

"You're not the first person to notice. And that's much better. Relax those shoulders and you'll be fine. Ready?"

Kaine retrieved his gear from the back seat, working his right side only. He added the small cache of weapons and magazines to the grab bag, and strolled towards the station. A grey brick Victorian building with tall chimney pots and a working clock, it was typical of the period.

Lara kept pace with him, but maintained her distance.

"What's wrong?"

"You have guns in your bag."

"Yes. For defence only and leaving them in the Beetle's a bad idea. Wouldn't want them falling into the hands of a car thief. My mother could break into that thing."

"It's not that, I was worried about metal detectors." She kept her voice down.

He snorted. "No worries there. Too expensive to install. I've only ever seen them at St Pancras International for Eurostar passengers. If we're unlucky enough to run into a spot check, I'll dump the weapons somewhere safe. Just try to relax. We're a couple off to the big city for a long weekend break."

They crossed the herringbone brickwork and reached the entrance. Lara stepped across to him and brushed his upper arm with a hand. "I know you're protecting me and, after everything we've been through, I trust you. Just wanted you to know I understand."

"Thank you," he said, enjoying the warmth of her touch through his thin shirt. "You don't know how much I appreciate that."

True to his years of training, Kaine pushed through the entrance first, scoping out the station before allowing Lara into potential harm's way. The doors led through to an impressive open space, high ceiling with black-painted wrought ironwork and tiled walls— cream above, bottle green below. It had the patina of age and differed little from hundreds of railway stations dotted around England.

Ticket machines ran along the left-hand wall and led to a glass-fronted ticket office. A London Underground-style grey barrier guarded the archway through to the platforms. The right-hand side of the station housed a shop, a cafe, and toilets.

They reached the back of a short queue—an elderly couple and two single men in business suits. Lara stood tall at his side, neck craned upwards, taking in the wrought iron roof struts.

"Relax, Lara," he whispered. "It's not that exciting."

"But it is. Look at that beautiful scrollwork."

The time ticked slowly. The female half of the couple searched through a handbag the size of a postal sack. Tension built in Kaine's neck. He relaxed his shoulders and took a huge breath. He spoke again, this time a little louder. "I'm going to check out the shop, love. Fancy a sandwich for the journey?"

"Good idea. Anything but egg mayonnaise. And don't forget some water."

Kaine took his bags with him to the newsagent and made his food choice without losing sight of Lara. He also took the opportunity to screen everyone else in the station, but found nothing suspicious. He split a twenty for the groceries and pocketed the change, but not before counting it carefully. Fieldcraft for beginners—when in enemy territory, blend in with the natives. His clothing screamed "working man strapped for cash" and his type didn't throw money around, unless he was "down t' pub of a weekend".

By the time he left the shop and wolfed down a chocolate-coated power bar, Kaine had loosened up and felt almost human.

Lara, finished at the ticket booth, stood at the station barrier with her back to him, head straight ahead, shoulders unnaturally stiff. The moment Kaine saw her new posture, he knew something was wrong. He scanned the concourse, but nothing had changed. For a fleeting moment, he considered making a discreet exit, but that would have left Lara alone to cope with whatever had spooked her. No way could he do that.

With his eyes wide, ears open, and senses on full alert, Kaine sauntered towards her, slowing when he reached the ticket kiosk. Attached to the wall above the ticket clerk, a small TV showed a newsreader in full flow. Behind him, the headline read, "Disaster in the North Sea." The tickertape banner scrolling along the bottom of the screen gave the salient facts—"83 passengers and crew die in horrific plane crash. Terrorist attack suspected. Full bulletin at 12:30."

Kaine reached Lara and looked at her. Tears brightened her eyes but had yet to fall. Her chin trembled.

"Please hold it together, Lara. I'll explain on the train. I promise." The words sounded hollow in his ears. Pitiful. "I understand how you must feel."

She turned to look at him, doubt and fear etched on her face.

"Explain it?" she whispered. "How can you explain that? Did you do it? Did you shoot down that plane?"

"Not here, Lara. Not now. I told you not to believe everything you heard."

He reached out a hand but she shrank away as though his touch might be poison. Her tears fell and they hurt him more than the bite of Red's hunting knife.

"Eighty-three people," she whispered, backing away until stopped by the barrier.

"It's not what you think," he said, realising how pathetic he sounded. "Please, Lara. Give me until King's Cross to explain."

"What's to stop you shooting me and throwing me from the train the moment we're out of the city? The moment you've finished with me."

"I would never do that. Here, take this."

Grimacing against the weight, he held out the grab bag, but she made no move to take it.

"All my weapons are in there."

She wiped the tears from her cheeks and shook her head. He placed the strap over his shoulder again, taking care to keep the bag away from his wound.

Behind them, three passengers entered through the main doors. Each bypassed the ticket machines and used passes to open the barrier. Kaine stepped closer to Lara, keeping his voice low but firm. "Either listen to what I have to say, or I'll hand myself over now. In that case, the bastards we're running from will kill us both. They may kill others to get to us, and if I'm in custody, I won't be able to stop them. Your choice."

"Y-You can explain that?" she said pointing behind her to the ticket office.

"Yes. At least my part in it. What time's our train?"

Eyes scanning the station, she hesitated before answering. "We're on the 12:27, arrives in King's Cross at 15:10. There's a change at Retford." She coughed. "Over one hundred and forty pounds for a so-called super off-peak return. Completely ridiculous."

She spoke up as a man in the red jacket of a train operator passed within earshot. With her action, Kaine relaxed a little. She'd given him some leeway.

"Thank you, Lara."

Once through the ticket barrier and onto the platform, they stood in stiff silence for five unbearable minutes. In the short time he'd known Lara Orchard, her opinion of him had become important, too important, but he didn't want to lose her trust. He wanted, needed, her to believe in his relative innocence. Even if she were the only one in the world who did.

While she stared at a poster advertising weekend coastal breaks at "Unbeatable Prices", he spent the time planning how to explain the mess he'd dragged her into.

Luckily for his blood pressure, the red-liveried loco arrived bang on schedule. Miracles, it appeared, did happen occasionally.

They found a near-empty compartment at the front of the train. Kaine took the aisle seat, with his back to the engine. It commanded a good view of the carriage. Unable to reach up without stressing the stitches, he stored the Bergen and the grab bag on the seat beside him. Lara sat opposite, her face a blank mask.

The moment the train pulled away, she wrinkled her face into a frown and raised an eyebrow at him.

"Thank you," he said. "For giving me a chance. And back at the farm, you were brilliant."

She deliberately ignored his compliments and said, "What should I call you?"

"Ryan Liam Kaine."

A brief head shake of disbelief. "That's your real name?"

"Yes. Why?"

"Liam was my father's name."

"Irish?"

She nodded. "On his mother's side."

"Ah. I wondered how it squared with your Anglo-Saxon surname."

She blinked and looked at him as though he'd said something daft. "Orchard is my married name, dummy."

Bloody idiot.

"Of course. Sorry. Missed too much sleep recently. If it means anything, my family came from Ireland, originally. About fifty years ago."

The train gathered momentum. The driver exercised the two-tone horn.

"Okay, Ryan Liam Kaine," she whispered, leaning forwards and resting her forearms on the table that separated them. "Let's have your story. From the top."

He leaned close to her, trying to make it look as though they were close friends passing the journey in pleasant conversation.

How much would he give for that to be true?

CHAPTER NINETEEN

Thursday 10th September – Lara Orchard

Aboard a train, heading south, UK

A million different thoughts raced through Lara's sleep-fuddled mind as she studied Ryan Liam Kaine—if indeed, that was his real name.

Handsome, in a rugged and self-contained way, and fighting exhaustion—according to the dark rings under his brown eyes. Thin lips, square jaw, dark hair flecked with silver, just about long enough to show the start of soft waves. His chin sprouted two or three days' growth, but his was no fashion statement, no designer stubble. On him it was a by-product of days spent battling for survival. She'd already seen his lean, well-muscled body in the treatment room.

What wasn't to like? Under different circumstances, of course.

At dawn, the most pressing thing in her life had been to ensure Lady Sundowner's survival. Now, a little over seven hours later, she was running for her life with a man—a man the headlines would have her believe was a mass murderer—who bore a vague resemblance to Ollie. Not so much in his physical appearance, but in the troubled expression on his careworn face.

Ollie had looked and acted the same way after returning from his first tour. The same sadness in the eyes, driven by the vile things he'd witnessed, the things he'd done, the things he couldn't talk about. The look that told Lara part of her husband would be forever lost to her. And then the real loss when the two uniformed men arrived at her door with the message all military wives dread but half expect. Impossible to prepare for.

Kaine carried his pain in the same way as Ollie, but there was something else behind the injury, a desperation and a firm determination to fight on.

Who was he, this Ryan Kaine? A military man used to battle—the way he coped with the rib injury proved he was what he said. How anyone could operate so well with such a wound was beyond her. He hadn't even accepted the painkillers she'd offered for fear they'd dull his reactions, spoil his aim.

Most people she knew would have ended up in a hospital bed, a quivering mass of self-pity, with a lesion as severe, but Kaine suffered in silence. Darn it, he barely even flinched when lifting the bag with its load of weapons and the heavy military backpack.

His eyes roamed the carriage, continually studying the few fellow passengers. She searched too, but without knowing what to look for. Six people. An elderly couple, lost in their separate paperbacks. A young mother fussing with her baby. The child gurgled and waved chubby arms. Two single men three booths apart, one in his thirties, but carrying way too much weight, the other knocking on the doors of retirement. None seemed to be taking any interest in them.

Kaine took a breath. "Ever heard of the SBS?"

Lara shrugged and shook her head. She was in no mood for a pop quiz.

"What about the SAS?" he whispered.

That, she did recognise. "Of course. The Iranian Embassy, Ranulph Fiennes, the explorer, and the one who writes the book.

Chris Something-or-other." She matched his volume and, like him, barely moved her lips.

Kaine nodded. "The Special Boat Service is the Royal Navy's version of the SAS, only we do our stuff in boats. Think of us as the UK's Navy SEALs, but with more class and skill."

She refused to smile at his pitiful attempt at humour.

"What does this have to do with"—she glanced around the carriage again, checking for prying eyes and cocked ears—"what happened last night?"

"You asked for the whole story, and I'm setting the scene." Another pause for air. "I spent the best part of twenty years in the Royal Navy, the last eight with the SBS. I expected to pull another ten and retire on a half-decent pension." He pulled back his shoulders and winced. Lara stole a quick glance at his rib area. No seepage, thank goodness. There was a limit to the number of times she could stitch a wound.

"Didn't work out the way I'd planned, though," he continued, speaking low and always keeping one eye on their surroundings. "Government cutbacks turned me and half my operations group into civilians. Think about that for a sec. I'd spent my whole adult life training to protect my country's interests and at aged thirty-nine, they assigned me a hammock on the scrapheap. I had all these mad fighting skills and an intimate knowledge of state-of-the-art weaponry, but bugger-all else."

Lara recalled a similar conversation with Ollie when he was offered early retirement. If only he'd taken it, maybe none of this would be happening.

"What did you do?" she asked.

For a few moments before answering, his head turned towards the window, apparently watching England's green and pleasant land flash past the window. In reality, his eyes roved, studying the other passengers through the reflections in the glass. "I applied to join the police force, but certain things on my record put the kybosh on that idea."

He stopped talking when a woman wearing a red suit arrived to punch their tickets. When she left, he opened the grocery bag and spread the food on the table. Lara chose the cheese and tomato roll and a bottle of fizzy water. She drained half in one thirsty glug. It had a taint of plastic, but quenched her thirst. Kaine took his time over his drink, a couple of sips, no more.

She wiped her mouth with one of a pile of paper napkins that fell from the bag and unwrapped the roll. "Keep going, please. I can listen and eat at the same time."

"Anyway, after the police rejected me, I spent a year or so contracted to a firm offering close protection for rich city types. You've seen them? Men and women in dark suits and sunglasses defending the rich and famous?"

"Did you work for any celebs I'd know? Would I have seen you on the news ... in the background?" she asked before taking a bite out of her roll. Not good. Tasteless, rubbery cheese and the tomatoes lacked any seasoning. Could anyone eat tomatoes without salt?

Darn it girl, concentrate.

He shook his head. "Doubt it. A couple of top bankers, a Saudi prince, a Russian oligarch. Arrogant arseholes the lot of them. I hated it. The money was good, but life isn't all about the cash."

He lowered his eyes and bit into his ham and salad baguette. Made a face. He didn't look as though he enjoyed it any more than she was enjoying her plastic cheese roll.

"You resigned?"

He chewed fast and swallowed before answering. "In a manner of speaking."

Still chewing, she made a rolling-forward gesture with her free hand. She was finding it more and more difficult to keep her expression neutral. He spoke as though each word sliced through his throat. How difficult must it be for a man used to keeping secrets to reveal so much to a complete stranger? And he'd yet to reach the sensitive information.

"Let's just say my contract was not renewed."

"Why not?"

He winced. "The company I worked for didn't expect a junior staff member to educate one of their fee-paying clients on the correct way to treat an employee."

Kaine took another bite.

Darn it, this was like birthing a foal on a winter's night, in the middle of a field, in a snowstorm. "You can't stop there. Full disclosure, remember?"

He swallowed, rewrapped the baguette, and dropped it into the bag. Stalling and looking none too happy about the words "full disclosure", he took another sip of water.

"Okay," he whispered, "the Saudi prince backhanded a waitress when she spilled his wine and, I ... broke his arm."

Lara raised her eyebrows to relax the frown she'd worn since seeing the news bulletin. He still hadn't explained how he'd received the rib injury, or his part in the deaths of those eighty-three passengers.

"Keep talking."

"After the close protection job, I spent a year as an instructor at an outdoor centre in the Scottish Highlands. We specialised in corporate team building. You know the sort of thing. Adventure breaks for whingeing middle-managers who'd pull a muscle uncorking a bottle of Beaujolais Nouveau and suffer a nosebleed if they climbed the stairs too quickly."

Lara allowed him a slight smile. "You lasted a whole year? I'm seeing a pattern here. Can you move on now, please? Get to the point." She showed him her watch. "We'll be reaching Retford soon."

"Getting there, ma'am."

He rolled the crick out of his neck and sank back into his seat, but his gaze kept flitting around the carriage, ever watchful.

"I didn't have the patience for wiping the arses of a bunch of management types and started looking for a change. Then I had a stroke of luck."

She moved a part-chewed wodge of food into her cheek and spoke out of the side of her mouth. "Continue."

"A few years ago, another round of defence cuts encouraged my former commander to take early retirement. Gravel has—"

"Gravel?"

"It's safer if you don't know his real name. Gravel has connections. He's an Old Etonian, plugged into the Old Boy network. He contacted me through the VSC." She raised a finger to interrupt, but he added, "The Victory Services Club. Affiliates are serving and former members of the UK's armed forces. We can contact each other through the club and still maintain a low profile, if you understand what I mean."

He paused before ploughing on. "Gravel started a highly specialised consultancy. I'm one of his most senior operatives."

Lara frowned. The information sounded ominous. "What ... sort of consultancy?"

He leaned forwards again, flinching against the obvious pain. "No, no. It's not what you think. I'm no hitman."

She searched his eyes for signs of guilt or deception, but found none.

He continued quietly, rushing his words. "The consultancy has contracts with governments, blue chips, and major insurance companies. One of my roles is to head our Hostage Extraction and Negotiation Unit. Very hush-hush. No official wants to be seen negotiating with kidnappers or terrorists. ... Do you remember Molly Devonshire?"

Lara closed her eyes for a moment. Why did she recognise the name? A memory surfaced. An ecstatic face grinning from the pages of a newspaper. A woman waving as she disembarked an aeroplane. Gatwick Airport on a sunny day.

Lara nodded. "A UN aid worker. She was kidnapped in The Sudan and turned up a fortnight later apparently unharmed. Refused to say what happened to her. That was you?"

A smile. Sad but nice. She returned it.

"We were lucky with Molly. Our in-country intelligence turned out to be spot-on. Doesn't always work out so well. Over the past three years, HENU has been dropped into hostile territory seven times, mainly in Africa and South America. Five times we were successful."

Despite her shock at seeing the news headlines, Lara started to see that a good man sat before her—he'd demonstrated the fact time and again—but she still wanted the full story. Kaine would refuse to give it if she let him know she'd formed any kind of positive opinion of him. "So what happened last night? A hostage negotiation went wrong?"

"No. That was something else entirely. A different service we offer. Apart from hostage negotiations, the consultancy also works with some of the world's biggest arms manufacturers. You won't recognise the names, they don't advertise on the TV, but we're talking multi-billion-pound international conglomerates.

"Gravel and I have full MoD and NATO accreditation to test and certify a wide range of military equipment. Weapons that work in the factory, or on the firing range, aren't always effective under real world conditions." His lips stretched into a wistful smile. "You'd be amazed how many weapons malfunction when exposed to adverse conditions, like salt water. What we do is all above board and official."

They locked eyes and made an emotional connection. Her heart flipped and she took another sip of water. "How above board and official? What exactly do you do?"

"If a company wants to sell military arms or equipment in Europe or to NATO, they need field certification. Our consultancy is one of a very few companies who can provide the service. Gravel mostly handles the schmoozing, the paperwork, and the broad-brush planning. I deal with the practical elements. That's what I was doing last night."

"Oh my God, you *did* shoot down that plane?"

The revelation hit her hard. Her heart slammed against her ribcage, her skin tingled, she struggled to breathe. If he was telling the truth, Kaine had made a horrifying mistake and had eighty-three innocent deaths on his conscience. If he wasn't...

She had to find out.

He stared through the dirty glass window again, apparently unable to continue. He tried to keep his expression neutral, but his neck muscles tightened, he jammed his teeth together, and for a moment, she would have sworn the cabin lights twinkled off fluid building up along his lower eyelids.

"Tell me." She tried to make it sound like a plea, but it came out like a demand.

He turned to face her, but kept his eyes fixed on his hands. "According to Gravel, my target was an unmanned drone. I had no reason to disbelieve him. We've carried out dozens of similar trials.

"The prototype missile I used was supposed to have a minimal payload. Enough ordnance to destroy a small drone. Gravel's job was to co-ordinate the operation with the British Airports Authority and the MoD. He assured me I had a twenty-minute window of clear airspace. I saw the paperwork, Lara. It was all in order. I swear to you."

His voice broke and he looked at her; his tear-filled eyes melted her heart.

"Everything went to plan until I pulled the trigger, and then ..."

Lara's throat tightened. She wanted to reach out to him, but held herself in check. She wasn't ready for that.

He took another gulp of water. It looked as though he struggled to swallow.

With his voice below a whisper, he walked her through the details —the fishing boat's last moments, his swim, and his fight in Cleethorpes. On reaching the part where he collapsed at her front door, he stopped talking and gave her time to absorb the information.

The world stopped for a moment as the silence stretched between them, heightening the whoosh of wheels on track and the intermittent clacking as the train passed over the points.

Lara reached out. He grabbed her hands and held on tight as though they were a lifeline, an anchor. The pain in his eyes matched the hurt she'd seen in Ollie's eyes before he'd left her for the final time. She sympathised with Kaine. Carrying the burden of all those deaths alone must have been unbearable.

"I ... can't imagine how you must feel. Those poor people."

He released her hands and pressed his clenched fists into his lap, trying to hide them beneath the table.

"Oh God. Sorry. What a stupid thing to say."

She could be such a darned fool.

"No. It's okay."

He clamped his mouth closed as though he had nothing more to add. She let minutes pass before speaking again. "You're sure this Gravel person is involved?"

He pulled in a ragged breath. "Certain. No one else knew where I planned to park the Citroën overnight."

She rubbed the ache from her forehead.

Kaine continued. "You don't know how sorry I am to have dragged you into this mess, but after Cleethorpes, I acted on impulse. Self-preservation. If I'd known how well-resourced they were, I wouldn't have gone within ten miles of your place."

"Then you'd have bled to death."

"Possibly. But you'd have been safe."

Lara blinked. Tears spilled. She wiped them away with her fingertips. "Damn it. I hate weepy women."

"I'd cry myself, but ..."

He rubbed his eyes and eased forwards, wincing against the pain.

"The Principal, any idea who he might be?" she asked.

"No. He could be working for any one of a dozen arms manufacturers. My part of the certification protocol is always blind. I'm given the weapon, its anonymised operating manual, and a few hours for familiarisation. Before I take possession, the people who commission the trial remove any identifiers—manufacturers, badges, logos. Occasionally, companies will pay us to test a random batch of a rival's product. They're hoping we'll give it a big fat 'Unserviceable' badge."

"That sounds unnecessarily complicated."

Kaine tilted his head. He had a way of looking at her as though sighting a target, but strangely, she sensed no danger from him. "The process is designed to avoid bias."

She shivered. "So, you don't even know who made the launcher that blew up in your face?"

He paused as though bringing back a painful memory. "The ... weapon bore some similarities to a device made by a French outfit.

One of the biggest weapons manufacturers in the world. Highly respected. We've worked for them off-and-on since Gravel started the company. Unlike most firms in the industry, there's never been any hint of scandal. No sanctions busting. No rumours of bribery or corruption. I really can't see them risking their reputation on something so ... monstrous ..." He rubbed his face. "Hell, Lara. I've been a bloody idiot. I can't believe anything Gravel's ever told me. It could all be bullshit. I need to have a chat with the bastard before he disappears into the sunset with his spoils. First though, I need to find you somewhere safe to stay."

Right. As though she was going to let that happen. Kaine would do anything to protect her. He'd demonstrated that back at the farm. She could trust him more than a bunch of unknown mercenaries, or faceless police officers, which was why she'd stick closer to him than the plaster dressing his wounds.

She tapped an index finger on the tabletop. "May I ask another question?"

"Of course."

"This MoD certification, do they have your fingerprints?"

"Yes. As a licensed firearms and explosives specialist, the MoD and the Home Office have a full biometric workup, including a DNA sample and retinal scans. Why?"

She chewed the inside of her lower lip for a moment. "Given all you've done since Cleethorpes, everything you've touched and the blood you've dripped over two crime scenes, shouldn't the police have identified you by now? Why isn't your photo plastered all over the news?"

Kaine's knowing smile told her the same thought had crossed his mind. "That, Dr Orchard, is a very good question, and one I can't answer right now. Perhaps someone high up is dragging their heels to keep the field free for the Principal and his attack dogs. It's only a matter of time though. Wouldn't surprise me to see my ugly mug plastered all over King's Cross station."

"It's not that ugly."

Darn, she'd done it again—spoken without thinking. So unlike her. She needed a good eight hours quality sleep in a soft, warm bed. Alone.

Her comment made him straighten. "I wasn't fishing."

"And I wasn't biting." She took a fresh napkin, dabbed her eyes, and twisted it into a rope. "What's our next step?"

Kaine cleared his throat. "As I said, *my* next step is to find you a safe place to hide before I have a chat with Gravel."

"Oh no," she said, just as firmly. "We don't have time for that. We need to act right away."

"No. Your safety comes first." He sliced his hand through the air between them. "End of discussion."

The rail track took a long, slow curve to the left. Sunlight burst into the carriage, glinted off the metal nameplate on Lara's medical bag, and flashed in Kaine's eyes. He snapped his head back into the shadow of a carriage support. He smiled, rested his forearms on the table, and rubbed his hands together.

"You've thought of something?" she asked.

"Maybe."

Darn. He'd reverted to stealth mode.

"If you have a plan, can I help?"

He studied her for a moment before answering. "Possibly."

Excellent. He hadn't dismissed her offer out of hand. "Will it be dangerous?"

"Not for you." He checked his watch. "We reach Retford in a couple of minutes. I need you to promise me something."

"I'm not making any promises I don't want to keep."

"Bloody hell, woman. You are infuriating." Despite the harsh words, the softness in his quiet voice told her he didn't mean it.

"So, sue me. What do you want me to do?"

"If there's trouble at Retford, do as I say without question. Please?"

Lara grinned. She felt better than she had all morning, more certain and, unaccountably, less scared. Her heart tripped faster.

"That, Ryan Liam Kaine, I will promise."

CHAPTER TWENTY

Thursday 10th September – Afternoon

Retford Station, Nottinghamshire, UK

Changing trains at Retford—a station with a single platform—involved a tense twenty-three-minute wait for the delayed connection.

Kaine, buoyed by Lara's reaction to his revelations, ushered her close to the station wall and stood guard, eyes raking the platform, on full alert while trying to appear relaxed. His right hand gripped a Maxim, cocked and ready, hidden under the sweater draped over his arm.

Lara remained quiet, studying the posters advertising the latest London theatre attractions.

Five other people dotted the platform. At the far end, some thirty metres away, an elderly couple held hands, locked in quiet conversation. They sheltered from the drizzle under the platform's canopy.

The young mother held her child in her arms, a buggy beside her stuffed with the supplies needed to service the kiddie.

Much closer, within ten metres, a twenty-something man with a backpack at his feet and a guitar case in hand, kept shooting furtive glances in their direction. The wind whipped his long hair around his head.

Kaine's defences flared. He put himself between Lara and Guitar Man, but kept an eye on the older folk. Grey hair and wrinkles didn't guarantee innocence. Didn't prove weakness either.

Guitar Man turned to face them. Frowning, his hand came up, reached inside his jacket ...

Kaine grabbed Lara's arm, ready to push her to the ground. He twisted enough to aim the hidden Maxim at Guitar Man's heart.

...and came out holding a comb. He started working the tangles out of his straggly hair. He smiled, nodded at Lara, gave Kaine a surreptitious thumbs up, adding a knowing wink.

Kaine released Lara's arm, dipped his head, and smirked. Silent man-talk for, "Yes, mate. She's gorgeous, and she's mine. You can look if you like, but that's all."

The express to King's Cross arrived in a cloud of spray and they clambered into a carriage even emptier than the one from Lincoln Central.

Lara collapsed into her seat.

"God, that was terrifying," she whispered, gasping. "The man with the guitar kept looking at you and I could have sworn that middle-aged couple was going to pull machine-guns out of their cases and ... Oh Lord. I'm not cut out for this line of work."

He shook his head. "You were brilliant. A natural. Did you notice the newspaper on the bench?"

"No, I was too scared watching the other people. Why?"

"The headlines read, 'Flight BE1555, Police Baffled'. Normally, I'd hate the cliché, but it puts me in the clear as far as an official search is concerned."

She took a white handkerchief from her handbag and wiped her face before leaning into the corner formed between her seat and the window.

"Okay, Ryan. Out with it. What's the plan?" she asked, glancing around to make sure they were alone.

What a woman. Unstoppable.

"We'll reach King's Cross in fifty-five minutes, give or take. Let me work through the details for a while. I promise to run the idea past you before we arrive."

"Is there anything I can do in the meantime?"

"Get some sleep. It's likely to be a long night."

Slowly, cat-like, Lara stretched her arms and flexed her fingers. She kicked off her shoes and lifted her feet onto the seat. "I'm too keyed up to sleep, but if you don't mind, I will rest my eyes for a while. I was up all night, too."

"Lady Sundowner, right."

She hid a yawn behind the hankie. "Impressive. You have a good memory."

"I try."

She lay back and Kaine studied her while planning the evening's operation. In rest, she looked even more beautiful, but so vulnerable. Anger and guilt battled inside him. Guilt for placing her in danger. Anger at Gravel and the Principal for causing it.

God, what a mess.

Lara stirred. Her eyes opened. She arched her back in a luxurious stretch and yawned. Kaine couldn't stop himself yawning in sympathy. He watched her in rapt fascination. How wonderful would it be to see her wake every morning?

Hell, Ryan. Don't go there.

Kaine punted the daydream into touch. With the whole world and his dog hunting him, why torture himself? He rubbed his eyes. What he wouldn't do for eight hours' shuteye—he'd try to catch a short nap in London before the night's work.

"Sleep well?" he asked quietly.

Lara frowned and turned her hazel eyes towards him. "I slept?"

How could she look so good on so little rest?

"We're ten minutes out."

She sat up, stretched again, and reached for her water bottle but found it empty. Kaine passed his across. She took a swig, swirled it around her mouth before swallowing, and offered it back.

"Finish it. We'll get some more at King's Cross."

"Thanks."

Fascinated, he watched her empty the bottle in one final pull, crush it flat, and replace the top. Then she rummaged through her bag and fished out a small hairbrush.

"While you were asleep, I 'borrowed' a smartphone from one of the passengers."

She pulled the brush through her shoulder-length hair, making it shine in the sunlight. He could have watched her all day.

"Wasn't that a little risky?"

"I didn't ask and gave it back before she noticed. The police still haven't released my name to the media, so we should be okay at King's Cross. I also phoned a couple of friends who've agreed to offer us their not-inconsiderable support."

"Will they reach King's Cross before us?"

"Not a chance."

"In that case," she said, leaning forwards in her seat, "I can be your lookout at the station in case there's a heavy police presence. What's it called? Running interference?"

Kaine grinned and shook his head slowly. "Only if you're playing American football. I appreciate the offer, but we should be okay to reach a safe house I know in Enfield. We can stay there until tonight."

"What happens tonight?"

"Tonight, Lara," he said, dropping the smile, "I hope you're going to help me coerce information from a man I used to call my friend."

As promised, he gave her an outline of the plan. At first, she was horrified with her part in the proposed operation, but eventually, he managed to talk her around, arguing that he could see no alternative and challenged her to come up with another plan. Although she couldn't find a better way that was satisfactory to Kaine, she did ask a few relevant and probing questions and answered a couple of his medical ones. Shortly after they'd ironed out a few wrinkles together, the train clanked slowly into King's Cross station.

"You ready?" he asked.

"As I'll ever be."

He stood and held out his hand. She didn't hesitate to take it. A sign of her trust that made his omissions more difficult to swallow.

Kaine couldn't bring himself to tell her that after she'd helped facilitate his "little chat" with Gravel, he'd take her to his old platoon sergeant in Croydon. He would set her up with a new identity and help spirit her out of the country. She'd be safe, and they'd probably never meet again.

He could think of no better way to protect her.

CHAPTER TWENTY-ONE

Thursday 10th September – Sabrina Faroukh

SAMS HQ, London, UK

Sabrina was certain the guilt showed in everything she did, everything she said. Every expression on her face gave her away. At any moment, she expected someone from security to grab her by the neck and march her into Patel's office. Then she'd disappear, as they'd planned to make Ryan Kaine disappear. But he'd outsmarted them. He'd escaped, as had Dr Orchard. Thank the Good Lord.

But it didn't happen. Everyone treated her the same way they did every other day. Some smiled a welcome, some turned away, jealous of her success, others ignored her completely. By the time she reached the twelfth floor, she could at last breathe normally. It had taken all her self-will to make it to her office and she wasn't going to fail now. Behave normally, and she might just make it through the next few days. Somewhere deep inside, she felt the end game approaching, and she needed to be ready for it.

First though, she had to find Ryan Kaine, and she couldn't do it from home. For that, she required the massive resources of SAMS' electronic infrastructure.

She reached her desk, nodded to her colleagues, rewarded Gary with a special warm smile, and logged on, unable to ignore the worms of fear crawling up and down her spine. It would not take long to find out whether the daytime security sweeps had discovered her morning's surveillance trickery. The moment she registered on the system, any unauthorised activity they'd detected would raise a silent alarm. Minutes later the goons would arrive and she'd vanish faster than the morning mist on a summer's day.

She waited.

The desk phone rang. Her heart stopped then started again, beating too fast. She picked up the phone.

"Hello?"

"Ms Faroukh?"

"Yes."

"Shafiq Patel here."

Merde!

"I see you've just signed onto the system. How are you this evening?"

Sabrina swallowed and tried to speak normally. "I ... I'm fine, sir. Thank you, sir."

"Excellent. Excellent." He spoke quickly, almost cheerfully.

"I did not think you worked this late, sir," she said, trying to appear less than terrified.

"I've just finished a conference call with potential clients in China. It's given me the chance to speak to you now rather than keep you waiting until tomorrow morning. I know how tiring night shifts can be. Do you have a moment to pop up to my office?"

Her first reaction was to grab her bag and run, but the guards would catch her at the first security point. Lord, why had she returned to work? She should have run home to *grand-père* Mo-Mo.

"Ms Faroukh?"

Answer him!

"Sorry, sir. I'll be right there."

"Good. See you in a moment."

Before leaving her desk, she dug through her handbag and found her mobile. Without removing it and keeping her actions hidden from the all-pervasive surveillance cameras, she entered a four character sequence and hit send. The communications dampening system within Sampson House would block the message, but if her bag ever made it outside the restricted zone intact, her emergency signal would be received. It would not do her any good, but at least her people would know to start looking. To cover her actions, she removed a lipstick and mirror and made some running repairs.

She stood and, with heart pounding and chest heaving, walked slowly towards the lifts. The route took her past Knowitall's office. The cluttered desk filled the small room. From her first day in the department, she suspected he kept it messy in an attempt to demonstrate his heavy workload, his importance to the company—an indispensable asset. Of the creep himself, there was no sign.

One of the two lift doors stood open. She entered and hit the button for the executive floor. When the doors slid shut, the airless steel box took on all the charm of a brightly lit tomb.

CHAPTER TWENTY-TWO

Thursday 10th September – Gravel

Devil's Dyke, West Sussex, UK

Graham Valence tapped the earpiece of his hands-free mobile.

"Phone home," he called, loud and clear.

The in-car mic picked up his voice and the atonal electronics plinked. The call connected, but transferred to voicemail.

"Gail, it's me. Pick up, angel. ... Okay, I guess you're in the shower. Listen, I'm about thirty minutes out. Traffic's a bitch as per usual. I'm stuck at the Devil's Dyke lights again. Had a great day. Cold and wet, but successful. Gasping for a drink, a hot meal, and a cuddle. But not necessarily in that order." He laughed. "See you soon. Toodle-pip."

After spending the day on the Solent, deliberately *incommunicado*, he'd built one hell of an appetite. The *Early Bird* could be a handful in a choppy sea, but the comforts of hot food and a warm wife would soon ease the ache from his bones and round the day off to perfection.

Sixteen hours at the boat's wheel gave him plausible deniability. Sure, it was a pity he had to feed poor old Ryan to the fishes. He'd miss the uptight and holier-than-thou prick, but not enough to lose any sleep over. Business was business, after all, and bloody lucrative business at that. Last thing he needed was an honest man holding him back, and that's exactly what Ryan was—an honest man in a dishonest world. But alas, he was no more. A dead senior executive. Deceased, along with the others on that plane.

Too bad all those people had to die, but he could see the pragmatism. Hide one death amongst so many others and you'd muddy the clearest of waters. A tragedy, a disaster, beat your chest in anguish, but one man's adversity was another's golden opportunity. After all, somebody always benefitted from other people's miseries. Back in 2007, the speculators profited when the bankers fucked up, and the public paid the price in worthless property and lost pensions.

Fuck 'em all.

He and Gail weren't going to suffer because of other people's screw-ups. Losing all their savings wasn't his fault. The greedy city arseholes, the bankers and the hedge fund managers, gambling with other people's money—they were the ones to blame. So what if he had to break a few laws to correct the drift, to right the uneven keel?

DefTech was safe, insulated. He'd seen to that.

The self-destruct mechanism in the missile launcher and the massive charge he'd set on *Herring Gull* had wiped away all Kaine's links to his firm.

Poor Ryan. Always so careful, so detailed, so precise. He'd walked Valence through every aspect of the operation, right down to the fishing boat he'd hired for the night, through a bunch of intermediaries. He'd made it so damned easy. A shaped charge planted in precisely the right place ensured a fractured keel and a fast scuttling. Only a few bits of flotsam would have remained on the surface, but the fast tide would have dispersed it overnight. By morning, there'd have been nothing left but empty sea and a missing hire boat.

Superb.

With the late, departed Ryan lying crushed in the wreckage at the bottom of the North Sea, Valence wouldn't have to watch his back for the rest of his life. The perfect end to a perfect operation and an extraordinarily profitable one.

He tapped his fingers on the leather steering wheel, keeping time with Beethoven's Piano Concerto Number 5. Eventually, he'd hum along during the rousing parts and feel so much the better for it. Music preserved his sanity during all the excruciating commutes. Without it, he'd have stroked out years ago. High blood pressure was a family curse. The music helped, as did the medication and Gail, but the only real cure would be early retirement and to do that he needed money. Hence his move to what Ryan would have called the Dark Side.

Naïve prick.

Meanwhile, he had to stay cool or he'd end up killing the arsehole commuters that insisted on slowing his journeys. What right did the fuckers have to hold him up?

He made a gun with his right hand then lined up his target—a mop-haired kid in a beat up, rust-bucket Fiat Uno—and pulled the trigger in time with a musical crescendo.

Valence smirked.

If only all his problems could be sorted as easily and quickly as an imaginary bullet into the base of an unsuspecting motorist's skull. Once more, he spent a brief moment lamenting the loss of Ryan Kaine, his longest-serving colleague and one-time friend. Such a disappointment, but life goes on.

At least it did for Valence. Ha!

The lights at the T-junction changed to green. He feathered the throttle, playing the "How many of the dozy fuckers ahead of me in the queue will pull their fucking fingers out in time to beat the next red light?" game.

Why didn't the morons have their cars in gear *before* the lights changed? Damn them. If they did, they wouldn't hold everybody else up.

Useless cretins.

Five cars rolled through the lights before they changed. Five! He counted the motors still left in the queue—seventeen. Five minutes between red lights, five cars per change, meant twenty more minutes of his life wasted in yet another traffic jam, plus the time he'd spent already. Still, another two or three off-the-books contracts and he and Gail would be away to warmer climes. There were no traffic jams in the middle of the Caribbean.

Should he call Gail back with a revised ETA?

Nah, she probably needed the extra time to put the finishing touches to dinner. Special occasions were worth the wait and it wasn't every day you added two million smackers to the retirement fund. He ran the calculations. Eighty-three victims—eighty-four if he included Ryan—worked out at a little under twenty-four grand a piece. Didn't sound too bad if he said it quickly enough. What value did you put on a life? Bugger all if you didn't know them. A conscience had no value. A conscience never paid the bills.

The lights changed. This time, seven cars beat the red and still the scruffy-haired lout bobbed his head in time to some high-tempo noise. Maybe he wasn't listening to music. Perhaps the annoying prick had Tourette's. Valence shot him with his imaginary gun once more, but the kid still kept bopping. Meanwhile, on his sound system, the Concerto reached the slow melodic part that never ceased to bring a tear to Valence's eye.

What a Goddamned softie he'd become in his middle years.

The dashboard clock flashed 19:27, and the watery late summer sun kissed the western rooftops. Wouldn't have to wait long for autumn.

If the bloody lights didn't change soon, autumn would arrive before he reached home. Bloody England with its knackered roads and permanent gridlock. Come to think of it, he'd done Ryan a favour. At least the soft bastard wouldn't have to sit in any more queues.

After Beethoven's masterpiece ended, Valence hummed a chorus of *Always Look on the Bright Side*.

While messing about on the sea, he'd powered down his mobiles—both the registered one and the burner—and refused to access his emails all day. The dying art of remaining incognito for a whole day in the Information Age took practice, yet was essential in his line of work. Getting away for a few undisturbed hours was the main reason he'd bought the Fairline Targa and kept it moored in Havant. The fifty-five foot, six berth, Volvo-powered beauty served a number of functions. A legitimate business expense, it kept his marine hand in, it gave him an impressive venue to schmooze major clients, and afforded him plenty of opportunities to disappear whenever the need arose. Such as the day after Flight BE1555 fell from the skies.

He'd made sure to say "Hello" to the Harbour Master before casting off and "Goodbye" when he'd docked that evening. An excellent alibi for the day. Not that he'd need one with Ryan eventually taking the blame.

It was still relatively early, and he considered checking in with a few contacts, Rudy Bernadotti, for example, but decided against it. Rudy had left strict instructions not to call until the initial uproar from the tragedy had died down, and the last thing Valence needed was to upset one of his prime golden geese. Nope, he'd keep his head down, stick to the plan, and maintain silent running for a month or two.

One thing about sitting in traffic, it gave him plenty of time to ruminate. How much had his life changed since meeting Gail?

She'd stolen his heart so easily and after three years of marriage, he loved her as much as he had on the first day they met.

Kismet?

Karma?

Who knew, but nobody on the planet, alive or dead, did it for him the way she did. He'd been a hollow shell before they met and nothing had been the same since. And damn, she was a dynamite lover, too. No one had ever touched him the same way Gail did.

Gravel Valence, you incurable old romantic.

The lights changed once more. This time, he squeezed through on the cusp of red-and-amber and gave the finger to the arseholes blaring their horns as he cut in front.

He stamped on the accelerator, and left the overtaken head-banging yob sucking on his exhaust fumes. With luck, he'd make the original ETA, have time to change for dinner, and down a nice apéritif before an early night of passion.

"Lovely jubbly."

Valence's smile widened. He snicked the Alpha into top and barged into the outside lane. What a great day to be alive.

———

Valence slipped the key into the lock and turned it. The front door opened silently.

"Hi honey, I'm home," he said, allowing a cheesy grin to crease his face.

Silence.

The lights in the lounge and kitchen shone brightly, but the house echoed to an unnatural stillness. No ambient mood music to welcome him back, no aroma of the evening meal to make his mouth water, no called greeting from a loving wife.

He removed his coat and hung it on the hook.

"Gail?"

He stopped, listened again. More silence. Something felt wrong. His hackles rose. Fear pulsed through his system, the internal warning bells in full activation.

The office.

His Walther P99.

Valence rushed along the hall, slipped through the open office door, and dived silently into the chair behind his desk. Bottom drawer, left-hand side. He pulled it open and ...

Empty.

"You looking for this, old buddy?"

Fuck!

Filling the doorway and wearing a grim smile, Ryan Kaine held the Walther in a rock-steady grip. He aimed the weapon at Valence's left eye.

Valence stopped breathing. The bugger never missed.

"Jesus, Ryan. What the f—"

"Surprised to see me?"

"I ... Hell, you nearly gave me a fucking heart attack, you bugger. What on earth are you doing in my house carrying my gun? Stand down, man. Explain yourself."

The stiff grin didn't waver. Nor did the gun.

"Oh, very good. Nice save, *sir*. Keep that up and I'll be nominating you for a BAFTA. Not quite Oscar material, yet. Needs polish. You'd have to show more emotional depth."

Valence leaned forwards to stand, but Ryan shook his head and motioned with the gun. He sat, rested his forearms on the desk, and flattened his hands on its polished surface to stop his fingers trembling. His bouncing left thigh rubbed against the kneehole inside the desk.

He raced through the options.

Rush him? No chance, not with Ryan standing on the other side of the desk and holding the gun, bullet chambered, trigger finger active.

Bluff it out?

The only way.

Ryan couldn't know the truth, not so soon. Keep him talking, wait for an opening. Damn it, he clearly survived the bomb, but how the fuck did he get past the wet team in Grimsby?

"That's better," Ryan said, entering the room and closing the door behind him. "Behave yourself and you might still be breathing at sunrise."

Valence swallowed. He was in big trouble, and he knew it. But he was still alive, and there was still a chance, but ...

Oh Christ, Gail. Where was she? He clamped his jaws shut, balled his hands into fists, and waited for Ryan to make a mistake.

There had to be a first time, didn't there?

CHAPTER TWENTY-THREE

Thursday 10th September – Evening

Gravel's Farmhouse, South of London, UK

Kaine had to hand it to Gravel. A moment of pleasure squeezed past Kaine's operational calm as he could almost see his former best friend running through the options and coming up empty. Kaine had given himself plenty of time to arrange things to his satisfaction, knowing he could predict Gravel's next moves.

"You are a murdering bastard," Kaine said, outwardly calm, but fighting the bile rising to his throat. "Eighty-three people. How could you?"

"You're wrong, Ryan. It's not what—"

Kaine lifted the Walther until the sights lined up with the middle of Gravel's forehead.

"Stop playing me for an idiot."

Gravel raised his hands, palms out. "I'm not."

"Tell me about Flight BE1555."

Gravel licked his lips. His eyes searched the room before locking with Kaine's once more.

"It was a tragic mistake. You must have programmed the guidance system incorrectly. You accidentally hit the wrong target."

Kaine shook his head. "I entered the transponder code exactly as you dictated, and we double-checked it together. No mistake. You set me up to commit cold-blooded murder. Who booked the contract? I want the name of the Principal."

"I don't know."

Gravel placed his hands flat on the surface once more. He'd never give up the information easily, but Kaine had all the leverage he needed trussed up not ten metres away. He opened the office door with his free hand, keeping the Walther fixed on its target.

"Okay. Time's wasting. Stand up."

Gravel kept his seat, hands still in full view. "Where are we going?"

"To the kitchen. Come on, up you get."

Gravel's head dipped and he glowered at Kaine from beneath dark eyebrows. "What for?"

"You'll find out." Kaine jerked the Walther upwards.

Gravel shot to his feet. His chair slammed into the display cabinet behind him. A polished silver golf trophy wobbled, but settled back and remained upright. Kaine adjusted the pistol to maintain a clear shot at his target's centre mass.

"Take it easy, *Major*. I wouldn't want to be responsible for another 'accident'."

The major pain in Kaine's backside clenched his fists again, but kept his hands low down at his sides. "You break into my house and have the gall to threaten me? What do you want?"

"Answers."

It was Gravel's turn to shake his head. "And I've already told you. I don't have any."

"You'd better, or there'll be blood spilled tonight for no reason."

Gravel's eyes narrowed. "I've been threatened by worse people than you, *Captain* Kaine. And don't forget, I've known you for years. You couldn't kill an unarmed man."

Kaine sneered. "That was before you had me murder all those innocents. Things like that can change a man."

Gravel bent at the waist. He rested his knuckled fists on the desk and stared into Kaine's eyes. "I didn't make you do anything. You fucked up, not me. Give yourself up and take the consequences."

Kaine nodded. "I'll admit to pulling the trigger, but I knew you'd deny any wrongdoing, which is why I have a present for you. Would you like to see it now?"

"What are you —"

"Come on. Let's go unwrap it, eh? Listen carefully, though. Make one move I don't like or expect, and I'll shoot. My first target will be the knee. Excruciating, or so I've been told. We both know it won't kill, but will incapacitate, and it won't stop me asking my simple little questions. The human body has two knees. And if that doesn't loosen your tongue, I'll start on the elbows. Then I'll go for the ankles, toes, fingers. One by one. Need I continue? I have plenty of ammo."

"You've gone mad," Gravel said, his voice calm and controlled. "You won't shoot me. Don't have it in you."

"We'll see, old buddy."

Gravel should have been angry or scared, but all Kaine saw in his former superior's behaviour was restrained confidence and maybe a hint of arrogance. That would have to change. He took a pre-looped heavy-duty cable tie from his pocket and threw it on the desk. "Put that around your wrists and pull it tight with your teeth. I'll check it's nice and secure."

"No."

Kaine squeezed the trigger. The Walther barked loud in the close confines of the small office. The bullet shattered the glass of the display cabinet behind the older man's head. The pieces tumbled to the carpet. A silver trophy of a man in "plus fours" swinging a golf club crumpled and fell.

Gravel ducked and raised his hands. A red line appeared on the tip of his left ear.

"Christ sakes, Ryan. You shot me. You fucking shot me!"

"The cable tie. Do it. Now." Kaine said, cool and calm, the gunshot still ringing in his ears.

With teeth gritted and jaw muscles bunching, Gravel worked the plastic band around his wrists and tightened it as instructed. Kaine confirmed its tension by the way the skin around the ligature creased.

"Kitchen. Now."

Gravel's frown deepened.

"No."

Kaine stepped forwards and grabbed the major's upper arm. His captive lunged, the point of his elbow aimed at Kaine's throat.

Prepared for the move, Kaine sidestepped the awkward attack and cracked Gravel on the back of the head with the pistol butt, hard enough to stun, but not enough to incapacitate. Gravel crumpled to his knees, shaken and dazed.

Kaine pulled the cursing, struggling man up by his hair, pushed him through the hall, and dumped him unceremoniously the wrong way into a chair. He forced Gravel to sit, legs astride, arms draped over the back, able to see his little "present".

"Surprise," Kaine said.

"No!" Gravel howled.

His eyes widened and he tried to stand but Kaine held him by the shoulder and ground the gun's muzzle into the base of his neck.

"You bastard. You fucking bastard!"

For the first time, Gravel's voice broke. Real emotion showed through the complacency.

"Language, *Major*. There's a woman present."

On the other side of the table, blindfolded, gagged, and securely tied to a stout wooden chair, Gravel's wife sat trembling and cowed. The moment Kaine had entered the kitchen with his captive, she started squealing behind her gag, clearly unable to tell what was happening.

Kaine blocked her out. He was past the point where anything mattered except identifying the Principal.

"What are you doing?" Gravel asked, his voice deathly quiet in the near-silent room—silent, save for Gail's whimpering and the inordinately loud tick of the clock on the sideboard.

Kaine handed Gravel another cable tie, this one unfastened.

"Thread it through the chair's spindles and the tie holding your wrists, and secure it tight. If you stand or screw up in any way, I'll shoot Gail in the knee as promised. I don't want any interruptions during our little *tête-à-tête*."

Kaine trained his gun on Gail's knee and watched Gravel follow his instructions.

"Gail," Gravel said, voice little more than a whisper, "it's me, darling. Don't worry. Everything will be okay."

"Aw, so touching. Pity she can't see how big and brave you are. Pity she doesn't know you're a murdering bastard. Or does she?"

The older man flinched. An almost imperceptible hitch of the left eyebrow, but enough to put Gail's innocence in doubt.

Gail too? Surely not.

How far did the conspiracy stretch?

Kaine leaned forwards, resting his free hand on the table. "Shall we begin?"

The darkness of fear touched Gravel's eyes. He shot a look at his wife, and then at Kaine, who chuckled. "You'll see her bleed and hear her scream, unless you answer the questions to my satisfaction."

"Please don't harm her. She's all I have."

From behind her gag, Gail screamed and struggled against her restraints. The chair bounced on the tiled floor, but Kaine had tied her hands to the chair's arms and her feet to its legs, and the chair was strong, solid. Gravel's eyes filled with hate and tears, but Kaine's mind brought back the fireball in the sky over the North Sea.

"What about the people on that plane? What about their families? Eighty-three people dead and for what? Money?"

"You killed them, Ryan. Not me. You're the fuck up."

"Who's the Principal?"

Gravel started at Kaine's sudden change of direction.

"I don't have that information. We keep the separation. Chinese

Walls, you remember. I have no idea who calls the shots or pays the bills."

"Bollocks. Who's the Principal?" Kaine repeated.

"Why don't you fucking listen? I don't know," Gravel said. "Now end this nonsense!"

Kaine forced his shoulders to slump. He sighed and walked around to Gail's side of the table. "This is your fault, Gravel. Remember that."

He removed Gail's blindfold, but left the gag—a cloth and duct tape wrapped five times around her head—in place. She blinked hard until her eyes grew accustomed to the light, and then sought out her husband. With tear-stained cheeks, a runny nose, and an angry but not terrified expression, she shook her head violently, puffing out her cheeks, trying to tell Gravel something. Then she turned to Kaine and made a sound, a cross between a nasal whimper and a part-suppressed growl.

"Yes," said Kaine to Gail. "you're right. I'm using you to force dear Graham to talk. How much you suffer is up to him. Shall we see how much he really loves you?" As he spoke, Kaine heard derision in his voice. "Do you know what he's been doing since leaving the army, Gail? Do you know what he does to pay for this lovely house, and the Fairline in Havant, and those exotic holidays?"

She closed her eyes. Sweat glistened on her face. She knew! She did know, and she didn't care.

Gravel's voice cut through Kaine's questions. "Don't listen to him, Gail. He's the man who shot down that plane last night. He's a madman."

Kaine continued as though Gravel hadn't spoken. "You know what Gail? I reckon you *do* know all about it. I'm right, aren't I? Can see it written all over your botoxed face. Excellent. That's going to make my job a whole lot easier. You see, I don't normally go in for hurting innocents, but if you knew and approved of what Gravel organised, you are a part of it and not a non-combatant. Interesting conundrum."

The frantic, frenzied way she shook her head and squealed did nothing to change Kaine's mind.

"Don't do it Ryan," Gravel screamed. "For the love of God, please don't!"

"Gail, here's what I think." Kaine raised an index finger and tapped his lips. "I think you are in this up to your pretty neck. You know all about how your loving husband tricked me into shooting down that plane. And that's why I'm here in your home uninvited. That's why you are about to suffer. You know what? I'm not even sorry. You deserve everything that's coming."

Gail looked up through tear-filled blue eyes, mascara running in thread-like lines down her cheeks—the ghastly parody of a Goth.

Kaine continued. "Over the past few years I had come to think of you as a friend, but that's gone now. If, as Gravel says, I'm a madman, a mass murderer, I've nothing to lose, have I? What are two more deaths when I already have so many on my conscience? I've killed others since then. People who tried to kill me. But they don't count. Unlike the passengers on Flight BE1555, those men chose their fate."

He rested a hand on her shoulder and turned to face his former boss. "Gravel, who paid you to shoot down that plane and why? If you answer those questions, I'll go and we'll never need to see each other again. Simple as that. I won't ask again."

From his hunched position straddling the dining chair, Gravel shook his head and a sneer creased his lips.

"Don't worry, darling. He won't hurt you. I attacked him in the office. He could have shot me and didn't. He's not going to do anything."

Gail dipped her head and stared at the trail of blood dripping down Gravel's left ear.

For the first time since Kaine had shot him with his own gun, some of Gravel's old swagger returned. He forced his shoulders down and rolled his head from side to side, stretching the small muscles in his neck in an action Kaine had seen him perform a thousand times. When in his late thirties, the indestructible Major Valence broke a vertebra in his neck when an armoured personnel carrier overturned during a patrol in Iraq. In cold weather or at times of stress, he often complained of a stiff neck.

Kaine allowed him to continue talking.

"You heard that gunshot earlier, darling? Don't worry about my ear," Gravel said, a cocky smile stretching his face. "Ryan Kaine's the best shot I've ever seen. Hits what he aims at. Never misses. He's not going to hurt either of us. Doesn't have it in him.

"Although he did shoot down that plane, it was an accident, love. He didn't mean it. Either he made a mistake with the targeting, or the weapon we were testing malfunctioned." He turned to Kaine. "Don't you see, Ryan? There's a way out of this. You need to think rationally. I can understand how something like this could push a good, honest man like you over the edge, but I'm your friend. I can help. Free me and I'll come with you to the police. We'll explain everything. There'll be an inquest, of course there will, but we can clear this up together."

Kaine smiled. "How are you gonna do that, Gravel?"

"Sorry?"

"How will you explain everything without giving the police the names of the people who hired you? You just told me you don't know who they are. You're lying again."

Gravel didn't answer. He simply looked at his wife, implacable, unbowed.

"What's wrong, Major Valence? Are you more scared of them than you are of me? Or are you in so deep you can't drop them in the muck without swallowing a bellyful yourself?"

Speaking to Kaine, but looking at his wife, he answered. "I'm telling you nothing."

Kaine fired.

The bullet tore through Gail's thigh. Her cheeks blew out as she shrieked through the gag.

Gravel screamed. "You bastard. You fucking bastard!" He jumped to his feet. Kaine turned the smoking gun on him. Gravel stood still, chair dangling in the air, hanging from the bindings. He stared at the blood flowing from his wife's leg. The stain grew, stark red against the white cotton of her slacks.

He breathed hard, his chest rose and fell, a look of disbelief on his face. "You shot her," he said, the shock clear in his hushed tone. "You fucking shot her, you bastard."

"Yes, I am," Kaine said. "But I was born that way. Greed turned you into one. Now, sit down."

"I'm going to tear your fucking head off!"

"You're not going to get the chance. I said, sit down!"

In apparent astonishment, Gail looked questioningly at Kaine and then at the wound.

"Sorry Gail. Blame your husband. Not me."

Kaine lowered the gun and rested the muzzle on her quivering knee before looking at his main captive. "The next shot gives her a lifetime of pain. Who's the Principal and why did he have me shoot down that aeroplane?"

Hard man, Gravel Valence, crumpled into his chair, tears flowing. "Rudy," he said, the name torn from a reluctant throat. His eyes locked onto the expanding blood stain.

"Go on," Kaine said, encouraging him with another twitch of the gun on Gail's knee. Again, she shrieked.

"Rudolpho Bernadotti. I'll tell you all about him, but Gail, please. Help her. She'll bleed out."

Kaine grabbed a dishcloth he'd placed on the table for the purpose and pressed it over the wound. Gail didn't even shudder. The thread-like creases on her botoxed forehead barely deepened.

"Keep talking, Gravel," Kaine said, adding a sneer. "Better hurry, though. This is a bad wound. She doesn't have all night."

While Gravel spilled his guts, Gail shook her head and shouted through her gag.

Gravel talked for two solid minutes. When he'd finished, Kaine threw the dishcloth on the table and replaced Gail's blindfold. He skirted the table, drove the Walther's muzzle into the back of Gravel's neck once more, and sliced through the second cable tie with his Ka-

Bar hunting knife. "Okay, old friend, I've heard enough. You're coming with me."

"What about Gail? Help her, please."

"Medic!" Kaine called. Footfalls on the upstairs landing told him Lara was on her way. He yanked on Gravel's sandy hair, forcing him to stand.

"A medic?"

"That's right. Here to treat Gail. Now, let's go."

Kaine tightened his grip on Gravel's hair and pushed him towards the back door.

"Thank fuck," Gravel said and stopped struggling. "Where you taking me?"

"I've found a nice little spot in your garage where we can be alone while my medic deals with Gail's wound. That suit you okay, *Major*? Don't test me though, or I'll rescind the doc's instructions and then where will that leave dear Gail?"

Kaine removed the voice recorder from his shirt pocket, pressed stop, and left it on the table. He dragged Gravel through the kitchen door, along the garden path, and into the detached double garage. He'd prepared the next play area in advance.

The basic rules of warfare—know your enemy, know your battleground.

CHAPTER TWENTY-FOUR

Thursday 10th September – Lara Orchard

Gravel's Farmhouse, South of London, UK

Carefully, Lara cut away the gag. She left the bulk of the tape attached to the woman's hair, but kept the blindfold in place. Gail spat fluff from her mouth.

"Who's that?" she asked, struggling against her bonds. "Oh my God, who's there?"

"Keep still." As Ryan instructed, Lara deepened her voice and put on the best Cockney accent she could manage.

It sounded fake but was the best she could do.

"You're a woman?"

Lara didn't respond.

"Help me, please. The madman's trying to kill us."

"Is he?"

"Yes, he shot me."

"Yeah, that's right."

"You're helping that lunatic?"

Lara nodded before remembering her patient couldn't see anything. "Yes."

"What are you going to do to me?" the pitiful creature wailed.

"My job's to keep you alive until the captain's sure your hubby's told him everythin'."

"What happens then?"

Good question.

"Dunno. Don't wanna know, neither."

"Oh dear God. What happens then?" Gail repeated, urgency speeding her words.

Lara turned away, unable to answer.

"Help us. Please?"

"He paid me to patch you up. That's it."

"Do you know what he's done?"

"Nope. Don't care, neither."

Gail started tugging at her ropes again.

"Don't waste your time strugglin'. The captain knows how to tie a knot. Keep still and let me treat the wound."

Lara dropped her medical bag on the kitchen table—Gail jumped at the sound—and checked the patient's vitals. Racing pulse, panting, shiny pale skin, sweaty armpits. She looked in a bad way, but beneath the bloody cloth, as Ryan had promised, the wound was clean—a through-and-through. It bled a great deal, but she'd seen horses suffer worse injuries after running into barbed wire fences.

She opened the bag, removed the dressing kit, and cut away the trouser leg with a pair of round-nosed shears.

The sickly odour of flop sweat mixed with overly sweet perfume and drying urine assaulted Lara's nose—the unfortunate woman must have wet herself when Ryan shot her. Hardly surprising.

The wound track tore through superficial layers of the *vastus lateralis*, the outer thigh. From her distant memory, Lara dragged her knowledge of the anatomy of the human leg. No major blood vessels lay beneath the area, no large veins or arteries, no significant nerve bundles. A fleshy part of the thigh, Ryan chose it to do minimal long-term damage, but it still looked like a major trauma to Lara. Which was the whole point.

Lara gritted her teeth and carried out her task on automatic. She'd heard most of Graham Valence's confession from her perch on the upstairs landing. It had corroborated Ryan's story, as she hoped it would.

Most military men in Ryan's situation wouldn't have thought twice about hurting the people who'd betrayed him so badly, but he was better than that. Much better. Former SBS Captain and current vilified patsy, Ryan Kaine, had made her a promise and had kept it.

She swabbed the wound. The bullet had passed through the muscle, through the chair seat, and ended up lodged in the grouting between two granite flagstones.

"Ain't givin' you no stitches for the moment. I'll leave that to the doctors in case some splinters blew back into the wound. But I am gonna clean it. Keep still."

After she'd finished, Lara wrapped a compression bandage around the thigh, added a second over the top as a precautionary measure.

"Keep calm," Lara said. "Struggle and you'll increase your blood pressure. Might open that wound again and you'll bleed to death."

"Help me, please."

"Already have."

"Graham, my husband, he's told Kaine everything he knows. There's nothing more. Kaine will kill us both and you'll be responsible."

"I ain't responsible for nothin'. I'm only here to help with the injuries. What more can I do?"

"Call the police."

"Really?" Lara asked, acting surprised.

"Yes." Gail sat up straight, eagerness vibrated through her body. "Please. Please call the police."

"Really? You want me to call the cops after what you and your husband done?"

The woman's mouth snapped shut.

"Nah," Lara jeered. "I thought not."

Lara checked her watch. She'd been in the kitchen thirteen minutes. Two ahead of schedule. She wrapped the used dressings in a paper towel, closed the medical bag, and hurried to the back door. Despite the discomfort—sweat had formed at the fingertips and wrinkled her skin—she kept the surgical gloves in place. She'd promised Ryan not to remove them until he gave her the okay.

After stepping outside, she filled her lungs and let out a loud, piercing, incredibly cathartic scream. Then she returned to the kitchen.

Gail twisted at the waist. Following the sounds. "What was that?"

"Message for hubby. Gonna play the recordin' now. Wanna hear what I missed."

"Bitch. You fucking evil bitch."

Lara hit play on the recorder and started listening. Part of her agreed with Gail's assessment. Maybe she *had* turned into a bitch, but that didn't necessarily make her actions wrong.

Even though both Lara and Gail had committed illegal acts, Lara's were morally defensible. Of that she was certain.

Evil people—people like Gail and Graham Valence—had turned Ryan into a mass killer, and he only had one chance to expose them, bring them to justice, and clear his name. Once his name and face made the papers, it was all over, despite his claims about friends and hideouts and emergency bank accounts.

She'd seen the real life cop shows. The cops followed the shortest path through the evidence and usually got their man. That path, and all the "evidence" so far, led straight to Ryan Liam Kaine.

Second only to a mistreated animal, the one thing Lara couldn't stand was injustice. She'd seen it when her dad was fired from the newspaper for someone else's mistake and a few times during Ollie's military career, but nothing as abhorrent as this.

Ryan needed Lara's help and, darn it, she would do whatever he needed.

He'd pulled her into his world, into his life, and had cost her everything, but despite that, she wanted to help. She *needed* to help him clear his name.

Flaming heck!

The realisation shocked her to the core.

CHAPTER TWENTY-FIVE

Thursday 10th September – Evening

Gravel's Farmhouse, South of London, UK

Kaine stepped back to admire his handiwork. Garages could be wonderful places to store things—murdering bastards, for example.

Stripped to his boxers and bound to one of the two-storey building's foundation columns with three webbing straps, Gravel wasn't going anywhere without Kaine's say-so.

The straps secured Gravel's ankles, waist, and neck to the column. Kaine left his arms free—wrists still tied together—but placed the straps' ratchet clamps at the back of the column, well out of the reach of grasping fingers.

He'd locked the first two straps tight enough to allow very little movement, but left the one at the neck almost loose—to begin with.

Kaine stood in front of his former boss and patted him on the cheek.

"There you go. Safe and sound. I bought these straps at a service station on the way here. It pays to come prepared. Am I right, old buddy?"

"Go fuck yourself, you piece of shit."

Kaine slapped Gravel's cheek again, this time hard enough to crack his head back against the concrete. "Language, old man. Language."

"Fucking hell, Ryan. You shot Gail. You shot her!"

"She'll live. Probably. At least that particular wound won't kill her."

"I never thought you'd do it. Not really. What's happened to you?"

Kaine rounded on him, barely able to keep control.

"God's sakes, man. You made me kill all those people and you wonder what's happened to *me*!"

Gravel had the good sense to lower his gaze. "Sorry, Ryan. I'm so sorry, but they had me between a rock —"

"Oh spare me the self-pity, you bastard! You turned me into a murderer and I turned Gail into a bargaining chip. Hardly the same thing though, is it." He stared at his captive for a moment before continuing. "The way I see things, you only have a couple of options."

"Yes? And what would they be?"

"The first is to come with me to the police. You can confess everything and throw yourself on the mercy of the courts."

Gravel snorted. "Bernadotti has access to money. Big money. I wouldn't live to reach court. You said there's a second option?"

Kaine scratched his chin. The beard was so damn annoying. Couldn't grow quickly enough.

"Tell me everything you know about Bernadotti."

"I *have* told you everything."

"The hell you have. I need his contact details, address, phone numbers, both mobile and land lines. Who does he work for? What car does he drive? Does he use a chauffeur? Favourite restaurants? You know the sort of thing. A full dossier."

Gravel shook his head and struggled to swallow against the restriction caused by the strap wrapped around his neck. "I don't know that stuff, Ryan, but I can get it. You'll need to give me some time."

Kaine stepped closer. "What am I going to do with you?"

Gravel kept his head turned away, eyes lowered. He didn't answer.

Kaine smacked the side of his captive's head. "Answer me, you arsehole."

Gravel's blue eyes locked with Kaine's. No remorse, no fear, only hatred. Given the chance, he'd kill Kaine in a blink of those baby blues, but Kaine knew one way to break him down fully. He only had to wait a few moments longer.

"Now, where were we? Ah yes. Rudy Bernadotti. Tell me all about him."

Kaine stepped around the back of the pillar and clicked a notch on the top ratchet, tightening the neck strap. Gravel's bound hands reached up, fingers pulling, scratching at the strap. His face turned red. His purple tongue poked through a gasping, flapping mouth. The strangulated gargling wasn't a pleasant sound.

"Stop. Please. I ... don't know ... anything."

"Don't give me that bollocks. You never take on a new client without running a complete background check on him and his family. If he has a wife, you'll know her clothes size and the name of her hairdresser. If his wife has a dog, you'll know the name and address of the poodle parlour and the next appointment she's made to have the bloody thing clipped. So, I repeat, where does Bernadotti—"

A high-pitched scream interrupted his question.

"Oh God, no!" Gravel forced out the words, struggling to speak against the pressure of the strap constricting his throat. "What are you doing to her?"

"Me? What can I be doing? I'm in here with you. Oh dear. One of my friends must be getting a little too friendly with Gail. Can't blame him really. I mean, she's looking pretty hot since she had all that work done. What size are those implants? Double-Ds?"

He released the clamp. Gravel whooped air into starved lungs.

"You bastard!" Gravel coughed.

"Are we going through that name-calling routine again? If you want me to ask my men to go easier on her, I'll need some more information."

"Please, please stop. Ryan, you're better than this."

"Used to be!"

Kaine worked the ratchet again and snapped Gravel's head back against the column. He gagged, barely to breathe.

"You made me a killer. Everything that happens in here and to Gail is down to you. I can't be held responsible for my actions. After all, I'm a madman, a mass murderer, right?"

"God, Ryan," Gravel gagged, "stop this. Please, I've ... told you all I know. What ... more can ... I do? Kill me, but leave Gail alone. Please, mate. For old time's—"

"Old time's sake? Is that what you were going to say, old pal, old buddy? Eighty-three people dead and I should go easy on you 'for old time's sake'!"

Kaine reached for the ratchet again and for the first time saw real fear painted in red on Gravel's face. He dropped his arm. "Tell you what I'll do, Graham. I'll give you a little time to think about what you're going to tell me and look in on Gail. How about that?" He rubbed the top of Gravel's head. "I'll report back in a sec. Don't go anywhere, now."

Kaine double-checked the bindings and made sure Gravel had no chance of escape before leaving him alone to stew. He turned off the strip lights on his way out. As the instructors used to say in SBS Boot Camp—darkness and fear have a way of weakening even the strongest mind.

CHAPTER TWENTY-SIX

Thursday 10th September – Lara Orchard

Gravel's Farmhouse, South of London, UK

Lara scrolled through the recording Ryan left for her until she found the relevant section, immediately after the shot.

"*Sorry Gail. Blame your husband. Not me.*"

Ryan sounded flat, unemotional. Given the circumstances of the recording, Lara could tell that anyone hearing it might think him unbalanced. The words continued. "*The next shot gives her a lifetime of pain. Who's the Principal and why did he want me to shoot down that aeroplane?*"

Sounds ... the legs of a chair scraping on the floor. Heavy breathing, panting.

"*Rudy.*"

"*Go on,*" Ryan said, over Gail's muffled shrieking.

"*Rudolpho Bernadotti. I'll tell you all about him, but Gail, please. Help her. She'll bleed out.*"

"Keep talking, Gravel," Ryan ordered after a slight pause. "*Better hurry, though. This is a bad wound. She doesn't have all night.*"

Graham Valence spoke quickly. "*The real target—I don't know his name—was originally booked on a private jet out of Humberside International. That was the aircraft you were supposed to shoot down. But his plane developed mechanical trouble and he transferred to Flight BE1555. Bernadotti didn't tell me ... I swear to God, Ryan ... I didn't know.*"

"*I don't believe you,*" Kaine said, his voice quiet and emotionless.

"*It's true, I tell you. Honest to God. All those innocent people? You really think I'd knowingly kill them all?*"

"*How did you receive the transponder code?*"

"*Bernadotti sent me a text ... I passed it to you without knowing the actual target. Ryan, I swear—*"

A sharp slap cut short Gravel's snivelling.

"*You lying piece of crap. I'm supposed to believe you sent me targeting co-ordinates without checking the source location first? Where's your famed caution—*"

Lara switched off the recording. She moved closer to her patient and touched the woman's shoulder. Gail jumped.

"And you have the nerve to call me an evil bitch?" Lara growled. "Still want me to call the cops?"

Gail had calmed and her shaking stopped. Control had returned.

"A confession made under duress won't hold up in a court of law."

"Prob'ly not, but what happens when this Bernadotti fella learns your hubby's given up his name? What do you think he'll do to you both?"

Gail turned her head towards Lara's voice.

"Listen to me," she said quietly, "I did nothing. Help me, please. ... I'll make it worth your while."

"'Help me'? Not 'Help us'? What about your hubby?"

"I can't be held responsible for what Graham said or did. Rudy knows I wouldn't say anything to hurt him."

Rudy?

Lara's eyebrow shot up. Gail being on first name terms with the Principal added an interesting morsel to the knowledge pool. Valuable information Ryan might be able to use.

"Help me," Gail whispered. "I have money. I can pay."

Everything Ryan told her had proved to be correct. He knew how these people operated, and she was learning fast that Ryan's word was solid, trustworthy. She was also learning why he had no pity for these people and how he could be cold and calm when deciding what to do.

Time to act on her own initiative.

If these scumbags turned on each other so readily, they wouldn't be surprised if others acted in the same manner. Shocked that she felt confident enough in her role to ad lib, Lara dragged a chair close to her patient and sat.

"How much?" she asked, matching Gail's low volume.

"How much do you want?"

"Make me an offer."

"One hundred thousand pounds."

Lara gasped. "You'll give me an 'undred grand to call the cops?"

Gail shook her head with such violence, Lara feared she'd give herself whiplash. "No, no police. You were right. I can't involve the authorities."

"So, who should I call?"

"Give me a phone and I'll contact Rudy. He'll get you your money."

To add an extra layer of tension, Lara hesitated.

"You're in bed with a mass murderer. Ain't no way I'm trustin' you."

Gail opened and closed her hands. Pleading in the only way available to her. "Please, please help me. Rudy and I are special friends, you know? He'd be so grateful, he'll honour any debt."

"Nah. Too risky. The captain's real mad. Never seen him in such a state. He'd kill me if he found out."

"Listen ... listen. As a sign of good faith, I can give you half now. Fifty thousand pounds. It's all the cash we have in the house."

Lara allowed her breathing to speed up.

"Where? Where's the dosh?"

Gail's head lowered. "In the wall safe in Graham's office. Behind his chair. I'll give you the combination."

"I ... dunno. It's too dangerous."

"There's a gun in the safe along with the money. You can use it to protect yourself from Kaine. Please, please, please. Oh God, please."

"Okay, okay. What's the combination?"

"Enter 2-9-8-5 on the keypad and turn the handle to the right, not the left. Turn it to the left and it triggers the alarm in the local police station. You got that?"

Lara repeated the instructions.

"There's something else in the safe. Bring it back with you."

"What is it?"

"A burner phone. Graham uses it to contact Rudy. He thinks I don't know about it, but Rudy tells me everything."

"Okay, we got a deal. But if you scream and the captain comes back, you're on your own, understand?"

Gail nodded. "Thank you. Oh God, thank you."

Lara looked up. Ryan stood framed in the rear doorway. He smiled at her and mouthed, "Everything okay?"

She gave him the thumbs-up and opened her hand. She needed five more minutes. He nodded and ducked back out through the door.

Lara found the office, opened the wall safe, and grabbed all the contents—envelope stuffed full of cash, gun, mobile phone, and a concertina file full of official-looking documents. She closed the safe again, hit "reset" on the keypad, and returned to the kitchen.

Gail hadn't moved and hadn't screamed. "Who's that?"

"It's me," Lara whispered.

"Did you find everything?"

"Everything but the mobile."

"What? Are you sure?"

"Positive."

Lara approached the captive. "Our deal's off. I can't trust you."

"No, listen. Graham must have moved it. Let me call Rudy on my mobile. He'll answer and you can talk directly to him."

"Where's your handbag?"

Gail hesitated.

"Hurry up, the captain won't take much longer. If your hubby cracks before we're done here. The deal's off. Got it?"

"Sorry, I was thinking. It should be on the coffee table in the lounge. Hurry, please."

Lara rushed to the lounge and returned with the mobile open at the directory. "What's the number?"

"It's stored under 'F' for Fitness Instructor," Gail said, her lower lip trembling. "Rudy and I usually meet at the gym in town."

"I'm dialling now."

She pressed the speaker key and held the mobile to Gail's mouth. "You're on speaker, I'll be able to hear everythin'. Play this smart and we'll both be in gravy."

Lara winced at her words. She had no idea where she'd pulled the expression from, but Gail seemed to understand the meaning.

Movement caught her peripheral vision. Back in the doorway again, Ryan shook his head. His pinched expression suggested he'd just sucked on a lemon. Lara poked her tongue out at him.

What did he expect? She hadn't been in the intimidation game that long. No doubt, she'd improve over time. Assuming they both survived long enough.

The call connected.

"Who's that?"

A man's deep voice. The question barked.

"Rudy, it's me, Gail."

"Gail?"

"Yes. Oh, it's so good to hear your voice."

"I can't speak now. Call me tomorrow afternoon."

"Rudy, no please—"

Kaine sliced his hand across his throat. Lara cut the call.

"Thanks, Gail," Kaine said, aloud. "That's all I needed. You can leave now, Doc. I'll take it from here."

Without a word, Lara left the room, closing the door to the hallway gently behind her.

CHAPTER TWENTY-SEVEN

Thursday 10th September – Late evening

Gravel's Farmhouse, South of London, UK

Kaine entered the kitchen, sat in the chair so recently warmed by Lara, and removed Gail's blindfold. She blinked hard and pulled her head away when her eyes found focus.

"Kaine!" Cold fury erupted from her mouth.

"Hi there, Gail. How you doing?" He gave her a welcoming smile, nice and friendly.

Her eyes darted left and right, searching.

"Don't worry. We're all alone. Only you and me." He waggled her mobile under her surgically-enhanced nose. "Thanks for this. Now I know you and dear Rudy don't have a secret name for each other, I'll be able to use this to arrange a private meeting. No fuss, no gunplay, no armed guards. Sweet."

"Where's Graham?"

Kaine leaned against the back of his chair and shook his head. "Really? *Now* you ask after him?"

"What have you done with my husband?"

"Never mind about dear old Gravel for the moment. The more important question is, what am I going to do with you?"

Her sculpted chin trembled and tears rolled down smooth cheeks. Gail turned her deep blue eyes on him and sniffled. "Please don't hurt me. I'm no danger to you." She lowered her eyes and thrust her cleavage at him. "Please don't hurt me anymore."

Kaine ignored the heaving breasts and studied the dressing. "The doc did a good job. The wound will leave a tiny scar, but you'll live. Call it a memento of my visit."

Still thrusting out her chest, Gail tried a different approach. "Rudy and I are only casual acquaintances. I was trying to use our relationship to strike a deal with your medical friend. You understand, don't you? Blindfolded and tied up in my own kitchen, I was terrified. I would have said anything to save Graham and me. Rudy means nothing."

Kaine scrolled through the mobile's directory. "Now that doesn't quite ring true. Why would you have his number listed under Fitness Instructor? I'm guessing you and dear Rudy meet up regularly to ... pump iron."

"It's not like you to be so crude, Ryan."

"Situations change a person."

"You've not changed that much. The injection to deaden the pain—"

"Yes, well. I have my limits."

"Ryan, I've always liked you. If you untie me, I'll prove it."

The tip of her tongue popped out and moistened her lips.

"For God's sake, Gail. Grow up. You're too old to be playing the nymphet and this is too serious a situation. All those people dead and you think a roll in the sack is the answer?"

Gail sucked in a lungful of air, but Kaine clapped his hand over her mouth and shook his head. "No, Gail. Screaming's not the thing either." He held his knife under her restyled nose. "Are you going to keep quiet?"

With wide eyes staring cross-eyed at the point of the blade, she nodded and he removed his hand. "Good. A couple of my SBS old buddies are on their way to keep you both company for a while."

"What? No, you can't!"

"It's either that, or I use the knife. You choose."

"You can't hold us captive forever."

"I'm not expecting to. After I've talked to Rudy and found out who's really behind this business, I'm handing everyone over to the police, myself included. The eighty-three families deserve answers. They also deserve compensation and I intend to deliver both. Whoever's behind this has deep pockets and I'm going to make them pay ... in more ways than one."

A triple knock on the front door announced the babysitters' arrival. He rested the knife on Gail's thigh, between the bandage and her knee. "Remember what I said about keeping quiet?"

She nodded.

He tapped the flat of the blade on her knee. "There's a good girl. Back in a tick."

Kaine closed the kitchen door, hurried down the hall, and opened the front door to his support team. Sergeant William Rollason and Corporal Daniel Pinkerton—two muscular individuals he'd known for more than a decade and trusted with his life—entered. Each carried two bulging holdalls.

"Rollo, Danny, thanks for dropping by."

"You called, we came. No problem, sir," Rollo said, taking in the oak panelling and the sweeping arc of the staircase—and checking the sightlines. "Nicest prison I've ever set foot in. How long we staying?"

"No telling. Could be a couple of days, could be a week. Any longer than that and I'll have already turned in my dog tags, if you follow me."

Rollo nodded.

Danny sniffed. "Suits me," he said and walked his bags into the lounge, where Lara waited for the next stage of the operation.

"Hello," she said, jumping to her feet and thrusting out her hand. "You must be Danny, we spoke on the phone."

Danny lowered his bags to the floor. He wiped his hands on his camouflage jacket before taking hold of hers and pumping as though expecting her to give out some beer.

Rollo grunted. "Danny, leave her alone, mate. She'll probably be needing that arm later."

Danny let go and issued an apology.

"Didn't hear you arrive," Kaine said, ushering them all inside the lounge, ignoring their banter, and closing the door behind him. "Where'd you park?"

"Up the hill behind your Toyota. Thought we'd keep our presence on the down-low until we finished our recce."

"Excellent." Kaine waved them into the settee and took the wing-back armchair, sinking into the soft upholstery. The fifty minutes of shuteye he'd snatched earlier in the evening hadn't been nearly enough to recharge his batteries fully. "Here's the sitrep." He turned to Lara. "Sorry, that's a Situation Report."

She tilted her head to the side and stared at him, a schoolmarm scolding her slowest pupil. "Ryan Liam Kaine, I was married to a soldier for eight years. I know what 'sitrep' means."

Rollo looked at Lara and then at Kaine. A half-grin formed on his weather-beaten face.

"Right. Sorry." Kaine scratched his irritating stubble, took a breath, and launched into it. "Gravel's in the garage strapped to a post and isn't going anywhere. I don't need to tell you how dangerous he can be, so use good judgement when you make him more comfortable. Gail Valence is in the kitchen, a little worse for wear, but Dr Orchard—Lara —assures me she'll be fine until Doc Sanders arrives from Parklands."

Rollo leaned forwards and rested his elbows on his thighs. "Old Sandy's on the case is he? Hope he's going easy on the sauce these days. Had the shakes pretty bad last time I saw him."

Lara's eyes bugged at the big man's words, but Kaine patted his hands in the air. "Rollo's kidding. Sandy's been teetotal all his life. Rollo, you ought to know better. Such slander is beneath you."

"Military humour was never particularly humorous," Lara said, reaching to the side of her chair. "Perhaps this will make you take things more seriously." She handed the concertina file to Kaine and the envelope to Rollo. "And that should take care of expenses for a few days."

Rollo opened his present and flicked through the banknotes. "How much in here?"

Lara shrugged. "I didn't count it. Gail said there'd be fifty thousand."

"Fifty grand?" Rollo said, smiling. "This ought to cover it well enough. You happy with half that, Danny?"

"I'm here, aren't I?" said the man of few words.

Kaine leaned forwards to cut off any further time wasting. "Okay, listen up. Every police officer in the country will be looking for me soon, but I'm not ready to hand myself over until I can prove I was set up. I need some quality time with Gravel's paymaster, Rudy Bernadotti. You three are my backstop."

"Us three?" Lara asked.

"Yes, you're staying here with Rollo and Danny," Kaine said, in a way he hoped sounded final. "I'll need a free hand to ask my questions without any more pussyfooting around."

"You tortured Gravel and shot Gail, and that's what you call pussy—"

Rollo interrupted. "You shot an unarmed woman? *You*?"

"Don't be too surprised, Sergeant. Before Gravel arrived, the doc injected her in the thigh with enough horse anaesthetic to deaden the pain from a shotgun blast. She didn't feel a thing." Kaine returned his attention to Lara. "What I'm about to do is dangerous and your presence will ... be a distraction. If I'm worried about you I won't be able to function properly. Sorry, but that's the way it has to be."

"But I've been helpful so far, haven't I?" she asked, sounding desperate and looking sideways at the two mercenaries.

"Yes, you have. I couldn't have come this far without you, but without any military training you'll be a liability in the field. The people I'll run into will make Gravel look like a primary school bully. And don't worry about these two," he said, eyeing Rollo and Danny. "They might look like a pair of savages, and in a fight, they are, but they're *my* savages. They'd lay down their lives to protect you. Wouldn't you, guys?"

"If I'm paid enough, Captain," Rollo said, winking at Lara.

Danny looked up and pointed at Rollo. "What he said." He removed weapons and ammunition from one of the holdalls and started making them ready.

"Besides, the difficult part's done." Kaine held up Gail's mobile. "With this, I have easy access to Bernadotti. Drawing him into a trap will be simple. Doc, you're safer right here."

To mark an end to the discussion, Kaine riffled through the compartments in the concertina file until he found a dossier marked "Operation Unmanned Drone II—OUDII".

"Here we are. Rollo, while I read this, check on the Valences. Make sure Gravel hasn't wet himself yet."

Lara snorted and crossed her arms. Rollo suppressed a grin and saluted Kaine on his way from the room.

"Doc?"

"Yes, *Captain* Kaine?" Lara snarled the words.

"I saw a lovely big kettle on the Aga in the kitchen."

Her eyes widened and her mouth fell open. "You want me to play housewife and make you all a cup of coffee?"

"Good idea, that would be lovely. Thanks so much for offering. White, no sugar, please."

Lara jumped to her feet, a deep flush coloured her normally pale cheeks. He smiled and raised his hands. "Okay, okay. If you're going to make a big fuss, I'll take it without sugar."

The mobile he'd taken from Gravel started vibrating. Danny looked towards the sound. Lara's mouth snapped shut.

Kaine raised a finger to his lips. "I've known Gravel long enough to pass for him on the phone. Keep quiet and get ready to make a move if we're sussed."

He picked up the mobile and accepted the call.

"Hello there, Graham Valence speaking."

Danny's appreciative nod told him his mimicry had passed muster.

"Mr Valence, you don't know me, but I have an urgent message for you and your partner, Ryan Kaine."

The caller, a woman, had a soft French accent. Kaine's immediate reaction was to hang up the phone, but her voice transmitted urgency. It made him pause.

"Who are you?"

"My name doesn't matter. You don't know me, but you and Ryan Kaine are in terrible danger. I … want to help. Please, you must listen to me."

"You have five seconds before I end this conversation and call the police."

"Good. That's what you need to do, Mr Valence. Contact Ryan Kaine and tell him to surrender to the police. His life depends on it. And while he's with the police, he should tell them to investigate a man called Rudolpho Bernadotti."

CHAPTER TWENTY-EIGHT

Thursday 10th September – Evening

Gravel's Farmhouse, South of London, UK

The mobile phone creaked under Kaine's tightening grip.

That name Bernadotti again. Jesus, what next?

"I'm putting you on hold, Ms Whoever-you-are. Don't hang up."

"Hurry, Mr Valence. I am in danger, also."

He hit the mute button.

"Danny carry on unpacking. Lara, you'll need to hear this."

Still with lasers shooting from her hazel eyes, she followed him to the hall. He released mute and hit the speaker key.

"Still there?"

"Yes, Mr Valence. What are you going to do? Can you contact Mr Kaine?" She spoke quietly, rushing her words.

"Possibly, in an emergency. Why?"

"He's in danger."

"You already said that."

"People are trying to kill him."

"What people?"

"A private army."

"What private army? You're making no sense, Ms ..."

"Call me ... Delilah."

"Okay, Delilah. Explain yourself."

"Tell Mr Kaine I tried to warn him and Doctor Orchard this morning at the veterinary clinic, but no one answered."

"You phoned? When exactly?"

She paused before answering. "Approximately ten fifteen."

Lara's widening eyes and the hand covering her open mouth told Kaine she remembered the hall phone ringing as they were leaving the farm. The woman, Delilah, might actually be telling the truth.

"You were a little late for the warning. You knew about the helicopter?"

"Yes ... I'm afraid I was responsible for sending them. Inadvertently, I promise you. I ... At the time, I had no idea what they were planning. You must believe me, Mr Valence. When I gave my bosses the location of Dr Orchard's clinic, I thought they'd send the police. Have you talked to Mr Kaine since the helicopter attack?"

"In a manner of speaking, yes."

"Excuse me?"

"Nothing. How did you find Kaine at the farm?"

"I tracked his car from Grimsby."

Kaine gritted his teeth. He knew it. Using the Citroën had been a schoolboy error. The injury and blood loss had screwed with his thinking.

Delilah continued. "It was my fault they sent a helicopter and a team of killers, but I didn't know. I swear I didn't."

"So, now you want to say sorry? Well, Delilah, I'm sure Kaine will accept your apology—if he survives the next death squad you send."

"Mr Valence, I gave information about your whereabouts to my bosses, but did not send the hit squad. In fact, I now know Mr Kaine was not responsible for destroying Flight BE1555. At least not intentionally. Please believe me. You are both in peril, your wife, too. As am I, if these people discover I am talking to you."

"What? How do you know all this?"

"That doesn't matter. Trust me. All three of you need to go to the police for protection."

"You mentioned a name earlier ... Bernie something? Who was that?"

"Rudolpho Bernadotti. He goes by the name Rudy. He's one of the men in charge here."

Kaine and Lara exchanged glances, her expression unreadable.

"Tell me about this Bernadotti character."

"I have only met him once. He is a dangerous man, Mr Valence. I want to help."

"Why?"

"I have learned things. Things that must be brought out into the open. All those innocent people were killed for money. This is simply not right. We have to stop them."

An idealist in this day and age? Could he believe her?

"Delilah, even if I believed you, Kaine can't go to the police without proof. They'll think he's a terrorist. Do you know how they treat terrorists these days? Where's Bernadotti right now? I'd need to bring him in with us."

"I don't know, but I can find him."

He hit mute again. "What do you think, Lara? Trust her, or hang up?"

Lara shrugged. "It's up to you, but she sounds genuine to me."

"We have Gail's mobile with Bernadotti's private number, but it wouldn't hurt to have a backup plan." Decision made, he reverted to his normal voice and unmuted the call. "Delilah, Graham Valence is up to his neck in this conspiracy. I'm Ryan Kaine. You and I need to meet."

"Mr Kaine? Is it really you? You're still alive?"

"Clearly. You offered to help me, but I'm not sure what you can do. Why should I listen to you?"

"I can give you access to Mr Bernadotti. I can be your eyes and ears here. Write down this number."

She read out a mobile number and he repeated it twice to commit it to long-term memory.

"I've been ... phone too long, Mr Kaine. Call me tonight ... eight o'clock. I might ... Bernadotti's locat—"

A high-pitched intermittent tone cut off her words. The alarm bells in Kaine's head turned into a warning claxon.

Hell!

"Get out! Lara, get out of the house now! Run to the car!"

He grabbed her arm and propelled her towards the front door.

She hesitated, shock and confusion written on her face. He pointed. "Go. I'm right behind you. Rollo, Danny!" he yelled. "Incoming!"

Kaine raced down the hall. He kicked open the kitchen door. Rollo stood over a wide-eyed and screaming Gail, slicing through her bonds with a combat knife.

"Incoming?" Rollo asked.

"Interference on the phone line," Kaine called, sidestepping past the big man and barging through the back door. "We've been lit up. I'll go for Gravel. Hurry. No idea how long we've got."

Cold night air hit his lungs, cooled the sweat on his face. High above his head, the ominous beehive buzz of a lightweight drone's electric motors drilled into his consciousness. It maintained an even pitch—no Doppler effect. No movement.

Kaine stopped and looked up, panting. The drone was stationary but oscillating wildly, struggling to maintain its position in a gusting wind. From its belly, the red beam of a laser sight bathed the roof with its targeting glow. A multi-directional gimbal maintained a static platform and stabilised the light. Towards the east, above the horizon, a white light flashed, growing larger as it approached.

He gauged the distance to the garage and estimated the time needed to release Gravel. Not enough.

Rollo and Danny could look after themselves and Gail, but Lara was his number one responsibility. She needed his protection. The distant white light drew closer.

No time.

He pulled the Walther from his belt and chambered a round. In a single movement, he took a two-handed grip, aimed, and fired three times.

The drone disintegrated, the red light vanished, but the white light still approached.

Kaine raced back into the kitchen.

Seconds. They had mere seconds.

CHAPTER TWENTY-NINE

Thursday 10th September – Lara Orchard

Gravel's Farmhouse, South of London, UK

Confused and scared, Lara stood in the front garden, her hair and clothes rippling in the growing wind at her back.

Incoming?

A bomb. How did Ryan know?

Rollo rushed through the front door, dragging a screaming Gail Valence, closely followed by Danny.

"Run, Doc. Run!" Danny yelled. He dropped the machine gun and grabbed her roughly by the arm.

He pulled her along with him. She tripped on one of the white-painted rocks guarding the path and fell, but he picked her up, threw her over his muscular shoulders in a fireman's lift, and bounded up the hill towards the road.

She struggled to free herself. "Let me go! I can run."

Danny skidded to a stop and lowered her. The second her feet touched gravel, she pushed him away and sprinted for the house.

"Ryan!" she screamed.

Eight metres away, a bright yellow light filled her eye, filled her mind. A silhouette appeared in the doorway.

"Ryan. Oh God. Ryan!"

She stopped.

He charged towards her, grabbed her hand, whipped her around. Lara didn't resist. She sprinted. Uphill.

"Come on, girl. Move!"

Ahead, in the distance, Danny had caught up with Rollo and helped him with a still struggling Gail. Fifty metres to the top of the hill, no more. Lara could manage that easily.

Broken images flashed as she ran. Ryan's back. His powerful arms. His strong, calloused hand in hers, gripping tight, reassuring.

They rushed past dark bushes and tall trees. Once through the open gates, they darted right and climbed some more. Tall grass underfoot brushed her ankles, whipped her trouser legs.

Cold air scorched her lungs. Her thighs burned. A stitch cramped her side, and still they ran. How far, she couldn't tell. Seconds, minutes, hours? But the hill stretched out above them.

They ran through thick, claggy mud, but Kaine didn't ease up until they'd crested the top and made it to the other side. Downhill!

Luxury.

Ryan dived headlong, pulling her down with him. He rolled on top of her, hugging her tight, breathing hard. His hand on the back of her head forced her face into his chest. Not quite the way she'd imagined their first embrace, but ... the earth moved.

The earth actually moved!

It punched up from deep underground and thumped the air from her lungs.

A fraction later, the explosion. An all-encompassing rumbling *boom* drowned out all other sound and echoed in the valley, returning to pound her again and again.

Then silence, save for the ringing in her ears and the sound of laboured breathing above and within her. A heavy weight lifted as Kaine rolled away.

"Lara, are you okay?"

She opened her eyes to the gloom. A dark shape above her, darker than the rest, moved.

"Lara, answer me, please. Are you okay?" Ryan said, the fear in his voice obvious.

"Next time, if you want a roll in the grass, just ask. Okay?"

Ryan laughed and hugged her again, this time with less strength, less ferocity. He held her for an age before releasing her and rolling away.

She reached out for him. "Don't leave."

"It's okay. I'm going nowhere. Just need to check on my men."

A hand caressed her cheek. A flickering yellow glow behind the brow of the hill outlined his profile. It formed a fiery halo. His eyes shone. He kissed her forehead and helped her sit.

"Stay there, I'll be right back."

He placed a hand on her shoulder, silently telling her not to stand. This time, she obeyed. She sat on the cold damp grass, backlit by flames, shivering. The wind knifed through her thin top. She hugged her chest and turned her back to the wind, minimising her profile the way horses and cattle sheltered from the elements. She was an animal fighting for her life, and the only one looking out for her was the man who'd dragged her into his world in the first place.

Ryan, bent at the waist to keep below the brow of the hill, ran to Rollo and Danny, both of whom lay prone, facing the destruction, faces lit by the flames. Of Gail, she saw no sign.

Rollo pointed over the hill and shook his head. Kaine frowned and turned to Lara, signalling for her to join them but keep low. She scrambled forwards on hands and knees. Her handbag dangled from the strap around her shoulders and dragged along the ground. She didn't remember rescuing it, but smiled in relief at the normality of its weight. With a handbag, she could still pretend life would be normal again, one day.

Twenty metres.

Lara hadn't crawled so far since childhood.

A clearly upset Ryan split his concentration between watching her progress and studying the destruction below.

The soft, damp grass cooled her palms and soothed the cuts on her knees. When had she cut them? Diving headlong before the explosion? No, she fell, and then Danny picked her up.

She reached the men, lay flat, and squirmed next to Ryan. He put a warming, comforting arm across her shoulders. She looked over the hill and down into the valley, and couldn't believe the sight.

The garage had been replaced by a crater at least five metres across. She couldn't tell how deep. What had once been a manicured cottage garden with a quaint potting shed and a two-storey brick garage, had become a war zone. The rear half of the house had disappeared. As far as she could tell, only the front façade remained intact, roof included. What had been a comfortable home minutes earlier, had become a burning pile of blackened rubble.

On the hill ten metres below and a little to Lara's left, a crumpled red and white cloth rippled in the blustery wind.

"She bit my arm and ran off, sir," said Rollo, showing the livid teeth marks inside his forearm. "I couldn't stop her."

"Okay, Sergeant," Ryan muttered. "Some people don't want to be helped."

Lara studied the fluttering cloth again—Gail's loose blouse. Her blonde hair caught the wind and danced like wisps of smoke. Something jagged stuck out of the left side of her head. Blood glistened in the firelight.

Lara closed her eyes. She'd seen violent death before, but in animals, not humans. Who wanted Ryan dead so badly they would kill so indiscriminately?

He leaned closer and whispered in her ear. "I didn't want this to happen, Lara. Believe me."

"I know. What caused all that?"

"A laser-guided missile," he said. "Lightweight, small charge, highly efficient."

"That was a small charge?" She opened her eyes and stared at him in disbelief.

He lifted his chin in confirmation. "That was a tiddler. You want to see the damage a twelve-inch naval gun will do."

"No, Ryan. I don't ..." The breath caught in her throat. "I ... I heard shooting before the explosion. Was that you?"

He nodded. "I destroyed the drone they used to light up the house as the target."

Rollo and Danny turned to listen.

"Not like you to shoot something without good reason, sir," Danny said.

"I had a reason," Ryan said, jaw set firm.

"Idiot boy." Rollo punched Danny's shoulder. "Feel that wind?"

Danny lifted his nose and seemed to sniff the air. "South-westerly. Force 6 or 7. Near gale conditions. Why?"

"When he took out the drone, the captain bought us time. Ten seconds, maybe fifteen."

"He did?"

Rollo pointed at the destruction. "If I figure it right, that thing was a Persuader MkV. Cellulose body, electric powered glide bomb. Launched by a jet from at least twenty miles away. To the east, just above the horizon. They're near silent and deadly."

"You sure?"

"Did you hear anything before it hit the house?"

Danny shrugged. "Nothing but a whistle, a crump, and then the boom."

"When the captain destroyed the drone, the Persuader lost its targeting resolution. It switched to auxiliary cruise mode and had to use its internal GPS. Probably slowed it down by about five knots. Maybe more in this crosswind."

Danny smiled at Ryan and formed a circle with thumb and forefinger. "Nice one, sir. I reckon we owe you, big time."

"And downing the drone would have disabled any infrared pictures it was broadcasting to the bad guys. They wouldn't have seen us scarpering. We might be in the clear for a while," Rollo added.

Ryan scowled at his friends. "Now's not the time to rest, gentlemen. We need to evacuate this place before the clean-up crew arrives, or the police."

"Is all that stuff true?" Lara asked.

Ryan shrugged. "Probably. I really just got mad and wanted to shoot something. The drone was as good a target as any."

Still staring at the destruction, Rollo shook his head slowly. "Drones, military-grade smart bombs launched from jets, an attack chopper? That amount of firepower costs serious money. Who the fuck are we fighting here, Captain?" He shot a glance at Lara. "Beg pardon for the language, Doc."

She smiled and shook her head. "Unforgiveable."

Ryan pushed himself up onto one knee, eyes scanning the valley beyond and around the destroyed house. "No idea, Sergeant. But I'm sure as hell going to find out. Okay people, let's move."

He helped Lara up and they hurried to the parked cars.

———

Ryan drove along dark country lanes for a mile before turning on the headlights. Rollo and Danny followed in their Nissan. They kept in touch via what Ryan called a "closed-link comms system". Whatever that meant. He assured her no one could overhear their conversation.

"How did you do that?" Lara asked once she'd found her voice again.

"What?"

"Drive in the pitch black without running off the road."

"The moon's out. There's plenty enough light to drive by."

"*And it helps when you have the eyes of a mountain lion. Over.*" Rollo said through the radio.

Ryan didn't react to the comment. "Munitions check. Sound off. Over."

Danny spoke first. "*Glock 17, four full mags. I had to drop the L85 when the doc fell. Over.*"

Lara twisted to face the back and tried to give him the evil eye

199

through the rear window, but the Nissan was nothing but a pair of dipped headlights. "I wouldn't have fallen if you hadn't grabbed my arm."

"Sorry, Doc. My bad. Over."

"But," she added, "I meant to thank you for helping and apologise for running off."

Danny grunted. *"You're welcome, Doc. Apology accepted. Over."*

"Rollo? Over." Ryan asked.

"One Glock, three full mags. How 'bout you? Over."

"Walther P99. Two full mags. Over."

"Since when do you use a Walther? Over."

"Borrowed it from Gravel. He won't be needing it anymore. Over."

"True enough. Rollo, out." Rollo's laugh contained little mirth.

"Lara, you'll find a ballistics vest on the back seat. Grab it and put it on."

She leaned over the seat and had to use two hands to lift the thing. She had no idea bulletproof vests were so heavy.

Ryan glanced at her. "Your head goes through the big hole. Pull the Velcro straps at the sides tight and there you go. That thing will stop anything but an armour-piercing sniper's round."

Lara shook her head. "What if the sniper's aiming at my head? I don't want it. If you aren't wearing one, then neither am I."

"Lara," Ryan said. "Please put it on. If we had more, we'd all be wearing them."

Although at least three sizes too large, once on, the vest wasn't too uncomfortable. One compensation for the weight, it kept her warm.

Ryan dropped a gear, turned right at a T-junction, and stamped on the accelerator. He checked the Velcro fastenings.

"Not exactly haute couture," he said, smiling, "but you won't be going near any catwalks for a while. Not that you'd be out of place in Milan, New York, or London ... Well, you know."

A compliment? He liked her? Protecting her wasn't just a sense of duty. He actually liked her. A flush warmed her cheeks, and her heart trilled.

If only they'd met in different circumstances ...

Ryan cleared his throat and concentrated on the road.

They drove north. After an hour of long silences interspersed with desultory chatter, Lara's curiosity took control.

"Where are we going?"

Ryan scratched his chin and took a moment to reply. "I have a friend, Mike, in a place called Long Buckby. He'll put us up while I work out my next move."

"*Your* next move?"

"We'll talk about it later."

"No," she said, adamant. "We'll talk about it now."

Ryan did that narrow-eyed, half-smile, half-grimace thing she'd learned to appreciate and even like.

"No, Lara. We'll talk about it later."

She recognised the next expression, too—his blank-faced stonewall, end-of-discussion, face. Didn't like that one quite so much.

"You'll like Mike's place. It's a working farm. Horses, cows and stuff. Be like home for you."

Lara clamped her mouth shut in case she said something she'd regret and settled back into her seat.

She dozed off and on, but woke by the time the eastern sky had lightened enough to welcome the dawn. They'd reached a motorway.

"Where are we?"

"M1 northbound," Ryan answered. "Just left the M25."

After Junction 7, Lara yawned. The dashboard clock read 05:43.

"We're about fifty minutes out. Too early to fetch up at Mike's front door unannounced, and the fuel light's just come on. Anyone need a comfort break? Over."

"*And breakfast?*" Danny said, sounding eager and bright. "*I could demolish a full English round about now. Maybe two. Toddington Services coming up in a few miles. Over.*"

Lara stretched her arms towards the windscreen.

"Yes, please," she said. "I could use a wash and a fresh set of clothes. Will I need to keep this thing on?" she asked, tugging at the vest.

Ryan looked at her from the corner of his eye. "Yes, you will. And you'll stay in the car until I buy you a sweater to cover it with."

Rollo's voice cut across her intended retort. "*The enemy's probably searching the major routes. Is it safe? Over.*"

"Calculated risk," Ryan answered. "They think I'm alone. Won't be looking for a group. We'll have to keep our guard up though. Over."

"*Always. Over,*" Rollo said

Danny grunted. "*Long as it doesn't interfere with breakfast, I'm with you all the way. Over.*"

Lara relaxed a little more. Less than four hours earlier, Rollo and Danny had been seconds from death, and yet they reacted as though the same thing happened to them all the time. They were prepared to risk their lives for nothing more than a few pounds and because Ryan asked them to.

Strange men, but so far honourable. Trustworthy.

Lara felt better than she had since escaping the carnage at her clinic.

CHAPTER THIRTY

Thursday 10th September – Rudy Bernadotti

Sampson Tower, London, UK

Rudy Bernadotti paced his private comms room in front of a bank of six TV monitors. Excitement tingled through his body, his heart raced, and sweat prickled at his scalp. The power he had over life and death, such a buzz.

Each screen showed a different black and white moving image of the carnage. Flames licked at what remained of Graham Valence's isolated home. The first screen showed the front of the house, which looked pretty well intact, apart from a few blown-out windows, but the back—shown on the other monitors—had been completely destroyed. It looked like a 3D rendition TV producers used on house renovation programmes to let the viewer know its internal structures. Only these pictures were the "before" part. The destroyed part.

The heat of the explosion had been so intense, it melted the wrought iron railings of the garden fence separating the house from the disintegrated garage.

Rudy focused his attention on the sixth screen, the one linked to the leader of the clear-up team.

"Report in, Tango One. What do you see? Over."

"One body. Female. In the nearby field. From the description, it looks like the wife. Can't confirm via facial recognition. There's no face left. No idea what she's doing outdoors this time of night. Want me to show you a close-up? Over."

Rudy curled his upper lip. "Yes please and take plenty of pictures. The police and MI5 might want our lab boys to run a facial reconstruction. Over."

"Doubt that, sir. When I said there was no face left, I wasn't kidding. Over."

The on-screen picture pointed at the ground. Tango One's military boots tramped through short grass, apparently up a steep hill, judging from the man's increased breathing. From the top of the screen, a foot rolled into shot. This one wore a woman's shoe minus its heel. The picture moved up a shapely body, clad in pale trousers and a loose top that flapped in the wind. Large breasts that didn't lie flat, even in death, bare arms exposed to the weather, but would feel no cold. A silver and gold watch on the left wrist looked familiar.

A frisson of delight rippled up and down Rudy's spine.

"Show me a close-up of the watch. Over."

The image zoomed in. The Rolex Oyster with the rose gold dial belonged to Gail Valence. He's seen it often enough. He gave a little fist pump. Another problem solved. The woman had more than outlived her usefulness. No use for her now with hubby out of the picture.

"Okay, show me what's left of the face. Over."

The image moved again, but what it showed didn't look like any human head Rudy had ever seen.

"Such a waste. What's that sticking out of her head? Over."

"Part of a house brick, sir. Have you seen enough? Over."

"What's wrong, Tango One? Don't like seeing the result of your handiwork up close and personal? Over."

"*Not really, sir. Not like this. Over.*"

"Any sign of a second body? Over."

"*No, sir. The area's flattened. The house is too unstable to search, and there's a ruddy great hole where the garage used to be. I think we'd better withdraw before the local plods arrive. Don't want to explain what we're doing here. That okay with you, sir? Over.*"

"I suppose so. Make sure you get me plenty of high res pictures before you leave. The quality of these video images is crap. Base, out."

One by one, the pictures on the monitors blinked off as Tango One's sweep-up team disconnected. Rudy turned to Adam, his assistant and closest friend. They'd known each other since secondary school. Rudy trusted no one else on the planet the way he trusted Adam. He'd call it love—if he knew what love was.

"What did you tell them?" Adam asked, waving at the blank screens.

Rudy's smile turned into a sneer. "Same thing we told the useless dead twats who fucked up at the vet's clinic. Fucking mercenaries thought they were wiping out a terrorist cell for a covert branch of MI5."

"Why would MI5 launch a wet raid on British soil? Wouldn't they have sent in the police or the army?"

"As far as Tango One is concerned, the evidence MI5 gathered couldn't reach a court of law because it would have breached the Official Secrets Act. I tell you, love, these ignorant squaddies will do anything if the price is right."

"You really are a sneaky bugger," Adam said, and the way he spoke—with breathless adulation—showed he didn't mean it as an insult.

"Bring up the last two minutes of the drone's digital stream."

Adam played his fingers over the keyboard. A monochromatic image appeared on the first monitor, showing squares and lines in differing shades of grey.

The index running vertically down the left side of the picture showed time and date, the flight duration, latitude and longitude, and the altitude—ninety-seven metres.

It took a great deal of concentration for Rudy to work out what the image depicted, but slowly, the outline of a house and garage emerged. The buildings stood in an isolated patch of land surrounded by fields, hundreds of metres from the nearest neighbour. Rudy recognised it as an aerial view of the Valence home in happier times, before the cruise bomb arrived.

"Is that the best image you have?"

Adam wrinkled up his nose in the cutest way. "Sorry, I've run it through our best enhancement program, and that's as good as it's going to get. Infra-red photography sucks."

Six hot spots showed up as white dots on the picture, one in the garage, one in the front room, two in the hallway, and two in the kitchen.

The altitude reading fell to thirty-five metres and the buildings increased in size on the screen. The picture rippled and the image colour-shifted to light red.

"Pause there. What's that?"

"The drone just lit the house with the targeting laser," Adam said. "And that's when I gave the order to launch the missile."

"This picture is fucking horrible. Are those white dots people? I can't tell."

"The computer recognition programme suggests they might be humans, but the static ones might come from different heat sources. Those in the kitchen could be a kettle or a cooker. Only one is moving, and that's definitely human."

"Why didn't you send up a drone with a better camera?"

"I had to compromise," Adam said, his doe eyes opened wide in apology. "The laser targeting module is heavy and only left room for a tiny camera."

"Why didn't you send up a surveillance drone as well?"

Adam winced. "I can't operate two drones simultaneously in the dark with that crosswind. I'd have had to draft in another operator and thought it best to limit the scope of the operation to need-to-know. Don't be mad at me, Rudy."

"I'm not mad, love," Rudy said, smiling. "It's just that you know how much pictures mean to me, and I hate not knowing what was going on. Roll the movie along."

One of the dots in the hallway rushed towards the kitchen, the others remained relatively stationary in relation to their positions inside the buildings. The moving white form exited the building, moved along the path between house and garage, and stopped. The splotch changed shape and a flower erupted, brighter and more intense around the blob. The image fizzled with horizontal lines of static before the screen blacked out.

Rudy turned from the screen and looked right at Adam. "What happened?"

"That man shot down the drone."

"Really? Play that part again. This time at half speed."

Adam reran the film and Rudy took in the screen metrics.

"Jesus. The drone was hovering at thirty-seven metres, and that man hit it with his first shot. Fuck, that's good shooting with a handgun."

"How do you know he wasn't using a rifle?"

"Speed. He dropped to his knee, raised the gun, and fired in more or less one movement. A rifle would have taken longer to shoulder and aim. That was a reaction shot. I've read Graham Valence's military records. His marksmanship is good, but not that good." Rudy stared hard at the screen. "Think about it. A near-vertical target in the dark and with a gusting wind? No, the guy who made that shot had very special skills." Rudy frowned. "You know what I think?"

"Do tell," Adam asked, tilting his head.

Always looked so damned cute when he did that.

Rudy ran a hand through his overlong hair. It needed a trim. He'd have the pinch-faced Margareta book him an appointment in the morning.

"I think the bastard who shot down our very expensive piece of military hardware was none other than Ryan Kaine."

"Are you sure?"

"Think about it. How many men in the UK could have made that shot? And how many of them would have been anywhere near Graham Valence's house tonight?" He rubbed his hands together. "How long after we lost contact with the drone did the Persuader strike?"

"Not easy to say, I'm afraid. We had a problem picking up telemetry on the missile. Couldn't exactly ask the Navy or Air Traffic Control to track its flight path, but judging from the time of release to the time of detonation, I'd say eight to ten seconds."

"Excellent. You know what that means?"

Adam shot him one of his knockout smiles. "Again, do tell."

"I think, dear Adam, we can safely say goodbye to both Graham Valence *and* Ryan Kaine. How about that? Tonight, we killed two annoying birds with only one stone. An expensive stone perhaps, but if a job's worth doing, it's worth spending money to do it well."

"I couldn't agree more. No one within fifty metres could have survived that explosion. Are you going to call Sir Malcolm with the good news?"

"Oh no, my love," Rudy said, holding out his hand, "that old tosser can wait. You and I should celebrate first. Come here and give me a kiss."

CHAPTER THIRTY-ONE

Friday 11th September – Lara Orchard

Newport Pagnell Services, M1, Buckinghamshire, UK

Lara pushed her plate away.

"You done?" Danny asked, pulling it towards him even before she nodded.

He wolfed down her abandoned sausage and mopped up the yolk with her last triangle of toast.

"Don't know where you put it all."

"Need to make the most of the opportunity, Doc. In the field, you never know when you'll get the chance to eat again."

"We're not in the Afghan desert, Danny," Rollo said. He'd finished his extra-large breakfast and was leaning back in his chair, nursing his second jumbo mug of coffee, eyes scanning the forecourt.

"Still," Danny said, "can't hurt to be prepared, right?"

Before they'd allowed her to leave the relative safety of the Land

Cruiser, Ryan had scouted the shopping concourse and returned with a man-sized T-shirt in blue. He apologised for the colour, saying it clashed with her hazel eyes, but most of the clothes shops had yet to open and it was the best he could do.

That he'd noticed her eye colour came as a nice surprise, but it shouldn't have. From her limited experience of seeing Ryan Kaine in action, she doubted he missed much.

On the walk from the car to the main Moto building, the three men had surrounded her, making her feel very small, but very safe. Half an hour later, with a wash and a huge breakfast under her belt, she felt great, but would have done almost anything for a fresh set of underwear.

Ryan promised they'd wait for the clothes shop to open as everyone needed a change of clothes. He actually said, "We all stand out like refugees from a civil war."

They'd chosen the quietest table at the back of the food hall near the service area. Rollo and Danny sat opposite her and Ryan, their backs to the wall, facing the entrance. She and Ryan kept their caps on and heads down, making sure not to look up at the CCTV cameras.

"Everyone happy?" Ryan asked and received nods and satisfied murmurs.

Lara tapped the table when she'd have rather raised her hand. "Can we discuss things now?"

Ryan nodded and drained his tea.

"Suppose there's time."

Everyone leaned forwards, but Rollo and Danny kept scanning the concourse which had started filling with early morning travellers. She started with a question that had been worrying her since the explosion. "This Delilah woman. Do you think she set us up?"

"Possibly," Ryan answered.

"She sounded genuinely concerned to me."

He crushed the napkin he'd been playing with and dropped it onto his empty plate. "She did keep me on the phone while they targeted the house."

"You said interference on the phone line tipped you off?" Rollo asked.

"That's right, and the call disconnected mid-sentence."

"That crackling we heard?" Lara asked.

"Yes. Laser targeting interferes with microwave phone signals. It's one of the few flaws in what is otherwise a very good covert targeting system."

Lara had a thought. "Do you get the same crackling with landlines?"

"Not really, they're closed and the lines are insulated. Why?"

"I was just thinking. Why did she use Gravel's mobile and not his landline? If she'd done that, we'd all be dead now, wouldn't we?"

Rollo raised his hand for silence as a middle-aged woman hurried past on her way to the toilets and then spoke. "She has a point there, Captain. If Delilah found Gravel's mobile number, she'd certainly have access to his landline number, too."

"Alternatively," Lara said, "if she was working with the people who fired that bomb, wouldn't she have co-ordinated the timing better? Wouldn't she have ended the call *before* they turned on the laser?"

"You're suggesting we should trust her?" Ryan asked, rubbing his eyes and trying to stifle a yawn.

He must have been exhausted. Lara wished he'd had the chance for more sleep. She'd insist on taking over the driving for the final leg of their journey.

Lara shook her head. The questions could go round in circles forever. They might never find the answer. "Who knows. I don't suppose you managed to save that concertina file?"

"Sorry, Doc," he said. "Highly remiss of me, but I was busy trying to save our lives at the time." A rueful smile creased his craggily handsome face.

"How much of the Bernadotti dossier did you manage to read?" she asked.

"Skimmed a few pages. Delilah's call interrupted me before I reached the useful stuff, but I know enough to ask her a few searching questions."

"So, are you going to phone her tonight, Ryan?"

Ryan looked enquiringly at Rollo who shrugged. As usual, Danny didn't have anything to add. Ryan stared at the print hanging on the wall behind his friends—an old-fashioned sports car moving at speed—before answering. "With Gail Valence dead, I've lost my easy access to Bernadotti. What other choice do I have but talk to her?"

"You could do as she suggested and present yourself to the nearest police station," Lara said, grabbing his hand. "I'll back up your statement, Ryan, and so will Rollo and Danny. Won't you guys?"

Rollo nodded half-heartedly. "Could do, but I'm not sure the cops will listen to a couple of old mercenaries like us two."

"Agreed. I certainly wouldn't want you ne'er-do-wells as my character witnesses," Ryan said, smiling. "But since you volunteered, after I drop you off at Mike's, I'm going to put you in contact with a guy I met in Afghanistan. He's now one of the boys in blue."

Danny injected himself into the conversation. "You know a Dibble?"

Ryan ignored him and threw a question at Rollo. "Did you ever hear of a lieutenant in Two Para called Giles?"

Rollo's eyes rolled up and to the right. "You mean 'Deity' Danforth, the Quaker? Yeah, I met him. Bloody good bloke in a ruckus, but a real bible-basher. Kept quoting the Gospels at us."

"Not that it matters, but Giles Danforth's a Presbyterian. What does matter is that he's a police officer based in Birmingham. He heads one of the Midlands Police's Armed Response Units. I'd trust him with my life, which is another reason I headed north after leaving Gravel's place. When we reach Mike, I'm going to give Giles a call. If he's the man I remember, he'll at least hear me out. My plan is for you and Danny to take Lara to him. I'll ask him to arrange protective—"

Lara thumped the table. A young family at the nearest occupied table turned to look, and she spoke in a whisper.

"I won't go. You still need my help."

"This isn't up for debate, Lara. Where I'm going, I can't have you around holding me back."

Lara's eyes started to water. She fought the tears.

"Listen to me, woman. Bernadotti and his people aren't messing around. They want me dead and don't give a damn who they hurt in the process. They're cleaning house. I should have known they'd target Gravel. Never should have taken you anywhere near them. It was begging for trouble. Don't you see? I'm probably going to die and I won't take you with me."

Lara sniffed and felt her lower lip tremble. Why was this so difficult? She'd known the man less than a day, but the thought of never seeing him again hurt more than she could have imagined.

"Will you at least wait until you've rested and that wound's had a chance to heal?"

The lines around his eyes softened and he caught hold of her hand. "Nothing's going to happen until I've spoken to Delilah. After that, I'll probably need a day or so to arrange things with Giles. Will that do you?"

She nodded, not wanting to speak and betray her emotions.

CHAPTER THIRTY-TWO

Friday 11th September – Evening

Newport Pagnell Services, M1, Buckinghamshire, UK

Refreshed after a shower and a full five hours uninterrupted sleep, Kaine sat in the same motorway services where he'd eaten breakfast with Lara and the guys that morning. The place was almost as empty. He wore black-framed non-prescription glasses, a baseball cap, dark leather jacket, black jeans, and rubber-soled work boots. Sitting directly beneath a surveillance camera, he stirred his coffee and stared at the clock on his phone, willing the time to pass more quickly.

His next move depended on a total stranger with a delicate French accent. An intolerable situation for a man in desperate need of reliable information. He didn't know her location or who she and Rudy Bernadotti worked for—an internet search on the man's name had netted a whole load of nothing. He was a ghost.

At 19:57 he lost patience, dialled the memorised number, and hit send. The call connected immediately.

"Hello?" Her voice was quiet, little more than a whisper.

Kaine could make out no background sounds on the line, nor an echo. As far as he could tell, she received the call in a quiet room with normal acoustics.

No help there. Move on.

"Delilah?"

"Mr K?"

"Yes. Hold on a second."

A plump cleaner in a green coverall swiped a mop over the tiled floor near his table. She looked at him and smiled. He smiled back. No fear or recognition on her face, despite the wall-to-wall media coverage since the police had finally released his name and photo as a "Person of Interest" in the crash of Flight BE1555. The cleaning woman turned her back, moved the "Wet Floor" cone a couple of metres further along, and pushed the mop around some more. His simple disguise seemed to be working. In real life, few people expect to become involved in a nationwide manhunt. Kaine doubted the woman had watched the news. Hopefully, she spent most of her viewing time watching soaps.

"Sorry. Are you still there?"

"Yes," Delilah answered.

"Is this conversation secure?"

"As secure as I can make it, assuming you are using a non-contract phone."

"I am."

"Then we would be very unlucky for anyone to hear this conversation but us."

Kaine coughed. "The way my luck's been running recently, that doesn't inspire much confidence."

"But you are still alive. You must have some force on your side. Allah, or God, perhaps?"

God? Yeah, right. Tell that to the people on Flight BE1555.

"Okay, less of the chitchat, tell me what you know about our mutual friend."

"Good, we should not use full names. Eavesdroppers have excellent automated search engines these days. I have worked on some of the best."

Kaine sighed. The woman was trying to teach him comms protocols when he'd written the book on the subject.

"What do you know about our man?"

"Very little at the moment. I only learned of his involvement last night. What information do you need? It would be best for you to ask me questions and I will find the answers if I can."

"Who does he work for?"

"The company is English, and its name begins with an 'S'. Biblical associations."

Sampson Armaments? Jesus.

Kaine finally understood his contact's choice of pseudonym. This particular Delilah might actually help him bring down a rather nasty Sampson. Despite the seriousness of his situation, Kaine almost laughed.

"How senior is our man within the organisation?"

"Board level, not that his name appears on the letterheads or the website. The company has an IT section devoted to minimising the digital presence of its senior executives and board members. What other information do you require?"

"Can you get hold of his personnel file?"

"That will not be a problem."

Interesting. Delilah either worked in the SAMS HR department, or had easy access to their computer files. Kaine bet on IT wiz. She mentioned working on impressive search engines. It probably meant she'd designed some of them.

"It would be helpful to know his pastimes, favourite restaurants. In short, I'm looking for areas of weakness in his personal defences."

She coughed. "I doubt you will find many. The company spends a great deal of time, money, and effort on personal protection. It would be bad publicity for any of their top executives to disappear or be caught in a compromising pastime, as you call it. Unfortunately, I will not be able to access the file until later tonight."

That soon?

His interest and excitement started to build.

"How much later tonight?"

Hesitation.

Had he pushed her too hard?

"I start work at midnight and will not have access to the data until the small hours."

Kaine ran the calculation. SAMS' Headquarters, Sampson Tower, stood within spitting distance of the Shard. Central London.

"How will you get the information to me?"

"By electronic dead drop. You can access it safely from anywhere in the world that has internet capability. I will call you tomorrow with the sign-in details."

A lifetime working for the military and his present situation threw up barriers. Kaine had a hard time trusting someone he'd never met, someone whose eyes he'd never read. "What's the nearest tube station to your work?"

"Why do you ask that?"

"I want to meet you face-to-face."

"No I cannot. It is too dangerous."

"Listen, Delilah, or whatever your real name is, you contacted me offering to help. If you want me to trust you, we have to meet."

She took a breath. Kaine could almost hear her trying to make the decision. In her place, he'd have ended the call and contacted the police.

"London Bridge."

Interesting. What was she playing at?

"What time?"

"The latest I can arrive at work without raising questions is a quarter to midnight. I have to pass through a security checkpoint. Can you reach London Bridge by eleven o'clock?"

"Twenty-three hundred hours? No chance." He lied. "Do you take a lunch break?"

"I have forty-five minutes at four o'clock. I usually take it in the canteen, but if the weather is favourable, I occasionally stretch my legs. The security guards would not find it unusual for me to leave the building at night."

"Excellent, you've answered my next question. How will I recognise you?"

"My hair is short and dark, with pink highlights. I will leave the building by the main entrance at a quarter past four and walk towards the station. Will that do?"

"Yes. I'll approach you."

She ended the call.

Could he trust her? Could he heck.

He drained the very average coffee and threw the empty cup in a bin on his way to the exit.

Kaine fired up his borrowed Land Cruiser and headed for the bright lights of London. Even taking his time, he could easily have reached London Bridge by eleven o'clock, but he had no intention of doing so. He'd miss the four o'clock meeting, too. The area around the Shard and the SAMS HQ offered little hiding place, especially in the middle of the night where any observer would be obvious. Central London at night wasn't the place for a fugitive, but the morning rush hour? That was a different matter entirely.

He trundled along the M1, keeping to the inside lane, at or slightly below the speed limit. Why risk arousing the attention of the police by haring around southern England?

His London safe house contained all he needed for a change of clothes, some food, and a place to think. His hidden armoury would also come in handy.

On top of everything else, he'd been using the same car for the best part of two days and it was high time to change his ride.

———

In London, Kaine hooked up with an old mate, Warrant Officer Rafael Avocet. A former Vehicle Artificer in the REME, Raffa was one of the best mechanics Kaine had ever met. In Afghanistan, he'd once rebuilt an engine overnight with little more than a Swiss Army knife, string, and chewing gum, while Kaine and his men held off a deadly insurgent attack. Raffa had saved a dozen lives that night and earned Kaine's undying respect.

Kaine traded his Land Cruiser for an early model VW Passat Estate GTi. Financially, Raffa—a self-styled "vehicle redistribution agent" in civilian life—received the better part of the bargain, but the Passat met Kaine's needs to perfection. Although its powerful engine ran more smoothly and more efficiently than it had when rolling through the factory gates some eleven years earlier, the tired and crumpled bodywork showed its venerable age.

He reached his Camden safe house in plenty of time to take a shower and luxuriate in a full three hours' sleep. His internal alarm woke him at 06:08. Surprisingly, he still felt tired.

Dressed for office work in the city and armed with a handgun, three full magazines, and a high-powered sniper's scope, Kaine hit the road within ten minutes of waking. He exited London Bridge tube station forty-five minutes later.

Up close, the Shard didn't impress half as much as it did from afar. The first dozen floors of glass and concrete looked the same as a million other skyscrapers the world over. Kaine's real interest focused on the twenty-three-storey building diagonally opposite—Sampson Tower, the world headquarters of SAMS Plc.

From his table in a delightfully old-fashioned greasy spoon, Kaine ate another full English, washed it down with two mugs of coffee, and kept his eyes focused on the impressive entrance to Sampson Tower. A polished chrome-and-glass portico housed a revolving door with a standard exit at the side.

The main flush of incoming personnel started arriving to complete their security sweep at around 07:45. Kaine's attention focused on the people leaving after their night shift. At 08:12, the rather striking, pink-haired Sabrina Faroukh blinked tired eyes against the bright morning, took a breath of city air, coughed, and strode towards the underground station. She stared straight ahead during her walk.

Kaine drained his mug, dropped a twenty-pound note on the table, and waited until "Delilah" turned a corner before leaving the café. No rush. She'd already told him the station she used for her daily commute.

By the time she reached London Bridge Station and the Northern Line platform, Kaine knew she was alone. He waited until she boarded a tube and took the carriage behind. She never left his sight for the whole journey. Apart from the occasional appreciative male glances—Sabrina Faroukh would turn heads in most crowds—no one paid her any undue attention. No watchers spoke into wrist mics, and no covert operatives studiously avoided looking in her direction. Anyone holding an open newspaper or book actually appeared to be reading. She was alone in a carriage crammed with commuters.

Kaine ticked one item off his list, no tail from the office. Maybe the woman spoke the truth after all. He had two more pinch points— the end of the train journey and her home, wherever that turned out to be.

She disembarked at Clapham Common and ambled the rest of the way home, in no apparent hurry. It took her twenty minutes to swim against the prevailing pedestrian tide before she reached the southern end of Stormont Road.

Home for Sabrina turned out to be a large Victorian villa over-looking Clapham Common. A low wall retained a tiny front garden, laid to concrete paving. Four steps led up to a storm porch shielding a large oak door. She stepped inside. From his position across the road, Kaine caught a glimpse of a wide entrance hall painted cream, a wall unit with six pigeonholes for post, staircase to the right, and an internal door. She approached it with keys raised. Behind her, the front door swung shut on an automatic closer.

The postage arrangement showed that the villa had been

converted into flats. Sabrina lived on the ground floor. That she had an impressive apartment in an expensive part of London demonstrated how well SAMS paid its IT staff.

Perhaps Sabrina Faroukh wasn't the low-level IT staffer she proclaimed.

A worry.

He hated surprises or confusion. In the field, when details don't line up, people die.

Kaine considered scrubbing the mission, but the woman represented his best chance of reaching Bernadotti easily and quickly, and he'd placed riskier bets before.

On the plus side, a five-year-old with learning difficulties could have picked the Yale latch on the front door, which didn't have a security intercom system. As for the Victorian-style casement stays on the windows? Disgraceful. Why her insurance provider hadn't demanded a security upgrade was beyond him.

Kaine sat on a bench on the far side of the park from the villa, reading an abandoned tabloid and studying the people and the late commuters. None warranted his attention.

After ten minutes, he tucked the paper under his arm and toured the neighbourhood streets. A corner shop on Lavender Hill sold sweets in jars. He bought a quarter pound bag of pineapple chunks. Again, nothing triggered his internal defences.

During his recce, he'd found an alley behind Sabrina's house that led to what was, by London standards, an enormous rear garden.

A two-metre-tall brick wall surrounding the villa's rear garden offered the illusion of security, but the rusty lock on the wooden gate presented no challenge. Kaine worked the lock with a set of picks— he hadn't carried them on *Herring Gull* and wouldn't make that mistake again. He slid through the part-open gate and hid behind an untrimmed privet hedge that ran around the inside of the wall. The hedge was likely someone's way of softening the ugly brickwork, but the same someone clearly knew nothing of personal security. Kaine didn't even have to crouch low to remain hidden from the house.

He took out his sniper's scope, sharpened the focus, and watched his target potter around her kitchen, yawning and stretching the whole time, her expression a mix of thoughtfulness, worry, and fatigue. She half-filled a kettle and scooped two heaped servings of coffee into a glass filter system. While the water boiled, she entered another room, presumably her bedroom, and emerged a few minutes later, hair tied back and dressed in a skin-tight leotard. She had a firm but rounded figure that demonstrated the virtues of regular exercise. Early twenties, large brown eyes, full-lips, of Middle Eastern heritage and colouring. Spying on Sabrina Faroukh wouldn't be too onerous.

Kaine offset his stalker's guilt by arguing that he was acting in Sabrina's best interests as well as his own. Conceivably, SAMS security people could have intercepted Sabrina and Kaine's telephone conversations—he had no idea how good her clandestine skills actually were. SAMS might be using her as bait, but the absence of a tail suggested she'd been telling the truth. No way was he going to let his guard down, though.

Things were good to go. With the scope still to his eye, Kaine took out his burner phone and hit the last number dialled, the only number he'd called on it. Sabrina scrambled for her handbag and answered.

"Hello, Delilah."

"What happened? Where were you?"

"Something came up."

"I was terrified. You don't know what I had to do to access this information. On my way out of the office, it seemed that every security guard in the building was looking at me. It was as if they knew I'd done something wrong. I felt sick and you didn't even show or call. And then it felt as though I was being watched all the way home."

On her homeward journey, she'd looked cool and relaxed. Kaine smiled. The woman's senses hadn't let her down. She showed promise. Now all she had to do was convince him to trust her.

"I told you I was busy, and don't worry about the terror, it gets worse with time."

"Are you deliberately trying to scare me?"

"Get over yourself, Delilah. I have a few problems of my own, like being hunted by every police officer in the UK, not to mention the foot soldiers our mutual friend has set on my tail."

Through the scope, Kaine saw her frown and bite her lower lip. "I'm sorry, but you are used to being a target. I am not. In fact, I don't know how to cope."

In the background, a kettle came to the boil.

"Better make your coffee, or is it tea?"

"Coffee. I'd usually choose green tea, but—" Her head snapped up and turned towards the window. "Where are you?"

Kaine grinned. Sabrina Faroukh had good instincts. "Did you find the information I wanted?"

"Yes."

"Where is it?"

"On my laptop's hard drive."

"How did you manage to get it?"

She answered while pouring the hot water into the cafetière. "Don't forget Mr K, I've read your file. How can I be gentle here? Let's just say I doubt your IT skills would stretch beyond booting up a laptop and leave it at that. Do you really want me to explain how I hacked into one of the most secure IT systems on the planet? Do you need the details of how I piggybacked an encrypted file onto a telephone call a colleague made to his wife? Would it make a difference to you if I told you I bounced the signal around three continents using seven different satellites, one of them military? Would it?"

Kaine smiled into his phone. "Point taken."

"You still don't trust me, do you."

"Trust has to be earned."

"You say you're close, why not meet me now?"

"That could prove operationally problematic."

"What do you mean?"

"I can't break cover in the daylight. You mentioned sending me access details."

"Later this morning I will create a secure website and give it the surname of your first SBS unit commander in Helmand Province.

223

Add 'dot org'. The password will be the call sign they gave you in your final mission in Iraq. There will only be one page on the website and it will contain the file you need. Is that clear?"

"Yes. How long will that take you?"

"Not long," she said, pressing the plunger on her filtration system.

"Great. Now all I have to do is find myself a nice safe internet cafe to read the files. I'll contact you again if I need to."

"Is that it?"

"It is."

"I thought you wanted to discuss this in person?"

"Ideally, but that won't be possible."

She poured the coffee, added a splash of milk from the fridge, and took a sip.

"I read Mr B's dossier overnight," she said. "There is a hole in his security you might be able to use."

"Really? Where did you do your military training?" he asked, more aggressively than intended.

As far as he could tell, she'd played it straight so far, but he had no intention of taking tactical advice from a novice. Despite that, he needed her, so he apologised.

"Sorry," he said. "Didn't mean to offend. I'll be in touch soon."

He ended the call and continued his surveillance, hoping she would do nothing to make him suspicious—like, for instance, make another call.

She didn't.

Over the course of the following half hour, Sabrina finished her coffee while tapping away at her laptop—setting up his secure website and encrypting the file, he assumed. After that, she completed an aerobics session in front of the TV in her lounge and disappeared into the bedroom once more.

Convinced she was alone, if not yet completely certain of her honesty, Kaine retraced his steps to the front of the house.

Stormont Road hadn't changed—still no suspicious parked cars, still no loitering pedestrians. With his internal warning system dormant, but his eyes and ears open and alive to sudden alarms, he climbed the steps.

Within five seconds, he'd picked the lock, stepped into the hall, and closed the door behind him. Pistol drawn, he stood still, listening to the creaks and groans of the old house as it woke under the warmth of the rising sun.

CHAPTER THIRTY-THREE

Saturday 12th September – Sabrina Faroukh

Stormont Road, London, UK

A hot shower usually worked wonders, but hours of tension had left Sabrina's nerves frayed, and Ryan Kaine's phone call had left her emotionally drained and physically tense. She'd completed her promised task and that should have been the end of it, but something in Kaine's tone made her think they had unfinished business. He treated her with suspicion, as though she were the enemy, and that was hardly surprising, considering his situation and considering what he'd faced since shooting down the aeroplane. How he coped with the guilt, she could not imagine.

Still, she had done everything she could do while preserving her primary objective and that was an end to it. Why then, did she feel so ... unfulfilled?

Why did she feel so guilty?

She dragged the extra-large T-shirt she used as a nightdress over her head and brushed her hair until it shone.

Her stomach rumbled. No chance of sleeping with an empty stomach. A bowl of cereal would suffice until breakfast. She strolled through to the kitchen, poured a half-bowl of muesli and added milk.

A rough hand clamped over her mouth, another grabbed her wrist. A prickly, bearded chin pressed against her cheek. Her legs turned to water. She slumped, but the man held her tight against his chest. Too shocked to struggle, she trembled, unable to fight against the man's strength.

Sabrina couldn't scream. Could barely breathe.

She felt nothing but rock-hard muscles and the pure animal power of the man holding her.

Dieu. Death feels like this?

"Please don't scream. I'm not here to hurt you." The man spoke with a quiet control, his voice familiar.

Ryan Kaine!

He released her mouth and wrist, and turned her to face him. Raising a finger to his lips, he tapped his ear and waved a hand around the room. She nodded her understanding.

Kaine reached into a pocket. Sabrina tensed again.

A knife? A gun? What did he want?

His hand came out carrying an electronic device the size and shape of a large cigar—an electronic signal scanner.

She stood back and watched him sweep the kitchen with the wand. Once finished, he took her wrist again—this time more gently —and dragged her from room to room as he repeated the process. Clearly a careful man, Kaine kept hold of her until they returned to the kitchen.

Sabrina watched him watching her. She rubbed her wrist, not that it hurt.

"I thought you were one of the SAMS security guards come to kill me," she said, her voice strained.

"Please excuse the unannounced visit and the rough handling. I didn't want you to pick up the bowl and drop your muesli all over the laminate flooring."

She stood up straight.

"Laminate? So much do you know. The floor is solid oak parquet. My grandfather laid it himself."

What a ridiculous thing to say to a trained killer. As though the composition of her flooring mattered to anyone but her.

The strength returned to her limbs, and along with it, an anger at the man's audacity. There she stood, metres from a known killer and she felt only anger at his intrusion, not fear. What was wrong with her? Kaine could snap her in two with his bare hands, yet she sensed no aggression in him, only caution, tension, and an underlying weariness.

His mouth curved into a thin smile. "My apologies again. Mind if I have a cuppa? I'll make it while you finish your breakfast. Or I suppose you'd call it supper? Shift work can mess with your body clock."

The gall of the man. Sneaking into her house and scaring her half to death, and then helping himself to a drink.

She scoffed and pointed to the bowl on the table. "How can I finish something I have not yet started?"

"Touché. I guess it's my fault we're getting off to a pretty rough start. Can we do it over?"

He stuck out a hand. Sabrina ignored it for fear he might crush her fingers and continued rubbing her wrist.

"Okay, fair enough."

He dropped the window blinds, filled the kettle, and took a mug from the wall cupboard without searching, as though he already knew where she kept them.

"Have you been spying on me?"

Kaine leaned his back against the surface, facing her. "Since you left work this morning."

She prepared to shout at him, but he raised his hands in mock surrender. "Easy there, partner. I followed you from Sampson Tower, but it was as much for your protection as mine. I wanted to make sure you didn't have a tail."

Kaine had a plausible answer for everything, but at least he kept his distance, and his demeanour wasn't in the least bit threatening. Despite the fact she'd never met a killer before, and rarely had male visitors in London, she felt no menace from him. In fact, she felt strangely relaxed in his presence. Ryan Kaine's aura exuded a calm honesty. Strange in a man with so many deaths on his résumé.

"The scanner," she said, "you still don't trust me?"

"Don't read too much into that. I wouldn't put it past SAMS to bug all its senior employees."

"Senior? Me? Before last night, I was nothing but a low-ranking computer analyst."

"What happened last night?"

"My boss called me into his office. At first I was terrified, but he promoted me. Either as a reward for my efforts in finding you at Lodge Farm, or as a bribe to keep me quiet. I do not know. Anyway, what made you think I was senior?"

Kaine patted the granite surface he was leaning against and made a big effort to appear impressed by the high ceilings and the luxurious fittings. "The mortgage on this place must be astronomic. Rental would be even higher in an area like this. SAMS must pay you a mint."

So, he didn't know everything, and she had no intention of disclosing anything more than completely necessary to keep him happy.

"Wrong. My maternal grandfather bought this house in 1953 and converted it into flats. He keeps the ground floor for the family and rents out the others. I'm paying a fraction of its true market value."

Sabrina met Kaine's steely gaze while speaking. No evasion. No equivocation. To appear honest, she had to be honest—at least up to a point. Another of *grand-père* Mo-Mo's expressions drove into her head, "*If you have to tell a lie, keep it as close to the truth as possible. That way, you will find it easier to maintain the deception.*"

229

Did Kaine believe her? Possibly. At least he didn't scoff. Nor did he leave.

He broke the brief silence. "My mistake. I apologise. So, the Bernadotti dossier. Can I read it now?"

She dragged a chair from under the kitchen table, sat, and attacked her soggy cereal.

"The file is on my laptop," she said between mouthfuls, "but I have read it and have a good memory. Why don't you quiz me while I eat? After that, I will load the file onto a USB pen along with some other information I've managed to find. You know how to use one?"

"If you mean one of those little gizmos you plug into the side of a computer, I think I can manage."

"In that case, I will delete the website I wasted my valuable time building."

As though she had all the time in the world to pander to his every whim.

"Sorry about that, but I do appreciate your efforts. Where do you keep your teabags? Real tea, not those fruit infusions."

She pointed to the caddy next to the kettle.

"Thanks." He took a bag, dropped it into the mug, and poured the boiling water. "What do you know about Bernadotti? Ever met him?"

Kaine added a splash of milk and took the seat opposite. He kept his back to the wall and faced the door. He avoided crowding her. A nice touch, and one she appreciated.

"Once or twice, but only *en passant.*"

"Impressions?"

She paused for a moment to recall the man responsible for all the deaths. "Tall, imposing, powerful, good looking. He spoke quietly with a gentle English accent."

"That's what he looked and sounded like, but what were your impressions?"

"I could not wait to get away from him. His eyes were dead. Cold. You know? Not a man I would invite home for coffee." She pointed her spoon at Kaine's mug. "Or tea."

He nodded and took another deep sip without blowing across the top first. Apparently, he was immune to scalding hot water as well as bullets and knives.

"Not that he would accept my invitation, if you understand my meaning," she added.

Kaine leaned forwards stiffly, curling to protect his left side—perhaps he was not immune to knives after all—and rested his elbows on the table, mug close to his lips. "Enlighten me."

"When we met, I had the distinct impression he preferred other company. The man at his side, for example. His deputy, Adam Akers. Bernadotti looked at him differently. However, I doubt he would turn down sex with a woman if she had something he needed. Sorry, am I making myself clear?"

"You seem to have learned quite a lot about him from two passing meetings."

The whole time he sat drinking his tea, Kaine never relaxed, always remained alert. Sabrina started to understand how he had survived for so long against such heavy odds.

"Mr Kaine, a woman in a man's world needs to read situations carefully. It does not take me long to size up a person's true intentions. For example, I feel no threat from you."

Sabrina surprised herself. She would not normally be so candid, but something about Ryan Kaine made her want to trust him. A known killer had broken into her home. Her internal defences should be screaming, but here, in her kitchen, just the two of them, it felt almost natural. Two long-time friends sharing a quiet drink.

"Tell me more about Bernadotti," he asked, staring into her eyes. No doubt searching for evasion.

"For example?"

"Home address, hobbies and pastimes. On the phone earlier, you said you'd found a hole in his security. Care to explain?"

Sabrina finished her muesli and pushed the bowl away. "Now you are interested in my ideas?"

He shrugged. "Impress me."

A challenge? She would accept. "The only weak link I saw is when he visits his trainer."

"Trainer?"

"Bernadotti has a black belt in Tae Kwon Do. He has one-to-one training sessions with a man with an oriental name."

Kaine smirked. "Tae Kwon Do. Right."

Sabrina expected Kaine to express worry or disappointed, but he seemed decidedly unimpressed.

"I have the address of his dojo and his training schedule."

"Good."

Kaine placed his mug on the table and released a heavy breath that on someone else could have been a sigh. For an older man, he had a good physique. Lean, powerful. Not too heavily muscled. The toned body of a working man, not the useless muscles of the narcissist who pumped iron for looks alone. It was a pity he chose to wear a grey-flecked beard, which did nothing but age him. No doubt he used it to hide his face, but he could not hide the pain and sadness in his haunted eyes.

"He has a black belt, second dan, if that means anything."

Kaine scoffed. "It means he's skilled enough to impress his sensei during a bout on a dojo mat."

"Am I right, though? You should target him after he leaves the dojo, when he is tired?"

"Possibly. You didn't happen to access the man's medical records?"

Kaine gave nothing away. Didn't he trust her yet? So frustrating, but in his position, Sabrina would be equally guarded. In fact, wasn't she doing exactly the same thing to Kaine? After all, she certainly didn't want him knowing her true intentions.

"Yes, I did," she answered. "For insurance purposes, SAMS insists that all its senior executives have annual medical assessments. Bernadotti's latest report is dated nine weeks ago."

"Excellent. That's all I need." Kaine stood and held out his hand again. "Now, Ms Faroukh, do you have that flash drive?"

"That's it? No '*thank you*'? Not even a '*well done*'?"

"Thank you. Well done," he said, his face expressionless. "Can I have the flash drive? Please?"

The absolute gall of the man. Take, take, take.

Sabrina jumped to her feet and stomped into the lounge. She returned with the drive and threw it at him. Kaine caught it right-handed and dropped it in the same pocket as the scanner.

"There you are," she snapped. "Happy now?"

Kaine frowned. "What's the problem?"

"You act as though you are doing me a favour by accepting the information I risked my job to steal. What is *your* problem?"

"What do you expect me to do?"

"Tell me what you're planning, so I can help."

Kaine's eyebrows shot towards his hairline. "Really? Is that what you expect? You want me to tell you my plans when I haven't made any yet?"

Merde.

Yet again, he made sense.

"Well ... put that way, I suppose you are right. I would have expected a little more gratitude though."

"Even if I did have a plan, I'd keep it to myself. The less you know, the safer you will be."

She dipped her head. "I apologise, Mr Kaine. Since I learned that SAMS arranged for you to kill all those people, my nerves have been in tatters."

He stood. "Apology accepted. The world must be a scary place for you right now."

Sabrina nodded.

If he only knew.

Kaine skirted the table and stood in front of her. Close, but not too close. He thrust out this hand again. This time, she took it.

"Friends?" he asked.

She nodded. "Friends."

As if that were possible. Alas, not so.

"After I leave this house, I doubt we'll speak again. You need to think about finding yourself another job. SAMS doesn't have much of a future."

Sabrina stood and met his gaze. They were nearly the same height, which surprised her. After reading Kaine's dossier, she'd imagined him a giant of a man with a powerful physique, when in fact, he was average-sized enough to blend into a crowd. He probably found that useful.

"Mr Kaine—"

"Call me Ryan."

"Ryan, you have no need to worry about my employment situation. I am very good at what I do. There are many firms who would snap up a woman with my skills. I plan to remain at SAMS for a few weeks in case you need me. I will keep my secure phone, too. Call me. Don't call me. Whatever. It is entirely up to you."

"Thank you, Ms Faroukh—"

"If you like, you can call me Sabrina. But not on the phone."

The creases on his forehead deepened and aged him further. "Because of those clever automated eavesdropping algorithms you helped build?"

"Correct."

Kaine touched his forehead in salute. "Thanks for everything, Sabrina, I sincerely appreciate the effort you've made and the risks you've taken. I hope we never meet again. If we do, it'll mean I couldn't get what I needed from the man with the black belt second dan in yoga."

"Tae Kwon Do," she corrected.

"Oh yes, that's right. Scary Korean self-defence system, recognised as one of the oldest and most deadly martial arts in the world. I'll bear that in mind when I invite Rudy for a chat."

Kaine's smile took years from his stony face. It was a nice smile. It melted some of the ice in his eyes. Given time, Sabrina could grow to like such a smile. A pity his life would probably end soon.

She stepped closer. "Ryan, please be careful. Trust no one."

His smile didn't falter. "Thanks again, my young worrywart. Goodbye, and have a long and successful life."

He turned and disappeared as silently as he'd appeared, leaving Sabrina to wonder what danger she'd helped him walk into this time. She suddenly felt very small, very alone, and very, very guilty.

Sabrina turned towards the east and, for the first time in years, she prayed.

CHAPTER THIRTY-FOUR

Monday 14th September – Giles Danforth

Midlands Police Annex Building, Birmingham, UK

Inspector Giles Danforth settled back in his chair and rubbed his tired eyes. As head of the Midlands Police Armed Response Unit, he loved every aspect of his job but the darned paperwork. It never seemed to end. Certified request forms when drawing weapons from the armoury. Declaration forms when returning them, detailing the ammunition used, where it was used, and under what circumstances. Another form to return the unused ammunition. Certificates of equipment worthiness. Regular certification of personnel fitness for duty and separate forms to confirm them as fit for special operations. Medical reports. Terms of reference updates and modifications. Equipment upgrades ....

May the Good Lord give me patience.

The phone on his desk bursting into life nearly gave him palpitations. Giles jerked forwards and snatched the handset from its cradle.

"Inspector Danforth here."

"Giles, it's me, Ryan. Ryan Kaine. How are you my old friend?"

Calm voice. A voice Giles recognised from a dusty place in hell.

"Who? ... Lord above, Ryan! The whole country's looking for you, man"

"Do you believe what they're saying about me?"

"You, a terrorist? Never."

Giles answered automatically and had never been more certain of anything in his life. His heart raced at the thought of talking to a fugitive, but he tried to keep the tension and excitement from his voice.

"Thanks, Giles. Knew I could trust you, but ... God forgive me, I did shoot down that plane."

"You did what!"

"Long story, but I was set up, and I'm going to prove it. And, after I have things wrapped up in a neat and tidy package, I need to hand myself over to someone I can trust."

"And you've chosen me?"

"You're the only police officer I know personally."

Giles needed time. Time to calm down. Time to think. He paused a moment before speaking again.

"Ryan, listen carefully. I head an Armed Response Unit in Birmingham. The Humberside Police is leading this investigation, along with the Air Accident Investigation Branch and probably HOATU."

Ryan snorted.

"What the hell's HOATU?"

"The Home Office Anti-Terrorist Unit."

His friend, the fugitive, levered out a derisory laugh. "Huh. A bunch of spooks in suits?"

"Be serious, will you, Ryan? I'm going to have to report this conversation. You know we're being recorded, right?"

"Yes, I rather thought you might be."

"If you like, I could contact the investigative team in Hull and find out who you should talk to."

"No, I'll only hand myself over to someone I trust. There are too many hotheads out there ready to shoot first and make up the answers to questions later. They won't give me a chance to tell my side of the story, and I don't want to meet my maker with this stain on my reputation. It's you or nobody."

"Ryan ... this is impossible—"

"Are you going to help me or not?"

"Wait. Give me a second to think."

"I'll give you five. After that, I'm hanging up."

Giles waved across the office to his second-in-command, Sergeant Roger "Bob" Dylan. He pointed at his phone and tapped his ear.

Bob took the hint and picked up his handset. Before answering, Giles waited for the tell-tale click of the new-fangled phone intercept they'd been given in the last funding round. The recordings wouldn't be admissible in court, at least not yet, but they'd provide useful background information.

"I'd like to help you, Ryan. I really would, but what can I do?"

"Arrange a time and place for a meet, and I'll do my best to make it. Assuming I survive this afternoon."

Giles swallowed.

"Why. What's happening this afternoon?"

"I have a rendezvous with the someone who can tell me who's ultimately responsible for my shooting down Flight BE1555. Whoever he is, the man's powerful, and well protected. No idea whether I'll survive, but if I do, I'll clear my name and provide a full explanation for the disaster."

"Listen Ryan, I can offer you protection if you come in unarmed, but if you have evidence of a plot, you'll need to speak to a detective."

Giles could hear Ryan's breathing and the sound of traffic in the background. If he could keep his old friend on the line for a few minutes, the techies in the Comms Room might be able to find a location.

"Ryan, are you still there?"

"Yes, I'm here. Are you running a phone trace?"

From his desk, Bob grimaced, made a rolling forward signal with his hand, and then raised two fingers. Two minutes to home in on a location.

Ryan spoke again. "Don't worry about trying to find me, I'll be moving from here as soon as we've finished talking. You mentioned a detective. Have anyone in mind?"

"Yes, in fact I do."

"Go on. I'm listening."

"Ever heard of a DCI David Jones?"

"No ... why should I?"

"You remember the Hollie Jardine abduction last year and that trouble they had down at the National Crime Agency a little while back?"

After a moment's hesitation, Ryan said, "I heard about them, yes."

"DCI Jones and his team ran those investigations."

"Okay, what about him?"

"He's a friend of mine. You can trust him."

"Can I? Can I really?"

"Yes."

"We'll see. Play him this tape and tell him about the real me. Don't let him believe the crap the media will be spewing."

Giles snorted. "No need to worry on that score. David Jones is his own man."

Ryan coughed and paused before speaking again. "Okay, I'll call you back as soon as I have something concrete. Assuming I live that long."

"Do you want DCI Jones' contact details?"

"No thanks, I'll only go through you."

Giles winced. He expected as much. "Right ... Okay. Leave it with me."

"Thanks, mate. One more thing, ask DCI Jones to find out all he can about three armaments companies, SAMS, ESAPP, and BSAL."

The line clicked and the call ended.

"Bob? Anything?"

The sergeant screwed up his face. "Sorry, sir. He's in north London. Camden's as close as they could narrow it."

"Darn it."

"What do you think? Is he serious about giving himself up?"

Giles thought for a second before nodding. "I've never known a more serious or honest individual than Ryan Kaine."

"Honest? A mass murderer?"

"He claims extenuating circumstances."

"Don't they all? Anyway, what next?"

"Next, I call David Jones."

"Good plan. Hand it up the food chain. You're better off out of it, sir."

"Don't be daft, Bob. One way or another, you and I are going to end up right in the middle of this thing."

Bob raised his eyes to the ceiling.

"Yeah, thought we might be."

CHAPTER THIRTY-FIVE

Monday 14th September – DCI David Jones

Holton Police HQ, Birmingham, UK

DCI Jones ended the call from Giles and leaned back in his chair, frowning.

How long since his last cuppa? Too long.

He stood and crossed to the kettle on the tray resting on top of the grey steel filing cabinet—his pitiful attempt at a hospitality area.

"Coffee, Philip?"

Jones' second-in-command, Detective Inspector Phil Cryer—he of the spectacularly good memory—crossed his arms and stretched out long in his chair.

"Nice one, boss. I'm gasping."

Any day now, Facilities Management would finish refurbishing Phil's new office and he'd be able to start carving out his own little police fiefdom. Until then, they'd continue sharing the same cramped space they had done for the best part of four years. Not an issue for Jones, but having to break in a new partner would be.

He half-filled the kettle from a bottle of water and threw the switch. As Phil's Aston Villa mug contained the dregs of his last brew and the office didn't have a sink, he used a spare. His own big mug, already cleaned and dried from its last brew, stood ready and waiting. While the kettle boiled, he turned to his subordinate.

"What do you know about weapons manufacturers and MoD procurement?"

Phil looked up from whatever he was doing on his computer. "Only what I've read in the press."

"Give me all you have on an organisation called SAMS. S-A-M-S."

In company, Phil would often make great play of closing his eyes, scratching his head, and straining to recall facts and figures, but he knew better than to try those theatrics when he and Jones were alone. Phil Cryer's eidetic memory rarely failed him, and once again, he spared Jones the onerous chore of trawling the internet.

"Okay," Phil said, drawing out the word. "Sampson Armaments and Munitions Services Plc. A multi-billion-pound weapons manufacturer and consultancy. The majority shareholder is Sir Malcolm Gareth Sampson. MG to his friends. Headquartered in London, with manufacturing bases throughout Europe. It also has subsidiaries in South Africa and Belize, of all places.

"SAMS has been supplying equipment and consultancy services to NATO, the MoD, and the UK police for the past three decades. They ran into financial difficulties recently after losing significant bids to supply equipment to the MoD and other EU countries. Their major rival is a French company called—"

"Don't tell me, ESAPP?" Jones interrupted.

"Yes, that's right, boss." Phil frowned. "How did you know?"

"It's one of the companies Giles wanted to discuss with us, in about"—Jones checked the time on the wall clock—"ten minutes, traffic permitting."

"Giles is on his way over?"

"Yep. He says he has some information on the Flight BE1555 investigation. Wants our help with something."

"Okay, I imagine he knows the prime suspect, Ryan Kaine?"

Jones smiled. Phil's speed on the uptake was one of the reasons he'd invited him onto the team in the first place. He wasn't simply a memory man and could use the information at his disposal to make connections other detectives missed.

"What makes you think that?"

"Don't be daft, boss. The PNC holds a copy of Kaine's military file. I've just finished looking it over."

"When did the MoD release it?"

"An hour ago, when you were in with the Deputy Chief."

The kettle clicked off and Jones did the business with the hot water. In the office, they had to put up with little cartons of long-life milk. Luckily for Phil, he took his coffee black with sweeteners since starting his new health and fitness regime.

That was quick. It normally takes them weeks to release that sort of information. Someone must have put on some pressure. Did Giles and Kaine ever serve together?"

"Not exactly, but they were in the same theatres of operation on more than one occasion, and when you said Giles wanted our help, I—"

"You put the facts together like any good DI?"

Phil puffed out his chest. "Still getting used to the title."

"You will. Okay, so what about our friends across the Channel, ESAPP?"

Phil took his reserve mug and sipped the liquid tar before answering—how Phil drank the evil stuff, Jones would never know.

"Right. ESAPP, European Small Arms and Personal Protection, A/S. Based in Paris, about thirty percent bigger than SAMS, in financial terms. The two companies have been at each other's throats for years.

"Last year, ESAPP tried to acquire Blaby Small Arms Limited, but the UK Government scuppered the deal on the grounds that it would be against the national interests. Rumour has it SAMS applied certain pressures."

"Interesting." Jones walked his mug back to his chair. "BSAL happens to be the third company on Giles' list."

"Makes sense," Phil said. "Part of Giles' job would be to keep abreast of upgrades to weapons and personal protective equipment."

"And how do you happen to know so much on the subject?"

"The FT ran a major exposé on defence procurement a few months ago. Caught my interest over breakfast one morning."

Jones shook his head. Phil's reading speed defied belief. He read five or six times faster than average, with the same retention as a High Speed Computer Cluster—or so he jokingly claimed.

"What did the articles say about BSAL?"

"Originally a Midlands engineering firm formed in 1901 to supply the British army with bolt-action repeating rifles. Since the mid 1970s, the company's fortunes have been on the slide. Their Phelps-Mack .38 handgun is considered obsolete and they only sell to third world powers. However ..." Phil paused for another slurp of coffee.

"However?" Jones prompted.

"...since receiving an EU grant to build a state-of-the-art ceramics facility, they've made some impressive claims."

"Such as?"

"At the most recent Military Trade Fair in Poland, BSAL unveiled prototype models of their latest ceramic equipment. They showed off an ultra-lightweight handgun, the P-MC .45, and their latest whole-body protection system, the P-MC WBPS. They claim to have worked out a new way of layering the silicate prior to firing that renders the product stronger and lighter than anything else on the market. They also say it's cheaper to produce and uses less energy. They'll be claiming its environmentally friendly next."

"Move along, Philip." Jones lowered his tea and placed the mug on the coaster, making sure the handle ran at forty-five degrees to the corner of the desk.

"If BSAL can support their claims in a series of upcoming proving trials, they'll be able to raise millions to upscale their production process. After that, they're likely to corner the market in small arms and body armour for the next ten to fifteen years. In the process, they'll put a huge dent in the profits of some very large companies, including SAMS and ESAPP. A few of the smaller ones might even go to the wall."

The office door opened and Giles entered without knocking. He nodded at each of them in turn. "Mind if I come in, gentlemen?"

"You are in," Jones answered, feigning annoyance.

"True enough. Better close the door then, stop this vicious draft."

Giles drew up the only spare chair—the one in front of Jones' desk—and moved it back against the filing cabinet so he could see both Jones and Phil without having to crane his neck.

Jones didn't wait for him to settle. "Better repeat what you told me over the phone, for Phil's benefit."

The broad-shouldered ARU man grinned. "I guess Phil's already filled you in on the background?" In the absence of a negative response, he continued. "Now you're wondering what any of this has to do with Ryan Kaine and Flight BE1555?"

Jones answered with a question of his own. "Was there someone on Flight BE1555 of particular importance to BSAL, SAMS, or ESAPP?"

"Good question. No wonder you're the senior officer here."

"Phil's information helped."

Phil stood and made Giles a drink. The ARU man had never been known to refuse a coffee and occasionally even made do with a tea. Phil handed a over-sized mug to Giles, returned to his chair, and pointed at his computer screen. "BrightEuro Airlines released the flight manifest this afternoon. Want me to compare the names with the companies' personnel records, boss?"

"How are you going to do that?" Giles asked.

Phil held up his hands and waggled his fingers in the manner of an old-fashioned club magician. "Any company bidding for MoD contracts has to open their personnel files for vetting purposes."

"And you have access to those files?" Giles asked.

"Of course."

"How?"

Jones fielded the question. "That, Giles, is between Philip, me, and the Home Secretary."

"Ah," Giles said, tapping the side of his nose with an index finger, while Phil worked his keyboard. "Phil's temporary secondment to the National Crime Agency. Say no more." He sipped his steaming coffee.

Jones left Phil to concentrate on his research and focused on Giles. "What can you tell me about Ryan Kaine."

"I ... met him a few times in Afghanistan."

It wasn't like Giles to be so evasive. Jones added a little prod. "Any details?"

Giles took a breath. "I know him, David. He's no more a terrorist than you are."

Still more prodding needed. "And?"

"I spoke to him right before calling you."

Phil stopped attacking the keys and the office fell silent.

Jones waited for his shock to settle before speaking, trying not to shout. "You spoke to the most wanted man in the UK and called me rather than the Chief Constable of the Humberside Police?"

Giles lowered his mug to the tray and rolled his chair closer to Jones' desk. "Before I left my office, I asked Sergeant Dylan to upload the recording of my phone call with Ryan. It should be on the server by now. Want me to access it for you?"

The cheeky puppy.

"Inspector Danforth, I'm perfectly capable of logging onto the PNC and finding a file. What's the URL? I assume you added secondary password protection to the file?"

Giles' expression was a picture. Good job he'd put down his coffee mug or he'd have been wearing its contents down the front of his polo shirt.

Phil chuckled. "Close your mouth, Giles. The boss has finally accepted that IT isn't the devil's magic. Actually has his own laptop these days. It's true, I've seen the thing. He sends emails and everything."

Another damned puppy.

"Less of the sarcasm, Philip."

"Sorry, boss," Phil said, but his wink and smirk showed a distinct lack of sincerity.

Jones touched the mouse and his screen lit up with the yellow-on-blue Midlands Police logo. Giles helped him navigate to the correct cluster, and he hit play on the voice recording.

By the time they'd listened to the whole Giles-Kaine telecon twice, Phil announced he'd finished his search by pulling away from his keyboard and leaning against the back of his chair. To add emphasis, he interlaced his fingers and cracked his knuckles.

"Done," he said, "and I found nothing. No one on Flight BE1555 had links with any of those three companies. The list contains a few business travellers and some holidaymakers. That's it. No arms dealers or ceramicists."

"So, why was Ryan certain about the armaments link?" Giles asked. "Did you hear how worked up he was at the end of the call? He's not a man to lose his cool easily."

"Who knows?" Jones said. "Okay, Giles convince me not to hand this business over to the Humberside Police."

"That's just it. I'm not sure I can. The man I spoke to tonight didn't sound anything like the professional Ryan Kaine I knew eight years ago. He was completely different."

"In what way?"

"The Ryan Kaine I knew was cool, but never really one of the guys, if you know what I mean."

"Not really."

"Put it this way, for a man with his skills, Ryan was relaxed and friendly until we were under fire. Then, watch out. He dealt absolute carnage."

"What skills?" Phil asked.

Giles paused for a second and glanced from Phil to Jones and back. "You've both read his personnel file?"

Phil nodded. "Weapons specialist and a certified Marksman Grade 3."

Giles snorted. "I'm a Marksman Grade 3, and Ryan Kaine makes me look like a novice."

Jones raised an eyebrow. "You have to be kidding. Remember, I've seen you on the range."

"I'm good, David, but Ryan's world class. There can't be more than twenty people on the planet with his accuracy. Give him anything, rifle, handgun, knife, he's brilliant. You know the William Tell story?"

Phil answered what was probably a rhetorical question. "The man who shot an apple off his son's head with a crossbow?"

Giles smiled. "Ryan Kaine would have hit the stalk and left the apple undamaged."

"He's that good?" Jones asked.

"Never seen anything like it."

Giles was holding something back. Jones could tell from the hesitation and the way he brushed a hand through his wavy hair.

"But?"

"It's difficult to say, but Ryan was emotional during that phone call. Too emotional. And all that stuff about not making it back. He sounded desperate to me."

Jones tugged his earlobe. "If he is telling the truth and someone tricked him into killing all those people, him being desperate wouldn't be much of a surprise, would it?"

Phil spoke next. "What are you going to do, boss?"

"First, Phil, we're going to learn all we can about Mr Kaine—"

"Captain Kaine," Giles corrected.

"My apologies, Giles. After you've convinced me *Captain* Kaine is worth listening to, I'm going to have a word with my very good friend, the Home Secretary. She owes Phil and me a favour or two."

"The NCA case again?" Giles asked.

Jones shrugged. "I can neither confirm, nor deny ..."

Phil leaned forwards. "Are you sure you want to cash in that particular favour for a suspected terrorist who might turn out to be a nutcase?"

"That's up to Giles. What do you say, Inspector Danforth?"

Giles' brown eyes lost focus for a moment before fixing on a point above Jones' head. "In 2009, Helmand Province, I was leading a five-man reconnaissance patrol in the high mountains. Insurgents pinned us down. We were taking heavy fire. Ryan Kaine and his team heard our emergency comms. Saved my life, all our lives, and ... Let's just say, I owe him, David."

"That's good enough for me."

CHAPTER THIRTY-SIX

Monday 14th September – Rudy Bernadotti

Sampson Tower, London, UK

Freda held the small mirror up to the back of Rudy's head.

"It is acceptable?" she asked, removing the cut hairs between his neck and shirt collar with a soft brush.

Rudy checked the results of sitting still for twenty minutes, looking at himself in the full-length mirror—neck shaved clean, hair not too short, still full enough to look soft and natural—and nodded. "It'll do. Send your invoice to my secretary. Now clear your stuff away and let me get on."

The tubby *fräulein* bobbed her head, rolled her equipment in a towel, and hurried out of his executive bathroom. Rudy had used the mobile hairdressing service ever since making top management. SAMS offered all its board-level directors the option of in-house grooming services, and Rudy made good use of them all. Massage, aromatherapy, reflexology, *Feng Shui*, the lot. He worked hard, and the profit-share and bonus package were only fitting. Besides, it behoved him to spread his largess to the minions. If he didn't make use of the perks, the plebs would lose out.

Rudy stripped and stepped into his wet room. The prickle of tiny cut hairs annoyed him way past the level of intolerance. He soaped and scrubbed, towelled off in minutes, and dressed in the fresh set of clothes he kept in the office for such occasions. It paid to look your best when dealing with clients who spent big money on weapons of death and destruction.

He returned to his office, refreshed and ready to face the day. The intercom buzzed the moment his Armani-covered backside hit the chair. It was almost as though Margareta had been spying on him from her nest in the outer office.

"Mr Bernadotti, you have a call booked with Sir Malcolm in fifteen minutes."

"Thanks, beautiful. I hadn't forgotten. I'll be ready."

And was he ready for the ignorant, ill-mannered fuckwit.

Rudy pulled his chair closer to the desk and touched his monitor. Thin-client, state-of-the-art security protection, ultra-fast, the system opened up in the blink of an eye and stood ready for his command.

He paused for a second to centre his mind in preparation for the onslaught to his senses. It would not do his chances of taking over the company when Sampson retired much good if he couldn't present the facts without babbling. Rudy already worried that Sampson had started to suspect that his penchant for the kill outweighed the minimum requirements of the job at hand.

In truth, he could have eliminated the Professor after the plane landed at Schiphol Airport, but that wouldn't have given him the second-hand rush of killing all those people. No, he'd have to survive off that high, and the other, minor kills, for a while. For the time being, he'd rein in the worst of his desires.

Rudy dived into the folder he'd worked on before Freda arrived and scan-read the bullet points and the executive summary. Tango One had uploaded the encrypted pictures and .mov files to the SAMS server within minutes of leaving the Valence house. Knowing how sensitive Sampson could be when it came to blood and gore, unless he'd caused it first hand, Rudy had sanitised them for the internal report. The original, unedited files were safely locked away on his external hard drive for his personal consumption and delight.

The images remaining on the company servers would still upset most unprepared individuals, but few lily-livered morons would ever have the opportunity to open the files. The clowns in Whitehall and the government who licensed the munitions industry seldom spared a thought for the end result of the product.

The intercom squawked.

"Yes, Margareta?"

"I have Sir Malcolm on line one."

"Thank you."

He hit the speaker button and leaned back, hands clasped behind his head. "MG, how are you this fine morning?"

"Don't give me that 'fine morning' bullshit. What the fuck happened last night? You torched half of Hampshire!"

Rudy could imagine the veins at the old man's temples distending. With any luck, the old bastard would stroke out. Keeping his voice neutral, he responded. "One small explosion in a quiet backwater is hardly Armageddon, MG. Have you opened the file I sent you?"

"No. Give me the potted version."

"You can relax. Valence and Kaine are both dead."

"Are you certain?"

"I don't exactly have their dog tags, but you can be sure they're no longer a problem. We can move on to the next phase of the operation."

"Which is?"

"Another approach to BSAL."

"What exactly do you mean by 'approach'?"

Stupid old man. How thick did he think Rudy was?

"No, no, MG. Not that sort of 'approach'. Purely benign, I assure you. Another aggressive move against BSAL at this stage might bring with it a whole heap of official interest. I don't want to draw attention to our plans."

"Why haven't they started raising hell about their dead professor?"

Fucking hell. Do I have to do all the old bastard's thinking for him?

Rudy managed to kept the quality of his voice slightly above that of a middle school teacher talking to a particularly slow child.

"Two reasons, MG. First, they might not know he's missing yet. BrightEuro Airlines only released the passenger manifest last night and I've had a friend of a friend massage the data. Second, Sir Richard Blaby is hardly going to advertise the fact that the guiding light behind his company's world-beating technology is missing. Their stock price would plummet."

Sampson snorted in his usual erudite manner. "You've got all the answers, haven't you."

Bingo. The penny had finally hit the carpet. How long had it taken? Eight years?

"I try, MG. I do try. There's one more point you might have overlooked."

"Which is?"

"It might also be time to stick the knife between a few BSAL ribs."

"Explain yourself."

And now for the sneaky part.

Rudy rubbed his hands together. In terms of political machinations, Niccolò Machiavelli couldn't stand in the same room as Rudolpho Bernadotti.

"Let's put it this way, MG. If Sir Richard were to somehow find out that SAMS had discovered BSAL's little secret, he might be a little less strident in rebuffing your next merger approach. For 'merger' you can read 'takeover'."

Sampson coughed out a guttural laugh. Not the most attractive noise Rudy had ever heard, but better than the snorting.

"Rudy, my boy. You planned all this from the start, right?"

"Yes, MG. In fact, I have a long-standing meeting booked in Oxford this afternoon with my counterpart in BSAL. It would appear that the rest of the BSAL board is just about ready to throw Sir Richard under the nearest bus. They see their company as one step away from liquidation."

"Wonderful. You really have outdone yourself. If we couple our production capabilities with the advances BSAL has made in ceramics manufacture, SAMS will be unstoppable."

"Exactly. We'll have to move quickly to counter any governmental concerns over potential conflicts of interest, and with that in mind, I have another suggestion."

"Which is?"

"My assistant, Adam, knows the son of the Minister for Defence Procurement, Sir Christopher Fellows-Bolton. Would you like me to arrange a 'fact finding' visit?"

"Will it do any good?"

"Well," Rudy said, unable to keep the smile from his voice, "Adam can be quite persuasive when he wants to be."

"Okay, go for it, but you'll have to pull your finger out. They'll be closing the bidding process for the PPE procurement in three months. We'll need at least an outline Memorandum of Understanding between SAMS and BSAL in place before then."

"Agreed. I'll crack on with the two-pronged approach today."

"Keep me informed as to your progress."

"Of course, MG. Of course."

The fuck he would.

Sampson ended the call. Rudy replaced the handset and buzzed Margareta.

"Yes, Mr Bernadotti?"

"Tell Adam I want him in here."

"Right away, Mr Bernadotti."

Two minutes later, his door opened and the blond-haired, blue-eyed supermodel swaggered in, grinning fit to crack his gorgeous face. "Did he go for it?"

Rudy raised a finger to his lips and signalled for Adam to close the door before answering. "Of course. Told you I could manipulate the senile old fart."

"You did indeed. Is my visit to Sir Christopher still on?"

"Yep. Do what's necessary to make sure he supports the takeover."

Adam winked and didn't bother taking a chair. "No worries on that score, love. Sir Kit's son, Tony, is married to a junior royal. Any hint of a family scandal will ruin the old boy's chances of a peerage, not to mention he's partial to a bit of rough. I could squeeze his nuts until they pop and not only will he love the experience, he'll thank me and keep it to himself."

"Get on with it then, and spare me the gory details."

"Jealous?"

"Fuck off. You have your instructions."

"Full expense account as normal?"

"Of course. Wine and dine the old queer at Gordon Ramsey's place. Then take him to the casino and hang the bill on the company's promotions budget."

Adam blew him a kiss, twiddled his fingers, and retreated to do what he did best—lay down his body for Rudy's cause.

Next came the logistics.

He peeled back the cuff of his shirt sleeve and checked his Rolex. 11:35. Plenty of time to make his Oxford meeting. People to smile at and palms to grease.

Rudy stood and turned to the Degas print of a ballerina *en point* hanging on the wall behind his desk. He released the catch holding it in place and swung it open to expose his wall safe. A six-digit combination released the lock, and he tugged open the door to free his SAMS PKM .45—a less expensive duplicate of the overpriced Walther PPQ M2. He stuck it into his leather shoulder holster and covered the assemblage with the jacket specifically tailored to hide the bulge. It would take a metal detector to show that he walked around England's capital armed. Not that it mattered, considering he was one of only a few hundred civilians in the UK legally entitled to carry a concealed weapon.

He completed his weapons package with a ceramic dagger housed in a diver's calf sheath, fully aware of the irony of taking a ceramic knife to a meeting at BSAL. No telling when he'd need such protection in an increasingly dangerous world.

Rudy left his office and opened the door to the reception area. Margareta looked up at him from behind her desk, a thin-lipped gash stretched into a hideous smile. One day, when she'd outgrown her usefulness, he'd get rid of the crone, but not yet, not while she was so tight with MG's equally decrepit PA, Petra Langham.

Margareta and Petra had started at the firm when SAMS was little more than a machine shop with a single MoD contract to refurbish decommissioned handguns and rifles from the British Army. SAMS' value-add proposition was to resell the clapped out weapons to Third World dictatorships at vastly overinflated second-hand prices. The MoD were thus able to proclaim its environmental credentials while at the same time showing support for "nascent democracies in developing countries". Meanwhile, SAMS grew fat on the proceeds.

The short of it was that by tolerating the ghastly Margareta, Rudy could maintain his close surveillance on the old bastard.

"Margareta," he said, giving her the benefit of his ten megawatt smile, "how are you this morning? May I just say how splendid you look?"

The middle-aged woman reddened and touched the nape of her wrinkled neck. "Thank you, Mr Bernadotti—"

"Lord, how many times have I asked you to call me Rudy? I mean, we've been working together for nearly five years and I wouldn't be able to operate without you."

She lowered her head and looked up through bushy eyebrows.

For fuck's sake, had the woman never heard of tweezers?

"Mr Bernadotti, you are too kind. A car is waiting, but Mark called in sick this morning with an upset tummy."

"Oh dear. Has he been eating at the Savoy Grill again? Perhaps we pay him too much."

Rudy laughed at his own joke and Margareta covered her thin lips with claw-like fingers.

"Oh, sir, that's so cruel. Mark sounded rather discomfited. At one stage, he actually threw up."

"Am I expected to drive myself to Oxford?"

"No, sir. Mark organised a relief driver. Sergeant-Major Peter Sidings is a fully vetted employee of Conqueror Security Services. I checked his *bona fides* personally. Mr Sidings has MoD and EU security clearance, and is highly qualified in defensive driving techniques." She tapped her keyboard and Rudy looked over her shoulder at the screen.

She read out the details.

"Two tours of Iraq and three of Afghanistan, one as a civilian driver to Bruno Di Marco, the MD of Venti Construction. They are the firm that rebuilt half of Kabul."

"Yes, I know their work. That's an impressive CV."

"They have provided excellent references. Here's his ID photo."

"Oh dear, look at that mugshot. He's likely to scare off any attacker. I'd be terrified to ask him to put his foot down if we were late for an appointment."

She placed her left hand to her throat. "That is somewhat harsh, Mr Bernadotti. I'd say he was rugged. His face has character."

Rudy touched her shoulder through her matron's blouse—the closest he'd ever willingly get to her skin. "If you're trying to make me jealous, Margareta, it's working. I'll have to make sure you don't meet the rugged Sergeant-Major."

She tittered.

"He's waiting for you in the car park, Mr Bernadotti, Lower Ground Floor, Level 2. The security guard has confirmed his ID."

"Excellent, I won't be back until after you've gone home."

"Very good, Mr Bernadotti."

The express lift whipped him down to LG2 and slowed with a stomach-lurching jolt. No matter how often Rudy rode it, he'd never get used to the speed of the descent. So fast, it felt like jumping off a high cliff.

Heights. His one fear. His one weakness. He'd tried therapy, hypnosis, acupuncture. All bloody useless.

He shuddered at the main reason he'd washed out of parachute training, back in his army days. One of his few failures in life, but something he rarely dwelt on. In the end, his failure had been a blessing. If he'd made it as a paratrooper and not a sniper, he'd never have met MG Sampson, and the arsehole wouldn't have taken a raw, but promising, Second-Lieutenant under his very wealthy wing.

At the time, SAMS had a sniper's package under development and needed an expert marksman on the payroll to test the equipment and schmooze the bigwigs—a role for which the young Rudy was created in the womb.

From such inauspicious beginnings, Rudy's lifelong plan had been born. One day, he'd run SAMS. Everything he did in business life focused on that single goal.

The lift doors opened and Rudy stepped into the security bay. A uniformed security guard nodded. "Morning, Mr Bernadotti. How are you today?"

"Fine thanks, Alexis. You?"

Alexis nodded. "Your ride is the black Mercedes, sir. The new driver doesn't say much, but his credentials are valid. Would you like me to call him over so you can check him out before I open the security door?"

Rudy stared once more into Alexis' gorgeous eyes and wondered whether the handsome Greek batted for his side. Historically, the Greeks had been open-minded about matters of the heart. One day, when he had more time, he might broach the subject.

"Yes. Let me see what our reticent driver looks like."

Alexis swivelled his chair to face the front and leaned closer to the microphone stand on his desk. He pressed the button at its base.

"Sergeant-Major Sidings, please report to the security kiosk."

The driver's door to the Mercedes opened and a wiry man of about average height slid out. He donned his chauffeur's cap and marched smartly towards them. Neatly trimmed dark beard, military bearing, blue eyes, long face, crooked nose. No oil painting. If anything, the photo ID flattered him. Jesus, but the bloke looked hard. Not the sort of man you'd pick a fight with in a back street pub, despite his lack of stature.

In short, perfect.

The driver reached the security screen and stood at attention.

"Sidings?" Rudy asked.

"Yes, sir."

"I don't like the look of you."

The driver remained stone-faced. He didn't speak. Rudy cast a sideways glance at Alexis. "You're right. Not the most talkative chap in the world, is he?" He returned his gaze to the driver. "Nothing to say, Sergeant-Major?"

"No, sir."

"Excellent. I prefer my drivers quiet. Did Mark tell you where we were going?"

"No, sir."

The man had an overbite, which caused a slight sibilance when speaking. Not too annoying, but probably might explain why he didn't say much. "Do you know your way to the Oxford University Science Park?"

"Magdalen or Kidlington, sir?"

"Kidlington."

"Yes, sir. I know it."

The man would do. No evasion, eyes steady, and small enough to take down in a fight. In any event, Rudy had his gun and his dagger and, according to the output of the hidden scanner he stood before, the Sergeant-Major's pockets contained nothing but a fountain pen, a wallet, and a mobile phone.

"Okay Alexis, you can open up."

Sidings stepped aside as the blast-resistant door slid open, and he led Rudy to the car. He held the nearside rear door open, and Rudy slid inside the secure passenger compartment. Tinted glass and soft leather seats—a protective womb for his safety and comfort.

Despite the rain-spattered exterior, the car had that new show-room aroma of polish and rich leather, the smell of luxury and security.

Sidings rolled the car out of the underground park, turned left, and headed towards London Bridge.

"Which way are you going?"

"A40 and M40 is best this time of day, sir."

"ETA?"

"With no traffic snarl-ups, approximately ninety minutes."

"Okay. I'll need to get some work done. No radio, no talking."

"Very good, sir."

Rudy lowered the panel in the back of the front seat to form a table and took a file from his briefcase. After thirty minutes, they'd reached the start of the A40, making better time than expected. At the same rate, they'd arrive ahead of schedule.

Sidings' smooth driving style gave Rudy no cause for concern. He took a bottle of Evian from the fridge, poured out a glass, and relaxed into his seat, sipping as he read.

CHAPTER THIRTY-SEVEN

Monday 14th September – Rudy Bernadotti

Stuffield Airfield, Lincolnshire, UK

Rudy's lips tingled. A pounding between his temples felt as though someone had stuck his head between the jaws of a vice and was slowly cranking the handle.

Fuck's sake, it hurt.

His tongue, thick and dry, stuck to the roof of a furry mouth. He tried to groan, but no sound came out. Head, arms, and legs—he couldn't move them. Something held them in place. Tape across his eyes blinded him, but he could open his mouth. At least he could breathe.

Oh dear Christ. What's happening?

Thumping in his head. Thirsty. So thirsty.

"Please ... water."

He shivered. Why was he cold?

Cold air chilled his bare skin. Naked? He was naked!

What the fuck?

A hard chair, not the soft leather seats of the Mercedes. The car! The chauffeur, what was his name? Tidings, no, Sidings.

Rudy tried to clear his head. Tried to focus. The last thing he remembered before waking to a nightmare was being in the Mercedes. What did he do? Poured himself a drink of water. Drugged?

No, no, no.

Despite all his precautions, the bastard drugged his water. Anger bubbled past the fear and the self-pity. Pure rage.

He fought against the restraints and screamed, "Where the fuck am—"

Crack.

Lights sparked at the back of his eyes. The unexpected slap nearly tore his head from his shoulders. It burned his cheek and brought with it the sweet, exultant taste of blood and terror. Blood, from the inside of his cheek, cut by his teeth, and the terror of imminent death. He loved the fear he saw in others when he dished out the pain, but being on the receiving end wasn't so good.

Oh God, what's happening?

"Hello, Rudy. Have a nice snooze?"

He yelped in shock.

The whispered words—more terrifying than a shout—poured into his ear from a mouth so close, Rudy felt the man's warm breath.

"Who—"

Another slap, this time to the right cheek and even harder, made him bite his tongue. More blood, and the shame of wetting his underwear, the only piece of clothing he felt against his clammy skin. Chill air wrapped his body. Cold. It was so, fucking cold.

Anger. Rage. Feel the passion. Draw warmth from it. Use it.

Rudy flexed his fingers, testing their mobility.

"I'm asking the questions, Rudy, my man. Open your mouth again and it better be in answer to one of them, or you'll be missing an important piece of your anatomy. Let me see, what should I take first? Toes ..."

The cold, sharp edge of something metallic and sharp bit into his left big toe.

Oh, God, shears.

Rudy roared and tried to tear his foot away, but the bindings prevented movement.

"...fingers ..."

The shears released his toe intact and moved to his left hand. Metal cut into his little finger. Rudy roared again.

"Bastard!"

Use the anger. Use it!

"...and eventually, that limp dick."

Rudy growled through a mouth clamped shut, waiting for the inevitable, but miraculously, when the shears released his finger, they didn't return.

The man moved close again. What was that smell? Pineapples?

"I'll decide what to remove depending upon my mood and your answers. No lack of choice to begin with. Each amputation will be excruciating but non-fatal, at least not at first. But before I start down that route, I'll fire up my blowtorch. Cauterised wounds prevent blood loss, but do nothing to numb the pain."

Rudy shook his head.

What did the bastard want? A robbery? That was it, a simple robbery. Sidings had seen his Rolex and had taken the opportunity. Fucking animal. How dare he?

Just wait, Sidings. Just you fucking wait.

Rudy knew who the thief was, and he'd make fucking sure the man would pay.

Oh, shit, no!

He realised something. He'd seen the thief, and Sidings knew it. The driver had no choice but to kill Rudy. Kidnapping and torture would mean decades in prison. But, Alexis had the man's ID and work record. Could Rudy use that? Dare he risk speaking? What should he do? Beg? Plead? Bribe? Threaten?

No, not threaten. Sidings might lose control.

Wait. Bide your time. He'll make a mistake.

A rubber-clad hand touched his bare shoulder. "Scream if you like. No one will hear you up here."

Up here? Where?

The voice passed behind him, from left to right.

"Oh will you look at that, the mass murderer's shivering. Is he cold?"

Mass murderer?

Rudy stiffened. A cold realisation bathed him in a biting terror more bitter than the icy air. Wind ruffled his recently trimmed hair and freeze-dried his sweat. Outdoors, they were outdoors. Birds twittered in the distance over to his left, but low down, so not in the trees. An aviary?

The man said they were "up here". Shit! They were on a roof.

"Eighty-three deaths on your hands, you evil sod." The man spoke barely above a whisper, making it so difficult to hear, Rudy had to concentrate hard.

"Thing is," Sidings continued, "you only have twenty fingers and toes, and one prick. Twenty-one body parts in exchange for all those lives. Not enough. Not nearly enough."

The man was going to kill him.

Concentrate, Rudy. Concentrate.

He said eighty-three deaths. That narrowed the field. Who was it? Graham Valence or Ryan Kaine? Did it matter? Yes. Valence would take a bribe, he'd shown that, but Kaine? Would he? But no, it couldn't be them. Both men were dead. Rudy had seen the video footage at the Valence house. They couldn't have survived everything SAMS had thrown at them.

Impossible.

A partner then.

Kaine or Valence must have told a friend to exact revenge in the event of their deaths. How did that help Rudy? Without information, he was blind, helpless. Dead.

"Then again, as well as fingers and toes, you have eyes, ears, a tongue, legs, arms. I'll apply tourniquets to keep you alive. And the paramedics will come and work their miracles. What do you think, Rudy? I could leave you with stumps for arms and legs, blind, deaf, dumb, helpless, and dick-less. A lifetime of unrelenting mental and physical torment. But is that enough for you to pay for all those deaths, all those grieving families? Nah, I doubt it."

The man stopped talking. The silence stretched on for an eternity. Far worse than the taunting, the threats. Somehow, even the birdsong stopped.

Say something, you fucker. Speak, damn it!

Rudy shivered as another gust of cold air sliced through him.

"You made me shoot them down." The whispered words, terrifying.

"Kaine!"

Rudy tensed, waiting for the slap, or the bite of the shears. Neither came.

"Yes, Rudy. Captain Ryan Kaine, at your service. You made me the most hated man in the UK. Although I shot down that plane, you're the one responsible."

Rudy shook his head, opened his mouth, but said nothing.

"Okay, Rudy. You can speak."

"It ... it wasn't me," he said, making the words spill out in a tangle. Playing a part, telling Kaine something he probably already knew, waiting for the mistake. "It was my boss, Sir Malcolm Sampson. I had no idea—"

The gut-punch struck like the blow from a sledgehammer. Air exploded from Rudy's lungs, but he couldn't replace it. His chest tried to open but he couldn't breathe. Suffocating in fresh air.

Dying.

He was dying.

"Stop lying. I said you could talk, but I won't listen to lies."

Eventually, the breath came. Tiny wisps of life-giving air.

Another blow would end him, but Kaine held off long enough for Rudy's lungs to inflate again. And again.

Breathe. He had to breathe. While he lived he had hope. A small chance. But a chance, nonetheless.

"Okay, okay. No ... more ... lies. Ask me ... anything and I'll tell you the truth, but please ... don't hurt me anymore."

That's it, Rudy. Lay it on thick.

If he escaped the chair in one piece, Kaine would pay. Fuck would he pay! Rudy imagined all the ways he could make the bastard suffer, if only he were free. The images warmed him. Strength flowed through him.

Again, the gloved hand gripped his shoulder. "You are a pathetic creature. Flight BE1555—why?"

Rudy took the gamble of his life. The whole truth might allow him to live a little longer. And while he lived, he had the possibility of survival. He'd talk. Play along. Stay alive and he might just find a way out of the mess.

"Have you ever heard of BSAL?" Rudy asked, panting hard—again, for show.

"Blaby Small Arms Limited."

Rudy nodded. "Yes, yes. A British manufacturer of handguns and personal protective equipment." He took another breath. The air tasted good. So very good.

"Rudy, imagine I know a little about the munitions industry. Stop stalling. No one's looking for you. No help is on the way."

The locator.

Rudy had almost forgotten about the implant.

Help *was* on the way. It had to be.

Kaine didn't know. He couldn't know about the locator beacon. When Rudy failed to make the appointment in Oxford, the alarm would be raised. That was his way out.

Stall him. Keep him waiting. Stay alive.

People would come. SAMS security people would come! Or maybe T5S, the subcontractors. Or Adam. Yes, Adam would move heaven and earth.

"I ... I'm not stalling. I promise you. ... BSAL is about to corner the market in military-grade ceramics. They have an R&D facility in

Oxford. That's where I was going today. It was headed by Professor Sergei Petrovic, a ... a Ukrainian. He developed a method of creating ..."

Rudy talked and talked, for what seemed like hours. At times Kaine interrupted to clear up a point or make him repeat a statement, presumably for a recording. But it didn't matter. He was still alive and staying alive was the only thing that mattered. And making sure he wasted enough time for the cavalry to find him and rain the fires of hell down onto this insignificant bastard who thought he could kidnap Rudolpho Bernadotti and get away with it. Once that happened, the recording would be destroyed, so he told Kaine everything.

Eventually, he ran out of things to say.

"Thank you, Rudy. Nearly done. Now I need your computer IDs and the passwords for your laptop, your home PCs, and the one at work."

Rudy swallowed. Kaine wanted access to the system to find hard evidence.

Keep him dangling. Stay alive long enough to give Adam time.

"I'll gladly give you access to my personal devices, but there's nothing on them of use to you. Contact numbers, personal correspondence, accounts, nothing more."

He hesitated, waiting for a sign that he was on the right track.

"Go on, Rudy."

"You want proof, right, Kaine? Enough to clear your name? Everything important is on my work system, but the SAMS IT security department will have changed my passwords the moment I went missing. How long has it been since you took me?"

"Twelve hours."

Twelve? It couldn't be. Kaine was lying. It wouldn't take Adam that long to find him. Adam *was* on his way. He had to be. Rudy snatched at the lifeline and held on tight.

"If I've been out of contact for twelve hours, the administrators will have put a hold on all my login codes. If I don't contact them within twenty-four hours, they'll exclude me from the system altogether. To regain my user rights, I'll have to report in person to the CISO, the Chief Information Security Officer, Shafiq Patel."

"That seems a little drastic."

He believes me!

Rudy had to keep going. His life depended on it.

"It's true. I swear it. Eighteen months ago, a Bolivian drug cartel kidnapped one of our South American representatives. We changed the security protocols in case they tried to beat the information out of her."

"If you read my file, you'll know I worked that case."

Of course. Rudy should have remembered. "Mr Kaine, only I can get you into the system, and I will. I promise."

The grip on his shoulder tightened. So strong. A crushing force.

"And I'm supposed to trust you. Is that right, Rudy?"

"Yes, oh please, God. Yes! You've beaten me. I'll come with you to the police and tell them everything," Rudy begged. "Sir Malcolm organised it. Planned it all. I'll turn Queen's evidence. Anything, but please don't kill me."

Dial it back, Rudy. Don't overcook it!

"Sorry, Rudy, I don't believe you."

"Please listen. If you've recorded my confession, it won't do you any good. It's clearly been obtained under duress and won't be admissible in a court of law."

"My thoughts exactly. So sorry, I have to go. Things to see, people to do over. You understand."

An arm cradled his head and the hand on his shoulder slid around to his neck. A thumb reached the notch behind the jaw just below the ear and pressed.

Pain seared his brain, immediate and excruciating.

Debilitating.

Jesus!

"No please. I can give you the proof." He could barely force out the words. "Give me a chance, please. I'll give you Sir Malcolm. He's the one with the power. He's the one to blame."

The thumb pressure eased and the agony diminished to match the throbbing of his racing pulse.

"He's a multibillionaire. He can release funds for you—"

The thumb pressure increased again.

"If ... if not for you, then for the families. You can make him set up a trust fund or something. I can help you. Listen to me. Please."

The hand and arm released and the pain stopped, but the relief was short-lived. The tape binding his eyes tore away, taking with it brows, lashes, and skin. Stinging in its suddenness.

"Shit!"

Daylight, blinding daylight. Rudy squeezed his eyes shut against the glare. The sun, low on the western horizon not strong enough to warm, but plenty bright enough to sear his eyeballs. Still daylight? He was right. It hadn't been twelve hours. More like six. Adam hadn't abandoned him.

They were high on a flat, asphalt roof in the middle of a desolate expanse of nothingness. Trees on the right but ...

Where? How high?

Oh fuck, how close to the edge?

Rudy looked down and peered into oblivion. His chair was perched centimetres from the roof's edge! Six storeys above a cracked concrete apron. The fissures rippled as his vision faded. A space, wide open and isolated.

The height terrified him more than Kaine's threats.

"Pull me back! Dear Christ, pull me back, you bastard!"

He rocked back, again and again, trying to use his momentum to force the chair away from the precipice, but it didn't work.

"Help. Please, I'll do anything."

Kaine slapped the back of Rudy's head. "Do you think that's what the passengers on Flight BE1555 were screaming as they plunged to their deaths?"

Kaine grabbed the back of the chair and pushed. Rudy screamed and lost control of his bowels. The overpowering smell of excrement cut through his terror. He teetered on the edge of the abyss for a lifetime, howling for mercy.

Minutes. He hung over the edge for minutes before the bastard tugged and dragged the chair into the centre of the flat roof. It scraped on the cracked asphalt surface.

Rudy pulled air into burning lungs.

Bastard. He knows! He knows everything.

"Oh dear," Kaine taunted. "Little Rudy's soiled himself."

"You fucking animal!" Rudy screamed and straining against the thick duct tape binding his forearms and ankles to the office chair. "You fucking sadistic bastard."

Rudy threw himself so hard to the left, the chair teetered and threatened to fall. He stopped struggling, desperate to regain control. Any sort of control. "Cut me loose, you sick fuck. I'm going to kill you!"

Kaine raised an eyebrow.

"Really?" Kaine said, and a sardonic smile formed on a tanned face that bore only a passing resemblance to Sidings. "Is that a challenge?"

"Yes. Try me!"

No overbite, no hissing sibilance, brown eyes, not blue. Even the nose was straight, not crooked. A disguise? Fuck's sake. He'd been fooled by a disguise? How?

"False teeth, tinted contact lenses, and a wad of tissue paper in one nostril," Kaine said, as though reading Rudy's mind. "Doesn't take much to fool a man who thinks he's untouchable."

"And Mark, my driver? Is he—"

"Dead? Why? Do you give a damn?"

"I ... Yes."

Rudy spoke the truth, which surprised him.

"No need to worry. Mark and I came to a business arrangement. He told me what I needed to know, and I rewarded him handsomely. Wouldn't be surprised if he was aboard a flight to the sun round about now."

"He lied to me?"

Kaine smiled. "Shocking, isn't it? People actually lie. Who'd have thought it?"

How'd he fucking do it?

"Your credentials ... they were perfect."

"Yes. I've used the Sidings identity a number of times in the past. You'd be amazed how often my services are needed in military hot spots."

Keep playing for time.

Rudy needed to stretch it out for as long as possible. Adam would come. He would.

"The water bottle in the car. Drugged?"

Again, Kaine nodded. "A horse tranquiliser. Once I knew your weight, from your last physical exam, a medic friend of mine helped me calculate the dosage. We wanted to incapacitate, but not kill. A tricky task, but worth it in the end. If you hadn't taken the drink, I'd have found a messier, more physical way to subdue you. It wouldn't have been difficult."

Despite the cooling, hardening mess between his legs, Rudy started to regain his equilibrium. As long as he concentrated on Kaine and didn't look at the building's edge, he'd be fine. He rotated his ankles and wrists and flexed his fingers and toes. In the unlikely event of Kaine giving him the opportunity to fight back, he wouldn't want stiffness or cramp slowing him down.

"Still," Kaine said slowly, "all this leaves me with quite a dilemma."

"Yeah?"

"What am I going to do with you?"

"What do you mean?"

"Well, I can't exactly march you into the nearest police station armed only with this recording. As you said, you can always scream coercion, say I tortured you into a confession. I don't have any independent proof. And I can't keep you locked up, not indefinitely. I'm only one man, working alone."

"Sampson Tower ... I can get you inside!"

Kaine shook his head and continued as though Rudy hadn't spoken.

"No, I need to be able to move around freely, and I can't do that with you in tow."

Frowning, Kaine shook his head, as though considering his next move. He even scratched his head.

"What to do? What to do?"

Then he smiled again, this one wolfish.

Oh God, what now?

"So," Kaine said, stepping closer, "you still up for that challenge?"

"What?"

"If I cut you free, are you still going to try and kill me?"

What? A trick. No way. Rudy wasn't going to fall for such a crock of bullshit.

Kaine reached behind his back. His hand reappeared clutching a six-inch hunting knife. The honed edge glinted in the light of the setting sun.

"Well?" he asked.

"You're going to cut me free and then we're going to fight to the death?"

Not possible. Kaine couldn't be that stupid. Could he?

"Unless you want me to gut you in the chair."

"Are you serious?"

Kaine sneered. "Yep. I'm going to beat you to a bloody pulp. Been looking forwards to this ever since I learned of your involvement. All those people, dead because of your greed. I'm going to have such fun."

What? He is *serious!*

This was Rudy's lucky day, after all. The fucker didn't know everything.

"Wait," Rudy said, "I-I've been tied here for hours. Can't feel my hands or feet. It wouldn't be a fair fight."

Kaine sneered. "You want a fair fight? You want a better chance than you gave the passengers aboard Flight BE1555?"

Rudy didn't have an answer for that one and snapped his mouth shut. Earlier, Kaine had accused him of being untouchable. Well, the cocky fucker would soon learn the truth of his words. Assuming he wasn't just bullshitting.

"Tell you what," Kaine said, stepping closer and waving the blade under Rudy's nose. "I'll cut you free and step back to the centre of the roof, well away from that nasty, scary edge. After that, you can take as long as you like to recover. Stretch out, do your warm-up exercises. Hey, now here's a thing. I'll even let you throw the first punch. How about that? Do we have a deal?"

Christ, the man was a total moron. He hadn't completed his background research. Couldn't possibly know about Rudy's martial arts training. Rudy tried not to show the excitement of hope. How many people had been fooled by his looks, his apparent softness, his unmarked face? In Rudy's case, the lack of battle scars didn't mean he ran from a fight. No. It simply meant he rarely took a hit. Undefeated in all his official bouts. Who needed the locator implant? Who needed Adam riding to the rescue?

Kaine didn't know Rudy's skills. Of course he didn't. How could he? But no, it could still be a trick.

"What's to stop you shooting me with my own gun or slicing me open with that pig sticker?"

"Nothing but my word." Kaine's sneer widened. "Your gun's still in your holster in the Mercedes, along with that fancy ceramic dagger of yours. As soon as I cut you free, I'll put my knife away. I don't need a gun or a knife to take you apart."

Jesus.

The arrogant prick was actually going to do it!

When he'd woken, there had been little hope, but Rudy was going to live. He was going to tear the stupid fuckwit's arms off and stuff them down his middle-aged throat.

"Okay, *Captain* Kaine. You have your deal. Now, cut me loose."

Bring it, old man. Bring it!

CHAPTER THIRTY-EIGHT

Monday 14th September – Evening

Stuffield Airfield, Lincolnshire, UK

Starting at the ankles, Kaine sliced through the tape, taking extra care when freeing the killer's wrists. Expecting the worst usually gave him the edge.

As promised, he retreated to the centre of the roof, re-sheathed the dagger, and waited.

The control tower of the abandoned aerodrome had proved the perfect place for a chat with the psychopathic sociopath. He'd learned all he could, but despite Bernadotti's guilt, Kaine couldn't bring himself to kill the man in cold blood. It would have made him no better than the people he was trying to take down.

Kaine had long since ruled out the possibility of dragging Rudy to the police. As the man so rightly said, without independent proof, it would be Kaine's word against Bernadotti's, and SAMS could bring the might of a multi-million-pound legal department to bear in support of its employee and its owner. They would do anything to preserve their "good name".

Bernadotti was right—a confession forced under duress would be inadmissible in court, but that wasn't the intention. No, the intention had been to generate intelligence, and Bernadotti's spewed confession had given him just that. All doubts Kaine had relating to the real guilty party had disappeared with the snivelling creature's words. MG Sampson bore the ultimate responsibility. Sampson had sanctioned the crime. No doubt remained.

The coerced confession wouldn't be enough to clear Kaine's name, but Bernadotti still had to die. In this instance, vengeance was Kaine's.

He'd kill the animal, but not in cold blood. As with Red in Cleethorpes, Kaine couldn't kill someone without giving them a fighting chance. He offered Bernadotti a fair fight and a better deal than anything Bernadotti had given the eighty-three passengers or the Valences.

Kaine crossed his arms and waited with calm patience as Bernadotti pushed himself tentatively from the chair. The designer underwear didn't look quite as fresh as they had done earlier and were a little baggy around the seat. No matter, the creep wasn't going to be worried about his clothing for too much longer.

Bernadotti stretched and rotated his legs, hips, waist, lower back, shoulders, and neck using the fluid movements of a martial arts devotee. Kaine had seen it all before. He'd faced the best of the worst.

Let's see what you've got, Rudy.

"If you're thirsty, there's a bottle of water by the wall," Kaine called, pointing to the doorway leading to the staircase and freedom. "I promise you it isn't drugged."

The Senior Vice President of Security for SAMS stepped out of his baggy underwear and allowed his junk to dangle in the breeze. He shuffled forwards in a trained fighter's first attack position, arms extended at chest level, leading with his left foot.

"I'll drink later. I'm ready, Kaine." He beckoned with his fingers. "This is going to be fun."

"Sure you don't want to loosen up some more? You've been sitting in that chair for quite some time. Wouldn't want you crying foul."

"Shut your mouth. You're going to eat shit."

Kaine grinned. "That's a weird thing to say, considering what's running down the backs of your legs. One rule I forgot to mention before we start."

"A rule in a street fight?"

Kaine sniffed the air. "Stay downwind, eh?"

"I'm going to slap you down, old man. And then I'm going to fuck you up the arse."

Kaine shook out his arms, rolled his shoulders, and waited.

Rudy started dancing. A reasonable facsimile of an Ali shuffle mixed with Bruce Lee panache. He threw chops and jabs, but stayed out of reach. Kaine turned with him, keeping face-on to the prancing black belt, second dan.

"I'm waiting, Mr Baryshnikov," Kaine said, shaking his head in dismay. "Promised you the first punch, remember?"

Rudy leaned back and snapped out a head-high kick, all the power coming from his hips and thighs. The simultaneous scream added nothing but effect. A wonderful example of the Hollywood action hero. The kick hit air, ten centimetres from where Kaine's nose had been.

"That all you have, son?"

"Just loosening up."

Rudy lunged, telegraphed a left jab to the chin, but followed up with the real attack, a rabbit punch to Kaine's left kidney, designed to incapacitate.

Kaine twisted clear of both strikes and snapped out his right arm, hard and fast. The knuckles of his curled index and middle fingers landed flush on Rudy's Adam's apple. Cartilage crunched. Bone snapped.

Rudy collapsed to his knees, hands scrabbling at his throat. Eyes wide, mouth open, he made a hideous gagging, gargling noise as he tried to breathe. His skin flushed.

Kaine flexed his fingers and stood over the dying killer.

"If you believe in a God, you could try praying, but I doubt you'll find forgiveness. Better hurry, though. I've just crushed your larynx and snapped your hyoid bone. You have maybe two minutes before you lose consciousness."

Tears fell from terrified eyes. Rudy toppled forwards onto the asphalt, still fighting to breathe. He curled into the foetal position, feet twitching.

"In case you think the sedative slowed you down, think again. It cleared from your system within the hour. I'm no cheat, Rudy. It's just that you're not very good, and I've been in the killing game far longer than you have."

Rudy reached out a hand, either for help, or to hurt, but Kaine stepped back, out of range.

"And don't worry about my not having your access codes or a way to get to Sir Malcolm, I'll use my own methods. Bye-bye, Rudy. Burn in hell."

Kaine watched the light drain from Rudy's eyes and counted off a full two minutes before placing two fingers on the carotid pulse. Strange things could happen with the human body. He'd heard of people surviving hideous crush injuries. Although he felt no pulse in the neck, swelling could mask it enough to confuse a non-medic, and he didn't want to place his fingers anywhere near the man's femoral artery.

"Sorry, Rudy, I think you're dead, but I have to make sure. Can't have you reanimating to ruin my plans, such as they are."

Kaine took out his dagger and pressed its point into the white of Rudy's left eye. The corpse didn't so much as twitch. No one alive could lie still with such a nick.

"Once again, I apologise."

Kaine reached into his jacket, retrieved Bernadotti's mobile, and covered the mouthpiece with a cloth before dialling 9-9-9. The emergency operator answered within seconds.

"Emergency, which service do you require? Fire, Police, or Ambulance?"

"Police please. I'd like to give the location of a dead body."

"Excuse me, sir. Can you repeat that, please?"

"No. You are recording this call. Hit replay when I'm done. Tell the police they'll find a body on the roof of the control tower at Stuffield Airfield, Lincolnshire. Thank you for your time. Have a wonderful day."

Kaine ended the call, but left the phone powered up to act as a beacon. After all, he didn't want some innocent kids exploring the old airfield, to stumble across a body and have endless nightmares. The Navy had taught him to be the responsible killer and tidy up after himself. As the saying went, he was "policing his brass".

He wiped down the mobile with the cloth and stuffed it under the body. The clouds massing on the western horizon threatened rain and, waterproof or not, he didn't want the phone damaged.

Kaine ran from the roof, down six flight of stairs, and dived into the Mercedes. Bernadotti's mobile would no doubt have a locator beacon which activated the moment he powered the thing up.

"Damned technology," he muttered.

Kaine had killed with his bare hands before—on eight separate occasions—but he'd always suffered a reaction afterwards. Doubt, regret, guilt, or a combination of all three.

The nebulous thing some might call a conscience would usually wait until the quiet times, after the fury of the battle had passed, when the fires of adrenaline had washed from his bloodstream. It would latch upon his doubts and ask the inevitable questions.

"Did you have to kill him?"

"Could you have found another way?"

"Could you have left him alive, subdued but alive?"

By the time he'd slipped behind the wheel of the Mercedes, Kaine already had the answers. He felt no remorse. Rudolpho Bernadotti deserved to die. If anything, Kaine had been too generous. He could have made the death more painful, drawn it out much, much longer, but Rudy's bloodless end brought its rewards.

He checked his hands. No tremors, no blood, no bruising. A quick and clean kill. In fact, his clothes looked almost as fresh as when he'd bought them that morning. He still looked every bit the first class chauffeur coming to the end of a long day.

Circumspection was in order. There was no telling who'd reach the body first—the police or a SAMS clean-up crew.

Ignition on, he fired up the big V8 diesel, threw the car into drive, and floored the throttle. Built for comfort not speed, the big car took off with the wallow of an oceangoing tugboat and rolled along the cracked and pitted runway, a legacy from WWII. He aimed the tugboat towards the woods at the rear end of the airfield, the opposite direction he expected the police to come from.

Whereas seventy years earlier, the place would have roared to the sound of Spitfires and Hurricanes taking off and landing, now nothing remained but ghosts. The ghost he'd added that day wouldn't match the others for valour or honour.

The Mercedes gathered speed. He turned right at the end of the runway, heading south, and the road behind him disappeared in a fireball of yellow and flying tarmac.

CHAPTER THIRTY-NINE

Monday 14th September – Evening

Stuffield Airfield, Lincolnshire, UK

The Mercedes lurched.

"What the hell?"

Kaine glanced over his shoulder. Low on the southern horizon, the black wasp outline of an attack helicopter grew larger. A puff of white and the trail of a rocket indicated another launch.

He gritted his teeth and mashed the accelerator pedal into the floor mat. The missile closed, aiming slightly left of its target. Kaine hauled the steering wheel to the right and lifted the little lever to activate the parking brake. The Mercedes bucked, the rear end slid, and the missile shot past.

The second explosion destroyed a single-storey concrete outbuilding. Shockwaves buffeted the car and threatened to snatch the steering wheel from Kaine's grip. He fought the wheel to correct the slide, punched the "sports mode" button on the console, and stamped on the throttle once more. The big car shot forwards, rocked by a third explosion. Bullet holes stitched the concrete to his right. He yanked the steering wheel left and aimed the car at the perimeter fence.

Bullets ripped through the Mercedes' boot, tore through the rear passenger compartment, and destroyed the passenger's headrest inches from Kaine's left shoulder. The windshield cracked and frosted in an instant, obscuring Kaine's view. He tore Bernadotti's pistol from his pocket and shot twice through the glass. Using the butt as a hammer, he smashed a hole in the screen large enough to see through. Ahead, the fence loomed—rusted chain link, held up by age-rotted concrete posts. He drove for a gap and raised his forearm to protect his eyes.

The car tore through the fencing as though it were made of string. It bounced, jumped, and ploughed through the yellow blanket of gorse between the fence and the treeline.

If he could reach the deeper woods, there'd be cover and time to think. How many more times would he underestimate the opposition? How had they found him so fast?

A fourth explosion cleared a hole in the undergrowth in front of him, but the slowing Mercedes carried enough impetus to plough straight through and slam into the base of a young oak. Four airbags deployed in a white cloud of protection, and the seatbelt dug hard into his shoulder. The car squealed in the agony of mechanical death and rocked back onto the soft springs. The powerful diesel engine continued to scream, and the drive wheels kept spinning, digging deeper into the mud and roots. Kaine killed the engine.

Silence.

Dazed and shaking from the adrenaline spike, Kaine punched open the driver's door and clambered into the gathering dusk. Oncoming darkness, the one thing on his side, would be of little use when the chopper arrived with its expected infrared camera.

He had seconds, no more.

The chopper shot past, barely clearing the treetops. Without aiming, Kaine emptied the clip of the SAMS PPQ at the body of the aircraft, not expecting to do anything other than make the pilot think a little. A lack of further explosions suggested they'd shot their load of missiles.

Kaine needed thermal as well as visual cover. He reached into the driver's compartment, pulled the boot release lever, and struggled through snagging, scratching bushes to the back of the car. He snatched up his camouflaged Bergen. With it, he had hope. Not much maybe, but better than without.

Around him, the air pinged and crackled with gunfire and flying bullets. Splinters exploded from the trees, fizzed through the air.

Carrying the Bergen high to protect his head and back, Kaine ran hard. He weaved through the trees, found a fern-covered, muddy hollow, and dived headlong, scrambling under the wide fronds.

A searchlight from the chopper's underbelly cut through the dark, sweeping left and right, turning dusk into day.

Pushing the Bergen ahead of him, Kaine crawled, scrambled, and hid behind a tree. He hugged the coarse trunk, gulped in air, and waited. How long did he have? Seconds.

He blinked to clear his vision. Slowly, his breathing settled.

Any minute now, the chopper would find him, his body heat would show up white and bright on the IR camera's screen. But no, the searchlight found the dead Mercedes—thirty metres from where he hid behind the tree—and lit it bright. Cannons attached to struts under the airframe cracked, and the car exploded into an orange fireball, throwing Kaine's position into relatively greater darkness.

Kaine smiled.

The blaze would obscure his heat signature. They should have left the car illuminated and under surveillance until the backup foot soldiers arrived to check for survivors or bodies. Now, they'd have to wait until the fireball died. The error gave Kaine time to think.

What were his options?

No telling when the backup team would arrive or how many troops it would contain. Stay and fight, or run? No real decision there. No humiliation in running from superior forces.

The threatened rain arrived. Slowly at first, a gentle mist, but growing into penny-sized drops that completed his evening. Rain reduced visibility and helped the hunted, not the hunters.

Kane tore off the sodden jacket of his suit and dropped it at his feet. He unclipped and unzipped the Bergen's top flap, yanked out the lightweight camouflage jacket, and pulled it on. The Bergen's left side panel stored his water flask, his Sig P250, and three spare magazines. He checked the load and took off, heading west, deeper into the woods and further from the runway.

The changing note of the helicopter's rotors told him the pilot was preparing to land. Weird. Why not climb and use his IR scanner? No way could Kaine have damaged the thing with random shots from an unfamiliar weapon.

Breathing hard, he stopped and turned. The chopper backed away from the flames and settled onto the runway. The aurora from the searchlight picked out the three men who emerged. Bent at the waist, they ran to the edge of the trees. One approached the burning car, raised his arm to shield his face from the heat, and shook his head. The trio backed away and formed a huddle.

The leader, a stocky man with an abnormally large head, used hand signals to issue his orders. Another move that helped Kaine. It appeared that no one had told them their target was a military man. Compartmentalised intel might make sense in big business, but it led to bad decision making in the field. Bighead told them to split. One was to search north, another south, and he would head west, towards Kaine.

Before moving off, each man dipped a hand into a pack and strapped NV goggles to their heads. Another bad move. The glow from the burning Mercedes would render the goggles useless until they'd cleared the area.

The hunters' mistakes gave Kaine reason to change his plans. Less than one hundred and fifty metres of light woodland separated him from Bighead. At the pace the man moved—too fast for a proper search which showed a ridiculous sense of superiority—Kaine had perhaps two minutes to prepare. He removed the Bergen and hid it at the base of the nearest tree. His chauffeur's shiny shoes didn't offer much protection from the wet, and the leather soles produced little traction, but they were all he had. He took a sprinter's one-kneed stance, braced his rear foot against the base of a tree, and waited.

Bighead marched steadily towards him, head turning left and right, the green optics signature from the NV goggles giving away his position.

Rain poured from thick black clouds, drowning sound and reducing vision. Even the weather was on Kaine's side.

Some sort of sixth sense must have warned his hunter. After tramping through the woods as though on a Sunday afternoon stroll, he stopped less than ten metres from where Kaine hid in the undergrowth and dropped to one knee. His large head swivelled and he sniffed the air.

Kaine held his breath. Backlit by the searchlight, Bighead presented an easy target for the Sig, but a shot would give away his position.

He waited.

Bighead released his left hand from the grip of the H&K SA80 he carried in the ready position and raised it to his mouth.

"Eagle Eye this is Black One, are you listening? Over." He spoke loud enough for his voice to overcome the pulsating throb of the chopper's rotors and carry easily to Kaine.

Bighead, Black One, pressed a finger to his earpiece and frowned. "Repeat that, Eagle Eye, these comms units are shit. Over."

He listened for a moment before adding, "No, no sign of the target. Have you rebooted that IR camera yet? ... About fucking time. Get up in the air and start your flyover. Don't want to be here all night searching the scrubland for this fucker. Over. ... Yes of course the orders call for both to die. No prisoners, they said. Remember who you've got down here and make sure of your targets though. I don't want my men taking friendly fire. Over."

After another slight delay, he spoke again. "Black Two and Black Three. Report. Over."

The chopper's engine roared as it took to the air. Black One turned to watch it rise. Under the cover of the increased sound, Kaine stood, raised his Sig, and took careful aim. He couldn't risk a head-shot, not if he wanted to avoid damaging the man's comms unit. No room for error or sympathy. He squeezed the trigger.

The Sig bucked, and the bullet tore through Black One's throat. Clean and final. The .45 calibre slug nearly removed the man's head. The dead man crumpled like a wet newspaper and fell onto his face.

The chopper, Eagle Eye, climbed higher, took a position over the car wreck, and hovered at about fifty metres. Kaine knelt beside the body, fusing their heat signatures. He ripped the H&K from the man's dead hands, checked the safety and its readiness, and rested it on the lifeless back, within easy reach. Then he took the comms unit from Black One's wrist and bloody ear. He wiped the earpiece clean on the man's tunic, worked it into to his own ear, and hit the press-to-talk button.

"Eagle Eye, this is Black One. What do you see? Over."

"*Black One, this is Eagle Eye. Apart from the torched car, I only see three heat signatures. Over.*"

"What?" Kaine yelled, knowing the distortion from the field system and the noise of the rotors would mask any differences between Black One's voice and his. "Are you fucking kidding me? Someone drove that Merc and shot at us. Is that scanner working properly? Over."

"*That's an affirmative, Black One. The scanner is fully operational. Over.*"

The rain increased in strength. Kaine had no idea how long it would take for Black One's body heat to dissipate in the downpour. Not long.

"Keep looking, Eagle Eye. Black Two, report. Over."

"*Fuck all on over here, Black One. Nothing but brambles, thorn bushes, and trees. No way anyone could have passed through here without tearing themselves to shreds, and I can't see no blood. Over.*"

"Stand by, Black Two. What about you Black Three? Over."

"*It's clear this side, Sarge, but I ain't happy. Like I told you in the chopper, this is fucking wrong. Over.*"

"Explain yourself, Black Three? Over."

"Firing missiles at a civilian car when we haven't confirmed the identity ain't right. Christ, it might have been a bunch of kids out for a joyride. Over."

"Black Three, this is Eagle Eye, you're being paid well enough. Quit your fucking bellyaching and get on with it. Over."

Kaine allowed himself a thin smile. With that one display of conscience, Black Three might just have earned himself a reprieve. He saw a chink of light in the darkness. A chink of light that changed the dynamics of the situation. He hit the PTT button again.

"This is Black One. Eagle Eye, any sign of our target? Over."

"That's a negative, Black One. I'm going to sweep westwards and see what's beyond that hill. I've still got a full belt of ammo in my port cannon and I'm itching for some target practice. The contract offers a bonus for a confirmed kill and I aim for us to collect before the ground team arrives. Eagle Eye out."

The helicopter banked to starboard and crabbed sideways, taking with it the worst of its heavy throbbing drone.

A follow-up team. No time to hang around.

With the exception of Black Three, these people didn't care who they killed. If they lived by the sword …

"Black Two, this is Black One, come towards me, but take a northerly tack. There's a small pond over here and the target could be masking his heat signature in some mud. Over."

"Hey, now that's a thought. I've seen the Arnie flick where he's fighting that alien. I'll be right there. Don't start the barbeque without me. Black Two, out." Black Two laughed, and his comms line clicked.

"Black Three, make your way to the runway and head towards me. Keep your eyes open. Black One, out."

Splitting and isolating the opposing force hadn't been as difficult as Kaine feared.

He slung the SA80's webbing strap over his shoulder, checked the magazine was full, confirmed the safety was engaged, and pulled back the charging handle.

Time to start work.

Fifty careful paces took Kaine to the edge of the woods and to a spot with a clear view of the runway. The rain still hammered down, but enough daylight remained for his purposes. He took a knee, raised the weapon, and released the safety. Rain slipped from the foliage in great heavy drops that ran down his hair and into his eyes. He blinked hard, but otherwise remained still. The lack of decent headgear made the wait interminable and his task more difficult, but he'd suffered worse. He braced his left elbow on his raised left knee, placed his trigger finger along the guard, slowed his breathing, and waited.

Not long now.

He focused on the target area, but kept listening.

The helicopter's low-pitched drubbing indicated its position as behind Kaine's left shoulder. It, together with the howling wind, would drown out any noise Black Two might be making. It opened Kaine up to a potential attack from his rear, but he'd sent the reprieved man the long way around. Black Three presented the more immediate challenge.

Movement!

In the distance, just within his visual range.

A man, Black Three. Moving slowly in full battle gear, head turned to his right, searching the woods, alert for signs of his target. The man looked the part, moved silently, kept to the shadows. Kaine might have missed the movement had he not been expecting it.

Twenty paces away.

He aimed at the man's throat.

Fifteen paces.

Not yet.

Kaine slid his finger onto the trigger, but added no pressure. He took a breath and held it.

Ten paces.

He added a little pressure and the trigger moved until the first-lock resistance engaged the red laser targeting light.

"Move a muscle and you're dead," Kaine called over the hammering rain.

Black Three stopped. His eyes closed and his lips compressed into a thin line.

"Lower your weapon ... that's right let it dangle from the strap. Now raise your hands high."

The man followed Kaine's commands, slowly and with exaggerated care.

"Good," Kaine said, standing, but keeping the laser on the target. "There are two ways this can go, Black Three. You die, or you live."

The man said nothing.

"What's it to be?"

"If you're going to kill me, get on with it."

Surly. Resigned.

Good.

"I don't want to kill you, man. I'm giving you the chance to walk away from this alive."

His shoulders jerked back. "What?"

"I heard what you said about firing on civilians. My fight isn't with you. If I let you go, will I regret it?"

"What? Who are you?"

"Ryan Kaine, formerly of Her Majesty's Navy."

"Fucking hell!"

Black Three's arms lowered a fraction, but Kaine twitched the muzzle of his SA80. "Keep those hands high and answer my question."

"Captain Kaine? I had no idea they sent us after you."

"So, you were just following orders?"

"No ... well, yes. Sorry. They told us we were after a terrorist cell who'd kidnapped one of their directors. Then we heard your phone call to the emergency operator. Fuck, you killed Bernadotti? Why?"

Kaine stepped back into the shadows. "Long story, but believe me, I did the world a favour. Is the safety on your rifle engaged?"

"Yes, sir."

"Remove the magazine, hold it by the muzzle, and drop it to the ground behind you. If it goes off, you'll be dead before it bounces."

Black Three followed his instructions.

"The weapon's empty, sir. I promise."

"Drop it now."

The rifle clattered to the tarmac two feet behind him.

"Take out your sidearm and do the same thing ... good. Now remove your earpiece and stamp on it ... okay, there's not much time before your mate arrives. I'm not going to offer him the same terms. Answer a couple of questions and you can go. Backup's coming, right?"

"Yes, sir. A six-man team's on its way from Boston. They're only about twenty minutes out."

"Who do you work for?"

"Target 5 Security, T5S. A private defence firm. We've been on standby since ... BE1555 went down."

"What's Black Two's name?"

Black Three licked his lips. "Klaus Bucholtz, but everyone calls him Bug. Evil bastard. Out of control. I think he's probably a bit touched." He tapped his temple with his middle and index fingers. "T5S shouldn't employ sickos like Bug."

Kaine's earpiece crackled, either Bug or the pilot was trying to raise him. He ignored it for a moment, but time was passing and he had a decision to make.

"Permission to speak freely, sir?"

"Be quick."

"Did you do it?"

"What?"

"Shoot down Flight BE1555."

"Yes, but not intentionally. Bernadotti set me up."

Even to Kaine, his answer sounded weak, pathetic, no matter how many times he said it.

"All those people. You poor bastard. Is that why ... I mean, Mr Bernadotti?"

"Yes. What's your name."

"Stefan Stankovic, sir."

"Can I trust you, Stefan?"

Stankovic stood taller. "Yes, sir."

289

in the general direction of Black Two. He closed his eyes to protect what little night vision he'd managed to acquire with the background fire and searchlight, and clicked the switch. A beam of light brightened behind his closed lids. He waggled the torch.

"*Yeah, yeah. I got it. Over.*"

"Take a bearing and follow it to me. Over."

Kaine threw the switch again and opened his eyes. The helicopter's throbbing increased in volume.

"*Roger that. Be right with you. Over.*"

"Black One, out."

Two minutes later, the rustling of broken branches pointed out Kaine's target. He released the safety, selected automatic fire, and raised the SA80 to his shoulder. With daylight all but gone, he couldn't afford finesse.

"Where are you, Black Two? Over."

The rustling stopped ten paces to Kaine's left.

"*I should be right on top of—*"

Kaine emptied the magazine into the bushes. Bug's agonised scream cut off mid burst, and he fell, nearly ripped in two—dead before his face ploughed into the brambles.

With the multiple-parps of the SA80 still ringing in his ears, Kaine raced away from the bodies, making space.

"Eagle Eye," he screamed, panting. "This is Black One, are you there? Over."

"*Reading you loud and clear. Over.*"

"We're under attack! The target must have taken Bug's gun. Stinko and I are under fire. Over."

"*Useless fucking squaddies want the flyboy's help again. Where are you? Over.*"

"Heading for the runway. Come help us. Shit, he's hit Black Three. Stinko's dead. Fuck. Where are you? Over."

The helicopter's chopping drone grew louder. Kaine reached the edge of the woods and reloaded. Thirty rounds should be enough. He'd already downed one helicopter, another shouldn't be too hard to manage with a rifle.

"*Christ. I see one hot signal and two fading. Is that you by the edge of the runway, Black One? Over.*"

"Yes, it's me," Kaine answered quietly, without using the comms unit—his hands were full of SA80.

The chopper closed. Searchlights flared, leaves and branches fluttered and swayed. Yet again, the rain smashed into Kaine's eyes. The acrid stench of aviation exhaust filled his nose. The chopper descended. Kaine couldn't miss.

"*I repeat. Is that you, Black One? Over.*"

"Say goodbye, Eagle Eye."

Kaine aimed at the tail rotor and squeezed the trigger. Once more the SA80 bucked and spat as the magazine emptied.

Sparks flashed. The tail rotor disintegrated and the aircraft lurched backwards as the pilot lost control. It yawed to port, rolled anti-clockwise, and slipped backwards into the trees. The boom struck first. The fuselage whipped up and around, the main rotors spinning, chopping, strimming. Foliage and undergrowth flew through the rain.

Kaine ran, arms pumping, knees raised, crashing through the apron of bushes. He made the runway and sprinted. The explosion started with a whump and grew to a roar. Scorching wind buffeted his neck, nearly knocked him off his feet.

Sucking air and coughing as the cold spray entered his lungs, he sprinted across the runway to the control block and crashed through the main door.

Inside, the silence deafened.

"Captain?" Stankovic yelled. "Is that you?"

Kaine hit the stairs, climbing fast. "Yeah."

Panting, lungs and thighs burning, the injured ribs stinging in complaint, Kaine reached the landing below the top floor and stopped. His shoulder scraped the concrete wall.

"Don't shoot, I'm coming up."

Kaine would soon learn whether he'd made the right decision to trust Stankovic. He popped his head out, half-expecting to have it blown apart. Nothing.

The man he'd spared, lit by the orange flames, lowered his rifle and stuck up his thumb. "Don't take many prisoners, do you, Captain?" He smiled.

"They wanted me dead. What was I supposed to do?"

"Point taken. That was just about the best bit of shooting I ever saw. Sixty-odd metres up into the night, with the rain in your face. There aren't many who could make that shot in those conditions."

"I got lucky."

"Yeah, right." Stankovic slumped onto his haunches, back against the graffiti-covered wall. "So," he said. "What now?"

Kaine shook his head. "No idea. Why haven't the police or your mates arrived?"

"My team isn't due for another ten minutes, and I wouldn't be surprised if SAMS intercepted your call to the emergency operator."

Ten minutes? Kaine assumed the mop-up crew would be right on him. Time worked differently in a fire fight.

"What are they armed with? Any heavy artillery? Anti-tank, anti-structure weapons?"

Stankovic shook his head. "Nah. We travel light. The heavy-duty stuff is held in reserve. The commander didn't think we needed it since we had air support. Fat lot of good that did." He shot Kaine a wry grin. "No one told us who we were going up against. Our briefing notes said you were part of a terrorist cell with a grudge against SAMS senior employees. Can't blame them, mind. Most of SAMS' equipment is badly made knockoff crap. Kept falling apart in Helmand. Couldn't cope with the dust. Every time we complained, the SAMS reps blamed us for not servicing our weapons properly. Me? Given the chance, I'd choose H&K original over SAMS crud any day of the week."

Kaine allowed the man to ramble. Some people like to think when in danger, others like to babble. No doubting which camp Stankovic fell into.

"Is there a call signal? A password?"

He shook his head. "Don't think so. At least if there is, I wasn't told it."

Crap. That potentially made things more difficult. Now for the most important question.

"Can I rely on you in a gunfight?"

Stankovic wrinkled his nose. "Sorry, sir. Some of those men are my mates. I'm not going to help them kill you, but I won't do anything to help you kill them, either." He paused for a moment. "Are we cool?"

Fair enough. Kaine couldn't have relied on a stranger anyway.

"I'd expect nothing else," he said, pointing his SA80 through the open doorway at the pale corpse lying on the roof. "See him?"

When Stankovic turned to look, Kaine reversed the rifle and stabbed the butt into the back of the young man's head. He slumped to the floor.

"Sorry, son."

Five minutes later, Kaine had him trussed with his own belt and shoelaces, and with the three heavy duty cable ties he'd taken from his Bergen. By the time he'd dragged the young mercenary to the safety of an adjacent windowless room, Stankovic started showing signs of life.

Blood from the split scalp dripped down his neck and stained the collar of his fatigues. Still, the state of his laundry would be the least of his worries if he turned on Kaine.

"God," he said, grimacing and blinking hard, "what'd you do that for?"

"Sorry, Stefan. Couldn't take the risk you'd change sides in the middle of the fire fight. Don't struggle, or those cable ties will slice your wrists open. Stay in here where it's safe. If I survive I'll release you."

"And if you don't?"

"Your mates are going to find you and rip the piss out of you forever. Oh dear, oh dear. Fancy being taken prisoner by a wizened old man with arthritic hands and a bent back. Either way, you'll live if you keep out of the crossfire." He patted the man's shoulder. "Keep quiet when your men arrive, or I'll be forced to hit you again and I wouldn't want to damage my weapon on your thick skull. Wouldn't want to, but I'd have no choice. Are we clear?"

Stankovic nodded and winced against the movement. "I've seen what you can do. Six-to-one are fair odds. You won't hear a peep out of me, sir."

"Fair enough. Now, excuse me for being too friendly."

Kaine searched Stankovic's pockets and his rucksack, and found five magazines for the SA80. That, together with the ammo he'd taken from Black One, would suffice.

Seconds later, car headlights lit the runway.

"Damn. Your friends have made good time. Wish me luck?"

"Sorry, sir. Can't do that."

Kaine nodded and crawled out onto the roof. The rain had eased, but the wind's howl had increased with the onset of night. Flames from the downed helicopter still flickered, but with much less vigour than earlier. Metal glowed red, but the rain had protected the trees and scrub land. An environmental disaster averted by nature.

Nice one.

He crawled to the edge of the roof, leading with the Bergen, and lay prone behind it in a shallow puddle. He rested the barrel of the SA80 on top and set up his firing position.

The vehicle below, big and square, slowed as it approached the aerodrome gates. Kaine could barely make out any details in the failing light. If the battle extended into total darkness, he'd be done for.

He watched the approaching vehicle and ran through a quick weapons check. His SA80 had stood up to the earlier challenge well enough, and now he had Stankovic's H&K as backup. Both were loaded and ready. Sixty rounds at his disposal. If he needed to reload, it wouldn't matter. He'd be meeting St Peter at the Gates.

His earpiece crackled. He tapped it and it burst into life.

"Black One, this is Blue One. Are you receiving me? Over."

The vehicle—a black Mitsubishi Shogun with a custom shell, bull bars, and detachable side searchlights—crawled along the runway, full beams lighting its way.

With the Shogun still moving, the front passenger opened his door, stepped onto the sill, and clung to the mountings of the roof rack. He played the searchlight over the burnt-out Mercedes and swept the beam along to take in the smouldering helicopter.

Not the cautious approach Kaine would have chosen. He shook his head. He'd seen boy soldiers in Angola with better fieldcraft skills than this lot.

If Kaine had been running the patrol, he'd have evacuated the Shogun before they'd passed through the entrance gates. Then he'd have spread his team wide and made them approach the site on foot, taking cover in the shadows. As it was, these guys had yet to develop any natural night vision and presented a nice bunched target.

If he didn't need the Shogun intact for his getaway, he'd have opened fire and killed the lot of them where they sat in their comfy seats.

Somewhere in the chambers of his fast-pumping heart, he held out the hope that he could get the drop on the mop-up crew and maybe talk them into surrendering and leaving him with the vehicle. Yeah, and Cinderella was a real princess who really did live happily ever after with no mortgage, no tax problems, and no trouble with the in-laws.

"*I repeat. This is Blue One. Are you receiving me? What the fuck happened here? Over.*"

Kaine pressed the PTT button.

"Blue One, this is ... Black One." He panted, trying to sound hurt, faltering. "Where the ... fuck have you been? Missed one hell of a ... party. Over." He finished with a tired, wet cough.

"*Report Black One. What happened? Over.*"

So far, Blue One hadn't called Kaine's bluff and seemed to be taken in by the deception. These guys should have agreed on a password.

"We took out the target, Blue One, but not before the fucker downed Eagle Eye, Bug, and Stinko. The mother got me in ... in the leg, over."

"*Where are you, Black One? Over.*"

Kaine followed the Shogun's progress through the SA80's scope and lined up the crosshairs on where the driver's head would be. He'd played the sniper before and had hated every shot taken from the covers, but in a fight for survival, he only knew one way.

"Twenty paces ... east of the wrecked chopper, Blue One. Can you ... see me waving? Over."

The Shogun jerked to a halt and reversed until it was once again level with the burning wreckage and with Kaine. Five men jumped out and, without warning, four of them started firing into the trees. One didn't.

"Stop!" Kaine screamed. "What the fu—" He released the PTT button and shook his head.

Had he been rumbled?

The firing stopped, as did the rain. Even the wind seemed to ease as though in mourning. Fifty metres away on the far side of the runway, a chorus of ragged laughter drifted into Kaine's ears.

His earpiece crackled again.

"Can you hear me, Black One?" The voice, laughing along with his men, took on a much less military inflection. *"Did the nasty Kaine shoot you in the leg? You shouldn't be so fucking careless then. All the more reward money left in the pot for the rest of us. Blue One, out!"*

After witnessing the callous act of treachery, Kaine had no reservations. Even if these guys did offer to surrender, he wouldn't accept it. He wanted to open up, kill the lot of them, but still he hesitated. If they'd move away from the Shogun he'd have them.

Their strident voices carried on the wind.

A tall man, with one shoulder hitched slightly higher than the other, stood at the edge of the huddle, half-shrouded in shadow. Vaguely familiar, and the one who hadn't fired, he turned his back to his companions and shouted over them to the driver. "Your orders, sir?"

The driver's door opened and a man—so short he barely showed over the roof of the Shogun—got out. "Go find Kaine's body. We need proof of death to collect that bonus."

Kaine watched high fives and back slaps from all but the man with the sloped shoulders and the driver. The group moved to the front of the Shogun and stood in the full glare of the headlights. Kaine couldn't miss.

He took no joy in the slaughter, but they all had to die. It was them or him. His first shot took away the top of the driver's head. The others turned, confused, scattered, but not before Kaine's burst of automatic fire killed two more.

Three targets left.

The stooped one dived backwards into the dark, but the remaining two scrambled for cover behind the Shogun. Neither made it. Kaine's second burst emptied the magazine and hit them both low. One man screamed as his left leg crumpled beneath him, the knee disappearing behind a spray of crimson. The other collapsed into a foetal ball, within touching distance of the car's bumper. He didn't move.

Only the tall man remained, but he'd melted into the black. Fast reactions had saved his life and landed Kaine in real trouble.

He grabbed Stankovic's rifle and rolled to his left as a flash of orange in a halo of smoke erupted from the darkness of the far side of the Shogun. It was closely followed by the sharp crack of gunfire. Kaine's Bergen jumped under the impact of a bullet.

Another burst of orange and another crack, this one a little to the left of the first, made the Bergen jump again. The surviving soldier changed position and fired again. The third bullet whistled past the Bergen and disappeared into the night. The man with the stoop was good. A worthy opponent with deadly skills.

Kaine pulled back from the edge and returned to the deeper shadow of the wall. He hit the PTT button. "You, in the trees, nice shooting, but you're nowhere close."

"*That you, Captain Kaine?*"

"Yeah, who's that?"

"*Pete Coughlin, we met in Angola.*"

"Pete Coughlin? Cough? Thought I recognised that shot-up shoulder of yours. How've you been?"

"*Not bad, thanks. You?*"

299

Cough's weapon spat again and the brickwork to the right of Kaine's Bergen erupted.

"Funny man. Why the hell is a soldier like you working with that bunch of thugs?"

"Ever since the banks fucked up the world's finances, pickings have been slim. World recession ain't as good for soldiers of fortune as some might think. I've had to feed off scraps for the past eight years."

"Shame."

"I heard you and Gravel were doing okay. Was thinking of contacting you for a job, but ... How is the old boy?"

"Dead, as is his wife."

"Christ. Are you shitting me?"

"Nope. The guys paying you blew them up the other night with a laser-guided smart bomb."

"Fucking hell. Anything to do with that trouble you're in?"

"Everything to do with it."

"You've been shafted, am I right? Never believed for one second the Ryan Kaine I know would knock a civilian plane out of the sky. By the way, I know you're nowhere near where I'm aiming. Just wanted to show you I haven't grown soft in my old age."

"Yeah, I could see that from the way you moved by the Shogun."

"Hope there's nothing important in that Bergen. No family heirlooms."

"Nothing but clothes."

Silence stretched out for a minute. Kaine took the opportunity to descend the steps, one by one. At each landing, he peered through a glassless window, checking for movement.

"Not sure you'll believe me Captain, but can I tell you something?"

"I'm listening."

"Blue One only briefed us after we left Boston. If they'd told us you were the target, I'd never have accepted the contract."

"Why not?"

"You know why not, sir. I've got no argument with you, and none of these guys were in your class. Didn't have the first idea who they were up against. I tried to tell Blue One to back up and take things slow, but you

saw him, right? Short-arse with a Napoleon complex. Wouldn't fucking listen."

Kaine understood, but time was passing and he couldn't let the standoff drag on too long. He needed to make tracks.

"Any suggestions as to how we end this, Cough?"

"Not a one. Did you really have to kill Stinko? He was a mate and a good guy."

The hairs on the back of Kaine's neck tingled. Here might be his way out.

"Stefan Stankovic is still alive. He's with me on the top floor of the tower, safe and sound but a tad uncomfortable and probably suffering from a headache."

"You shitting me again?"

"Nope. You have my word."

"How come you let him live? Know him from somewhere?"

"Nope. He just made the right noises over the comms traffic. I don't kill people for the hell of it, Cough. You know that."

"Yeah. I do."

"Does this change things?"

The comms line degenerated into light static for a few interminable seconds.

"Captain! Don't shoot. I'm coming out." Cough's natural voice sounded over the wind.

A shadow behind the Shogun moved forwards, slow and steady. It fused into a tall, slim man, rifle held horizontally above his head. Cough passed in front of the vehicle and stopped in the funnel of light. He'd removed the magazine from the weapon, but Kaine couldn't tell whether a shell remained in the chamber.

"I'm putting my weapons down," he shouted, lowering the rifle to the tarmac and following it with his handgun.

He stepped forwards half a pace but stayed within the light.

Kaine breathed again.

"Leave the guns where they are and come to the tower. Top floor, room on the left side of the stairs. Slowly. I won't shoot if you play it straight."

As Coughlin started moving, Kaine ducked into the blackest part of the landing and hid behind a rusted metal filing cabinet. He waited until his old friend passed him on the landing, then stepped out and cocked his SA80. Coughlin stopped and raised his hands.

"Shit, Captain. You really don't trust anyone, do you?"

He'd trusted Gravel, but that hadn't turned out too well.

"Hands against the wall, shuffle backwards with your feet. More. That'll do."

He patted Coughlin down, came up empty, and stepped well away. "Sorry about that, Cough. You can relax now and turn around."

The tall man turned and lowered his arms, a dark scowl creased his face. "Is this the way you treat all your friends. I trusted you not to shoot, and you still act as though I'm your enemy?"

Kaine shrugged and added an apologetic smile. "I did say sorry."

Cough started to form fists but relaxed his hands when Kaine moved his SA80. "Is Stinko really upstairs or was that so much bullshit?"

"Stefan?" Kaine yelled. "Tell Pete Coughlin you're okay before the two of us come to blows."

"Pete, that you, man?" Stankovic yelled. "Can someone please come up here and cut me free? I've lost all feeling in my fingers and toes."

Cough relaxed and smiled. "Glad I trusted my instincts about you, Captain. Are we going up to him?"

Kaine lowered the rifle and shook his head. "Oh no. Two against one in a small room aren't good odds. There's a price on my head."

"Jeez, man. Haven't I proven myself enough?"

"Yeah, but you said times were hard and I'm worth a lot of cash to someone. I need to remove that price on my head before I can rely on anyone with military training."

Cough's frown relaxed and his expression changed to one of disappointment.

"Don't worry though," Kaine said. "The minute I free myself from this mess, I'll contact you and stand you to a couple of pints at your favourite local. Pay you back for the money you lost on this contract too, if I can."

Promises were easily given, especially when the odds suggested he wouldn't survive long enough to pay out.

"Fair enough. What next?"

"Are the Shogun's keys still in the ignition?"

Cough nodded. "The engine's still running."

"Good. Off you go then." Kaine pointed the way up the stairs with the rifle and the tall man turned to go. "Oh, and Pete?"

"Yeah?"

"Thanks for ... well, you know."

"Yeah, I know. Good luck out there, sir. You're going to need it."

Kaine waited for the second reprieved man to climb halfway up the next flight before he turned and ran. He took the stairs two at a time, his hand using the rusted metal railings for guidance. Once on the ground, he sprinted for the Shogun.

CHAPTER FORTY-ONE

Monday 14th September – MG Sampson

Sampson Tower, London, UK

MG, telephone handset mashed hard against his ear, listened to the fuckwit's miserable excuses. The anger built slowly, but inexorably into heart-pounding, eye-popping, teeth-grinding fury. The slow breathing exercises recommended by his cardiologist worked just about as well as fucking usual.

"Escaped? What do you mean, he escaped? You had Rudy Bernadotti's locator beacon, all the men you asked for, *carte blanche* on equipment and ordnance, and you still let the fucker get away? What fucking use are you and your so-called security company? What the fuck am I paying you all those millions for, damn it! What happened?"

The man on the other end of the line, T5S's CEO, spluttered. "It's difficult to say, Sir Malcolm. The picture is confused."

"Confused? I'll remind you of that comment the next time you bid for one of my security contracts. What the fuck happened, man?"

"The reports are still coming in, Sir Malcolm."

"'The reports are still coming in'," MG repeated, turning his voice into a wheedling, whining travesty of the other man's delivery. "Tell me what you *do* know."

"From what we can gather, eight of my contractors are dead and two are missing in action. We lost the helicopter—"

"*Another* fucking helicopter? For fuck's sake! This bastard Kaine's costing me a fortune. What else?"

"Apart from the dead men, you mean?"

MG put his head to the window and rolled his forehead against the cool glass, but it did nothing to help with the growing, needling headache.

"Those men are your responsibility, not mine. If you'd sent professionals, Kaine wouldn't have bested them. So, yes, apart from the dead men, what else?"

"A Mitsubishi Shogun is missing, but we did find Mr Bernadotti's body."

"So he's definitely dead?"

"He is."

MG shrugged. Good job. The fucking poof was getting far too big for his size elevens. "How did he die?"

"The on-scene medic suggests he took a single blow to the throat."

"What? Rudy Bernadotti was a black belt in something or other, and you say one blow killed him?"

"That's right, Sir Malcolm. One punch to the throat and he suffocated."

"Any sign of torture? I mean, did he suffer?"

"They found him naked with wide red marks to his wrists and ankles, but apart from the trauma to the throat and neck, and an eye wound, the body is undamaged."

Shame, but the fucking queer probably suffered worse when paying for rough sex.

"What of the local police. Are they at the scene yet?"

"No, Sir Malcolm. We managed to head them off. The site is a disused WWII airfield. The MoD uses it for military manoeuvres. War Games, you know? I suspect that's why Kaine chose the site in the first place. It's pretty isolated, a few farms and very little else. We're keeping the police away. Telling them it's a hot fire zone. I'll have a clean-up crew in there by daybreak. They'll have the place fully sanitised by midday. Is that acceptable?"

"It'll fucking have to be, won't it. Just make sure nothing comes back on me or my company."

"Absolutely, Sir Malcolm. As far as anyone is concerned, War Games are part of regular army activities. They never warn the locals in advance and they're well compensated for the noise disturbances. Everything will be properly managed, I can assure you. No one will ask any questions."

"And the 9-9-9 call Kaine made?"

"Intercepted, Sir Malcolm. Kaine used Mr Bernadotti's mobile and we had it covered. Probably thought he was being clever not using his own phone. Idiot."

MG scoffed. "How much of an idiot could he be if he killed eight, or was it ten, of your men? Wish I had that sort of idiot on my payroll. And talking about payroll, what's the reward on Kaine's head?"

"Half a million pounds."

"Double it."

"A million pounds?" The man's voice lifted a few notes. "Who's eligible?"

"Anyone giving us information leading to Kaine's death, so long as the police aren't involved. Can you deal with it? Send out the information and handle the claims? That sort of thing."

"Of course, Sir Malcolm. T5S is happy to help. And just to be certain, the reward is open to members of my company, over and above our usual finder's fee?"

Greedy bastard.

"Yes. Let the free-for-all begin. Just bring me Kaine's head or incontrovertible proof of his death."

MG rounded his shoulders to ease the stabbing cramp forming at the back of his neck. The last bit of information helped a little. Maybe the situation could be contained after all. One of the joys of having money and power was the number of times you could buy your way out of trouble.

"So, back to details. You think Kaine used the Mitsubishi as a getaway car?"

"Yes."

"Surely you have a tracker on the bloody thing?"

"We do."

"I sense another 'but' here."

"He drove it three miles to a petrol station, swapped it with an ancient VW Golf, and was last seen heading west on the A46. After that, we lost him."

"No traffic cameras out there in the sticks?"

"There are a few speed traps, but he didn't trip any."

"Right, send the car's details to the SAMS traffic surveillance team. Perhaps they can pick up where you failed."

"Already done that, Sir Malcolm. I gave them my report before calling you. Thought you'd prefer it that way."

Things were looking a little brighter, but despite that, T5S would remain on the SAMS preferred contractors list only until the end of the current contract. One fuck up was one too many. No need to lumber SAMS with a dud. Plenty of similar firms had sprouted up all over the place since the fall of the Soviet Union and the enlargement of the EU—God bless it. Free movement of people across the borders gave plenty of scope for acquiring the services of cut price cutthroats.

MG smiled at his play on words. Whoever had called him an illiterate prick in the press could kiss his arse and read his bank balance.

"That's the first decent thing you've done all night. If your people's information is accurate and Kaine's still on the road in that Golf, my traffic monitoring team will find him."

"It is accurate, Sir Malcolm. We took the details direct from the real owner of the Golf. He was rather upset when we took our

Mitsubishi back. Stupid bugger thought he'd traded the car deal of the century."

"Send in your full report the minute you have it. You know the proper channels."

"I usually deal directly with Mr Bernadotti. To whom should I address the paperwork?"

To whom?

Who did the guy think he was, the fucking queen?

"Use the standard email address. Adam Akers is the interim CSO. He'll be handling the workload moving forward."

"Will that be all, Sir Malcolm?"

"For now."

MG cut the man off before he could launch into the usual sycophantic farewell. Fucking peasant could twist in the wind waiting for his next contract, unless they found Kaine. If they did that, there was still a chance of redemption for T5S.

He stared through the window at the Shard. The ugly-arsed monstrosity dwarfed Sampson Tower. Its top fifteen floors or so—the part that tapered into a broken point—glowed white against the dark sky. Who the fuck gave permission for all that light pollution?

The idea of someone over there in that hideous piece of modernist crap staring down at him made MG's teeth itch. The damned thing ruined his view of the river, too. Since they built it, he could no longer see the Houses of Parliament or the London Eye.

A complete fucking disaster.

What would happen if a salvo of missiles from one of his company's fighter jets tore into the place? It would certainly improve his view. If he could arrange it so that the thing came down without damaging Sampson Tower, or without the destruction being linked back to SAMS, it might be worth the risk. He rolled the idea around in his head for a few moments until the image of the Shard's obliteration calmed his raging thoughts.

Reluctantly, he dismissed the idea.

"Ah sod it!"

As his father used to say, "Don't piss on your own doormat."

So true.

He pushed away from the window and dropped into his swivel chair.

"Petra!"

Why use the intercom when she was only in the other room? The interconnecting door opened and his long-term PA popped her mousy head into his office.

"Yes, Sir Malcolm?"

"Who's in charge of the IT suite tonight?"

She stepped fully into the room and tapped the screen of her tablet. "Edvard Kypers, Sir Malcolm. Shall I get him on the line?"

"Yes please, and then you can go home. I won't be needing you any longer this evening."

"Thank you, Sir Malcolm."

"And there's no need to rush in tomorrow either. You've been pulling long hours recently."

"That's okay, Sir Malcolm. I don't mind. I'll be in at the usual time. Bright and early. Eight o'clock."

The little woman bobbed her head and played with the diamond studded pendant he'd given her for her tenth anniversary as his personal dogsbody. He rarely saw her without it. Only cost him a few quid, but the gesture worked well enough. Probably the first time a man had ever given her anything more than the brush off.

How easy it was to manipulate the little people. He hadn't given the poor cow a pay hike for three years. "We live in such tight financial times," he'd said. "Government cuts to military spending. You know how it goes, Petra. As soon as the company's finances recover, you'll be first in line for a pay rise."

Yadda, yadda, yadda.

The phone on his desk buzzed. He picked it up and waited until the line clicked before speaking.

"Kypers? What's happening with that Golf and Ryan Kaine?"

CHAPTER FORTY-TWO

Tuesday 15th September – MG Sampson

Sampson Tower, London, UK

To make him appear more professional, MG clicked the intercom button.

"Yu can send him in now, Petra."

The door opened and the well-dressed form of Shafiq Patel sauntered into the office, adjusting his garish pink silk tie as he approached the desk. He'd always considered the Paki an oil-stain on the carpet, but never had the opportunity to prove it before.

"Good evening, Sir Malcolm," the creep said, in his snobbier-than-aristocracy accent. "You asked to see me?"

Didn't fucking ask, I fucking ordered!

MG didn't reply immediately. In business, it often paid dividends to allow the underlings to squirm.

Patel's eyes swivelled in his head, sizing up the office like he was casing the joint.

MG clicked through the file on his computer. The evidence was irrefutable.

"How long have you been working with Ryan Kaine?" MG said, bald and to the point.

Patel stood still. Confusion scratched into the usually unlined face. "I ... Excuse me, Sir Malcolm? What was that?"

MG pointed at his desk monitor. "It's all here, Patel. Emails, money transfers, offshore bank accounts. You've been helping this killer escape justice for money. And now Rudy's dead. You contemptible bastard."

Patel's frown deepened. He started shaking. "That ... that's simply not true, Sir Malcolm."

"Are you calling me a liar?"

"No, well, yes ... I mean of course not, but I ... Sir Malcolm, I would never do that. Rudy is ... was, my friend. We're all in this thing together."

"Don't fucking lie to me, arsehole!" MG slammed his fist down on the desk. The shockwave vibrated into his elbow, numbed his fingers.

Shit, when would he learn to stop hitting things with his bare hands?

"I have a copy of the email you sent from your home computer, dated last Sunday evening." He pointed to the TV screen on his wall which slaved the monitor on his desk. Patel turned to look at the image—the blown-up transcript of an email message.

MG gave him time to read the text.

"You set Rudy up. You are directly responsible for his death," MG said, his voice lowered into a quiet growl.

Patel's swarthy features blanched a few shades. A sheen of sweat popped out on the greasy bugger's forehead and beaded on his upper lip. He threw up a trembling hand to wipe his mouth. "No, I didn't. That email isn't real. It's a forgery."

"Once I was made aware of your treachery, I had it verified independently. You sent it to a dummy website and Kaine accessed it overnight on Sunday at an internet cafe in Hammersmith. On Monday morning, he snatched Rudy."

"No, no. I didn't do that. My God, I would never do that, Sir Malcolm. You know why. I'm too closely involved. Heavens, I sent the helicopter to the vet's farm. I wanted Kaine dead as much as you and Rudy did."

MG leaned back in his chair and sneered. "A helicopter with two backup road teams. No one should have escaped that setup, but Kaine did. And he took the vet with him. Now I know how he escaped. You called him with a warning. The farm's phone records prove it."

Patel's mouth worked but only strangled sounds emerged until he swallowed and tried again. "Whoever told you I did this is a liar." He squeaked the words, lower lip trembling.

"A member of your staff. She—"

"Sabrina?" Patel yelled, stepping one pace forwards. "Sabrina Faroukh? It was her wasn't it? She's the one. You must believe me. She's the one talking to Kaine, not me. Ask Joshua Knowles. He's been suspicious of her from the beginning. Please. Ask Joshua."

MG sighed. Sabrina had warned him Patel would try to shift the blame onto her.

"I can't ask Knowles. He no longer works for SAMS. I'm not having a man who subscribes to kiddie porn sites working in my company. Think what it will do to our public profile, our credibility."

This was such fun. He should have sold tickets. Unfortunately, the recording of this "interview" could never reach the public airways.

Patel pulled himself up to his full height. "What? Joshua Knowles a paedophile? I don't believe it. He has a family."

MG lowered his voice even further. "Don't you dare contradict me. Knowles admitted it not one hour ago when I presented him with the evidence. Begged me not to tell his wife and children. The only reason I'm not calling the police is ... well, I don't want PC Plod marching through these offices in their size twelve boots."

Patel stood still, mouth opening and closing like a drowning guppy. "It's not true, it can't—"

"You miserable fuck. I don't want to hear another word out of you. You're fired." He flicked a button on his desk phone. "Petra, you can let them in now."

"Certainly, Sir Malcolm."

The door opened and two burly men in the pale grey uniforms of the SAMS in-house security team marched in and stood either side of Patel. When he tried to push them away, the men grabbed him under the armpits and held him steady.

"Sir Malcolm, please ... wait. I can explain."

Patel tried to wriggle free until one of the guards squeezed the inside of his upper arm. He shrieked and froze.

MG stood. "You aren't allowed anywhere near your desk. HR will send your personal things along once the items have been checked. A severance package has already been organised. Don't expect much. And Patel?"

SAMS' former Director of Information Security looked at MG, eyes wide and shining.

"If you breathe one word of what transpired during your time here, I'll contact T5S and ask them to pay you a visit. Do you understand what I'm saying here?"

Patel closed his mouth and swallowed. MG waved a dismissive hand. The security men practically had to drag Patel's limp form from the office.

MG rubbed his hands together. "You can come in now, my dear."

The delectable Sabrina Faroukh stepped through from his private bathroom. A bright smile graced her flawless face. That simple expression alone was worth the money he expected to lavish upon her, and the body below it promised untold pleasures to come. The thought that she might enjoy a spell in the Chair tripped through his mind, stimulated the parts only special things could reach. No need to rush things, though. The Chair wasn't for everyone.

"Now, my dear. How can I thank you for bringing these matters to my attention?"

He stepped around his desk and drew closer, expecting her to back away. She held her ground and stared at him through unwavering dark eyes. Fuck, she was outstanding. Heat radiated from her, bringing with it an exotic fragrance he couldn't name. Her full lips pouted and her silk blouse revealed just enough cleavage to show promise. She had a trim waist, flat stomach, wide hips, and a pert arse you could bounce apples off. The pink highlights in her hair, he could do without, but the rest? Yes, she would do very nicely indeed.

She lowered her eyes.

"I don't know, Sir Malcolm."

Coyness? How delightful.

"It would appear SAMS is now short a senior IT Director. Would you like to be considered for the position?"

She gasped. "Are you serious, sir?"

MG laughed. The girl was priceless.

"Of course, Ms Faroukh. Consider yourself the latest addition to the SAMS executive directorate. Now, how would you like to celebrate your promotion?"

He reached out, but she slipped sideways out of his reach and pressed her hands together, fingertips to her lips.

"Sir Malcolm, I have some more information, but I'm worried. Will you listen all the way though before asking any questions?"

MG's senses fired.

What the fuck next?

"Go on."

Her eyelids fluttered. "I'm a little thirsty. Could I please have a drink?"

"Of course. What would you like? Whiskey, wine?"

"I don't drink alcohol. Could I have a tonic water with a twist of lime, please?"

"Certainly. Take a seat while I pour."

MG waved her to the corner where the leather Chesterfield suite gathered around the full-length observation window and took in the magnificent, if interrupted, view of London. He watched as she slid gracefully into one of the single chairs. Playing hard to get made a nice challenge. Most women threw themselves at him in the hopes of gaining favour. This one differed and as a result, made him take greater interest. He poured her drink and helped himself to a large brandy. Celebration time.

Their fingers touched as she took her glass and sipped. Once in his seat across from her, he waved a hand. "The floor is yours, my dear. Please begin."

She lowered her glass to the coffee table, giving him a perfect view of her nicely curved assets as she leaned forwards. Did she know what she was doing? Some women didn't understand the effect they had on men, but most did. Which camp did Sabrina Faroukh fall into?

"Five days ago ... last Thursday, I noticed unusual activity on the company servers."

She wants to talk work? Damn, what a shame.

He wet his lips with the cognac and leaned back into the sofa. The soft leather sighed as it accepted his weight.

She continued. "Someone was spending inordinate amounts of time trawling through the company's personnel files. Most particularly, the IT personnel. The person targeted a number of individuals, people in the department most closely involved in finding Ryan Kaine. Including Joshua Knowles ... and me."

MG straightened.

"I tracked the activity back to that internet cafe in Hammersmith and told Mr Patel. He dismissed my concerns as paranoia and told me to carry on with my work." She leaned forwards again and took up her glass. "This confused me. After all, we were supposed to be looking for anomalies that might lead us to Kaine. Then I got to thinking about the reward and the fact that Knowitall—sorry, that's my pet name for Joshua Knowles—had already taken credit for my finding Kaine at Lodge Farm. I didn't want the same thing to happen again with Mr Patel. Am I making sense, so far?"

"Yes, I'm following you. Please continue."

"Thank you."

She paused to sip her drink, and then set the glass on the coffee table once more. Her hands trembled almost as much as Patel's had done. The poor thing was terrified. MG almost felt sympathy.

"Mr Patel's reaction worried me," she continued. "I thought he and Knowitall were trying to steal the reward for Kaine's capture from me. A man in your position can't possibly understand what five hundred thousand pounds would mean to someone like me. I started investigating Patel's online activity. That's when I discovered he was sending information to an external site. At first, I didn't know what to do, and then something happened that terrified me into silence." Her lower lips trembled.

MG leaned forwards, his interest definitely aroused in more ways than just the physical.

"Tell me."

"I met Ryan Kaine."

"You did what?" MG jumped to his feet and stood over the girl.

She cowered away and he took a pace back. Intimidation could wait until it was absolutely necessary.

"It's not the way it sounds, Sir Malcolm. He broke into my home and threatened to kill me."

"He did what?" MG modified his tone to show concern, not anger. The beauty was clearly terrified and shouting wouldn't help.

"Yes, Sir Malcolm. Kaine knew all about me, my work, my education, my family background. He's a scary man. Evil. I was petrified."

MG took hold of her hand. She didn't flinch at his touch. A good sign.

"What did he say?"

"It's not what he said, but the information he had on me. Do you see? That's when I knew who Mr Patel was talking to. It became obvious he sent my personnel file to Ryan Kaine!"

She pulled her hand from his and took another drink, the glass shaking, rattling against her teeth.

"What else did Kaine say?"

"I thought I was going to die. He had that desperate look of a killer and knowing what I do about him, the way he murdered the observation team in Grimsby and the people on the plane ... Oh God. I should have spoken up. And now Mr Bernadotti's dead and it's all my fault. If I'd told you or the police sooner, he might still be alive. I'm such a coward."

Tears threaten to spill from her huge eyes.

"Shush, my dear. Rudy knew the dangers. He would have taken every precaution, but Ryan Kaine is much more cunning than we gave him credit for. I give you my word, Ms Faroukh, or may I call you Sabrina?" She sniffed and nodded her consent. "I give you my word, Sabrina. We will catch this murderer and bring him to justice."

Bollocks to justice. The bastard's going to die slowly.

She sniffed again and tried to dry her eyes with her fingertips. He gave her one of his monogrammed handkerchiefs. She dabbed away the tears and used it to blow her nose.

The woman blew her nose on three-hundred-thread-count Egyptian cotton, for fuck's sake! Still, with a body like hers, she might be worth it in the long run.

"And I think I can help," she said, offering the handkerchief, which he refused to take.

Touch the soiled cloth?

As if!

"How?"

"Kaine threatened to kill me and my family if I didn't help him. To get rid of him, I promised to send him some information. What else could I have done?"

MG jumped to his feet. "You mean to tell me you know how to contact him?"

She wiped her eyes again. "No, but he gave me this." From her handbag, she took a small mobile phone. "He said it was untraceable."

MG formed fists. "He's going to call you? When?"

"I don't know, he didn't say. I'm supposed to keep the phone fully charged and powered up at all times. Oh God, what should I do? He'll kill me if he knows I'm talking to you. I know he will. He was as close to me as you are and I could smell death on him. And now I learn he's killed Mr Bernadotti. Why? Why is he doing this?"

"I have no idea, Sabrina. Anyone who shoots down a civilian plane and kills all those people has to be unhinged."

"No, no, that's not what I meant. Why did he kill Mr Bernadotti, and why does he want to attack SAMS in particular?"

"Who knows? Maybe he has PTSD. Or perhaps he blames SAMS for creating all the wars in the world when all we do is provide the best defence equipment to legitimate governments at the lowest possible price."

He sat on the arm of the chair and took both her hands in his.

"Do you know what this means, my dear? We have him."

"Sorry? What are you saying?"

"With your help we can capture him."

"But the man's a terrorist. Deranged. Shouldn't we contact the police?"

MG thought about patting her naïve head, but decided that might be too patronising. He certainly didn't want the girl thinking of him as a father figure, unless she preferred it that way.

"My dear, Sabrina," he said, ladling on the empathy and the charm. "SAMS operates in the most hazardous regions of the world. We have our own private army that is significantly better trained and equipped than the under-resourced officers of the UK Police Service."

He lowered his head and kissed the back of her hand, delighted to discover she offered no resistance.

"No, what we must do is set a trap and lure him into it."

Her frown returned.

"But I can't have anything to do with killing."

"Oh my dear, who said anything about killing the poor tortured soul? No, we'll subdue him and present him to the police, safe and sound. You have my word."

She smiled up at him.

Outwardly, MG remained calm. Inwardly, he jumped up and down, punching the air. With the girl's help, Kaine was his.

Yes, got the fucker.

CHAPTER FORTY-THREE

Tuesday 15th September – Lara Orchard

Long Buckby, Northants, UK

Lara tested the area around Ryan's scar again. He barely even winced under her probing fingers.

"I've never seen a cut that deep heal so quickly."

Ryan smiled. "A fast repair mechanism is helpful in my line of work. All I've ever needed is rest and decent food. Having a good personal medic helps, though."

Tears welled and she lowered her head.

He caressed her cheek with a gentle hand. Her skin warmed beneath his touch.

"Lara, without you, I'd have given up days ago."

She held his hand and he didn't pull away. "What rest have you really had since the ... crash? A few hours snatched here and there."

"More than I deserve, but we're nearing the end."

"When you returned from the meeting with Bernadotti, you were exhausted."

"Yes, but I've had a full night's sleep since then. I'm fighting fit."

"Do you have to go? You read Sabrina's dossier on Sampson. He's surrounded by a protection team. The only time he's alone is when he's in the loo. It's too dangerous, Ryan. Please don't go."

He stared at her. Fire burned behind his eyes. "Don't worry about me, Lara. Sabrina's information is extensive. I know how he thinks, how Sampson operates, what he does to relax. I have all his security details and know its strengths and weaknesses."

"What weaknesses? It'll just be you against, what, four heavily armed men? That's not to mention the building's standard security patrols. You shouldn't go."

"I'll have a few things in my favour. For a start, they won't be expecting me."

"Can't you take someone with you. Rollo and Danny are more than capable. And you must know others willing to help. The two men you spared at the airfield, for example."

"You want me to risk the lives of my friends just to save my sorry arse? No. Being alone actually helps in some circumstances. Anyone I come up against will be an enemy. The opposition will delay a split second before acting. That's my first edge."

She shook her head. He was making it sound too easy. "Please stay here, Ryan. I've grown used to seeing your ugly mug around Mike's place."

"Ugly? You said I wasn't ugly. What's changed your mind?"

Lara sniffled. "I didn't mean it."

"What part? The bit when you said I wasn't ugly, or the bit when you said I was. Women are so confusing."

"Stop it, Ryan. I know you're trying to make me smile, but I won't."

"Okay. So can we agree on rugged? Chiselled? Distinguished?"

He arched both eyebrows.

Her body almost dived forwards to meet his lips. Oh how she wanted to kiss him at that moment, but couldn't. It was too soon, far too soon, and everything was adrenaline mixed with fear and concern for her patient. If he died because she'd not done a good enough job ... he'd never clear his name, and she wouldn't be able to live with herself.

A slight cough from Ryan broke her daydream and she looked up at the first man she'd even thought about kissing since Ollie. "You know we have enough to take to the police. They'll open an investigation and you'll be exonerated."

Again, he cupped her cheek with a strong, calloused hand. Again, she held it against her face.

"No. All we have is circumstantial evidence forced from Bernadotti and Gravel under duress. There are powerful forces at play here, Lara. Sampson is influential. Wouldn't surprise me if the UK Government was involved somewhere along the line. Military procurement is a murky business. Brings billions of pounds to the Exchequer."

She gripped his hand tighter. "Why don't we send the evidence to your policeman friend or this DCI Jones and go into hiding? I know I'd have to come with you, Ryan. Considering the people we're up against, I understand that. I have some money set aside, and we can—"

He shook his head. "Cash, isn't a problem. My work pays well—or it used to. I have funds hidden away. I could run and hide, but what about the victims' families? You expect me to turn tail and lie in the sun, while the man responsible for all those deaths carries on raking in his billions?"

"Not forever. Just until the police can clear your name. Please?"

"No, Lara. I need to finish this now."

She wouldn't have been surprised to hear him add "or die trying", but that sort of melodrama didn't suit his style. So much like Ollie. And, like Ollie, once Ryan's mind was made up, there wouldn't be a flaming thing she could do to change it.

She pulled away from his hand and sighed. "How long before you have to leave?"

He looked over her shoulder to Rollo and Danny, and his frown deepened.

"Sorry, Lara. I'm going now. Sampson's already beefed up his personal security since Bernadotti's death. If I wait any longer, I'll miss my opportunity. Sabrina is giving me a way in. It has to be tonight."

Lara's mouth fell open and she stuttered, "But... but you don't have a plan or backup or anything."

He forced a smile and took both of her hands in his. "When this is over, you'll be free to go back to your clinic and your hairy wee beasties, okay? And when I come knocking next time, I won't bring the uninvited guests, but I will cook you breakfast, if you'll let me."

She sniffled, battling the tears, knowing deep in her aching heart he was lying and they'd probably never meet again.

Ryan signalled to Rollo, who marched forwards and stood at her side.

"Look after her, Sergeant."

"Will do, sir. You can rely on me."

Ryan nodded to the big man. "I know, Rollo."

He turned and, without another word or a backwards glance, hurried to his car and sped away. When his Passat turned the corner and was lost to her sight, Lara relaxed her control and allowed the tears to fall.

Alone.

She was alone again.

Rollo cleared his throat. "Sorry, Doc, but we need to go."

She pulled a tissue from her pocket and blew her nose. "Can you give me a moment, Rollo? I'm—"

"Take all the time you need in the car, Doc. We need to get a hurry on."

He placed a firm hand in the middle of her back and guided her towards the farmhouse. Mike Procter—a grizzled seventy-three-year-old with a sailor's white beard, twinkling eyes, and a ready smile—stood in the doorway. In the five days since their unannounced arrival, he'd fussed over her like a kindly uncle, and he clearly loved Ryan like a son.

For Ryan to have such loyal friends showed the calibre of the man. He didn't deserve the life Sir Malcolm Sampson had forced upon him and she wished she could do more to help him make things right.

"God, please keep him safe."

At her side, Rollo sighed. She nearly missed his mumbled, "Where he's going, there is no God."

CHAPTER FORTY-FOUR

Tuesday 15th September – Late evening

The M1, Heading South, Near London, UK

The phone line clicked. Kaine clamped his gloved hand over his free ear to block out the background traffic noise. On the nearby M1, traffic crawled by northbound, but flew past on its way towards the city. The reverse of the morning rush hour flow.

"Jones here."

Curt and to the point. Kaine smiled. With those two words, the detective had already met some of his expectations. Giles' description hadn't been wrong.

"Detective Chief Inspector David Jones?"

"Yes."

"My name is Ryan Kaine."

"Is it?"

No hesitation. No wasted words. No bluster.

Excellent. A good start.

"Did Giles Danforth contact you?"

"He did."

Kaine sighed. Any more monosyllabic, and the conversation would become tiresome. "What did he tell you about me?"

"The fact I'm still on the line should indicate something. How did you find my private number? Giles would never have given it to you."

Better.

"You're right. Giles didn't give me your mobile number. I have alternative methods. A number of your colleagues are searching for me, Mr Jones. You'll understand why I didn't call your office or landline. I'd rather you didn't trace this call."

"I've read your service record, Mr Kaine. It tells me you are an honourable, trustworthy man. Why don't you come in so we can talk face-to-face?" The detective spoke without inflection, his gentle Midlands burr business-like but not hostile.

Kaine relaxed a little. Despite his reservations, talking to DCI Jones might work out well after all. The man hadn't wasted time with superfluous questions or angry threats. In fact, his tone showed a quiet patience. To coin a tired phrase, David Jones might be a man with whom he could do business.

"Originally, I did say I'd only talk to Giles, but I thought a direct approach would save time. You see, I've read your dossier, too, Mr Jones. Very impressive. An old-fashioned copper—"

"Less of the 'old'."

Kaine grinned. "My apologies."

"Accepted."

"You were in the army before you joined the force—"

"We call it the Police *Service* now."

"Yes, I know, very PC. So, you've spent your whole working life serving and protecting others. We're much the same, you and I. Our weapons might differ, but—"

"Captain Kaine, what do you want?"

"I'd like to arrange a meeting. Soon. Maybe as early as tomorrow. When I hand myself over to you, I'll be unarmed. Neither you nor your men will be in any danger from me. On that, you have my word of honour."

"You expect me to trust the word of a suspected terrorist?"

"I hoped you would, but won't be surprised if you don't. By the time we meet, if we meet, you'll be in receipt of some information to demonstrate my good intentions. As you know from Giles, I admit to firing the missile that brought down Flight BE1555, but there are other forces at work here you need to know about. I don't expect your forgiveness, Mr Jones, but I do expect you to weigh all the evidence before making your decision."

"I'm listening. Go on."

Here goes.

"Later tonight, two of my colleagues will call on you. Their only job is to deliver Lara Orchard safely into your protection."

"Dr Orchard's working with you?"

"No. Absolutely not. It's a long story, but if I'd left her at the farm, they'd have killed her."

"They? Who are 'they'? SAMS, ESAPP, or BSAL?"

Good. Jones *had* been taking an interest.

"Dr Orchard has all the evidence I've amassed so far. A recorded confession, paper trails, and bank statements. They all point to my relative innocence, but it's useless without the full story, and I'm attempting to get that tonight."

Kaine waited for the disconnect, but the line stayed active.

"Mr Jones, are you still there?"

"I am."

Jones said something else, but a fire engine passed by, sirens blaring, and drowned out his response.

"Sorry, Mr Jones. You'll have to repeat that."

"I said, on your mission tonight, are there likely to be any injuries or fatalities?"

Is this where Jones ended the call?

"Possibly, but only in self-defence on my part. I can't speak for the others."

"I"—Jones cleared his throat—"understand."

Interesting.

"When you meet Dr Orchard, ask her anything and she'll answer to the best of her ability. I've told her everything I know and everything I suspect. Please listen to her. She's an innocent who needs your protection. Call Giles now and ask for his backup. My friends will stay with Dr Orchard until he reaches your cottage. After that, I ask you to let them go free. I repeat, they have nothing to do with this mess other than to protect Lar—Dr Orchard."

"Why don't you come in with them? Make things official. Together, we could make a case. I'm not without influence."

"Sorry, Chief Inspector, that's not an option. The man I'm after is protected by some very powerful people. Before we meet, I need information from him that will stand up to serious investigation."

"Really."

A flat reply, non-committal.

"I have few expectations of surviving tonight, Mr Jones, but if I do, I'll bring irrefutable proof, signed, sealed, and delivered to you at Holton Police HQ. I might even wrap it up in a pink ribbon and tie a love bow."

"You're coming in? Giving yourself up?"

"If I survive tonight. That's what I said, and I'm a man of my word."

"I'm looking forward to meeting you."

"Keep your fingers crossed for me, then. Goodbye, Mr Jones."

"If you repeat what I'm about to say, I'll deny it. Good luck, Captain Kaine."

Jones ended the call. Kaine stared at the silent phone for a moment before throwing it into the nearby hedge. He took a brand new unregistered mobile from his pocket and tapped a memorised number.

Rollo answered instantly. "Is it safe, sir?"

"Yes. Jones is alone and expecting your arrival. Are you close by?"

"Yes, sir. I can see the lights in his front room from here. Pretty place this, and he has a nice little home."

"Never mind about that. Put Lara on."

After what sounded like cloth being dragged across the mouth-piece, she spoke. "Ryan, are you okay?"

"Please don't worry about me, just listen to what Rollo and Danny say. Everything I've learned about DCI Jones tells me he's a good man. He and Giles will keep you safe."

"Did you talk to ... Delilah?"

"Not yet. I'll call her after speaking to you."

"Please don't do this. It's too dangerous."

"Sorry, Lara. It's the only way. If you trust me, trust Rollo and Danny."

She choked off a sob. "Be careful, Ryan. If you don't come back safe and sound, I'll kill you."

He laughed. "Don't know how you'd manage that. Bye now."

Kaine ended the call, said "Have a good life," to no one, and dialled again. He waited for Sabrina to answer.

CHAPTER FORTY-FIVE

Tuesday 15th September – Sabrina Faroukh

Sampson Tower, London, UK

The mobile buzzed. Sabrina snatched it up.

"Delilah?"

"Mr K."

"Did you find what I needed?"

"Of course," she said. "I'm sending the information to you now. I've uploaded a file to the website to show you the floor plan, locations of the guard posts, and their patrol schedules. The penthouse suite is like a prison. Are you sure this is the right way?"

"I am."

"You're going alone?"

"Yes."

"That's suicidal. The guards have shoot to kill orders. You'll be cut to pieces."

"Sampson has to pay for his crimes. Are you ready to doctor the video surveillance?"

"Yes. I've set the sixty-minute closed loop to run along the route I've laid out on the plans. It will start at one o'clock exactly. If you haven't reached the penthouse by one minute to two, then—"

"Understood. No changes to his itinerary?"

"He has a reservation at The Ritz for eight and a driver booked to return him home at midnight. His security team has been briefed accordingly."

"So, he'll be at the penthouse after that? Just him and his four-man Praetorian Guard?"

"Correct."

"You're hacking skills are extraordinary."

"You gave me no alternative."

Sabrina cut the call, swivelled her chair, and looked up at Sir Malcolm, making her smile timid and hopeful. He stood over her, dominant and powerful. A multibillionaire with the world at his mercy.

"Did I do well, Sir Malcolm?"

Sampson ran the tips of his fingers down her neck and along her bare shoulder. She trembled under his touch. The halter top, chosen to expose as much flesh as decorum allowed, did its job of attraction.

"No need for such formalities. Call me MG, Sabrina. And yes, that was perfect."

She allowed her smile to remain. "You read the report I gave you, MG?"

"I have indeed and am very impressed. It's the reason I allowed you into my home."

He leaned closer. Sabrina held her breath. What would she do if the man actually tried to kiss her? Could she accept his advances without vomiting?

A knock on a door she hadn't noticed before spared her the dilemma.

Sampson's grin puffed out his fleshy cheeks and added an extra chin. "No need to be alarmed, my dear. That will be Adam, my new head of security. Rudy Bernadotti's interim replacement. Shall we continue our chat over dinner?" He straightened and held out his hand, which she took and stood beside him. "Anton Grimaldi, my personal chef, has prepared pan-fried John Dory with mushrooms, broad beans, and wild strawberries. I hope you eat fish."

"It sounds wonderful." And it did, although Sabrina doubted she'd be able to eat given the tension rippling through her stomach.

The side door opened. A tall, sandy-haired man entered and stood in the open doorway. Handsome in an aloof sort of way, he stared at her through slits for eyes.

"Adam," Sampson said as they approached the newcomer, "come in. Meet the company's newest Deputy IT Director, Sabrina Faroukh. She's taking over from Joshua Knowles."

"Good evening, Ms Faroukh."

Sabrina nodded, intimidated by the tall, broad-shouldered man with the quiet voice, the deep frown, and the blue eyes that seemed to see right through her.

Sampson half-turned. "Adam here will protect you while you're under my roof."

"Do I need protecting?"

"My dear, we all need some kind of protection. But after tonight's events"—he showed his teeth, mostly implants, and placed his hands together as though in prayer—"we will both be much, much safer."

Sabrina swallowed hard. "Thank you, Sir Malcolm."

The smile dropped from Sampson's face to be replaced by a pained frown. "Tut, tut, my dear, I thought we were friends. It's MG, remember?"

"Sorry, MG, but this is happening *trop vite* ... too quickly for me to take in. Although, I shall adapt."

"Of course you will," Sampson said and pointed beyond Adam. "Dinner is being served and you can't have John Dory cold."

Sampson Tower sprouted from St Thomas Street in a phallic thrust of concrete, glass, and chrome, and Sabrina had expected the penthouse suite to reflect the same hard-edged modern style, but no. Sampson's interior decorator had thrown everything but a suit of armour at the place and had eschewed minimalist chic for mock baronial splendour.

From the intricate pattern of the oak flooring, to the marble columns, and through to the heavy drapes and French polished furniture, the main reception room could have graced the centrefold of Country Homes and Gardens Magazine. All it missed was a roaring fire in the grate and hunting dogs lying on the hearth rug, soaking up the heat.

She expected the same thing of the dining room, but rather than the twelve-setting dining table with a butler ready to supervise uniformed waitresses performing silver service, the room was intimate. A small table set for two.

"Don't look so surprised. This is my private eating space. The overblown splendour of the main reception is to impress the punters. Most of the arseholes I invite up here expect Sir Malcolm Sampson, the uncouth barrow boy, to deck out his gaff like some sort of country castle. There's a posh dining hall next door." He indicated the wall behind Sabrina. "Me? I prefer this intimate little place for my favoured guests."

Sabrina shot a glance at Adam as he took a defensive position between Sampson and the kitchen, hands clasped behind his back, standing at military ease, unblinking eyes fixed on her.

"Ignore him, my dear. Try to enjoy your meal. As I said earlier, Adam is here for your protection as much as mine."

"Really?"

"I haven't worked my way to the top of a cutthroat business without picking up a number of enemies along the way. For now, Adam's job is to keep me and my special guests safe from whoever might want to turn me over."

"Turn you over?"

"Sorry. I forgot you aren't English. I mean Adam offers protection from people who might want to do me harm. As you told Ryan Kaine, I have a team of bodyguards at my disposal, but Adam is the best of the best."

Sabrina imagined Sampson saying the same about the late unlamented Rudy, whose skills didn't stand up against those of Ryan Kaine.

A dark-haired waitress wearing a plain black dress under a frilly white apron arrived to serve the starters—smoked salmon, red caviar, toast, and a green salad. She poured Sabrina a glass of sparkling water and Sampson a white wine. He tucked into the food with gusto. Sabrina picked at her salad, but ignored the fish eggs.

"Mind if I ask a question, MG?"

"Feel free."

"What happens if Kaine has someone watching The Ritz who reports that you didn't show for your dinner reservation? Won't that make him suspicious enough to change his plans?"

Sampson heaped a spoonful of caviar onto a triangle of toast. "Very good. I can see you're not just a very pretty face."

"You flatter me, MG. I want to impress you with more than my ability to hack into surveillance systems and follow cars on motorway cameras."

She lowered her eyes and took a sip of water. Sampson knocked his wine back as though it were lemonade. He even smacked his lips.

"Don't worry about the Ritz. I employ a body-double for exactly this situation. You'd be surprised how many times I find it important to be in two places at once."

Sampson belched loudly into his napkin but didn't apologise.

"My car will deliver my lookalike fashionably late for my dinner reservation and collect him at the appointed time. At The Ritz, I always hire one of their private rooms, The Burlington. No one will get close enough to my man to spot the difference."

Sampson clapped twice, and the waitress returned to clear the plates and lay fresh ones. As with the starter plates, these had a gold crest and a motto in Latin Sabrina translated as—*Power Through Force of Arms*. While the plates were still hot, a man in a chef's hat carried a dome-covered silver platter. Their John Dory had arrived.

———

"Well, my dear," Sampson said, checking his ostentatious watch. "Nearly time for the main event. Adam will show you out. You wouldn't want to see what happens next."

Sabrina dabbed her lips with a napkin and stood. "Thank you for the excellent meal, MG."

"Think nothing of it. I hope we can do it again very soon."

He kissed the back of her hand and pointed her to Adam, who'd opened a different door from the one they'd entered.

She looked questioningly at Sampson.

"You'll leave via the service exit in case Kaine has the place watched. Follow Adam, he'll show you the way."

Sabrina leaned forwards with her cheek and Sampson kissed it with greasy lips. At the same time, he grabbed her arse cheek and squeezed. She squeaked and put her hand on his chest. "Please, MG, not in front of the help."

"Be seeing you later, Sabrina."

"I look forward to it, MG," she said, adding her best attempt at a coquettish titter.

She followed Akers through the empty kitchen and along a well-lit corridor leading to the service elevators at the back of the building. The rich sauce that coated the fish lay heavy on her stomach even though she'd barely picked at her food.

Akers stopped so abruptly she almost ran into him. He opened a door and stepped back to allow her access. She looked into a darkened room.

"Wait. This isn't—"

A hand thumped her between the shoulder blades. The force propelled her through the doorway. She staggered, tripped on the edge of a rug, and landed headlong on a single, unmade bed. She turned, panting, unable to catch her breath. Akers blocked the doorway, an index finger raised to his lips. In the other hand, he held a chrome-plated automatic pistol.

She grabbed her chest and opened her mouth.

"Don't bother screaming," he said, his cultured voice little more than a whisper. "This area's soundproofed. Nobody will hear you, and you'll only strain that throaty voice of yours."

"What are you doing? Please don't—"

"Sir Malcolm's orders. Relax, watch a little TV. We have all the channels. Sky Movies, Sky Sports, Freeview. If all goes well with Kaine tonight, I'll come and let you out in the morning."

"And if it doesn't?" she croaked, barely able to speak.

Adam smiled and backed out of the room, pulling the door closed behind him.

The electronic catch activated, and the door locked with a sharp metallic click.

CHAPTER FORTY-SIX

Wednesday 16th September – Late evening

Sampson Tower, London, UK

Dressed for a clandestine entry—rubber-soled shoes, black trousers, vest, and jacket—Kaine slipped into the underground car park before the shutters rolled into place after the latest departure. He had the place pretty near to himself. On his way to the predetermined hiding place, he counted seventeen luxury cars—all congregated near the security-controlled entrance—and thirty-three empty spaces. High-powered air conditioners and perfumed ventilation units kept the subtly lit car park smelling of freshly cut grass.

How the other half parked.

Silence boomed around him, thumped in his ears.

The underground parking level at night was a ghostly place full of dark corners, long shadows deepened by the emergency exit signs, and empty space. The one bright light came from the security booth he'd last seen on Monday morning. So much had happened since he'd collected Bernadotti for his trip to meet Death, it seemed like weeks ago.

A different guard manned the booth, not Alexis. This one, a slightly smaller replica of Dwayne "The Rock" Johnson. This Dwayne was bored and struggling to stay awake judging by the way he yawned, stretched his arms, and stood up every few minutes to walk some circulation into his legs.

This was the one strong point of entry Sabrina couldn't weaken for him. This, he had to accomplish for himself.

He hid behind a BMW 7 Series and bided his time.

The luminous dial on his watch read 00:32. Twenty-eight minutes before the video feed in strategic areas of the building would flicker and drop into a one-hour closed loop. At least that's what Sabrina promised. Everything rested on her ability to work her magic, but he'd made the decision to trust her and wouldn't go back on it now. This was the only way. For Kaine to earn any peace, Sampson had to pay for his act of barbarism.

For those innocent people.

In the muted darkness, waiting for his moment to act, Kaine once again saw the Buzzer erupt from the PAAS-4 tube and fly. He saw it arc through the dusky sky. Saw it hit the target. Saw lights blossom into an orange flower that hung in the air for a moment before plummeting into the North Sea. He imagined all the people inside the fuselage of death, screaming for their lives, praying to their gods, dying. Over and over again, he saw their deaths.

All for money. All for business. The business of death.

00:43.

Kaine squeezed a pair of soft foam earplugs into tight balls, popped them into his ears, and waited until they expanded before clicking his fingers. Happy with the temporary partial-deafness, he waited for young Dwayne to turn away or lower his head to a book.

Come on, Dwayne. Do something.

The security guard leaned back in his chair, stretched out his arms, and yawned to the ceiling—a wide-mouthed, close-eyed, luxurious yawn.

Good enough.

Kaine jumped up and landed, arse first, on the BMW's boot. The car's alarm erupted into raucous, intermittent horn blasts, coupled with a dazzle of flashing headlights.

He crawled five cars away, huddled into the deep shadow beneath a night black Jaguar XJ and waited for Dwayne to spring into action. Unless the security booth's designers had gone to the expense of fitting decent sound proofing, nobody could suffer the noise for long.

Kaine only had to wait a moment.

The door to the glass booth opened and Dwayne rushed out, computer tablet in hand, torch in the other, the beam leading his way. He reached the noisy BMW in time for the alarm to cut off, muttered something incomprehensible that included the words "German" and "shit-box", and turned on his heel. When he'd reached the halfway point, the BMW erupted again.

Dwayne yelled something, turned about-face, and marched back to the offending vehicle. He completed a clockwise circuit of the BMW, checking the bonnet and doors.

"Damn it all to fuck," he muttered.

The alarm cut out halfway through his rant, and Dwayne's expletive echoed around the car park.

The big guard glanced around the empty space, embarrassment darkening his squared-jawed, clean-cut features until he confirmed the car park as empty. He glared at the guilty vehicle, checked the number plate, and swiped an index finger up the screen of his tablet. On finding the information he required, he headed back to his sanctuary.

From the security of his hiding place, Kaine watched Dwayne pick up his desk phone and dial. He remained standing but kept his back to Kaine.

To reinforce Dwayne's annoyance, Kaine scuttled back to the BMW and kicked the boot again, before returning to the distant shadows.

Dwayne's head snapped around. He jabbed a finger at the car as though confirming his point to the person on the receiving end of the phone line, nodded, and then ended the call.

Kaine settled down to wait.

How long would it take the BMW's owner to respond to Dwayne's summons? Hopefully, less than seventeen minutes. Sabrina's promised surveillance downtime left very little time for error. He'd likely need every second of the hour.

On hands and knees, Kaine worked his way to the car nearest Dwayne's booth and lay prone. Too close for comfort, but too far to make the next phase a certainty. At least fifteen paces separated Kaine from the security door.

00:59.

Come on, for pity's sake. Time's wasting.

Dwayne checked his reflection in the window, straightened his tie, and turned to face the internal door. He must have heard someone approaching.

The door opened, and a harried-looking professor type in a white lab coat, frazzled hair, and thick glasses rushed in. Dwayne ducked his head in a short bow and escorted the new arrival towards the BMW.

"...disturb you, Dr Erwin. It's just started, but I was worried the battery might die. I wouldn't want you stranded here in the morning."

As the pair passed his hiding spot, Kaine pushed himself into a sprinter's starting position.

"Seems silent enough to me," Erwin said, hurried and impatient.

"It is now. I checked all the doors and the boot ..."

01:02.

Crouching low, Kaine sprinted across the gap, and slipped between the half-open glass door and the jamb. He made it through the kiosk without hearing a "Hey you, stop!" from Dwayne or Erwin and paused for breath in a brightly lit, but deserted corridor.

Barrier one negotiated, three more to go.

So far, Sabrina's information held up under examination, but the surveillance cameras looking down on him from the ceiling at every turn, gave him chills. Were they really transmitting dummy images, or was a beefy guard doing a double-take at his security monitor and reaching for a silent alarm? Either way, Kaine had made his move and had to play his hand according to the plan he and Sabrina had mapped out together.

01:03.

Fifty-seven minutes to go. No time to loiter. He ran through the architect plans he'd committed to memory. The emergency staircase lay at the rear of the building on either side of the service lifts. He raced down the corridor with the lens of each surveillance camera he passed beneath drilling lasers into the top of his skull. He'd conducted dozens of infiltrations in his career, but none in a twenty-three-storey tower in the middle of the world's financial capital, and never solo. He'd rarely felt as exposed or vulnerable.

The double doors leading to the service area were protected by a keypad security system that normally required both a pass card and a pin number. He grasped the handle and waited.

C'mon Sabrina do your stuff.

01:06.

A loud double click announced the lock's disengagement. He slipped into the stairwell and started climbing.

Twenty-three storeys, forty-six flights, each containing fifteen steps—six hundred and ninety in total—and each flight separated by a landing area. He started jogging, taking the steps two at a time, pausing at each floor to listen at the exit door for pursuers, and to take a few extra breaths. Save for the normal creaks and groans of a living, breathing building with its air conditioning, working lifts, and skeleton crew of night workers, and his laboured breathing, he heard nothing out of the ordinary. He reached the top floor, quads aching, lungs burning, sweating, but unmolested and hugely relieved.

He took a knee and gave himself a five-minute recovery break. The wound at his side burned from the exertion, but the stitches held together well enough. The picture of a teary-eyed Lara begging him to call off his suicide mission entered his head, unbidden. He dismissed it as a weakness he didn't need.

Suicide mission? Time would tell.

01:24.

He'd made good speed.

Kaine took deep, slow breaths to pay off the oxygen debt, and stretched his quads, hamstrings, and calves. In times past, such relatively modest exertions as climbing a few stairs wouldn't have taken so much out of him. Damn it, he was getting old.

He pressed his ear to the door, no sound of pacing feet, but carpeted floors the other side—if there were any—would dampen any footfalls. The architect's drawings Sabrina provided hadn't included notes on decor or floor coverings.

So far, Sabrina Faroukh had lived up to her word and Kaine owed her everything. If he survived the night, he'd have to think of a decent way to show his gratitude.

Leaving her life forever might be a good start.

The memorised floor plan gave him the layout of the penthouse suite. The door he leaned against opened into a service corridor connecting a utility room, laundry, storage rooms, kitchen, and guest rooms for the guards. At the far end of the corridor, a locked door led to Sir Malcolm's private accommodation, the great man's London home.

According to Sabrina's research, with the Chairman in residence, at least four men patrolled the penthouse. Two guarded the front entrance and its dedicated lift, another patrolled the service annex, and a fourth acted as his personal shield.

At irregular times during the night, the first three men swapped roles, and this presented Kaine with his next challenge. He had to neutralise the rear guard but, if possible, not fatally. Kaine had more than enough deaths on his conscience.

01:30.

The lock released exactly when promised.

He pulled open the door, slid inside, and stood still, back pressed to the wall. Subdued lighting cast by ceiling LEDs brightened a corridor that stretched out to the left and right. Muffled music filtered through the third door along on the left side of the hallway, the kitchen. A strip of bright light showed through the crack at the bottom of door.

A great time for someone's post-midnight feast. Kaine reached the door as it opened.

A tall, dark-haired man—the heavy body of a man used to pumping iron, hands full of sandwich plate and coffee mug—filled the opening. He stopped. Gasped.

Kaine's left jab shattered the big man's nose. A follow-up kick mashed the fleshy part of the guard's groin. He crumpled. The plate and the mug hit the floor at the same time as his kneecaps.

Surprise had worked in Kaine's favour, but some men recover more quickly from crushed testicles than others—one side-effect of steroid abuse. He jumped around to the back of the fallen guard, wrapped his right arm around the guy's neck and applied pressure to the carotid arteries.

The guard bucked and kicked. The squeaking rubber heels of his loafers made thick black scuffmarks on the floor tiles. Fingers reached for Kaine's forearms, tearing, scratching at his sleeves. Kaine wrapped his legs around the man's waist and clung on. Soon, the bucking slowed and the guard's arms fell loose at his sides.

After a seven count, Kaine, sweating and breathing hard, released the hold and dragged the guard inside the kitchen. The door swung closed behind them.

He checked for a pulse—slow but strong—and hogtied the guard with three of the heavy-duty cable ties he'd brought along for the visit. He couldn't use a gag for fear of choking the big guy, but the architect's plans told him the service areas were soundproofed from the living quarters. Time would tell.

The pantry proved large enough to accommodate the big man— not comfortably, but enough to allow him breathing space. With luck, he'd remain undiscovered until the cook arrived to prepare breakfast, by which time Kaine would be gone.

Or dead.

As he closed the pantry door, the guard's animal grunting showed he'd already started to recover. Kaine didn't want to be anywhere near when his friends finally released him.

He splashed tap water onto his face and straightened his clothing —he wouldn't want Sir Malcolm to be woken by a dishevelled seeker of vengeance. He had his pride.

Kaine hurried back through the kitchen and pressed his ear against the door before opening it and ducking through. He turned left and headed towards Sampson's quarters.

The final door opened into a reception room the size of a professional basketball court. Dimly lit, the place reeked of leather, furniture polish, and cigar smoke. Scanning anti-clockwise, he took it all in—overstuffed three-piece lounge suite under a viewing platform, cinema-sized TV filling half a wall, fully stocked bar, office desk and chairs. On the opposite side of the room, two wide steps gave access to a raised gallery area that led to the main entrance doors, three bedrooms, a gym, and a bathroom. Clearly, the designer had spared none of Sir Malcolm's money to create a home away from home—if your home happened to be a faux Tudor castle. For Kaine, the place tried too hard to be palatial, but succeeded only in being gaudy.

He allowed his eyes to grow accustomed to the light before heading silently towards the master bedroom.

The main lights snapped on with enough brilliance to land a Boeing 777. The gym door opened, as did the one to the master bedroom. Three men, all carrying semi-automatic handguns, all pointed at his chest, stepped into the room.

The TV screen burst into life. Sir Malcolm Sampson's contemptuous face appeared in living colour. "Welcome to my home, Mr Kaine," he said. "You can't imagine how pleased I am to meet you at last."

Movement to his right. He flinched before a blow crunched the back of Kaine's head. He fell into blackness.

CHAPTER FORTY-SEVEN

Wednesday 16th September – MG Sampson

Sampson Tower, London, UK

MG watched the process from a safe distance.

"Make sure he's clean, Adam. Wouldn't put it past the arsehole to hide a bomb up his jacksie."

MG chuckled. No doubt the raging queer would enjoy trying to find something stuffed inside another man's arse.

While the two other guards held down the unconscious Kaine, a po-faced Akers waved a small electronic wand over the bastard's near-naked body. The wand pulsed and clicked in his hand, and squawked as it neared Kaine's left forearm.

"What's that?" MG asked, stepping behind his desk. He hadn't survived in the cutthroat world of the international armaments business by exposing himself to personal danger.

Akers shook his head. "No need to worry, Sir Malcolm. It's a surgical implant. His ulna and radial bones are held together with steel pins and screws. It's in his military file. Kaine's a regular Robocop." He finished the sweep and stood back. "He's clean and unarmed. Apart from the implant, there's no metal on or inside his body."

"Good," MG said. "Stick him in the Chair."

———

When he'd first seen Ryan Kaine in the flesh, MG had been surprised and a little disappointed. Over the previous few days, he'd imagined the man as some sort of monstrous fighting machine, yet there he sat in his underwear, looking lean and fit, but not particularly powerful. Despite having read Kaine's MoD file and seen his photos, he'd never have suspected that a man with such a relatively small frame could have done all the tasks attributed to him. The guy looked normal. Nothing at all to worry about.

But MG knew better.

Kaine groaned. His head rolled up, and his eyes blinked open. Unfocused at first, confused, and then alert, taking in the room until they alighted on MG. Cold, dark hatred filled them. Then he looked down, snarled, muscles tensed as he fought against his bindings.

Fat lot of good that would do him.

"I see you've noticed the Chair, Kaine. I had my men bring it in from the games room. Lovely isn't it? Carbon fibre weaved with a non-conductive polymer and bonded with one of the company's most advanced adhesives. Very light and extraordinarily strong, it can withstand a direct impact from a truck travelling at over ninety miles per hour. I know, we've tested it on our deceleration track. Use the same material in our aircraft ejector seats. What's more, its surface is wipe-clean for ease of maintenance.

He particularly liked the wipe-clean aspect.

Kaine appeared to be listening, but said nothing. He twisted and turned, testing the restraints. Always searching for a way out, he'd never give up. Watching the man squirm and suffer was going to be delicious. A better thrill than inflicting pain on the tarts and rent boys he paid to take the punishment. Today though, there would be no limits, no holding back. No safe word.

Definitely no fucking safe word.

MG trembled at the anticipated delight. He couldn't wait to get started. Kaine was fit and strong. He'd last ages before succumbing to the torture and dying in a pool of his own blood and shit.

MG studied his handiwork.

He'd supervised placement of the manacles himself, just in case the hired help fucked up as they often did. As Dad never tired of telling him, "If you want a job done properly Malcolm, do it yourself."

A stainless steel chain looped around Kaine's waist and passed through a hole in the Chair's rear support. They'd chained and padlocked his ankles to the central pedestal. His wrists were hand-cuffed together behind his back and attached to the waist chain. A choke chain, wrapped around his neck, was fastened to the built-in head restraint. The whole assemblage allowed the prisoner minimal movement, but left his chest and stomach exposed and unprotected. It looked extremely uncomfortable.

As it was damn well meant to be.

He'd perfected the arrangement during his private sessions. He didn't use his title, Chairman, for nothing. Again, MG chuckled.

Kaine had cost him days in lost time and millions in money and equipment. Payback was going to be tough and very, very long.

"In case you're wondering about the chains and bracelets being a little ... old school in comparison with the seat, that's down to me, I'm afraid. You see, I just love the sound of clanking metal. Takes me back to my youth on the mean streets."

Kaine snorted. "Stop wittering, man. You're giving me a headache."

"Adam, he's slurring his words."

"Sorry, Sir Malcolm. I must have hit him a little too hard."

Akers didn't sound sorry.

"Not fucking good enough. I want the prick fully aware of what's happening to him. I want him screaming. Consider yourself seriously rebuked. In fact, I'm going to tell payroll to fine you one day's salary."

Akers bowed his head. "Yes, sir. I understand."

"But don't worry, I'll have them donate the money to the trust fund SAMS is setting up for the bereaved families of Flight BE1555. It's only fitting. The poor unfortunates need all the support we can give them."

Kaine's head lifted and his eyes burned.

"Angry, Kaine? Maybe you're not so badly hurt after all."

Akers smiled and stepped closer to the chair. "The trust fund is a wonderful idea, Sir Malcolm. I don't mind donating to a good cause. Can I start now, please?"

"In time, Adam. Let me savour the moment."

The jaw muscles in Akers' handsome face bunched. "You know what he did to Rudy, and he broke Bruce's nose."

MG grunted. "That was the Jock's fault for being so fucking slow and useless."

"Why didn't you warn him Kaine was coming?"

MG smiled. "If I'd made it too easy, Kaine might have smelled a trap and aborted. He's been bloody lucky so far, and I didn't want to give him any chances."

"But his nose ... and his privates."

"His bollocks? Yes, well that's unfortunate for Bruce and all his playmates, but I'll give you permission to repay Kaine in full for both Rudy and Bruce, but only when I'm done with him. How does that sound?"

"Perfect," Akers said, smiling. "Thank you, Sir Malcolm."

MG rubbed his hands together, not that they were cold. "Kaine, in case you were wondering, this man is Adam Akers. ... I see the name means nothing to you. Understandable, but when I tell you Mr Akers was Rudy's life partner, then ... Ah, I see you understand your predicament."

Kaine scanned the room as best he could, given the restrictions to his movement. Fighting the restrictive choke chain, he said, "Where are the other two? Too scared to face me? Shame, I'd like to make their acquaintance."

"Ha! Such bravado. Timothy and his partner have taken poor Bruce to hospital. They'll be back in a while, but Adam and I don't want any witnesses to the next few hours' entertainment anyway. Feel free to introduce yourself, Adam. Impress upon Mr Kaine how distraught you are at poor Rudy's treatment, but make sure he stays awake."

Barely in control, Akers rained blows on Kaine's unprotected face, chest, and belly—punches, chops, and kicks—and the whole time, he screamed obscenities. The deep cut in Kaine's side opened.

Not for the first time, blood trickled onto the beloved chair.

MG enjoyed the show. Kaine didn't. He tried to cover up and roll away from the worst of the punches, but the chains allowed him too little movement. For most of the attack, he tucked his chin into his right shoulder, scrunched up his face, and took the punishment without so much as a squeak. Not that MG expected to see any such weakness so early in the proceedings. Kaine's file described a man capable of sustaining immense physical punishment.

The upcoming few hours would test that statement to destruction.

After five minutes dishing out the bare-knuckle punishment, Akers, sweat stained and panting, stopped. He may not have been as good a fighter as Bernadotti, but what he lacked in skill, he more than made up for in enthusiasm.

"That's it, Adam. Take a breather. The night is young and Mr Kaine's going nowhere. Now you've softened him up, I need to ask a few questions."

Kaine raised his head. The left side of his face was an unrecognisable mess. His mouth, a bloody, swollen gash, twisted into a hideous distorted smile. "That all you got, Blondie? My little sister hits harder than that."

Akers screamed and leaped forwards. His hands found Kaine's throat, thumbs pressing into the jugular. Kaine's neck muscles and sinews stiffened, his face turned bright red, and still he smiled.

The fucker's insane.

"No, Adam. Stop!"

Akers snarled, but released his hold and backhanded Kaine across the face. He stood over Kaine, hands shaking, bruised knuckles darkening against his otherwise pale skin.

Kaine just smiled. He took three deep pulls of air, still grinning, still under control—apparently. He spat blood and a tooth onto the Italian marble floor.

No matter. Blood didn't stain polished marble. One of SAMS' crime scene clean-up crews would get to work on it in the morning. No questions asked, none expected.

"Why am I still alive?" Kaine asked.

His voice croaked, but his breathing had almost returned to normal.

"Good question, Kaine. Glad to hear you're awake and aware after that pummelling. You're still alive because you have some information I need, and because I want you to suffer. You might not answer my questions, but you will suffer."

Kaine looked at MG through his less-damaged right eye. "What questions?"

"Oh, nothing much. We have the copy of Rudy's confession you left with his body, but I want the original file. Where is it?"

"Bugger o—" Kaine coughed. Blood and spittle spilled from his mouth and dribbled down his chin.

MG watched the frothy mixture trail down Kaine's sweaty chest. He wondered whether the drip would join the blood oozing from the side wound, but it took a right turn at his bellybutton and fell the other side.

He sighed. "Yes, I thought you'd play the tough guy, but I have plenty of time. In fact, I've given the staff the day off tomorrow. You'll stay alive until I have the original recording, understand? Not saying you'll necessarily be in one piece, though. Who else have you told?"

Kaine shook his head.

"What does that mean? No you didn't make a copy, or no, you're not saying anything? Tell me or I'll let Adam loose again."

Akers raised his fists. "I'm going to kill you slowly, you bastard, and fuck you up the arse before you die."

Kaine hacked out a laugh. "That's what Rudy said before I killed him." He puckered his damaged lips and smacked Akers an air kiss. He might have added a wink, but it was difficult to tell with the left eye swollen shut.

Akers screamed and jumped forwards, but MG threw out an arm. "Later, Adam."

Reluctantly, the big queer backed away.

MG focused on Kaine once more. "Who the fuck do you think you are, breaking into my home and threatening my life? Did you think I wouldn't be ready for you? Stupid fuck. You've been lucky so far, but your luck has just run out. Coming here was a mistake. One that's finally going to cost you your life. And now, it's my turn."

Slowly, MG removed his jacket, rolled up his shirtsleeves, and aimed a flurry of punches at Kaine's stomach, right-left-right. MG tried to remember the last time he'd thrown a punch in real anger. Decades, but he clearly hadn't lost the knack. Kaine grunted each time a punch landed, but MG's knuckles bounced off rock solid abs.

MG had been in plenty of scraps as a youngster and had landed a few million punches in the gym over the years, but heavy bags didn't hit back and MG wasn't one for sparring. All that grunting, sweating, and flying blood and spittle—not for him. He even avoided punching Kaine's open wound—no telling what he'd catch. No way was he going to use gloves, though. Skin on skin. No fun otherwise.

Panting hard, MG backed away, and rested an arse cheek on the edge of his desk. He shook his head. "It didn't have to come to this, you know. Such a waste. I considered making a direct approach to bring you into the company. Even talked to your former boss, what was his name?"

The tip of Kaine's tongue flicked out to lick his lips. He glared at MG, still full of fight. Full of menace. Breaking his spirit was going to be fun.

"Valence," Akers said, helpfully, "Graham Valence."

"Thank you Adam, that's right. Also known as Gravel. Honestly, you men in uniform with your cute nicknames. Part of the bonding process, building the herd mentality. Groupthink, I believe it's called. Or I might have got that part wrong. Never mind, where was I? Oh yes, I told Rudy to talk to Valence a few months ago. Asked if we should bring you into the fold, as it were. You know what he said?"

No reply.

"I asked you a question, Kaine. What do you think he said?"

Still no response from the man in the Chair. Not surprising. Talking through swollen lips and moving the damaged, perhaps broken jaw would have been difficult.

"I'll tell you what he said. He told Rudy you were an honest man. 'Fucking Boy Scout' was the exact phrase he used, apparently. So when we needed a fall guy, guess who fitted the bill? No, no need to answer that one."

MG stretched his arms above his head and let out a huge yawn.

"Never underestimate the joy in a good stretch and a yawn, Kaine. One of life's simple pleasures. Bet you wish you could stretch out right now. You look so damned uncomfortable. I bet you're thirsty, too."

He walked to the wet bar and took his time to pour a large glass of water, delighted to see Kaine paying close attention. Punches and kicks were painful enough, but torture could take many forms. He took a deep, satisfying glug, smacked his lips, and emptied the rest into the sink.

"So, when we needed to kill Professor Petrovic, the BSAL ceramicist, you became the obvious choice of triggerman."

"Ceramics?" Kaine asked, slurring the word. "You killed all those people over pieces of clay?"

MG laughed. "I didn't kill anybody, Kaine. You did. And yes, it was for the money. If BSAL's safety equipment passed their trials, billions of dollars would have been wiped off SAMS' share value. Billions. And we'd have lost any hope of future PPE contracts. I've put my whole adult life into this company, and I won't see it fail. The jobs of hundreds of thousands of SAMS employees would be at risk, too. So what if a few people had to die? The casualties of war, Kaine."

"They were innocent civilians, you bastard," Kaine said, spraying blood.

"Innocent civilians? So fucking what?"

"Women and children."

"Again, so fucking what? If Petrovic's private flight hadn't been grounded, fewer lives would have been lost, but those are the breaks. It's a crying shame and all, but every cloud has a silver lining. Turns out the MoD is about to issue a tender for a defence system to protect civilian planes from anti-aircraft missile attack. Early warning devices and reflective countermeasures. The sort of stuff fighter jets use. You'll never guess which company is top of the preferred bidders list. Yep, that's right, good old SAMS. The UK's proud defender."

He laughed at Kaine's battered look of disgust and continued taunting. "Back in the seventies, we'd call that sort of thing serendipity. A happy accident. Great times the seventies. My father and I had just started the firm. Happy days. Lord how we've grown."

"I'm going to tear this whole structure down around your ears," Kaine mumbled, barely making sense.

"Really? And how are you going to do that chained to the Chair? Never know when to stop, do you, Kaine. Adam, there's a baseball bat in the gym. Why don't you go fetch it and we can have some real fun. I want to hear this fucker scream."

Akers shook his head. "I like the feel of knuckle against flesh. More personal that way."

He danced forwards and threw a wild left at Kaine's nose. Kaine turned and dipped his head. Akers' fist landed on skull. He screamed and pulled away, cradling one hand in the other. The skin around the prominent knuckle had split, exposing severed tendon and jagged bone. Blood poured from the wound.

"He broke my hand! He broke my fuck—"

"Pitiful," MG said. "Call yourself a security officer? Beaten by a man chained to a chair? Maybe I should wait for Timothy and his friend to return from the hospital. Go get the fucking bat. I want to ask our guest some questions. Let's see how feisty he is while I'm smashing his kneecaps."

Kaine said something, the words made incomprehensible by the blood bubbling through the battered lips.

"What's that?" Akers asked, leaning forwards.

More sounds burbled, but no meaning.

Akers pushed his face closer to Kaine's. "What did you say, arse—"

Kaine lunged. Mouth open, teeth bared. His jaw snapped shut. Teeth clamped onto Akers' nose.

Akers screamed. Started punching, scratching, clawing, but Kaine didn't let go. Still screaming, Akers pulled. Something gave way, and his head snapped backwards. His hand slapped to his face. Blood poured through his already-bloodied fingers.

"My nose! Oh God. My nose. He's bitten my nose off."

Akers kicked out at Kaine's shin, but missed and staggered away.

Kaine spat again and a piece of jagged skin and bloody cartilage landed on the floor beside his tooth. He grinned.

Wailing now, Akers scurried to the bathroom and kicked open the door. MG kept his distance from the chair. He valued his face.

"Well now, that was informative. I wondered whether he was up to the job. Clearly he isn't a fitting replacement for dear old Rudy. Thanks for that, Kaine."

He cocked an ear. The so-called soundproof bathroom door did little to muffle Akers' howling curses. "What can I say. Good help is so hard to find these days."

Kaine's head dropped and then lifted again as though fighting to stay conscious. MG wasn't going to fall for that old trick. The screaming from the bathroom brought to mind the phrase "once bitten ...".

He laughed aloud at the irony.

"Queers are so engrossed in their looks, he'll be out of his mind when he sees his face in the mirror. Doubt I'll be able to hold him off you when he comes back out. Better get that baseball bat myself. Back in a minute. Don't go away now."

MG whistled all the way to the gym. The next part was going to be deliciously brutal.

His aluminium bat stood in the corner next to his seldom-used golf bag, gleaming clean from its recent visit to the autoclave. You couldn't beat medical sterilisation equipment for removing unwanted DNA.

The pristine white grip tape, tacky, non-slip, fit his hands to perfection. He took a stance and tried a couple of practise swings. The bat let out a satisfying whoosh as it parted the air.

He pushed through the door. "Can't wait to get started. What's it to be first, Kaine? Elbows or kneecaps? You choose."

Bat raised high, MG swaggered though to the lounge. Akers had finally stopped screaming. Fucking baby could bleed to death as far as he was concerned. He took a pace forwards. Stopped.

What the fuck!

The carbon fibre chair stood empty.

The shiny chains dangled below the seat, still swinging. In the blood and spittle on the marble tiles lay three pairs of open handcuffs.

Movement caught the corner of MG's eye. He spun.

Ryan Kaine flashed a gap-toothed smile.

CHAPTER FORTY-EIGHT

Wednesday 16th September – Early morning

Sampson Tower, London, UK

Everything hurt so much Kaine struggled to dress after dealing with Sampson and Adam Akers, now dubbed Pinocchio.

Shoulders, back, stomach, knees, and chest all vied with his battered face for top spot on Kaine's chart of pain—his hit parade—but without doubt, the missing tooth won. The root throbbed with every beat of his heart, and he couldn't stop his tongue worrying away at the gap. His left eye, so swollen he could barely see though it, was probably the most significant short-term injury. It screwed with his depth perception and would hamper him if it came to a fistfight. On the other hand, being right-eye dominant, his shooting accuracy would remain unaffected.

He'd suffered similar damage before and his vision would soon recover—assuming he lived long enough for the swelling to subside.

The rib injury, open again and seeping, stung like crazy, but was a minor inconvenience in the grand scheme of things.

One little discomfort he didn't mind though, was the bruised knuckle on his right hand from landing a punch flush on Pinocchio's jaw. The squealing arsehole had collapsed faster than a paper umbrella in a thunderstorm.

He stood over a groaning MG Sampson, who'd taken Kaine's place in the carbon fibre chair. Spittle ran from the corner of the billionaire's mouth, formed a thin trail down his flabby cheek, and pooled on the collar of his silk shirt. Not a pretty sight, but a hell of a lot better than the reflection Kaine had seen in the bathroom mirror. The phrase "tenderised beef" came to mind. Good job he hadn't planned any photo shoots over the next few weeks. On the other hand, he might do well if he hired himself out for early Halloween parties.

Sampson groaned. His lids flickered. Pale blue eyes found Kaine's battered face and he gasped. He pulled away and tried to raise his hands, but the chains stopped his movement short.

"What—"

"Not very comfortable, is it?" he said. His words whistled through the gap where his tooth used to be.

"What did you do to me?" MG asked, voice trembling, barely above a whisper.

"I didn't touch you, old chap. You fainted away like a debutante at her coming out party. Never see anything so pathetic."

Kaine patted Sampson's cheek and stared at the dark stain spreading at the crotch of the billionaire's trousers.

"Oh dear. Those expensive trousers are ruined. It seems you don't mind dishing out the punishment. Now let's see how much you can take."

Sampson's lower lip trembled. Head still, his eyes searched the room.

"No use looking for help. Pinocchio's no good to you and I've barricaded both the front door and the tradesman's entrance. Thought it would be nice for us to spend a little quality time together.

Rudy seemed to enjoy my company. Until the end, of course, when he cried like a baby."

Kaine tried to smile, but a split on his upper lip opened and stung to hell.

"How's the fancy high-tech chair? In deference to your age and waistline, I've given you a little more wriggle room than you gave me, but I doubt you appreciate my generosity."

The Knight of the Realm, no longer the gloating thug he'd been a few minutes earlier, dropped his trembling chins to his chest. How far the mighty can fall.

Kaine sniffed. "That piss is going to stink before long, but you'll have to put up with it for the moment. I'll let you change your trousers before we leave."

Sampson's head jerked up. "Leave? Where are you taking me?"

"That remains to be seen. I haven't decided yet. Might take you with me to the police station, might not." Kaine straightened and took a step back to study the man. "Better pray I take you with me, though."

"Why?"

"If I leave you in the chair, it'll mean our negotiations won't have been successful and you'll be dead."

Sampson opened his mouth and sucked in some air, but Kaine raised a silencing finger. "Don't bother screaming. You had this place soundproofed, remember? No one will hear and you'll end up annoying me." He rested a hand on Sampson's trembling shoulder. "Believe me, old chap, you don't want that."

The fat man's jaws snapped shut. He turned his head to the panoramic window with its view of the London skyline. His eyes narrowed, lids formed slits. Here was a man who'd negotiated multi-million-pound business contracts all his adult life. Kaine could almost see the inner businessman replace the terrified captive. As he intended, the word "negotiations" had given Sampson hope. A thin smile appeared on his cruel lips.

The performance turned Kaine's stomach. When he thought of the people aboard the doomed Flight BE1555, he nearly lost control.

How easy it would have been to take Sampson's shiny baseball bat and start swinging. Start swinging and not stop until he'd pulverised every bone in the miserable overstuffed body. But no, Kaine needed Sir Malcolm alive, for now.

He gave the captive time to think, time to strategise. First would come the questions. He'd try to work out whether Kaine had room for compromise. He'd see if they had any common ground.

Kaine waited, battling the thumping headache, the dimming vision, and the bubbling nausea. Time wasn't on his side, but he couldn't afford to rush the next part. Everything depended on the upcoming verbal sparring.

Minutes passed before Sampson shook himself as though waking from a daze. He tugged at his chains and then looked up at Kaine. "How?"

Game on.

"How did I get free?"

Sampson nodded. Kaine raised his right hand, palm open, and Sampson cowered away as best he could, given the restrains.

"Don't worry, I'm not going to hit you. Not yet."

He showed Sampson his palm again.

"See this scratch?" he said pointing to the thin red line running through the muscular pad at the base of the thumb. "That's something your boy, Adam, missed when he ran that scanner over me."

"You were awake for that?"

"Of course. My Nan could hit harder than your boy Timothy—and I was prepared for the blow."

Again he smiled, and again the split lip made its presence known. Pity Lara wasn't around to apply some of her magic balm—a simple smile would help. He pressed a finger to the cut and continued talking.

"As you rightly said, Pinocchio is a poor excuse for a security officer. Shame about his nose, but,"—Kaine shrugged—"the fortunes of war, I'm afraid. Now, back to this." Kaine showed Sampson the scratch on his palm once more and tapped it with his fingers. "Whenever I go a-hunting, I always bring this little marvel with me in case I get into difficulty."

After making a great show of closing his eyes and turning his head, Kaine used the middle finger of the same hand to work away at the lower end of the scratch. After a couple of strokes, Sampson would have seen the hooked head of a thin white object protruding from the top of the wound, near the palm. Then, using the tips of his index and middle fingers as tweezers, he extracted an object the same length as a matchstick, but much thinner, from its meaty sheath. He brought his thumb into play and held it a precision grip the same grip he'd use to hold a key.

The operation took no more than a couple of seconds. Kaine opened his eyes and twiddled the article in his fingertips with the dexterity of a close-up magician.

Sampson watched in confused fascination.

"Takes a little practise to perfect the technique blind, but worth it don't you think? If you're wondering, this gizmo is a ceramic lock pick. For fun, I've practised opening handcuffs in the dark with tools very similar to this ever since I was a kid. Just like your carbon fibre chair, ceramics don't show up on metal detectors. Ironic, eh? This whole affair started with ceramics and now I'm ending it with the same material."

Sampson closed his eyes. "I should have used cable ties."

Kaine waggled his head. "Wouldn't have made much difference. I can open cable ties with this thing too. Just takes a little longer to locate the locking catch. They're smaller but I rarely fail."

He replaced the pick in its pouch and clapped his hands before remembering the bruised knuckle and his aching arms. Sadly, recovering from injury took longer with each passing year. No need to worry about retirement, though. No one draws a pension in prison.

"Now, what are we going to do?"

Sampson closed his eyes for a moment making ready for the game Kaine knew he'd attempt to play.

"If it's money you want, I have plenty. Name your price. I can wire it to your account from this room. Millions. Think what you can do with all that money. Escape. Buy an island in the Caribbean. Anything, but please don't hurt me."

Kaine held up his hand for silence. "But you've only just finished taunting me for being a Boy Scout. What makes you think I've changed in the past twenty minutes?"

"Think about it, Kaine. Six or seven zeros. Enough to set you up for life. You need never return to the UK."

Kaine played with his new beard. "Not much good if I don't live to spend it. What about that reward on my head? You've just upped it to one million pounds."

"You know it's a million?"

"With friends in T5S, I know many things."

"I'll cancel it. Make it known you're not to be harmed in any way. I have the power to do that. You know I have." Desperation bled through his words, causing them to run together.

"And what's to stop you setting more of your wet teams on my trail the moment I let you go?"

"I wouldn't. I-I promise."

"Don't bother, Sir Malcolm. I'm not listening. You can come out now, Delilah."

The kitchen door opened. Sabrina Faroukh walked in carrying a green plastic box. She took one look at Kaine and threw her free hand to her mouth.

"Sabrina, help!" Sampson screamed. "Call security. Quickly. Run!"

A frown wrinkled her forehead. "Why would I do that?"

Sampson's jaw fell open as he watched her place the box on his desk, open it, and scrabble around inside. Armed with what she wanted, she approached Kaine in the centre of the room and stood close. "Your face looks so much worse up close. Are you okay? It was unbearable sitting back, watching what those monsters were doing to you."

Sampson let out a strangled cry and struggled at his chains. "Bitch. You fucking bitch. I trusted you!"

Sabrina turned a steely glare on him. "Trusted me enough to lock me in a room against my will?"

Kaine dropped a hand on Sampson's shoulder once again. "Stop that. You'll only hurt yourself. Don't worry, I won't be dishing out the same treatment you gave me. I doubt your heart could take it."

Sabrina took Kaine's hand and led him to the desk. "Come here and stand still."

Reluctantly, Kaine obeyed and stood, awaiting more torture. She dabbed a cotton pad with antiseptic liquid and applied it to one of his many cuts. He jumped back. "Bloody hell, woman. Who taught you first aid, the Marquis de Sade? Take it easy."

"Stand still, you big baby."

"You try it from my side."

She attacked a cut over his eye and he managed not to react. Sampson needed to see a stone hard killer, not a baby crying for his mother. She wet a cloth with distilled water and gently washed the rest of his face. Removing the congealed blood made him feel a little better. Not a hell of a lot, but every little helped.

"Any sticking plasters in that box?"

He held up his hand and showed her his scraped knuckle. Sabrina applied a bandage with the same precision and care as she did with the antiseptic. Given the choice, he'd have preferred going another couple of rounds with Pinocchio.

"Open your mouth. Let me see that tooth." She lifted his top lip and made a sucked-lemon face. "Not so bad, but you'll need to see a dentist."

"No, really?" Kaine still couldn't stop his tongue worrying away at the new gap.

"Oh my Lord. Can you see out of your left eye?"

"Not much, but I protected the right, which is the one I use for shooting."

"I wondered why you tucked your chin in like that when Adam was hitting you. Does it hurt?"

"Only when I laugh."

"You want to laugh?" she said, innocence itself.

"No intention of it."

Kaine's mind jumped back a few days to a vet's surgery in the countryside. What would he give for Lara's gentle comfort? Still, no use wishing for things he couldn't have.

"Finished torturing me yet?"

"For the moment." She smiled sadly and touched his cheek. "I was so scared for you."

"What's going on?" Sampson asked, a look of disbelief on his flabby face. "Adam locked you in the spare room."

She looked at Kaine. "Do we have time for explanations?"

Kaine checked his watch, which he'd found on Sampson's desk. 03:46. Was that all? "The security shift won't change for another couple of hours. Carry on. I love a good story. Mind if I sit for a while? It's been a tiring night."

On his way to Sampson's enticing office chair, he took a detour to the wet bar, and poured a huge whisky into a cut glass tumbler. "Sabrina, would you like something?"

"Tonic water with a twist of lime, please."

"Coming right up. Carry on, lass. Put the man out of his misery."

Sampson cried out and tugged at his chains.

"No, no, Sir Malcolm. No need to look so scared. I didn't mean it that way."

He handed Sabrina her drink and dropped into the executive chair, sighing as he lifted each booted foot onto the leather-topped desk. Who could resist the luxury of stretching out in padded leather comfort with a drop of whisky to warm the spirits? He could grow accustomed to the high life, assuming he could find a way to leave the building without sustaining any further damage.

As it was, he'd be bruised all over by morning, but that was better than the alternative.

Kaine swigged the very nice single malt, bathing the exposed root in the alcohol. It hurt like stink, but after the initial spike of agony, the tooth settled down to an aching throb. He likened it to the banging-your-head-against-a-brick-wall approach to therapy. Stop head butting the wall, and it'll stop hurting.

Sabrina leaned against the edge of the desk in front of Kaine and faced the man in the chains. She had the floor and the look on her face confirmed that she enjoyed the experience. She started by wagging an index finger at the beaten man.

"What sort of idiot are you, for goodness' sake? You had Adam put me in a room with an electronic lock after having given me full access to your security system to lay the trap for Ryan. Did you not think I could put a time delayed opening on all the internal locks too?"

Sampson slumped back into the chair, head resting against the restraint, and eyes half closed. Kaine struggled to keep his good eye open and forced himself to stay awake.

"You were so smug," Sabrina continued, "you didn't think to change any of the passwords I used to access your security systems this afternoon. Not that it mattered since I have had plenty of time over the past three months to engineer a back door through all your firewalls. A dreadful lapse in security. If you take my advice, I recommend a complete system overhaul. I can put you in touch with some very good people."

She paused to sip her drink before ploughing on.

"Once inside that room, I only had to wait until one o'clock for the lock to disengage. After which, my main concern was to avoid your guards on my way to the control room near the rear entrance. I needn't have worried. You were so absorbed in torturing the captain, you wouldn't have noticed a herd of elephants running through the apartment."

"Fucking bitch."

"Hey," Kaine called, stabbing a finger in Sampson's direction. "Mind your language. Ought to be ashamed of yourself. Sabrina, did you do the business?"

"Of course."

"What business?" Sampson demanded, trying to exert some authority where none existed.

Kaine smiled and regretted it instantly as the splits in his lip opened up again. He doused them in whisky. The pickling process worked, after a fashion.

Sabrina leaned closer to Sampson, but made sure to keep well out of the range of his teeth. Clever girl.

"Since Ryan arrived, I've been sitting in your office recording everything you said and did."

"What?" The blood drained from Sampson's face.

Sabrina smiled. "I said, ever since Kaine woke—"

"Oh God. No!"

"Would you like to see and hear the important parts?" she asked. "You know, the parts where you admit to ordering the execution of all those passengers just to kill Professor Petrovic. All those people had to die to prevent your company's stock from falling. No? Are you sure? The pictures of you and Adam beating Ryan are rather ... visceral. In high definition, full colour, and stereophonic surround sound. I'm sure the police and the internet viewers will find them most enlightening. And don't forget, unlike Mr Bernadotti's confession, yours was not coerced."

Sampson swallowed hard. He stretched his neck to find Kaine. "What ... what do you plan to do with the recording?"

"Do you want to tell him, or shall I?" Kaine asked Sabrina.

"It was your plan. You tell him."

He finished the last of his malt and arched some of the stiffness out of his lower back before continuing. The whiskey helped, but too much would dull his reactions and much as he'd have liked to empty the expensive bottle, he resisted the temptation.

"Stop me if I get any of this wrong. As you know, I don't have much of a clue about information technology. As I understand it, you've sent the tapes to a proxy server and set a time delay on its transmission to the police and the major media outlets. You know who I'm talking about, Sir Malcolm. The BBC, Sky News, NOS, the Dutch Broadcasting Foundation. Not to forget the print media. The red tops and the broadsheets. Am I right?"

Sabrina raised her open hand and waggled it at him. "Apart from the fact that everything is digitised these days and we don't use tapes anymore, you are quite accurate. As you requested, here is the abort code to cancel the transmission." She handed Kaine a piece of paper. "Send that message to the email account I set up for you, and it will delete the recordings, just as you requested."

"When does the transmission go out?" he asked, his eyes fixed on Sampson.

"Nine o'clock this morning."

"A little over four hours. Excellent. I think we can hold out here until then."

Sampson struggled to sit upright. "Kaine, I'll pay for that piece of paper. Big money. God, if you play those recordings, public trust in SAMS will collapse. The company will fold. So many people, tens of thousands, will lose their jobs—"

Kaine snorted. "Worried about the employees? Do me a favour."

"Big money, Kaine. Think about it."

He paused before asking, "How big?"

Sabrina jumped to her feet. "Ryan!"

He waved her down. "I'm a wanted man, Sabrina. If I allow the recordings to go public, it'll prove I'm guilty of pulling the trigger. I can't spend time in prison. The claustrophobia would kill me. I need to run, but I'm not spending the rest of my life watching my back. New identity documents, reconstructive surgery, a safe place to live. All that takes money. What alternative do I have?"

"Ten million US dollars!" Sampson said, eyes wide and shining with fresh hope. His breathing rate had doubled during Kaine's outburst.

"One billion." Kaine countered.

"What? I can't raise that much in cash. Not tonight."

"How much can you find, right now, this minute? And think carefully, your life depends on it."

Sampson's eyes locked on Kaine's. "Three hundred and fifty million, in Euros."

"Bullshit."

Sabrina stared at Kaine as though he'd grown a pair of pointed horns and turned bright red.

"No," Sampson yelled. "I promise you. We keep a fund to smooth troubled deals in third world countries. I have full transfer privileges. No questions asked."

"A private slush pile for bribes?" Sabrina asked. "That is illegal."

Sampson ignored her interruption and focussed on Kaine. "Let me loose and I'll prove it."

Kaine snorted. "Yeah, like that's going to happen. Sabrina, you've been through the company's financials, is he telling the truth?"

She shrugged. "I don't know. There are a number of Swiss accounts, but I haven't been able to access them without his passwords."

"Which bank is the money in?"

"*Kirchenfeldt Kantonalbank*," Sampson spat out the answer, double quick. Sweat coated his face and soaked his shirt.

"I know that one," Sabrina said. "Unbreakable security. They use retinal scans."

"Can I pop his eye out and shove it in front of the camera?"

Sampson gagged.

Kaine made sure Sabrina blocked Sampson's view and winked. She stared angrily at him before answering. "No, the eye needs an active blood flow or the scan won't work."

"Pity. Will you help me transfer the funds into my private account? Please? It's important."

He reached out to touch her shoulder but she pulled away and refused to look at him. Kaine couldn't blame her. If their positions were reversed, he'd feel equally as disgusted.

"I will help," she said at last, "but only because of the way they treated you."

"Thank you. I won't forget it." Kaine turned to face their captive. "Okay, Sir Malcolm, if the money's there and you help us make the transfer, you have your deal."

"Yes, yes. Oh God yes. The money is there, I swear it." Sampson nodded so vigorously, Kaine worried the billionaire might hurt himself.

"Okay, let's do it. Account number and passcodes please."

Sampson tilted his head, his eyes narrowed into slits once more. "How do I know you'll destroy the recordings after I've given you the money?"

Kaine groaned as he struggled to his feet and approached Sampson, who tried to melt into the mesh of his fancy chair. Kaine leaned close, daring Sampson to bare his teeth.

"Let me put this in a way you can understand," he said. "Firstly, if you don't give me the access codes willingly, I'll make you give them. And, believe me, you won't enjoy the experience. Secondly, I have absolutely no intention of destroying the recordings or of giving them to you."

"What?"

"Those recordings are my insurance policy. No way I'm handing them over."

A tic pecked at Sampson's left eye. "In that case, why should I give you the money?"

"Because, I'll give you this piece of paper"—he patted the pocket where he'd placed Sabrina's note—"so you can cancel the transmission. Don't forget, you offered to pay for the note, not the actual recording. And look at it this way. If I'm living the life of a playboy on a tropical island, why would I incriminate myself?" Kaine paused a moment for the nugget to sink into Sampson's brain before adding, "Don't you see, Sir Malcolm? Giving me the money absolutely guarantees my silence."

A slow smile plumped out Sampson's cheeks.

"Mr Kaine," he said, "I think you and I have just reached an agreement."

———

The money transfer took less than fifty minutes to arrange and left Kaine marvelling at the efficiency of modern international finance.

Sabrina created the transaction on Sampson's laptop using the codes Kaine and Sampson gave her for each account. She hammered at the keyboard with a ferocity that confirmed her repugnance for the deal. Once the formalities had been completed and the codes accepted, she held the laptop screen up to each of Sampson's eyes in turn to complete the authentication procedure.

Kaine took great pleasure in hitting "transmit" and in a matter of seconds, the funds left the SAMS slush fund and entered one of Kaine's private accounts. Watching the numbers fall on one side of the screen and simultaneously rise on the other gave Kaine a peculiar thrill he didn't anticipate.

For the first time in his life, Mrs Kaine's son had joined the ranks of the world's financial elite. His personal account held three hundred and fifty-two million Euros, plus a few hundred thousand in change. If he'd been able to move without causing himself too much pain, he might have danced a jig. As it was, he couldn't even manage a fist pump.

Phase One complete. Now for Phase Two—extraction.

Sabrina still scowled at him. Her disapproval made him uncomfortable. The life of a millionaire had its drawbacks, but somehow, he'd cope.

"Satisfied?" she asked, slamming the laptop closed and dropping it onto the desk.

"Yes thanks, Sabrina. Very satisfied."

"What now?"

Despite his damaged lips, Kaine smiled and lowered his voice to a level only she could hear. "Now, Sabrina, I'm going to deliver myself, Sampson, and a copy of the recording to a police officer I know in Birmingham."

CHAPTER FORTY-NINE

Wednesday 16th September – Morning

Sampson Tower, London, UK

Sabrina grabbed Kaine's hand and pulled him away from prying ears. They put their heads together in a quiet huddle beside the bar.

"You aren't keeping the money?"

"Of course not. What gave you that idea?"

"I ... Well, you did!"

He snickered, feeling slightly better than he had minutes earlier. "Yes, I suppose so. A deception for Sampson's benefit."

She pushed her face towards his, still scowling. "I am waiting for an explanation."

"I plan to put the cash into a trust fund for the victims' families. It won't bring their loved ones back, but at least it will ensure they have some financial stability for the future."

"Really?"

"Did you seriously think I'd take the money and run?"

She sighed. "Yes, I did. You plan to administer the fund from prison?"

"Of course not. I hadn't thought that part through. To be honest, I didn't really expect to get this far." He massaged the nape of his neck —just about the only part of him that didn't hurt too much. "I'll need to appoint an Executor. Don't fancy the job, I suppose?"

She shook her head. "Oh no, not me. The temptation would be too great. I'm just a simple-minded IT geek."

He raised a stiff, bruised arm and touched her bare shoulder. "Nothing simple about you, Sabrina, but I understand what you mean. When I saw all that money clicking into my account, I weakened a little. Daydreamed about an island in the Caribbean with its own private airstrip, golden beaches, dusky maidens ... Ah well. As it stands, I'll probably be doing porridge the rest of my days."

"Porridge?"

"Never mind."

"What made you think Sir Malcolm would fall for your deception?"

"Greed is the one thing people like Sampson understand. Selling my soul was something he'd expect. He now thinks I have a reason *not* to release the recording, and I'm going to use that to get us out of here safely."

"How?"

"Sampson is our passport out of the building. Are you ready for a moonlit stroll to the car?"

"It is pouring with rain. No moon tonight."

"Okay, Ms Pedant."

"What are you talking about over there?" Sampson said, struggling with his chains again. "Let me loose. You promised!"

With his back to Sampson, Kaine raised a finger to his lips and winked.

"Yes," he said, turning to face their prisoner once again, "and I always keep my promises. But you have one more task to perform before I can let you go."

Fear crumpled Sampson's bluster. "What do you mean?"

"Not to worry, Sir Malcolm, it's nothing onerous. All you need to do is escort us from the building. Thanks to your friend Pinocchio, I'm in no fit state to play nice. I'd rather not have to kill any of your security staff tonight. Do we have a deal?"

The billionaire, who seemed to have aged by at least a decade since his return with the baseball bat, nodded. "You expect me to walk you through the building like this?" He indicated the damp patch on his trousers.

"Of course not. You can put on fresh clothes, but don't do anything stupid. I'm not a patient man."

Kaine raised the SAMS PPQ he'd taken from Akers and pointed it at the billionaire's groin. Sampson snapped his legs together as though it would offer some protection.

"Think about it. A man your age might not recover from non-surgical castration."

Kaine released the handcuffs, helped the trembling man to his bedroom, and stood over him while he dressed. It took him two goes to find the second trouser leg.

"Hurry, Sir Malcolm. I might just decide I don't need you after all."

"S-Sorry. I'm doing the best I can."

When Sampson finished dressing, Kaine jabbed the PPQ's muzzle into his kidney hard enough to make the old man grunt. "Just a little reminder. I'm in no mood for games and in case you think my reactions are too slow, you'll be my first target. Take the lead. Sabrina and I'll be right behind you. And remember where my gun's pointed."

Sampson walked towards the exit and paused alongside the bathroom door. "Adam. Did you kill him?"

"You mean poor Pinocchio? Do you care?"

"Not funny, Ryan." Sabrina said, shaking her head.

Kaine would have shrugged, but he was in enough discomfort putting one foot in front of the other. The drubbing headache had worsened since he'd started walking, causing yellow lights to ripple the edges of his vision. He'd have leaned on Sabrina, but any sign of weakness at this stage could still prove fatal.

"Well, Sir Malcolm? Would you like to open the door and see what I do to people who upset me?"

Sampson reached out a hand to the bathroom doorknob, but let it fall and carried on to the main entrance.

"Good decision. It's not a pretty sight, but think of it as my way of putting him out of his misery. He wouldn't have been happy spending the rest of his life in prison with those good looks, despite what happened to his schnozzle."

Sabrina looked at Kaine, her dark eyes questioning and a deep frown creasing her forehead. He shook his head and mimed a fist to the face and bound wrists.

"Wait a minute," Kaine said, pointing to a door beside the main exit. "Is that a cloakroom?"

Sampson nodded. Kaine opened the door and found a flat cap and a light woollen overcoat. The cap was a little large, but his bruises appreciated the lack of pressure. "Put this coat on, Sir Malcolm. I wouldn't want you catching cold. Sabrina? How do I look?"

"As though you were a nail who'd lost a fight with a hammer, but the hat helps."

"Excellent."

Kaine waited for Sampson to dress before prodding him with the gun once more. "Be cool and this will be over very soon. Sabrina?"

"Yes?"

"If we run into security, smile at them. It'll take their attention away from my face."

She rubbed his arm. "I'll try, but you are a real mess. So ugly."

"Gee, thanks. Keep an eye on our backs, I need to focus on this sack of dog turd."

The lift doors closed. Kaine hit the LG2 button. He stood close to Sampson and kept his face turned away from the security camera in the roof. The lift's mirrored walls showed his butchered face. He tried not to look.

As the lift descended, a wave of nausea rushed up from deep in his gut. He leaned against the wall, making sure to keep out of Sampson's eyeline. After two huge open-mouthed breaths, the feeling passed. He nudged Sampson. "What are you going to tell our friend in the security booth about our nocturnal departure?"

"Nothing. He wouldn't dare ask."

"For the sake of your testicles, I do hope you play this cool."

Kaine tapped the PPQ against Sampson's leg to emphasise the point, but the Knight of the Realm didn't look as though he had any fight left in him.

"What happens after I get you clear of the building?"

"Then, Sir Malcolm, I'll hand you the piece of paper Sabrina gave me, and I'll be on my merry way."

Sampson turned and glanced up at Kaine, hope brightened his eyes. "The paper. You promise?"

"Yes. And you know I never break my word. By the way, you don't mind if I borrow one of your cars, do you? Not the Rolls or the Mercedes. The Maybach will do. Plenty of power and a nice big boot."

The lift stopped and the doors whispered open. Kaine grabbed the back of Sampson's coat. "Nice and easy, Sir Malcolm. We're nearly done."

Kaine held his breath. If the guys monitoring the surveillance cameras had noticed anything suspicious, this is where they'd strike. Sabrina caught hold of his hand and squeezed. She, too, sensed the danger.

He pushed Sampson out first.

Silence. An empty corridor.

Kaine focused most of his attention on Sampson, but kept his ears attuned for the sounds of tramping boots.

They turned right out of the lift and walked along the same corridor Kaine had used after ducking past Dwayne. He checked his watch—05:58—a mere five hours had passed. Somehow, it seemed so much longer.

Once again, his tongue brushed the hole where a tooth used to be

373

and his eyes watered. If he didn't find a dentist soon, it would drive him nuts.

They stopped outside the door to Dwayne's security booth.

Kaine stuffed the gun into his jacket pocket and whispered in Sampson's ear. "Play it smart and this will all be over in a couple of minutes. Sabrina will drive."

Dwayne opened the door to Sampson's sharp knock and dipped his head in deference. "Good morning, Sir Malcolm. Which one today?"

"The Maybach," Sampson answered, curt and sharp.

"Yes, Sir Malcolm. It's fully fuelled and serviced."

"Get on with it, man."

Dwayne, apparently unfazed by Sampson's sharp tone, stepped behind his desk and unlocked a glass-fronted wall cabinet. Inside, a dozen keys hung on hooks, each labelled with the make, model, and owner's name. The first five hooks on the top row belonged to Sir Malcolm. Dwayne selected a set and offered them across. Sampson pointed at Sabrina and the big guard handed them to her. She smiled and thanked him. Dwayne did nothing to hide his surprise at the courtesy. The little things in life gave such pleasure.

Dwayne hit a switch, and the security door clicked open. He hit another, and the banks of strip lights flickered into life. They entered the car park.

"Thanks, Dwayne," Kaine said on leaving.

"It's Willem, sir."

Kaine preferred "Dwayne", but who was he to argue with a parent's choice in first names for their son? "My mistake, Willem. Have a great day."

"Thank you, sir. Are you okay?" he asked, looking closer at Kaine's face.

The gun's textured grip turned slippery in Kaine's sweaty hand. "Army and Navy Golden Gloves night at the O2 Arena. Sir Malcolm has been helping me celebrate."

"You won?"

Kaine twitched an eyebrow—it was all he could manage. "You should see the other guy."

"Think I'll pass on that, sir." Willem said, stepping aside.

The midnight blue Maybach—possibly the world's most expensive getaway car—stood poised, waiting. Its lights blinked when Sabrina approached with the keys. She didn't have to press a button.

Kaine opened the rear passenger door. "Get in, Sir Malcolm."

"But you said—"

Kaine pulled out the PPQ, hid it from Willem's view, and dug the muzzle into Sampson's groin. The man nearly doubled over. "I'll let you go when we're out of the building and I'm sure it's safe."

"But—"

"One more bloody word, and I swear it'll be your last. I'll take my chances with shooting our way out of here."

Sampson slid inside and Kaine followed him, slumping into the seat, thankful to have the padded leather take his weight.

Thirty more seconds to freedom. Kaine could hardly breathe for the tension.

Sabrina found the ignition button, and the big engine caught and purred. The roller grate guarding the exit rose, and they were on their way.

They'd done it!

Out they drove, out into the beautiful grey streets of London. Free and clear, for as long as it took for Kaine to reach Giles Danforth and DCI Jones in Birmingham. Three hours, maybe four, tops.

As they cleared the shadow of the Tower, a huge weight seemed to lift from Kaine's shoulders, taking with it some of the pain. At his side, Sir Malcolm Sampson sat forward, tense, clearly expecting a double-cross.

"Seatbelt on, Sir Malcolm. Wouldn't want any unfortunate incidents along the way."

"Where to?" Sabrina called from the front.

"I'm heading north. Do you have an exit strategy?"

She nodded. "I need to collect my passport and a few essentials from home. Can we go straight to Clapham?"

Kaine squeezed his eyelids together, trying unsuccessfully to relieve the strain of a pulsing headache. "No problem."

———

Twenty-five minutes later, Sabrina pulled into the alley behind her villa and turned to face him.

"Give me five minutes. No longer," she said, her eyes shining. "I imagine you and Sir Malcolm have things to discuss."

After she left, Kaine turned to face his captive. "Alone at last. I suppose you're worried I'll go back on my word and screw you over?"

Sampson trembled but didn't respond. Kaine reached into his pocket for Sabrina's piece of paper and held it up. Sampson snatched it from his hand and unfolded it. He turned the scrap over and held it up to the light.

"What's this?"

"That, Sir Malcolm, is a blank piece of paper."

"You mean—"

"That's right. There is no time-delayed message ready to wing its electronic way through the ether. The recordings are too explosive to hit the public domain. Please excuse the dreadful pun."

Sampson slumped into his seat. "A bluff?" The litterlout scrunched up the paper and threw it into the footwell.

"Yes, a bluff. As you said earlier, SAMS Plc is a huge employer and plays an important part in the UK's defence. With any luck, removing you from the board and placing it in temporary public ownership might save it for the future. Either way, you're done. I'm taking us both in."

"What? No, you promised," Sampson yelled.

One hand reached for the door handle, the other struggled to release his seatbelt.

"You promised!"

Kaine slapped Sampson across the back of the head.

"Sit back and behave yourself. I promised to give you that piece of paper and let you go, and that's exactly what I'm doing. You have the paper and I'm letting you go... on a trip to Birmingham. An acquaintance of mine is keen to meet us."

"You fucking bastard. What about my money?"

"It's not your money anymore, it's my money. But don't worry. I'll make sure it's put to good use. Now, I'm afraid you need to pop into the boot."

"What? No, I-I'm a claustrophobic. You can't—"

A wave of the PPQ was enough to silence him. "Aren't you glad I chose the Maybach? Told you it had a large boot. Guess what. If you behave, I'll let you have my torch. How nice am I?"

The abject terror on Sampson's face almost forced a change of heart, but the memory of Kaine's most recent boat trip hardened his resolve. He checked the streets were clear.

"Go on, Sir Malcolm, in the back if you please."

As Kaine applied the finishing touches to Sampson's restraints, Sabrina returned, overnight bag slung over her shoulder. She studied Kaine's handiwork and tilted her head in approval.

"You were right, Ryan. The luggage compartment is certainly very spacious. He appears more comfortable than you did in that horrible chair. It even has a deep pile carpet. It is what you would call snug, yes?"

"Snug's a good word. Don't suppose you have any duct tape?"

"Yes. Shall I get it?"

From his position curled into a tight ball in the boot, Sampson whimpered. "Duct tape? What for?"

"Going to wrap it around your head and mouth. Can't have you screaming all the way to Birmingham. This tooth is giving me a throbbing headache, and I won't be able to hear the radio."

"God, please. No." Big tears poured from pleading eyes. "I'll suffocate. Please, don't. I'll be quiet. Promise. Oh God, please."

Kaine crossed his arms and rated the performance. It appeared genuine. He doubted anyone could fake that quality of terror. "Okay, Sir Malcolm. You've made a compelling case. I'll leave the tape for now, but Sabrina, please fetch the roll in case our guest changes his mind."

"Okay. Be right back."

Sampson blinked away the tears and, between great racking sobs, said, "Thank you ... thank you."

Kaine reached a hand into his pocket and dropped a torch into the boot. "It's better than you deserve, but here's the light I promised. Not a single whimper out of you until I open this boot again. Understood?"

Sampson nodded and continued to gulp air through a wide-open mouth.

Sabrina returned with a large roll of silver tape. "This is what you need?"

"Thanks. We'll take it with us in case Sir Malcolm forgets his manners."

"I won't. God no."

Kaine slammed the boot closed.

CHAPTER FIFTY

Stansted Airport, Essex, UK

Dawn's grey light promised a dreary day. Heavy clouds hung low and threatening, but the flat expanse of Stansted Airport was as welcome as any transport hub he'd ever seen. Sabrina parked in the drop-off zone and they only had a few seconds to say goodbye. New friends thrown together in adversity destined never to meet again, Kaine found the parting more difficult than he'd expected.

He broke the silence, keeping his voice low. "I haven't had a chance to thank you properly for everything."

In the passenger seat, Sabrina looked through the rain-dotted windscreen. "That's okay. I was just doing my job."

He took her hand. "Who are you, Sabrina Faroukh?"

"For one thing, that is not my real name."

"No! Really?" Kaine said, allowing irony to tinge his voice. "As if I didn't know. Any clues?"

She smiled, released her hand, and offered it in a formal shake. "Sabrina LeMaître, *à votre service, monsieur.*"

"*Enchantée, mademoiselle.*" He pumped her hand twice before the surname triggered a memory. "LeMaître? Any relation to Maurice LeMaître, Chairman of ESAPP?"

"Mo-Mo is my *grand-père.*"

The information hit as hard as one of Pinocchio's jabs. "You were working at SAMS for your family?"

"Unofficially, and without *grand-père* Mo-Mo's consent. He worries too much for my safety."

"What were you doing? Surely not something as tacky as industrial espionage?"

Sabrina LeMaître turned in her seat to face him full on. "This is between you and me, agreed? It goes no further?"

"You have my word." Kaine crossed his heart.

"Silly man." Sabrina leaned in, pecked him on the cheek, and started talking. "Eight months ago, someone broke into our R&D facility in Reims and stole a batch of the prototypes of our latest surface-to-air missiles. The last time a similar event occurred, SAMS released a replica version of the device within months. It seems they have been stealing our research for years, but we have never been able to prove it. Without *grand-père* Mo-Mo's permission or knowledge, I decided to investigate.

"After creating the false identity of Algerian techno-wizard, Sabrina Faroukh, infiltrating SAMS was simple. The difficult part was working my way into the trust of that *putain*—"she nodded in the direction of the boot—"without making my skills too obvious. Imagine how I felt when I discovered you'd shot down Flight BE1555 with one of ESAPP's stolen weapons. I thought Sampson and Bernadotti planned to place the blame on us. I was incensed."

Kaine snorted. "Despite what happened at the veterinary clinic, it's lucky for me we ended up on the same side. So, what next for you?"

"Home to Paris for a long rest. I haven't seen my cat for three months. She will have forgotten me."

He hadn't taken her for a cat lover, but what did he know about Sabrina LeMaître other than he owed her his life?

"And after your reunion with Tibbles?"

"Her name is Cleopatra. After that, I'll go back to my IT job at ESAPP and try to ensure *grand-père* Mo-Mo never learns what I did here. He thinks I am taking an extended sabbatical to recharge my batteries. And now, I must return to Paris. London pales beside her."

Kaine carried her bag to the entrance and they stood under the impressive awning, sheltering from the pulsing rain.

"What happens next for you?" she asked, glancing at the Maybach behind him. "Are you still going to deliver Sir Malcolm and yourself to the police?"

"Are you worried for me?"

"Of course, and there is the money to consider."

"Ah yes, the money." Kaine watched the entrance to the terminal building for signs of jobsworth parking attendants ready to move them along. None seemed prepared to brave the weather.

"Since you're not interested in the role, I have an alternative executor in mind for the trust fund."

"Dr Orchard?"

He nodded. "You really do have all the answers, don't you? But yes, Lara seems a good fit. She's saved my life more than once. Reckon I can trust her with the trust fund—if you excuse yet another dreadful pun."

"I will make allowances for your injuries and your peculiar sense of humour."

"Thanks, but on a serious note, if anything happens to me, I'm relying on you to give Lara as much help as she needs. After all, you do know where the money is."

"But by handing—"

A wide-bodied aircraft took off in a howl of jet engines and drowned out her words. A taxi pulled up behind the Maybach and blared its horn. Kaine gave the driver the evil eye—he only had use of the one. The taxi driver lowered his head and made busy with something in the passenger's seat.

"Sorry," he said to Sabrina. "What was that?"

"I said, by handing over the evidence, you're giving up your protection."

He took a breath. "Yes, I know. But for the families of the victims, justice must be seen to be served."

She touched his cheek with a hand so gentle, his bruises only complained a little. "You are an honourable man, Ryan Kaine."

"Thanks."

"I did not mean it as a compliment."

Up on her toes, she kissed his less damaged cheek. "Take care, Ryan."

Sabrina turned and hurried into the terminal building. She didn't look back.

———

The small Fiat van chuntered along the M1 heading north, its ragged engine note drowning out the sound of wheels on tarmac.

"Can you hear me, Sir Malcolm?"

A muffled, "Yes," proved his captive still breathed—not that it mattered a whole lot to Kaine.

"Sorry it's not as comfortable back there as the Maybach, but that beast isn't exactly inconspicuous, and no doubt Timothy and his mates are on the hunt by now. They'll track it to Stansted quickly enough. Hopefully, they'll be checking flights for their missing CEO about now."

"Bastard!"

"Yep, I've already admitted that. Anyhow, not long to go now. We're on the M6, by the way. So far, the traffic's light. Give me an hour and I'll have you out of there."

"Go fuck yourself."

Kaine tapped the brake and the Fiat shuddered. "Any more of that language and I pull over and use the duct tape."

He greeted the silence from the back with a crooked grin. Surprisingly, the further he drove from London, the brighter and more awake he became. The lessening of his guilt seemed to lighten his load and ease his aches and pains. He'd have burst into song, but no doubt, Sampson's legal team would have called it cruel and unusual punishment. The facial injuries prevented him whistling, so he drove in relative silence.

"Soon be time for the news. Shut up now while I find out whether you've been reported missing."

BBC Radio 5 Live was part-way through a riveting review of *Yesterday in Parliament*, and Kaine struggled to concentrate on the latest debate on immigration numbers.

Motorway traffic built as they approached Coventry and their speed dropped to below fifty.

The female anchor ended the political segment and introduced a chirpy weatherwoman who announced that heavy rain was a distinct possibility in the Midlands. Kaine watched the wipers sweep back and forth across the scratched windscreen. "Now tell me something I don't already know."

In no hurry to reach his holding cell in Birmingham, Kaine eased the Fiat into the inside lane and allowed an aggressive "white van man" to scream past and tailgate the Saab ahead.

"We interrupt the weather report and go live to Bradley Adams in Stockport for a breaking story. Bradley, what do you have for us?"

"Hello, Annie. This is really heart-breaking news. I'm standing in a leafy suburb of Stockport outside the home of Matthew and Valerie Princeton, whose lives have been struck by tragedy for the second time in less than eight days.

"Mr and Mrs Princeton's oldest son, nineteen-year-old Matthew, was one of the passengers aboard the ill-fated Flight BE1555, so cruelly shot down by terrorists last week. It would appear that the family, already blighted by the death of one son, may also have lost a second."

"Oh, Christ Almighty."

Through tunnelling vision, Kaine reduced speed, his whole mind focused on the words spewing from the radio.

"*Martin, Mr and Mrs Princeton's fifteen-year-old son, has been reported missing from a school geography trip to the Grampian Mountains. The boys' teacher, an experienced mountaineer contacted the emergency services late yesterday evening. Mountain Rescue teams have been searching but weather conditions ...*"

Kaine listened to the complete report in a state of shock. Ahead, the traffic concertinaed and ground to a halt. To his left, green fields soaked up the rain. To his right, a freight truck filled the view, leaving him alone with his thoughts. The Fiat's ancient motor rattled in idle, running rough. In his rear-view mirror, the grill of another haulage truck hemmed him in. For the first time in Kaine's life, claustrophobia threatened to engulf him.

He stared at the radio. Listening, but praying he'd heard wrong.

The radio reporter interviewed a spokesman for the Princetons who told of the family's anguish and said they were making arrangements to travel north. The man's words sliced through Kaine's heart and reopened the wounds. He'd spent the days since the crash working on a form of redemption and from leaving Sampson Tower until the story broke, he'd found a tiny morsel of peace.

But now?

For the Princetons to face the loss of another son had to be crippling. Kaine struggled to see the car ahead through damp eyes.

The rage returned.

"Can you hear this, you murdering pig?" he screamed, half at the man in the back, and half at the broken face looking at him in the rear-view mirror. "Well, can you?"

Sampson clearly knew better than to respond. One peep out of him would have been enough for Kaine to have lost all control. Sampson knew a life fighting to avoid a prison sentence was better than no life at all.

Options flashed through Kaine's mind as the lane ahead finally cleared and the traffic started flowing again. Vague ideas formed and melted away on a wave of doubt. Others nudged into place and solidified.

A plan. Hopeless in its formation, desperate in its simplicity, essential in its scope. Kaine was used to making operational decisions in an instant.

What use was money to the Princetons while their remaining son could be dead or dying at the top of a Scottish mountain? Money couldn't help them, but Kaine could. Not from a prison cell, but he did know the Grampians—he'd run military survival courses in the region since the early 1990s.

In seconds, his plan coalesced—short, intermediate, and long-term. He'd had found a new life's goal. Adrenaline flowed, his heart raced, and he stamped on the accelerator.

For the first time since *Herring Gull*'s death, he could see a future. Ryan Kaine had a purpose.

He was reborn!

The Grampians were at least eight hours away, probably longer in the rust-bucket Fiat. Other than to upgrade his car, Kaine couldn't waste a second. He would tend to his wounds later.

He grabbed his mobile, dialled the memorised number, and hit the green button.

"C'mon, Giles, pick up!"

While the call connected, the needle on the Fiat's speedometer crept up slowly. It hovered at sixty-seven and stayed there. Too slow. He'd hire a faster car at the next services. Money wasn't a problem. Never would be again.

The mobile clicked. "DI Danforth speaking. How can I help?"

"Giles, it's me, your old mate from Helmand. How you doing?"

Despite exercising control, Kaine could feel the excitement speeding his words. Breathe. He had to calm down, take his time. The last thing he needed was to sound any warning bells.

"Fine thanks. What can I do for you?" The wariness in Giles' delivery pricked Kaine's excitement balloon.

"Are you alone, Giles?"

"Not exactly."

"Okay. Can I assume this call's being monitored?"

"Not necessarily, but stranger things have happened."

"Fair enough. I wanted to let you know there's been a slight change in plans."

"Are you having a problem?"

"Sort of. I still have a guest for the party, but I'm going to drop him at an alternative location."

Giles spoke again after a short delay. "Okay ... If I understand you correctly, you won't be coming to the party yourself, is that right?"

"Unfortunately not, I'm needed elsewhere, but I will leave a present with the guest."

"Are you sure? We were all looking forward to seeing you safe and sound. Helmand Province is a dangerous place and you've been alone for a long time."

"Don't worry about me, Giles. I'm in good shape," Kaine said, wincing as his bruised and swollen face made him a liar, "but I don't have much time to talk. Can you contact your friend, Davey Jones?"

"It's David, not Davey or Dave, but of course. He's dead keen to meet you. How long are you going to be?"

"Give me forty-five minutes and I'll call you back and ... Giles?"

"Yes, mate?"

"Thanks for everything, it's been an honour knowing you."

CHAPTER FIFTY-ONE

Wednesday 16th September - DCI David Jones

Stafford Services, Staffordshire, UK

The rusty green Fiat Fiorino stood exactly where Kaine promised it would be—on a grass verge, part-hidden by bushes and trees in Stafford Services, Northbound on the M6.

Police vehicles, with blue lights flashing, blocked the access road for fifty metres in each direction. With Phil Cryer and the rest of the team looking on, Jones gave the signal.

Giles Danforth and six of his men—armed, and in full body armour—fanned out and approached the rear of the small van. They took up firing positions less than ten feet away, crouching behind clear ballistic screens. Giles held up his hand and, using his fingers, counted down from five in silence.

At zero, one of his squad, Sergeant Dylan, rushed forwards

wielding a short crowbar. He punched the sharp end into the crack between the rear doors and with one quick movement, wrenched them open. He stood aside to allow Giles and the rest of his colleagues to view the inside.

Giles' demeanour changed, his whole body relaxed. He signalled his men to lower their weapons and stand down, and turned to Jones, a broad smile lighting his strong face. "You might want to take over from here, Chief Inspector."

Jones and Phil exchanged glances.

"Bit of an anti-climax," Phil said, standing tall, wincing a little when adding weight to his knee.

"You wanted Kaine to jump out wielding a sub-machine-gun?"

"No way. I've been involved in two shootouts in my life and that's more than enough for this officer's lifetime. Kaine mentioned a present. I expected balloons and party-poppers at the very least."

They walked towards Giles, who made safe his rifle and pointed it towards the ground. "I'd cut him loose myself, David, but thought you'd like the pleasure. He's messed his trousers, I'm afraid."

Jones pointed to his right. "DI Cryer's used to dealing with messy nappies. After you, Philip."

Phil sniffed the air inside the van and wrinkled his nose. "I'd rather not, boss. Might be best left to the paramedics."

"Maybe you're right," Jones said, taking in the view, but keeping well away from the stink.

Wild-eyed and snorting against the tape wrapped around his mouth and jaw, an overweight grey-haired man lay face-down on a pile of dusty sacks, hogtied with three heavy-duty cable ties. A white envelope pinned to the seat of his trousers contained something that looked like the outline of a USB stick and bore the inscription:

"My name is Sir Malcolm Sampson, Chairman of Sampson Armaments and Munitions Services Plc. I am a mass murderer. Treat me with total disrespect!"

Jones tugged at his left earlobe. "Now that's something you don't see every day."

CHAPTER FIFTY-TWO

Wednesday 16th September – Afternoon

The Scottish Border, UK

A watery sun and a blue sign, the Saltire, welcomed Kaine into Scotland. The M6 stretched out ahead, and the Toyota Land Cruiser—hired using his Sergeant-Major Peter Sidings credentials when he'd dumped Sampson and the Fiat—ate up the miles with power to spare. He'd made better time than expected, but his destination still lay at least three hours further north.

The news reports hadn't added much new information in the previous four hours. Young Martin Princeton was still missing, and the weather was still hampering the search.

Kaine tapped the Bluetooth earpiece, called out the numbers, and the hands-free system did the rest. Lara answered quickly.

"Hello?"

"Hi, Lara. How you doing?"

"Ryan? Oh my God. Ryan, are you okay?"

She sounded so damned good.

"Believe it or not, I've actually been worse. Are you alone?"

"Yes."

"There's been a slight change of plan. I didn't stop at Birmingham. I have something to do first."

"Oh my God," she rushed to say. "What's happened? Are you okay?"

"Turn on the radio and listen to the news."

"I have been. It's the Princetons, isn't it. You're going to help find their boy."

Kaine was so right about her. They'd only known each other a few days, yet Lara already understood him so well. "Yes. At the risk of sounding melodramatic, I think that's going to be my new role."

"What is?"

"Protecting the families."

"Of the victims?"

He hesitated a second before admitting it aloud.

"That's right. The eighty-three."

"I-I understand. At least I think I do."

Ignoring the pain of his battered face, he smiled, but didn't know what to say.

"Will you do one thing for me, Ryan?"

"If I can."

"Please be careful. The police are still looking for you."

"You know me, Doc. Being careful is what I'm all about. I *will* keep in touch. We have a future to discuss."

Kaine ended the call on Lara's gasp.

The END

THE RYAN KAINE SERIES

Turn the page for a preview of the next Ryan Kaine.

fusebooks.com/kaine

A FREE PREVIEW OF THE NEXT RYAN KAINE NOVEL

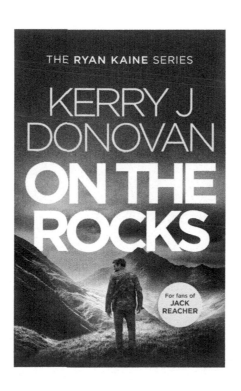

ON THE ROCKS - CHAPTER 1

Wednesday 16th September – Martin Princeton

Still raining.

Martin opened his eyes a crack.

Rained all bloody night. Hour after sodding hour. Didn't let up for a single second and he couldn't do a bloody thing to take shelter.

Pain. Nothing but pain.

Dawn had brought hope, but it also brought heavier rain.

He used to love Scotland. Hated the place now. Stupid country. Stupid weather. Stupid mountains.

Why didn't he stay home? Nah, he wanted to be with his mates. Wanted to run from the well-meaning neighbours and their flowers and their Goddamned sympathy for Mum and Dad. Not for him though. Nobody asked how he was. Nobody gave a toss about the little brother. They left him to fend for himself. Bastards.

And where did he end up?

Halfway down a cliff, alone, bleeding, and freezing to death.

A fuckup all my life. Everybody knows. Matt knew, but wouldn't say. Yeah, Matt knew.

Huge crushing drops fell onto his face, into his eyes. The cold had numbed his skin, and the freezing air sliced through his thin clothing.

So damned cold.

Why didn't he put on his heavy jacket when he had the chance? Too bloody stupid. That's why not. The other lads in the party, the ones with the muscles that made girls fawn all over them, they didn't wrap up warm against the cold and the rain, so he hadn't either. They'd shamed him into it and now he was going to die alone in nothing but a pair of jeans, a T-shirt, and a light summer jacket.

Pride and macho stupidity was going to kill him in the end.

Losing Matt in the plane crash, when was it? A week ago? Just a week? Jesus. Focusing on Matt's death had made him careless, and the mountains were going to make him pay.

Overnight, the darkness had been total. No stars, no moon, no light. Nothing to see and nothing to hear but the wind whistling through the rocks and his pitiful weeping.

He tried not to cry like a girl, but couldn't help it.

If dying alone in misery wasn't a good enough reason to cry, then what was?

Besides, up here, no one could see or hear him. No one to laugh at his blubbing.

Right on cue, a pulse of agony ripped up his left leg and into his knee. It was probably broken. Yeah, that's right. Martin Princeton, a weakling who got lost on a school trip. That's what they'd think of him—a pitiful weakling, a cripple.

Better to just die and get it over with than have them look at him with pity.

How long would it take to die? Would he last the day?

He knew people could survive without food for days, but the cold, the fucking cold.

He couldn't bear the thought of another endless night with nothing to focus on but the pain every time he moved and the blinding, screaming headache that clamped his temples so tight he thought his skull was going to explode.

Martin tried to keep still, but the shivering wouldn't let him. Each shudder fired electric shocks through his arm and leg. Music—his normal escape from the world—wouldn't come. Whatever he tried, he couldn't make the tunes play in his head.

It had already been more than a day and nobody had come for him? Why not? Did anyone know he was missing? Had anyone raised the alarm?

And what would happen to Mum and Dad now?

Again, he cried. Not from anger or self-pity this time, but for what his death would do to his 'rents.

They'd already been through so much since the plane crash. Mum collapsed into Dad's arms when the police broke the news that Matt had died aboard Flight BE155. One of the eighty-three people murdered by the madman, Ryan Kaine.

Ryan-fucking-Kaine.

Monster. Terrorist bastard. Fucking killer.

Ryan-fucking-Kaine killed Matt.

Oh, God.

His big brother was dead.

At least Matt had gone quickly. Always was the lucky one. Not like Martin. No, Martin was going to die alone on a bloody mountain. Exposure would get him, or gangrene. Painful and slow.

Matt died but Martin was still alive—at least for the moment. But he wished he was dead—ungrateful bastard.

Oh, God. Matt, I'm so, so sorry.

The big brother who'd tormented and teased him all his life, but who'd have taken a bullet for him, would never come back. He'd never see Matt again.

Fuck.

He'd never see anyone again.

He should have stayed with Mum and Dad. Should have stayed home. The sadness in Mum's eyes when he told her he was still going to Scotland despite Matt's death. He didn't ask. Didn't even bloody ask. Instead he'd been angry with her for insisting she walked him to school like he was a baby, too small to cross the road on his own.

"For God's sake, Mum. Stop crying. It's embarrassing," he'd said under his breath outside the school gates while the other lads stood by, trying not to smirk. "I'll be back in plenty of time for the funeral."

Why had he even said that? What was he thinking? She'd reacted as though he'd slapped her across the face. And he hadn't even apologised. He'd been a selfish bastard, didn't even say goodbye, and where was he now? Dying on a Scottish mountain, that's where.

Fucking idiot.

All because he wanted to see the eagles up close.

Stupid, stupid, stupid.

To think he'd fallen for it.

What would Matt have said?

"You're a complete moron, baby brother. What have I told you about reading between the lines? Don't trust anyone! You fuckup. Fancy letting Mum and Dad down like this now I'm not here to save your sorry arse."

He'd have said it with a kindly smile and maybe ruffled his hair, but he'd have said it just the same.

Sorry, Matt. Sorry for being a fuckup. Sorry for everything.

A raindrop fell on the tip of his nose and ran into his mouth. He licked the water away. No chance of dying of thirst in Scotland.

Had a better chance of fucking drowning.

He sneezed. The movement shot a light sabre through his leg, his shoulder screamed, and the crushing vice around his head tightened.

Martin pushed his free fist into his mouth, bit down hard on the knuckles, and screamed in silence. Once again, he let the tears flow.

He stared up at the jagged edge of the cliff face in the distance, the one with its recently crumbled ledge.

If there were any search teams, would the broken rocks point them to him? Could he last long enough for that?

Time passed slower than every single maths lesson he'd ever had with Ma Bancroft. Jesus, when would they put the old cow out of her misery? She had to be at least fifty.

Seconds, minutes, hours passed.

The rain lightened and finally stopped, but a heavy blanket of fog took its place.

Last night, before the sun set, the drubbing of a helicopter's rotor blades had given him brief hope, but the bloody thing had flown right over his position without stopping. The spotters hadn't seen him, but why should they? The rocks hid him.

Maybe the helicopter hadn't been searching for him after all. Perhaps someone else was lost on the mountain.

Oh, Jesus. Jesus.

They weren't coming. No one was coming.

He'd fucked up for the last time.

"Mum, Dad, Matt, I'm so sorry I let you down."

Martin closed his eyes to the cold grey mist and waited for death.

ON THE ROCKS - CHAPTER 2

Wednesday 16th September—Afternoon, Day 2

Two hours after crossing the border into Scotland, the fuel light on the dashboard flashed its angry yellow 'Feed me, feed me' message. Ordinarily, Ryan Kaine would have gritted his teeth, but the exposed root of his broken tooth throbbed and made it impossible.

From hiring the Toyota Land Cruiser outside Luton, a full tank should have been more than enough to take him all the way to the foothills of Ben Craed and part of the way back again. But, despite the risk of speed traps, he'd been heavy on the throttle and the high motorway speeds had returned to bite him on the arse.

The dashboard's digital readout showed seventy miles before the big SUV would start running on fumes, but the satnav told him he still had over one hundred to travel before he reached the Mountain Rescue Centre at Lodge Farm. The gas-guzzling monster drank diesel like an alcoholic preparing for rehab, and he needed plenty in reserve for a fast escape if necessary.

No alternative, he had to stop.

He slid a finger over the satnav's touch screen and ran the search.

Twenty-five miles to the nearest petrol station. Enough tolerance to keep the speed reasonably high, but only just.

At Luton, Kaine had hired the only 4x4 in the shop. He didn't need the added traction on the motorway, but it would probably turn out handy in the mountains. And the way the weather ahead looked, his destination in the Cairngorms would be challenging without low range.

By the time he took the exit road off the A84 and turned into the BP forecourt, the miles-left-in-the-tank showed three zeros. So much for the accuracy of the car's electronics.

Killian Services boasted a single-storey food court and shopping area, and a petrol station with four pumps, all in use. At 15:43, and with at least another ninety minutes on increasingly windy uphill roads still to go, the rest stop couldn't have been better placed. He pulled in behind a tired-looking Volvo and waited with growing impatience for the grey-haired septuagenarian to climb from his car and work out how to operate the self-service pump. In normal circumstances, Kaine would have jumped out to offer help, but he needed to stay below the radar until his police contact had time to start the process that would clear his name.

He checked his injuries in the rear-view mirror—lump above the left ear, left eye swollen almost shut, split lip, bruised cheek. Not pretty, and they were only the visible injuries. Stripped down to his briefs, he probably looked like tenderised beef.

Still, Adam Akers, the man who'd given Kaine most of the damage, had fared worse. Poor little Pinocchio hadn't earned his new nickname lightly. The thought of the man pleading with a plastic surgeon to reattach the tip of his nose made Kaine smile. The police would catch him soon if they hadn't already. No, poor old Pinocchio was the least of Kaine's problems.

He sat in the car, drumming his fingers on the steering wheel, and waited. One sight of his face might have shocked the old boy at the pump into a coronary and Kaine didn't need yet another death on his overburdened conscience.

Kaine stopped drumming long enough to search his pockets but came up empty. He'd finished the last of his sweets, the pineapple chunks, on the English side of the border and would resupply his energy fix in the shop when paying for the diesel, but only if the old boy ahead would ever finish refuelling.

Yet again, he'd chosen the slowest lane. Why? The other one had already moved ahead by one car, and a showroom-polished midnight blue Mercedes Benz S-class pulled alongside Kaine's Toyota. Two men wearing white shirts and ties with respectably short hair—one blond, the other dark brown—continued an animated conversation to the thumping techno soundtrack blaring from the car's infotainment centre. Kaine held his mobile phone to his right ear to obscure the undamaged side of his face and pretended to make a call. Fortunately, neither man paid him any attention.

While waiting for the old fellow to limp towards the kiosk, Kaine ran a continual search-sweep of the forecourt. There were two surveillance cameras—one on a pole with a two-seventy degree view of the pumps, the other one at a lower level, above the door to the shop. Both covered the pumps and were fixed. He'd place good odds on there being at least one more inside the kiosk, pointing at the till —to prevent theft by the shop worker rather than the customers— and maybe a second surveilling the stock. He'd have to keep his face averted from the lenses, but the peak of his baseball cap would help with that. A quick in-and-out to pick up some provisions and pay for diesel shouldn't prove too problematic.

The thirty-something Merc driver punched the car horn and rolled his hand forward in an aggressive hurry-up, trying to antagonise a turbaned man at the pump ahead. The Sikh man turned his back and continued filling his Renault. Another shrill blast of car horn drowned out the rumble of road traffic for a moment, and the techno drivel increased in volume as the Merc's passenger window rolled down. The passenger poked his blond head through the opening.

"Hey, Ghandi. Pull your finger out o' your fucking arsehole," he shouted, his accent pure Glasgow Southside. "We dinnae got all day tae wait for the likes of youse!"

The driver punctuated his younger mate's words with another loud blast of car horn. They laughed.

Thirty pregnant seconds later, his Renault filled, the Sikh man returned the nozzle to the pump and struggled to lock his car's fuel cap under the glare of the two well-dressed bullies. The driver revved the Merc's powerful engine and rolled his car forward until it all but rested against the Renault's rear bumper.

Along with the normal villains who passed into Kaine's sphere of influence, bullies rated high on his list of individuals to detest. He gripped the leather steering wheel tighter and tried to keep from jumping out of the car and having quiet words with the two.

The Volvo in front of Kaine finally moved, and he allowed the Land Cruiser to roll down the slight incline under its own weight.

The turbaned man slid into his Renault and drove his car into a bay in front of the kiosk, clearing the pump for Merc. The Glaswegian watched as the Sikh and his wife entered the kiosk, an angry scowl darkening his round and spotty face. Kaine could almost hear the man's racist mind whirring above the ear-splitting noise pounding from his car's stereo.

At his pump, Kaine selected Diesel SuperMax and, keeping his head down and his back to the pumps, he started the fill.

The Merc drew to a stop on the other side of Kaine's pump. The driver killed the engine and mercifully, the music died with it, leaving a light tinnitus ringing in Kaine's ears. The car's front doors clicked open and thumped closed, and the driver fiddled with the filler cap.

A shadow darkened Kaine's pump and its chrome side panels reflected a round, angry face.

Oh, dear. Here we go.

The Glaswegian dug a forefinger into Kaine's shoulder blade, just about the only place on his body that didn't hurt.

"Fuck's sake, man. What happened to your coupon? Your face?"

Kaine paused for breath.

Can I never catch a break?

He considered ignoring the big thug, but that would likely make matters worse. Kaine kept the fuel flowing and turned the left side of his face to the young man, making a point to show the difficulty he was having trying to see through his part-closed eye.

"My wife gets angry when I forget to put the loo seat down."

The Glaswegian took a moment before getting the joke. He guffawed, slapped the same place on Kaine's shoulder, and turned to his mate.

"Hear that, Purdy?"

The driver looked up from his filling task.

"What d'you say, young 'un?"

Purdy's accent came from south of the border, down Manchester way.

"This southern softie lets his wife beat him into plum jam. D'ya see his chops, man?"

"I think you'll find he's joking, George."

The backpressure of a full tank activated the off-lock on the nozzle of Kaine's pump. He withdrew it and tapped it against the filler tube.

"Is that right, pal?" George asked. "You taking the piss out 'o me?"

He edged half a step closer to Kaine and blocked his way to the pump.

"Do you mind, son? I'm in a hurry."

"No, mate, I don't mind at all. I asked you a question."

Kaine straightened and stared the man down.

Taller than Kaine by at least ten centimetres, George's shoulder muscles rippled beneath the shirt, stretching the seams. His collar and tie dug into his thick neck and, judging by the man's ruddy skin tone, seemed to cut off some of the blood flow to his head. It might have explained the man's low response rate. His biceps bulged, and a trim waist and flat belly showed off hours of gym work. He had blue irises, pinkeye, and rounded everything off with coffee-and-cigarette breath.

Lovely.

"A question you say?" Kaine asked, keeping his voice down.

"Aye."

"What question?" Kaine considered a smile, but George wasn't worth the discomfort.

"I asked, were you taking the piss?"

Kaine sighed. Much more of the halitosis and bluster would put Kaine over the edge and he couldn't spare the time to put the young blowhard in his place.

"Not at all, George. But, come to think of it, I will need the loo before I drive off."

"Funny man, eh? Purdy," he yelled to his mate, "this man thinks he's a comedian."

"Behave yourself, George. Can't you see the man's getting angry. Wouldn't want to rile him up or he might set his wife on us."

George's forehead wrinkled again and his eyes rolled up in his head as though lost in thought. Whatever he saw in the sky must have explained the gag, and he barked out a loud laugh.

"Brilliant, Purdy. You're the comedian, not this pussy-whipped arsehole."

George scoffed at Kaine, turned on his heel, and marched towards the kiosk.

Kaine replaced the fuel pistol into its holster.

"Sorry 'bout that, pal," Purdy said, without sounding the least bit contrite. "He's got anger control issues. A short fuse. You did well not to annoy him too much."

Purdy winked and added a contemptuous sneer.

Kaine jerked up his chin in a minimal acknowledgement of Purdy's half-arsed apology and headed for the shop. He pushed through the door and turned his face from the camera. On his way to the counter, he collected a cheese sandwich, a bottle of sugar-free lemonade, a chocolate bar, two individually wrapped slices of fruit cake, and a family-sized bag of pear drops.

Up front, George stood aggressively close to the man in the turban and his tiny wife. He kept edging closer until the Indian man, pushed up to the counter, had nowhere to go.

"Fucking holding me up again, Ghandi?" George growled into the man's ear.

The acne-scarred young woman at the till watched the spectacle from behind her reinforced glass security screen, but said nothing. Kaine marched forward, stopped within arm's reach of George, and smiled at the Indian couple.

"Everything okay here?"

George turned his head and smiled as though expecting to see Purdy. The grin mutated into a smirk.

"Hey, look. It's pussy-whipped short arse."

Geoge showed his back to the Indian couple and faced Kaine. Waves of highly spiced body spray leeched across the short gap between them, but Kaine held his ground. Showing weakness at this point would only escalate the aggression and the last thing he needed was to draw any more attention to his presence.

"Hello, George," Kaine said, playing nice when he really wanted to remove the man's head from his broad shoulders. "Why don't you leave this man and his wife alone and we can all be on our way. No fuss, no bother."

"You what?" George growled, leaning closer and misting Kaine with yet more halitosis.

Reluctantly, Kaine backed up a couple of paces, giving himself room to operate. Without looking away, he lowered his provisions onto a display shelf that held greetings cards and a stock of keyrings. He flexed his fingers, keeping his hands open, but prepared for action.

In the convex mirror above and behind the till, Kaine watched Purdy enter. The driver turned away from the action and towards the canned drinks vending machine.

George looked at his buddy and then at Kaine, clearly trying to make a decision. A vein at his temple distended and his face turned an even deeper shade of red. Kaine began to worry the kid might stroke out. He considered advising George to loosen his collar, but doubted the advice would go down particularly well.

In the mirror, Purdy fed two coins into the machine, pressed a button, and bent to collect his winnings—a silver can of cola. Still half-turned away from the till, he pulled the ring tab, and took a long, noisy slug.

George balled his hands into fists and cracked his knuckles. His jaw muscles tensed, and his nostrils flared, bull-like. The only actions missing to complete the image were for him to snort and maybe paw the lino with his hoof. Kaine had to force himself not to grin at the performance. The big fool was posturing for his older mate, but Purdy still hadn't looked up to appreciate the show.

"Steady, George," Kaine whispered, holding up his hands. "You really don't want to do this."

"I don't?"

"At least not in here. We need more room."

George's forehead wrinkled. "We do?"

His puffy eyes swivelled in their sockets as though taking in his surroundings for the first time. In the mirror, Purdy lowered his drink and looked towards them. When Purdy sighed and shook his head in apparent disappointment, Kaine dared to hope the older man would talk sense into his young mate and diffuse the situation. Kaine didn't really want to hurt the kid, but, never one to rely on hope over expectation, he turned and took a couple of sidesteps away from the counter. To defend himself properly, he needed to see both men simultaneously and neither in reflection.

The Sikh man hugged his wife, and the trembling shopkeeper reached for a phone, possibly to summon the police. Damn it, Kaine didn't need more company. Things were moving fast, but not in a direction he would have chosen.

Purdy threw the lock on the front door, flipped the hanging sign from 'Open' to 'Closed', and swaggered towards them.

"What you doing, George?" he said. "Causing all kinds of trouble without me?"

Great. Another fine mess.

George's lips peeled back in a savage smile that exposed a set of perfect teeth so bright, he must have just had them whitened.

"This arsehole's interfering with the natural order of things,

Purdy. He thinks I'm being too hard on these fucking towel heads. Thinks they need his protection."

Purdy kept approaching until Kaine held up his hand and showed his palm. All he needed was a pair of white gauntlets and he'd pass for a policeman on traffic duty.

"That's close enough, Purdy," he said, keeping his voice even and his tone pleasant.

The driver stopped five metres away, sniffed, and raised the can to his lips once more. He drained it in one long, glugging swallow and belched loudly when he'd finished.

Keeping his eyes on Purdy, Kaine spoke again. "George, why don't you let the nice couple pay their bill and go?"

The kid's cheeks flushed so dark, they matched the Manchester United kit on the toy bear sitting on the checkout counter.

Purdy wiped his mouth with the back of his hand and dropped the can. It crashed onto the tiled floor, the sound rattling through the quietened shop. An oppressive silence stretched out, broken only by the muffled sobs of the Indian woman. Purdy shifted his weight onto his back foot and crossed his arms, exuding an easy confidence.

"And if he doesn't?" Purdy asked, still smiling.

The words of Kaine's drill sergeant back at his SBS boot camp—a grizzled old cliché of a man—rattled around his head. "When in a standoff and outnumbered, consider your position carefully. If you can, withdraw. If you can't, stick the knife in first."

"Do you have an alternative suggestion?" Kaine asked.

George snorted, but said nothing and allowed Purdy to answer.

"I could kick your scrawny arse for upsetting George, or let him have some fun and do it himself. What do you reckon to that?"

Kaine made a show of checking his backside. "Scrawny? Never had that complaint before."

He scratched his week-old beard and pursed his lips as though considering Purdy's suggestion. Then, he nodded.

"That's an interesting proposition and you're certainly welcome to try, but do you mind if I make a counter proposal?"

Purdy shifted his weight again and uncrossed his arms preparing for action. He looked useful, as though he'd seen plenty of combat.

"Go ahead. Surprise me."

"Excellent. Why not let these good people get on with their lives? I'll pay their bill and mine, and then the three of us can go over to the cafe and discuss the possible effects of Brexit on immigration. What do you say?"

George finally found his voice again. "You a Paki lover?"

Without dragging his focus from Purdy, the one he considered the real threat, Kaine said, "Oh dear, George. You've got that so wrong." He half-turned to address the Sikh couple. "If you'll excuse me talking on your behalf?"

The man's grateful smile was enough to give Kaine permission. He returned his attention to George and spoke as though trying to educate a toddler, but kept half an eye on Purdy.

"Sikhism originated in the Punjab, George. That's India, not Pakistan, and your pejorative term is rather offensive. Very un-PC. If you insist on being a racist, at least try to ground your bigotry in fact. You ought to be ashamed of yourself."

"Huh?" George's face crumpled in confusion.

"Care to explain it to him, Purdy?"

Purdy nodded. "Yeah, okay. He just called you a moron, George. Happens he's right, but you're my moron and he's just earned himself a serious kicking." He jabbed a finger at the Indian couple. "You two. Fuck off and count yourselves lucky. Don't show your filthy black faces around here no more."

The Sikh man, arm around his wife's shoulders, stood tall and spoke directly to Kaine for the first time. "Are you going to be okay, sir?"

"Don't worry about me, Mr ..."

"Singh. Dalip Singh. My wife and I are grateful to you, sir. Are you sure we should go?"

"Please do, Mr Singh. These idiots won't hold me up for long."

George snorted again, but did nothing more than force the couple to step around him.

Kaine waited for Mr Singh to unlock the door and hurry his wife outside before speaking again, this time to the woman behind her security screen. "Did you just call the police?"

She nodded. "Aye, but they won't get here for half an hour." She threw a hand to her mouth as though realising she'd said too much. "Sorry, I ... mean they're on their way."

"No problem," Kaine said, running the timetable in his head. "Better call for an ambulance, as well."

George cackled, "That's right. You're gonna need one."

Purdy sighed. "He means for us, George. The fucker's still being a comedian."

In the courtyard beyond the window, a group of irate customers who'd been unable to activate the pumps, stood in a huddle. Mr Singh took centre stage, waving his arms and pointing to the shop. It looked as though he was trying to drum up support for a rescue attempt.

Kaine sighed. He'd only stopped for diesel and provisions, and things looked likely to escalate into a full-scale battle. Time to end this mess before the wrong people started getting hurt. He checked the time on the clock above the counter. The police wouldn't be too long.

"Tell you what, George," Kaine said, deliberately turning his back to Purdy, but keeping the mirror in view. "Why don't we save a bit of time? You tell me which one of you I should hospitalise, and I'll let the other play nursemaid until the ambulance arrives. Sound fair?"

In the mirror, Purdy nodded.

George threw a slow and telegraphed left cross at Kaine's jaw. Kaine jinked inside it, blocked the blow upwards with his right forearm, and snapped a stiff-fingered jab deep into the kid's armpit.

George screamed and collapsed to his knees, holding his right arm stiff against his ribcage. The colour drained from his face. His eyes stared wide, and his mouth opened and closed in a desperate fight for air.

Kaine stepped around and behind George, his back to the till and made ready for the attack, but a wide-eyed Purdy hadn't moved.

Kaine ruffled George's hair as though comforting an unruly schoolboy.

"Relax, George," he said. "Don't try to fight it. I paralysed your axillary nerve, but it's not permanent. You're in shock right now, but you'll be able to breathe normally in a minute or two. Maybe three."

George slumped against the newspaper display, tears formed on his lashes but were yet to fall.

Kaine forced his breathing to calm. Stunning the kid hadn't taken much effort, but the adrenaline had started to pump though his system and he needed to keep his reactions under control or he'd end up doing Purdy some real damage. Despite everything, he didn't want to inflict serious pain if he could avoid it.

Purdy's hand shot into his jacket and came out carrying an ebony-handled switchblade. A flick of the wrist and a twist of the fingers exposed the stainless steel cutting edge in all its shiny danger.

The shopkeeper screamed. George panted, breathing again as his nervous system began to recover from the pulverising blow.

Kaine stiffened and followed the arc of the blade as a grinning Purdy waved it ahead of him. He slid one foot in front of the other, advancing slowly.

Hell.

Kaine should have expected little else, but the dark-haired extremist might just have sealed his own fate.

"C'mon fucker. Come see what Purdy's got for you!"

Step-by-sliding-step, the man edged closer, keeping his balance and presenting a much more dangerous proposition than the lumbering George.

Purdy chuckled. "I'm gonna slit you wide open."

Kaine shook the tension out of his hands, grabbed a newspaper from the stand at his side and rolled it into a stiff baton.

Watch his eyes, Ryan. Take your time.

He sucked in a deep breath and waited for Purdy to make his first mistake.

AVAILABLE NOW

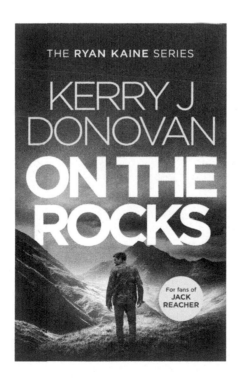

fusebooks.com/ontherocks

A FREE RYAN KAINE ORIGINS NOVELLA

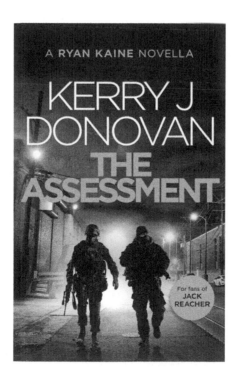

fusebooks.com/ryankaine

PLEASE LEAVE A REVIEW

PLEASE LEAVE A REVIEW

If you enjoyed On the Lookout, it would mean a lot to Kerry if you were able to leave a review. Reviews are an important way for books to find new readers. Thank you.

ABOUT KERRY J DONOVAN

#1 International Best-seller with *Ryan Kaine: On the Run,* Kerry was born in Dublin. He currently lives with Margaret in a bungalow in Nottinghamshire. He has three children and four grandchildren.

Kerry earned a first-class honours degree in Human Biology and has a PhD in Sport and Exercise Sciences. A former scientific advisor to The Office of the Deputy Prime Minister, he helped UK emergency first-responders prepare for chemical attacks in the wake of 9/11. He is also a former furniture designer/maker.

http://kerryjdonovan.com/

Printed in Great Britain
by Amazon

19727719R00246